THE SHUTOUTS

ALSO BY

GABRIELLE KORN

Yours for the Taking

THE SHUTOUTS

a novel

GABRIELLE KORN

ST. MARTIN'S PRESS
NEW YORK

This is a work of fiction. All of the characters, organizations, and events portrayed in this novel are either products of the author's imagination or are used fictitiously.

First published in the United States by St. Martin's Press, an imprint of St. Martin's Publishing Group

www.stmartins.com

Designed by Devan Norman

Library of Congress Cataloging-in-Publication Data

Names: Korn, Gabrielle, 1989– author.
Title: The shutouts : a novel / Gabrielle Korn.
Description: First edition. | New York : St. Martin's Press, 2024.
Identifiers: LCCN 2024022278 | ISBN 9781250323484 (hardcover) | ISBN 9781250323491 (ebook)
Subjects: LCGFT: Dystopian fiction. | Queer fiction. | Novels.
Classification: LCC PS3611.O74313 S58 2024 | DDC 813/.6—dc23/eng/20240517
LC record available at https://lccn.loc.gov/2024022278

First Edition: 2024

10 9 8 7 6 5 4 3 2 1

For Wallace

What happens when your head splits open
and the bird flies out, its two notes deranged?
You got better, I got better,
wildflowers rimmed the crater,
glitter glitter glitter.

—Dean Young, "Dear Friend"

THE SHUTOUTS

APRIL 1, 2041

My daughter,

The first thing I need to tell you—and after that I want to tell you everything—is that I never meant to leave you for this long. In a perfect world, of course, I wouldn't have left at all. I wouldn't have needed to. But this world, as I imagine you have learned by now, is far from perfect.

I know it's probably an odd thing, getting a letter in the mail. But I think this is the safest way to communicate. The digital surveillance has gotten so tight that no email would make it to you without the feds combing through it, not at this point. And with all that attention going into the virtual world, little is being spent analyzing what you can hold in your hands. At least, that's my hope. It's my bet.

So, here I am, writing you a letter. I'll write and send you one letter from every place I stop, as I cross the country to get back to you. It's already been a long, hard road, and I've barely gotten started.

I want to know you so badly. But you're almost a teenager now, which means you're nearly a woman, and I know from my own experiences that means you're wholly your own person, perhaps more like a stranger than my own daughter.

I also know that it's not fair for me to want to know you without also being available for *you* to know; not just the version of myself that I could invent to make you forgive me, but the truth. A truth that is not always beautiful. As your mother I do have this strange desire to only present you with things of beauty. I hate that you have to know ugliness. But my leaving, I know, was an ugliness. Perhaps the first you ever experienced. Perhaps just the first of many bad things that happened to you. I wish I knew. I hope that soon you'll tell me.

I've tried to call you many times over the past six years. When I first left I called every day. Your father never let me speak to you. He didn't want to hear about why I'd taken off, only why I wasn't back yet, since I'd left a note saying I'd return in a couple of days. He eventually blocked my number. I've tried emailing every combination of your name I can think of that might take me to you. I have a Google alert for you. I've checked the local school records, but all I can find is that you're still enrolled, which doesn't help me. In some ways I admire that you don't seem to be on social media (not a surprise; your father was never on it, either). I wonder if it's intentional. I don't know what your father told you about me. I imagine he didn't tell you about the calls. You must hate me. I deserve that.

So let me tell you why I'm writing to you now. I hope you believe my story once it's told. Of course, truth is subjective. I want to tell you my truth as best I can—the things I experienced and the things I came to know. What you do with that info is yours. Some of it might seem like a conspiracy theory, the rantings of a woman desperate to win her daughter back. Well: I am desperate. But I've also always been honest, maybe to a fault. I wonder if you remember that about me.

For the past four nights I've been sleeping in my car (well, technically it's not *my* car, but more on that later), which I honestly don't mind, but there were tornado warnings last night on the radio. I pulled off the highway and into a small rural neighborhood as the wind started to pick up. I knocked on the door of the first house I saw. No answer, all the lights off. No car in the driveway. I drove to the next one, a few miles down the road. An elderly couple opened the door, looking terrified at the sight of me or maybe it was just the trees behind me, threatening to snap right off their roots. I asked if I could stay the night and they shook their heads, closed the door in my face. I understand it, I guess. I'm a stranger. I probably looked a little feral, as I sometimes do. I drove as fast as I could back to the first house and peered in the windows until I could be sure there was no one there and then I used a rock to break a window and climb in. I braced myself for an alarm, but none came.

It's not abandoned; there's food in the fridge and clothes in the closets, evidence of a family everywhere. But when I got here it was late enough that I figured no one would come home at least for the night. I brought blankets and food down to their basement, where I hope I'll be safe. I'm writing to you using the light of a flashlight I found down here. I'm scared if I turn on lights, the neighbors will call the cops. I hope if they come home while I'm still here, I'll be able to explain myself before they, I don't know, shoot me. You'd think people would be sympathetic to a girl on the road in the middle of a storm, but who knows these days.

I am truly in the middle of nowhere, or at least, the middle of Idaho, which to me might as well be Mars. The road isn't paved, can you believe it? I'm not sure how long I'll have to stay here, or how long before these people come home. I was eager to move as quickly as possible toward you, but it seemed Mother Nature, as always, had her own ideas. Mothers, right? Ha.

If I make good time, my letters will reach you before I do, over the next few weeks. Hopefully this will prepare you for my arrival. Hopefully everything will get to you before your father finds it. That's why the return address says your father's sister-in-law's name. I doubt he'd open mail from your aunt to you. When you were little, you were close with her. I hope you still are, and that it's believable that she'd be writing to you.

When you read the last of my letters, you'll have a choice to make. But before I present you with that choice, you need to know everything that's going into it. Everything that's happened since I left.

I'll start from the beginning. Some of it might feel like too much information. I am not sure how much a girl wants to know about her mom. If it were me, I'd want to be spared the intimate details, but you're not me. I hope you are curious, that you want details, that you might even be hungry for the truth about me. If I'm wrong, I'm sorry in advance. Skip over things if you want. I just can't tell you the story of my leaving without the story of my heart, which I have followed over the years into various situations, some wonderful and some terrifying and dangerous. I like to imagine that you're like me in this way. You were always so brave.

Anyway. I've struggled to find the true beginning of this story, but I think it starts when I was a few years older than you: seventeen. And I was completely on my own.

Let me paint a picture. I was small. I had red hair streaked with blue. My face was covered with acne and freckles. I spent most of middle school practicing active shooter drills, and then most of high school learning remotely throughout the many pandemics that haunted the 2020s. I grew up in Queens, which maybe you remember.

Like a lot of my generation I was idealistic and rebellious, but also terrified, a ball of nerves, not believing in any of the systems that I was told were there to help me. The government? The public schools? The NYPD, for fuck's sake? They were all the enemy. I was good with computers, though. When we had to quarantine I'd program my computer to show myself nodding along in class while I lay in bed and stared at the ceiling.

I often felt that I was born into the wrong family, maybe (hopefully?) switched at the hospital by accident. There was no way these right-wing nuts—who worshiped at the altar of Fox News—were my mother and my father. They didn't even want me to get a COVID vaccine. I'd had to sneak away and get one while they zoned out in front of Sean Hannity.

When I was old enough to argue with them about politics, they said, "You sound like those Antifas." I shouted back, "Antifa just means anti-fascist. Do you hate Antifa because you love fascism?" They sent me to my room. They didn't know how to handle me, how to talk to me, even, so mostly they didn't.

It's also worth noting that this was a specific period of time. The world had entered a sort of doom spiral; so much attention and resources were being directed at cleaning up the damage being caused in real time by climate change–related disasters that it deterred any sort of focus on larger-scale, longer-term issues. Every day there was a new hurricane, tornado, flood, heat wave, virus, fire. So much goddamn fire. No matter where it was, the smoke seemed to always reach us, settling over the city and blocking the sun for days.

I didn't understand why everyone wasn't walking around screaming hysterically. How could you be aware of what was happening and go about your day as though everything was fine and normal?

I had become a wild thing, a street cat in a cage. Horrified by what I knew to be true: this world was on the brink of collapse. To not be taken seriously drove me not just to madness but to rage—and what is madness, really, if not rage with nowhere to go? I had a family who thought I was crazy, who *told* me I was crazy, which in turn made me *act* crazy.

As I learned more about the world, I tried to talk to my parents about climate change, about gun control, about abortion rights, and they rolled their eyes and told me to mind my own business. "What the fuck is wrong with you?" they'd ask me. "Why can't we have a normal, grateful daughter?"

I was prone to screaming, and sometimes violence. When my parents wouldn't turn off Fox News long enough to listen to me talk about how hard I found remote learning, I smashed the TV with my hands, bleeding all over the beige carpet; when they wouldn't stop buying red meat, I logged into their bank account and set up an automatic donation—for every dollar they spent on something that had been factory farmed, two would be donated to an animal sanctuary directly from their savings.

I was pretty proud of that one.

Instead of helping me learn to navigate the strange, terrifying world, on my seventeenth birthday, my parents gave me five hundred dollars in cash and asked me to move out.

They wished me good luck with tears in their eyes—always the victims—and then, after I stuffed everything I could into a backpack, a locksmith showed up to change the locks. They informed me they had switched banks, so I shouldn't bother trying to extort more money. I never saw my parents again. (I'm sorry for telling you they were dead. They *were* dead, to me, as I was to them.)

This, I believe, is where my story begins. Up until that moment, I could have been someone who lived a normal life, maybe. Perhaps there's some alternate universe where little Kelly doesn't get kicked out of her house, and instead goes to college, gets a real job. I'd love to see what she became.

So, imagine it. I'm seventeen, standing in front of my parents' apartment building in Queens, clutching an envelope of cash. At the time I told myself: *I'm free.* But I also couldn't stop shaking, not for hours, as I wandered around the borough wondering where I'd sleep that night.

I was pretty sure everyone was staring at me. Eyeballs leering from dark corners. I didn't think I had any friends whose doorsteps I could show up at. I was a weird kid, a loner. In hindsight I probably could have turned up just about anywhere familiar asking for help and gotten it; I realize now, as a mom, that I was underestimating the way grown-ups want to help kids in trouble. I could have turned to the parents of classmates or even my teachers, probably. But my parents had made it clear that I was worthless to them, and I took that to mean I had no worth. It took me a long time to unlearn that. I am, perhaps, still working on it.

My first thought was that maybe I could find myself an apartment, but the cash wouldn't have even bought me a month in someone's closet. And I didn't want to waste it on, what, two nights in a hotel? I bought a cup of coffee, drank it quickly, and then sat on the ground with the cup in front of me, looking as forlorn as I could, which wasn't that hard because I was feeling truly lost. A few people walking by dropped coins in it, but you have to keep in mind that we were in a recession, and inflation meant that their coins really wouldn't help me at all. I gave up begging pretty quickly.

I hope you never have to feel how I felt on that day. The terror, the loneliness, the absolute bewilderment of how quickly my life had changed. Like I was watching a video of myself as I walked the streets. I could even imagine the sad-girl music playing. Boo-hoo, poor me. But seriously.

My phone bill was paid through the end of the month (one last parting gift from dear old Mom and Dad), so I started Googling homeless shelters for kids. I found one in Lower Manhattan, but by the time I got there, it was almost dark, and a tired-looking woman with thinning hair at a desk said they were full for the night.

"You have to get here early to snag a bed," she said, her voice heavy and hoarse with a Queens accent. "I'm sorry, kid."

For the first time since leaving my home, I broke down. She slid a box of tissues toward me and watched while I wiped my face.

"You know, you might be better off not going in there," she said, looking around, as though she was telling me a secret. "Girls don't do so good after dark if they're alone, you know?"

That scared me. "What am I supposed to do *tonight*?" I asked.

"My advice? Go to the nearest hospital and camp out in the waiting room. If anyone asks, say your dad is in surgery."

It seemed like as good a plan as any. I thanked her and left, doing exactly as she said: I slept in a ball in the waiting room of a bustling emergency room. No one asked me what I was doing there. They left me alone.

In the morning I drank hospital coffee from a machine and used the public restroom and then I was out on the street again.

Instead of going back to the teen shelter, spooked by what the woman had told me, I spent that second day wandering. I mostly stayed in Queens, because it was familiar. I kept a wide radius around my parents' neighborhood, afraid I'd see them. I wasn't sure what I'd say if I did. Something like: *Look at what you turned me into.*

Around lunchtime I stopped in a bodega to get a Snickers bar and a bottle of water. I paid for it in quarters, and then ate while I roamed, trying to take the tiniest bites possible to make it last. I was starving.

At one point I rounded a corner and crashed into a man who reeked of alcohol and urine. Before I could apologize he grabbed me by my shirt and pulled me close. "Little girl," he said. With his free hand he roughly caressed my face, his jagged, dirty fingernails especially painful as they made contact with the cystic acne on my cheeks. I will never forget the look in his eyes, which told me he didn't see me as a person but as a *thing* he wanted; I imagined he'd stop at nothing to get it. I pushed him as hard as I could and ran until I couldn't run anymore.

Before I knew it, it was getting dark again. I stopped in the lit doorway of an apartment building and a doorman appeared. "Shoo," he said. "Don't loiter."

"Sorry," I said. "I was just . . ."

"Don't make me call security," he said. I left.

I wondered if I should try to get a job. If I should work during the day and sleep on the subway at night. But who would hire me? I was a mess. My only skills were that I knew my way around the backend of a computer, but I couldn't yet imagine how to parlay that into a paying gig. My résumé was blank. The pandemic meant that the years I could have spent working entry-level retail or service jobs after school were instead spent quarantining at home or, at best, babysitting the neighbors. I did love kids. But I knew nannying in my current state was off the table. Who would want me around their children?

By this point I had wandered almost to the edge of the borough, where Queens touched Long Island, the pavement giving way to empty fields and the sidewalks starting to widen. It was there, at the edge of a town that has since sunk into the sea, next to a row of shuttered businesses, that I saw a burned-out, boarded-up house, and heard music.

I don't know why I trusted this sight, this sound. Someone else would probably have been spooked. But I wasn't afraid. For some reason I just knew in my heart I was getting close to finding my people.

I was right. And thank god for that.

I walked around to the back of the building—which was sagging and smelled of mold—following the sound of the music. The overgrown yellowing grass was littered with garbage. Suddenly, the music stopped. A piece of plywood covering a first-floor window popped out, as though it had been kicked. Three young people wearing tattered black clothes stood in the window.

"What do you want?" a girl's voice said.

I took a step closer. "I just need a place to crash."

I could see them more clearly now. Two girls and one boy.

"Jesus Christ, how old are you?" the second girl said.

I stuck my chin out, tried to seem bigger. "Twenty," I lied.

"Yeah, and I'm forty," the first girl said. They all laughed.

I started to turn around. "Wait, wait," the guy said. "Are you alone?" His voice sounded nice, even concerned. "Do you need help?"

I stopped. No one had asked me if I needed help. I was disarmed by this simple question, this confirmation that I was still human. So I nodded. Gave in to the truth. "My parents kicked me out," I told them. "I'm seventeen. I have nowhere to go."

"Why'd they kick you out?" the guy asked.

"Creative differences?" the second girl offered.

"Something like that," I said. "If by *creative differences* you mean they love fascism, and I'm not evil."

They looked at one another, and then back at me. "Well, come, then," the first girl said. I wasn't sure how the decision had been made, but it seemed unanimous. They held their hands out to me and helped me climb through the window, and then boarded it back up behind me.

"I'm Vero," the guy said. He was very cute close up. Olive skin, thick dark hair that curled around his gauged ears. He was wearing a tank top and I caught a glimpse of a binder around his chest.

Vero gestured at the two girls beside him. "That's Madhuri and that's Cory." Madhuri was Indian, with long black hair parted down the middle. She was wearing fishnet gloves. Cory was white, and too skinny, with patchy short brown hair that she clearly cut herself.

"Hi," I said. "I'm Kelly."

It was dark inside the house and my eyes were taking a minute to adjust. Eventually I could make out shapes beyond where we stood. People lying in sleeping bags, huddled together in corners. Some were illuminated in blue light from their laptops.

"Come on, we sleep upstairs," Vero said, before I got a good look at anyone. "You got a sleeping bag?"

"No," I said. "But I'm fine on the floor." That was a lie: I'd never slept on a floor in my life.

He shrugged and I followed them up a few flights of stairs into the attic. Walking behind Vero I noticed he had a rattail and zits on his shoulders, which I realize does not sound appealing but trust me that it was; it was more of a sum-total thing. As a whole, Vero was magnetic. I also clocked a new-looking iPhone sticking out of his back pocket, no case.

The attic was drafty, with an A-frame uninsulated ceiling. There was one dusty window and three sleeping bags on the floor, barely enough room for me.

The sun had set completely now and the only light in the room was coming from a flashlight that Madhuri clutched. My three new acquaintances sat down on their sleeping bags in a circle, and I sat between Vero and Madhuri. They smelled worse up close, like old chicken soup, but I guessed that I wasn't exactly giving bouquet of roses, either. I hoped that soon I'd become nose-blind to their stench, as I had to my own.

Cory dug around in a backpack and produced a metallic emergency blanket, folded up into a small square. "Here." She handed it to me. "It's warmer than it looks."

I wrapped myself in it, immediately starting to warm up.

"Kelly, like the color," Vero said. "Kelly *Green*." He looked delighted.

"Here we fucking go," Cory said, rolling her eyes.

"What?" I said.

"Vero likes to nickname us," Madhuri said.

Vero was grinning. He pointed at Madhuri. "Madly," then at Cory, "and Coriander."

"Why?" I was starting to laugh. I couldn't remember the last time I'd laughed.

Madhuri sighed, clearly pretending not to be amused. "Because I do everything with *passion*."

"No," Vero said. "Because you're secretly insane. You have a surprise violent streak."

"And Coriander because my full name is Cory Andrews," Cory said. She grinned at me. "It's so dumb. I hate it."

I didn't think she meant that. I got the sense that it was an honor to be nicknamed by Vero. At least, that's how I felt.

"And now Kelly Green, because it sounds cute," said Vero. The word *cute* bounced around my brain.

"How come you don't have a nickname?" I asked Vero.

"I already chose my name," he said. "One of the many blessings of being trans."

It was a hard time to be a trans person. Not that it had ever been easy, but there'd been a rash of anti-trans legislation across the country; the right was focusing on trans people as a hot-button topic, banning surgeries and hormone therapies, and the left was mostly letting it go.

But Vero had called being trans a blessing. I loved that. We were all smiling. It felt warm and good and normal.

"Why are you guys being so nice to me?" I asked.

There was an awkward pause.

"We don't turn away other queers," Vero said. "It's one of our only rules. That and never call the cops, of course."

I stared blankly. Cory came to my rescue. "Even if you're not queer, it's okay," she said. "We have room. And anyway, you're already here."

I was still at a loss for words. It might sound ridiculous, but this was the first time anyone had asked me about my sexuality, much less made an assumption to my face about it. I'm not sure how visible I was to other people. I had been so nerdy and awkward that it's not like anyone in school ever flirted with me. I knew what I wanted, deep down, but it was all very untested. I was such a baby.

"I'm bi," I said. "Or maybe, like, pan? I don't know." The words surprised me as they came out of my mouth. The truth was so easy to say once I said it. In the secret crushes that swirled in my brain, gender had never been a factor. When I was little, I used to think that everyone felt like that.

"Join the club," Madhuri said. "I'm in love with both Coriander *and* Vero."

"No, you're not," Cory said, and pushed her.

Madhuri fell over dramatically, lying on her back with her arms and legs spread out. "No, I am," she said. "And that's why I can't date either of you. How could I possibly choose?"

I hadn't yet realized how much Madhuri and I would have in common.

"Vero and I could arm-wrestle for you," Cory suggested, though I didn't get the sense either of them was actually interested in Madhuri, nor she them. This was clearly just a game they played.

I picked the split ends of my hair, a nervous habit. Vero noticed and put a warm hand on my shoulder.

"You'll figure it out," he said. He was so gentle with me back then.

"What are your other rules?" I asked.

"No drugs," Madhuri said.

"No *illegal* drugs," said Cory. "We're not, like, straight-edge."

"We've just lost too many friends to fentanyl," Madhuri said. "It's in everything now."

Vero took a little thing of nasal spray out of his pocket and showed it to me. "Narcan," he said. "We can get you one, too."

I knew a little about the epidemic. I'd had classmates who vanished to go to rehab, knew of kids whose parents had died of overdoses. I was relieved that this was their take, until Cory said, "Well, moderation counts for a lot."

Vero and Madhuri looked pissed. "I hate when you say shit like that," he said. "Makes me so fucking nervous, man."

She shrugged. She didn't seem bothered. Her give-no-fucks attitude struck me—in all my naivety—as cool.

In the distance, we heard a siren. All of us froze, waiting to see if it was getting closer or farther away.

The sound faded. I wondered how often, if at all, people would try to kick us out of here; who owned this house at the edge of the world, and why it was vacant. Probably a foreclosure, I know now. So many people were kicked out of their homes by the banks in those years, with no one left who could afford to buy them again.

"Should we tell her?" Cory asked.

"Tell me what?"

They exchanged glances, smirks. Vero said, "We saw you, earlier."

"In the convenience store," Cory added.

I felt a hot rush of embarrassment turning my face and neck pink. "Oh," I said. They'd seen me clutching my candy bar to my chest, counting change from my envelope.

"No, no," Cory said quickly. "We thought you were cute. We thought you looked like one of us."

At this, I couldn't help it: I grinned. "That's so nice," I said.

"Anyway," Madhuri said, "we do have some things that we, like, stand for, but it's too much to discuss now. I bet you're tired."

"I know I am," Cory said. It was hardly past 8:00 p.m., but so dark it could have been midnight. "We follow the sun," she said to me, as though she could read my thoughts. "We'll wake up early. Lots to do tomorrow."

"Okay," I said. I couldn't imagine what they had to do. But I also couldn't wait to find out.

"First, do you have a phone?" Vero asked. I nodded, and he reached his arm out for it. Without really thinking about it, I gave it to him. He took everyone else's phones, too, and then wrapped them in a silver blanket. "Good night, phones," he said. And then to me, he explained, "This keeps them from using our phones to track us."

He didn't say who *them* was, and I didn't ask. I trusted him. I trusted all of them.

With these new people, I was shy, nervous, awkward. It was as though all my feral rage was left with my parents. Without them, I was just desperate to be accepted. I felt new. I felt that *this* was my real family, these queer kids living in squalor, and I needed to make them love me, keep me.

Let me pause here. I have always suspected that you might also be queer. I hope this doesn't piss you off. I hope I'm not overstepping. Please don't stop reading if this makes you mad. I'm trying to make up for so many years. I wish I could have been there to guide you through the first inklings of your queerness, as I'm sure they've already begun. Your father will be no help, but he also won't be upset. Maybe you don't need me to tell you that. He's more open-minded than he seems. It's one of the things I appreciated most about him.

Anyway. I didn't sleep well that first night, mostly because I was on the floor. (Vero had produced an extra fleece blanket, but I couldn't decide whether to sleep on top of it or under it, so I spent the whole night moving it around.) But it was also hard to sleep because I was so excited to be surrounded by these strangers who were so warm to me. We were all born into tumult, united by a rejection of the hand we'd been dealt. No one before us had to cope with what we did and because of that we all mistrusted adults as much as we'd come to lean on one another. I loved them all immediately.

I want to tell you the whole story of them, of me with them, of who we became, and how.

But for now, I've been writing for hours and my hand is hurting. Will you even be able to read my chicken scratch? I hope so. I hope that when this letter finds you, it will be welcome.

I'm going to take a break now, and try to get some sleep. I'll pick up where I left off in the morning, if I can.

I love you.

Mom

1

MAX

2078

MAX TUCKED THEIR LONG BLACK HAIR BEHIND THEIR EARS and cracked their knuckles. Then, as they'd done countless times over the course of their twenty-six years on earth, they began the rhythmic task of threading their loom.

The twine from the dried B3k stalk was tough, but their hands were calloused, and they were used to working the material until it softened. They pushed it through the large wooden needle and then worked it between the rows, precise and tight.

B3k was a legume with dark glossy leaves. It had once been contained to fields, but like an invasive weed, it now spread everywhere; it covered buildings, overtook trees, grew tall and dense along the footpaths that snaked through the compound. There was no reason to curb its growth: after all, the drought-resistant super-plant provided an entire day's nutrition and calories through its red beans, which had a sweet, muddy taste, like clean earth. With some salt it tasted even better. It could be baked, fried, boiled. It was the only thing they ate.

It was named B3k because, according to the lore, the scientist who developed it had tried three thousand variations of beans before landing on the one that could meet all their needs. Not just the beans, but the whole plant: even the stalks could be dehydrated, stripped, and turned to thread. The fabric that resulted was coarse, at times scratchy, but Max had never known another texture against their skin. It was a pale brown, the same color as the shirt on their back and the pants on their legs, and, really, nearly every piece of clothing and blanket and towel they'd ever seen, other than certain ceremonial robes worn by the elders, which were bleached beige from the sun.

Max's loom station was in a large open space filled with other people weaving. Max didn't mind being on textile duty. Here, in the quiet, it was almost like meditating. Elsewhere on the Winter Liberation Army compound, it was loud; raw materials clanging, kids screaming in play, particles being blasted into the air to reflect the sun and control the temperature. The usual.

The Winter Liberation Army was deep in the wilderness of what used to be Washington State, surrounded by redwoods and Douglas firs, moss and fern and creeks, often blanketed by a fog so thick you could almost hold it in your hands. The compound was impossible to find, if you didn't know where to look. No one could stumble upon it; it was out of range of the satellites that used to hover over this part of the world. The radios and cable and internet that used to connect people didn't even reach it. All this, of course, was intentional. The Winter Liberation Army—and the committee that ran it—did not want to be found.

Max was halfway done with a blanket they'd been weaving all week. When they finished, they'd be moved to the solar panel division, where they'd be sent on a run to the nearest landfill to scrounge for the aluminum and tempered glass that would be placed atop the glassy surface of the lake, soaking up the sun. The week after that, they'd help operate the machine that was pulling carbon from the air and sequestering it deep underground. After that, they'd be in the fields, helping harvest the beans.

Life, generally, was peaceful and boring. Sometimes it was challenging. Like everyone, Max had been taught to be some combination of engineer, chemist, farmer, biologist. The elders didn't want to get into a situation where only the technology's inventors knew how to make it. They could all do everything, anything that was needed.

In the soothing quiet of the textile warehouse, Max sat next to Sterrett. They'd been friends since childhood.

Max and Sterrett were among a handful of nonbinary people in the Winter Liberation Army, though at first Max had tried very hard to fit in with the boys and then with the girls. Neither label felt wrong, exactly, but neither felt totally right, either. Max was just Max.

It came as a relief to Max when, later, they proved incapable of growing a full beard. The thought of facial hair was horrifying. And, if they spoke quietly, which they usually did, their voice retained a kind of androgynous, midrange tone. They were comfortable in the space in between the genders other people were proudly claiming, and grateful for a body that reflected that feeling.

Sterrett had short black hair and dimples on their cheeks. When they were kids Sterrett was often covered in scratches and bruises; evidence of a rough-and-tumble energy, a child who was happiest when climbing trees. Like Max, Sterrett was shy, though Max knew that underneath Sterrett's quietness was something dark, something cynical, whereas underneath Max's surface was mostly earnestness, a tendency to take things at face value. Max had always been fascinated by Sterrett, even after a lifetime of friendship. That unknowable quality. They always wanted more.

Today they wanted more in a new way. Just a few nights prior, Max and Sterrett had been hanging out under the stars, goofing off like they always did at the edge of a clearing out of sight from the main compound, and the next thing Max knew Sterrett had pushed them against a pine tree, their hips grinding together, teeth knocking awkwardly, the rough woven tunic digging patterns into their skin. Sterrett kissed Max's neck and it sent a shiver down Max's whole body so intensely that they accidentally made a sound, something between an "oh" and a "shit" that made Sterrett laugh. Max was embarrassed by how easily they were turned on, but Sterrett wasn't judging. Before this moment Max hadn't considered Sterrett as anything more than a friend, but still they fell to the ground together, breathing into each other's mouths, and Max was surprised by how badly they suddenly wanted them, and how much they liked being wanted by them back. Max had accidentally grazed Sterrett's prickly B3k binder with their hands, and wondered for the first time if it was painful to wear.

Everything was different now that they'd crossed this line together. From the neighboring loom, Max couldn't stop glancing at Sterrett.

"Let's go," Max whispered finally, tying their remaining thread into a knot. "Hurry up and finish." Sterrett had to know what this meant; Max wanted to go to what had quickly become their secret meeting spot in the trees.

They smiled as Sterrett squirmed. "I want to," they whispered back. "But we have *services.*" Sterrett rolled their eyes as they said the word.

Max groaned, a little too loudly, and someone on the other side of them shot them a look. Sterrett was devoted to the rituals, insistent that they never miss one. They'd always been like that, even though they also seemed to hate going; a fascinating contradiction. Max wondered if Sterrett would ever explain it.

"Fine," they said. "But after . . . ?"

Sterrett nodded. "After."

The dome-shaped chapel was built atop a magnetized platform so that it could float two feet off the ground, a flash-flood measure that many of the main buildings had. There was a small set of stairs for those who needed them, but Max's long legs meant they could leap up without help. They pulled Sterrett up behind them.

Max's mom was in her usual seat in the middle, and Max slid down the pine pew until they were next to her. They always sat like this; between their mom and Sterrett. Sometimes they were joined by Sterrett's parents, but today it was just the three of them.

"Hi, my love," she said.

Max's mom was beautiful, with long shiny black hair and luminous olive skin. Max had her hair, but their face was different, their eyes wider and their nose more symmetrical, skin a darker brown, shoulders more freckled. They were constantly searching the faces of the older adults to try to find similarities, which might have given Max some sort of clue as to who could have fathered them, though they always came up short. Max's mom told them as much as she thought they needed to know—like that she and Max, like most people born into the community, were mixed race. Max was unsatisfied with this answer, though her vagueness was not unusual. The emphasis in the community was on their similarities, not their differences, not the heritages that might inform who they were as individuals. They were all told over and over by the adults in leadership that it did not matter; that their genders and races and where their ancestors came from were not as important as their one goal of living in harmony with the earth, slowing the change of the climate.

But Max didn't buy it. Even if it was a relic of the past, the past was why they lived like this in the first place, as they'd all been told.

Besides: there was evidence that it did matter. Max was reminded of it as they heard the clearing of a throat from the stage, indicating Len was ready to start the service. As Max liked to point out to Sterrett, if nothing mattered but living in harmony with the earth, why did everyone in charge look like Len?

Len was an ancient white man who wore a long robe of woven B3k material wrapped around his middle; ceremonial attire that he never changed out of, as far as Max knew. He was missing a few front teeth and had words tattooed on his hands, now wrinkled into illegibility. Before Len, another man had been in charge—the man who pioneered their way of life and thus maintained a legendary status among his followers—but he'd died of cancer many years ago, before Max was born. Len had been running things ever since, and though he'd been voted in by committee, which implied he was popular, Max always thought he had a strange energy to him, an undercurrent of slime that ran just under the surface. It showed itself in brief grimaces that flew across his face between practiced smiles. But you had to be paying close attention to catch it. Most people read him as charming, larger than life.

Len took his place at the pulpit and the crowd quieted. There were several hundred people who lived on the commune, and about fifty who could fit into the chapel at once. This was the second service; they were held back-to-back from early evening to late at night, and everyone was expected to attend one.

"Blessed be the clean air," Len said, and the people repeated his words and bowed their heads. Some rocked back and forth. "Blessed be the pure water and the cool temperatures and the bountiful harvest. Blessed be our restraint in procreation. Blessed be the earth we stand to protect. Blessed be winter, may we liberate it. Amen."

"Amen," Max said, no longer paying attention. They could have recited these words while unconscious.

Instead they tried to catch Sterrett's eye, but Sterrett refused to indulge them, staring straight ahead. Max nudged their knee so it touched Sterrett's, but this only made Sterrett jump, startled. They inched away from Max instead of toward them.

Max sighed. When it was just the two of them, Sterrett couldn't keep their hands to themself, but in public, it was like nothing had ever happened. Max wasn't sure if Sterrett was embarrassed or ashamed of what was happening between them, or perhaps it simply wasn't serious enough to let other people know. That was okay. Max wasn't sure how serious they were about it, either. It was fun, at any rate.

Meanwhile, the prayer continued as it always did. "Blessed be the scientists whose hard work and miraculous discoveries have allowed us to live freely outside. Blessed be the innovations that keep us separate from the rest of the world. Let us give thanks that we were spared from the dark lottery of the Inside Project and the influence of malicious forces."

Ah, the Inside Project. Max was a toddler when the United World Government announced the application process by which civilians could apply to live in the city-size structures that would protect them from the changing climate, though they couldn't tell if they actually remembered this happening or had just been told the story so many times. The Winter Liberation Army's leadership committee had known this was coming; it was the reason they'd separated from the rest of the country and began hoarding weather-proofing technology. Everyone else who didn't go Inside was more or less doomed—famously, there'd been no protections offered for the people left out, and no one had the technology they did. When

Inside was announced, the members of the WLA had already figured out how to survive in the wilderness. In fact, they'd spent years preparing to. All this was part of the history of this place; it had been drilled into Max as a child in school and was forever revisited during services, repackaged as prayer.

Onstage, Len began cutting a fresh B3k sprig and wrapping twine around it, signifying a new holy bundle.

Len held the sprig above his head. "What child asks the questions tonight?"

An eight-year-old in the front row stood. This, too, was ritual; once a week, a different kid took a turn asking a question. She had bruises on her wrists and snot crusted on her nose. Max couldn't remember her name.

Sterrett flinched.

"What?" Max whispered, but Sterrett only shook their head, refusing to engage. Sterrett was staring at the girl, unwilling, or maybe unable, to look away.

"Tell me your question, child," Len said.

"What's a birthday?" the girl asked. Her voice was high-pitched, but steady.

There was a murmur from the audience. Max tilted their head to the side. This was a word they hadn't heard anyone say in a long time, and its meaning hovered just out of reach.

Len smiled, bringing the sprig down to his chest. "It's a celebration of the anniversary of the day you were born."

"Why don't *we* celebrate it?" she asked. As the ritual went, she was allowed several follow-up questions.

But instead of answering, Len said, "You know why." He waited for her to figure it out.

"Because births are sad," she said, finally reciting what they'd all been taught, making the connection herself. "Because even though it has to happen sometimes, it's inherently wrong."

Len nodded. "Very good. Though we are grateful for our community and the lives we sustain, we don't believe in adding more humans to this earth. That's why we have the one-child policy, yes?"

The girl nodded.

At the mention of the one-child policy, Max's mom hung her head.

"Hey," Max whispered, elbowing her, but she didn't look at them. They didn't know why she'd have this reaction to something that had been preached to them thousands of times. Max felt frustratingly out of the loop; both their mom and Sterrett were acting so strangely and refusing to explain.

Len appraised the girl with his eyes. "Thank you for your questions. Soon you will be an adult. I look forward to what you will contribute to our society."

The girl climbed onstage to be blessed. Len ran the B3k sprig along her arms and legs. She looked uncomfortable, antsy. When he was done, he handed her the sprig, and she bolted, disappearing back into the audience.

"Blessed be the memory of he who sacrificed his life in the name of our precious resources. May his legacy forever inspire us to value the group over the self. Amen." Len pressed his hands together and bowed his head, and the people watching him did the same.

The ceremony was over. Sterrett got up and left before Max could say anything. Max's mom followed. Neither of them seemed to want to wait for Max, which was odd. Max joined the line of people waiting to file out of the chapel and then skipped the stairs and hopped directly down, landing lightly on their feet and bounding away.

They found Sterrett at their spot at the edge of the clearing, the same place where they'd first kissed a few nights ago. The air was full of the sweet smell of the B3k cooking nearby, and a fog had started to set in, blocking out the stars. Sterrett was sitting in the grass. Max flopped down on the ground next to them, and then lay on their side, head in hand. Sterrett didn't say anything.

"What's up?" they asked. "Are you okay?"

"I have to tell you something," they said.

"Anything," Max said.

"But you have to promise that it stays between us."

"We already have a secret between us," Max said. "You can trust me."

"I know I can," Sterrett said, and then was quiet for so long that for a moment Max wondered if they were changing their mind. Max put a hand on Sterrett's knee.

"When we were kids, Len used to . . ." Sterrett couldn't finish the sentence. They closed their eyes, turned pale, reliving something.

Max watched the color drain from Sterrett's cheeks.

"Used to what?"

Sterrett opened their eyes then, looking into Max's. "Don't make me say it," they whispered.

Max's stomach twisted. A white-hot anger was rising inside them, but they weren't surprised. This confirmed a feeling they'd carried with them for a long time. Len wasn't just unpleasant. He was something much worse.

"Does anybody else know?"

"I kept waiting for someone to notice," Sterrett said. "He'd leave bruises. But no one ever said anything, so neither did I. And now I feel like it's too late. Please, please don't tell." Sterrett's voice took on a different tone, pleading.

"I can't believe I didn't know," Max said.

Sterrett dismissed this. "Well, to be fair, I didn't tell you."

"Do you think he's doing it to other kids?"

"I know he is," Sterrett said, turning away from Max and lying on their back. Max lay on their back, too, so their shoulders and arms were touching. "You know Molly? The little girl asking questions?" Sterrett swallowed. "She had bruises on her arms. Just like I used to. And she's the right age for him."

When they were kids, Max had always noticed Sterrett's bruises, but thought nothing of them. Or rather thought they were badges of pride, something earned from playing hard. The shame of this—of not seeing what was right in front of them—was making it hard to breathe.

"Why tell me now?" Max asked.

"You're paying more attention to me than you ever have," Sterrett said. "I just didn't think I could keep it from you now that we . . ." they trailed off. "You know."

“You always make us go to services,” Max said. “I never would have gone if I’d known.”

“I’m scared to not go,” Sterrett replied. “I don’t want to attract attention. He’d notice if I wasn’t there. I missed a few, when we were kids, and he shamed my mom for it.”

They were quiet for a few moments. Sterrett’s skin was warm pressed into Max’s, and the grass was cool and prickly beneath their back.

Max said, “I can’t believe that no one has ever called him out for this.”

“If the others aren’t saying anything, there’s a reason,” Sterrett said. “I think he has too much power. No one would believe us. And anyway, I’m not sure what he’d do in retaliation. He’s violent.”

“I hate him,” Max said.

“Please? Promise you won’t say anything?”

“Fine. I promise,” Max assured them, while feeling like they were making the wrong decision. But it was Sterrett’s experience, not theirs. It wasn’t up to them to decide how to handle it.

The next morning, Max woke up to the loud chime of the breakfast bell.

They sat up and stretched. Their bed was a mattress on the floor in a huge room full of other mattresses. Morning light filtered lazily through the woven curtains, illuminating the faces of the people around them as they opened their eyes. All the single people slept in this room together. Only once they committed to a partner or partners could they be given privacy in a separate building that had apartments. Groggy, Max looked around, but Sterrett must have already gotten up.

Max rose and wandered outside to the long picnic tables. It was another temperate day, the sun barely piercing through the fog. Max was still trying to shake off the knowledge of what Sterrett had told them last night, like a bad dream. They weren’t sure how they could get through the day now that they knew.

They found their mom at a table alone, already halfway through her breakfast.

"Hi, my love," she said, as Max slid in next to her. They put their head on her warm shoulder, a bid for affection they hadn't asked for in a long time.

"What's wrong?" she said, putting her arm around them and pulling them closer.

"Nothing," they lied. "How are you? You seemed off last night."

"I'm okay," she said. "I'm going to visit the doctor later. I just feel a little sick."

"I'm sorry," they said. "Do you want me to go with you?"

"How about you meet me after?"

Max agreed.

It was their day off, and they had plans with Sterrett to go on a hike. They met at the base of the nearest mountain, which was on the edge of the community land. Max and Sterrett had stuffed their bags with food and emergency supplies—they'd all been trained in wilderness survival, should anything go wrong on a hike, which was allowed so long as they stayed within a specific radius that the committee said was safe.

They were quiet on the walk. That was something Max always appreciated about their friendship with Sterrett, even before they started sleeping together. Theirs was a connection so deep that it didn't always require words. Now, the only sounds were their footsteps and their breath and the birds and the wind in the trees. Sweat from Max's lip dripped into their mouth.

A few drones were flying overhead, spraying sulfur dioxide into the stratosphere to help dim the sun. Operating the drones was Max's least-favorite duty, perhaps because the payoff was impossible to measure. They couldn't compare the sun here to the sun elsewhere. They didn't know if it was even working, and that made the task unbearably dull.

That being said, there were worse things than drone duty. There was also a rotation that involved collecting human waste and turning it into fertilizer for the B3k fields. That one Max could really do without.

They reached the top of the summit, feeling high off the effort. "I'm starving," Max said, slightly out of breath. "Want to eat?"

But Sterrett didn't answer. Instead they stared off into the distance, the afternoon sun making the tips of their hair glow, and Max's heart skipped a beat as they realized Sterrett was crying.

"Hey," they said. "Hey. What is it?"

Sterrett didn't try to wipe the tears away. They were falling faster now. Snot dripped from their nose. Max wanted to fix it, but didn't know how.

"You haven't touched me since I told you," Sterrett said.

It was true. They were usually affectionate as soon as they were alone, but all day Max had stayed a few feet away, as though if they touched Sterrett, Sterrett might fall apart. The realization twisted Max's stomach in knots.

"I'm sorry," they said. "I didn't realize you would want to be touched after everything you've told me."

"How can you say that?" Sterrett said, their voice rising. "It happened a long time ago. I like feeling in control of my body. I like doing what I want with it. Which includes having sex with you. I'm sorry if that's too complicated."

Max held their hands up, a sign of surrender. "I didn't think about it like that," they said. "I'm sorry. You've been living with this for years and I only just found out." They stepped toward Sterrett, reached their arms out. "Can I touch you now?"

"No," Sterrett said, and then laughed. "Now I don't want you to."

"I swear on the earth," Max said, exasperated but smiling. "Fine. Let's just go back, then. I promised my mom I'd meet her after her doctor's appointment."

"Don't you want to eat?" Sterrett said.

They sat on the ground and pulled out their B3k, fried in small squares and heavily salted for the midday meal. They ate in silence. When they finished, Sterrett pulled Max into a hug, breathing them in. What a relief, finally, to be held.

"I'm sorry, again," Max said. "This is all uncharted territory. Us, I mean."

"I know," Sterrett said, from where their face was pressed into Max's collarbone. "It's okay. Sorry I got so upset. I think I'm just tired. You haven't been letting me get a lot of sleep lately."

"It's okay if it's more than that," Max said. "I can handle it."

Sterrett nodded, still pressed against them. "Thank you," they said.

They walked back in silence, holding hands.

As they hiked down the mountain Max tried to imagine what it had been like for Sterrett all these years, alone in the knowledge of what had been done to them. Or maybe not so alone in it—maybe other people knew and hadn't done anything. Just like they knew what was being done to that little girl and weren't going to do anything.

The sun was starting to set and the light was golden and dreamy, the fog having burned off earlier. Birds were screaming in the redwoods. Max's legs were tired from the hike, becoming liquid, and they had to focus on putting one foot in front of the other for fear of tripping. They were glad they'd eaten, glad Sterrett was with them, glad Sterrett was now something more than just their friend, something undefined but special, with promise. A surprise. There were hardly ever any surprises.

They followed the trail that took them back to the compound and then they took a shortcut to the brick building where Max's mom would be, straight through a particularly dense field of B3k, because it was quicker to fight their way through the overgrowth than go around it. They'd done so countless times and could deftly weave through the stalks, taking care not to step on too many beans.

Just before they reached the building, though, two doctors came out of the door and lingered there in the doorway.

"We'll have to report this to Len," Max heard one of them say.

Max and Sterrett were a few feet away, still concealed by the unruly stalks of wild bean plants, and at this they both held very still. Something to be reported to Len was something they wanted to hear about.

"Hopefully she'll allow us to take care of it for her," the second doctor responded. "I don't think I have the stomach to leave another one in the woods."

The doctors were walking down the path now, too far away for Max to hear the rest.

"What the fuck was that?" Max said. "They weren't talking about . . . second-borns, were they?"

Sterrett was white as the fog. "I think they were. I mean, *leave another one in the woods*? I've heard rumors that they do that, but I didn't think they were true."

"I didn't think so, either," Max said. "I thought that was just something the kids made up to freak each other out."

"That sounded pretty real," Sterrett said bitterly.

Max didn't know what to say.

Len being a predator, now second-born babies left in the woods? How could they reconcile all of it? How could they continue to go on as though everything was normal, knowing what they did?

Sterrett put a hand on Max's shoulder. "You're having big thoughts," they said. "I can see them on your face."

"I have questions," Max said. "About everything."

"It's a mindfuck if you think about any of this too hard," they said with a weak smile. "Welcome."

"I didn't know," Max said. "Or maybe I did. And I didn't want to see it."

"You did," Sterrett said. "You just didn't realize it. I don't think we could have been friends if you were totally oblivious."

"I did?"

"I mean, I think you did. You were the one who pointed out to *me* that all the people in charge are old men. Why do you think you noticed that, if not because part of you didn't trust this place?"

Max felt like the earth was moving beneath their feet. They needed to sit down. "I didn't know you noticed. When I had doubts."

"Of course I did," Sterrett said. "I've been here with you this whole time."

"Sterrett," they said. "I don't understand any of this. I don't understand how you've stayed here."

"Stayed here?" Sterrett repeated. "This is our home."

"But after everything you've been through. I don't know."

Sterrett shrugged, wouldn't make eye contact. Something was shifting. The suggestion of leaving had made Sterrett clam back up. "You get used to it," they said, so quietly Max had to strain to hear. "It's amazing what you can get used to."

"I can't get used to babies being left in the woods," Max said.

"Maybe we misheard." Sterrett shrugged again. "Maybe they were talking about something totally different and we're just being paranoid. What do I know?"

"A lot more than me," Max said. "Apparently."

"I'm sorry," Sterrett said. "You fuck me for a few days and suddenly your world turns upside down."

Max snorted. They hadn't thought about it like that, but Sterrett was right: since that first night together, everything had changed, in every way.

"It really has been . . . an illuminating period of time."

"You're welcome?" Sterrett offered.

But Max didn't have time to answer, because in that moment their mom emerged from the same building, her eyes puffy as though she'd just been sobbing. Max moved toward her, but Sterrett grabbed their arm.

"Wait," they whispered.

They froze, remaining hidden in the dense B3k stalks. Max's mother, clearly thinking she was alone, placed her hands on her stomach, then looked down at it.

"What are we going to do?" she said.

APRIL 2, 2041

Hello again.

I didn't realize how much emotion would go into recounting my past to you. Even just writing about my first night with Vero, Madhuri, and Cory has me hungover. And there's so much more to tell you.

I'm still in Idaho. I'd hoped to be farther by now, but the weather doesn't care about hope.

When I woke up in the morning, the sky was the clearest blue—the kind of deep gorgeous color you only get on this side of the country, where there's less humidity and pollution to refract the light—and the sun was almost painfully bright. I walked down the road for a bit, just taking it all in. The wind did some major damage while I slept, and power lines were tangled up in fallen trees. I'm thankful I found shelter when I did, even if it meant breaking and entering.

My car was okay, thank god, just a little dinged up. I got back on the highway and drove and drove through farmland and forest and mountains until my vision started to blur. I'm parked at a truck stop now, where I'll spend the night.

So: Where was I?

Oh. The first night in the old abandoned house, followed by the first morning.

I was awake before everyone else, and my stirring woke Cory up. "Do you want something to eat?" she whispered.

I nodded. My stomach was growling so loudly I wondered if she could hear it.

She got out of her sleeping bag. In the weak daylight, I could see her more clearly: skinny arms, face piercings—a lip ring and an eyebrow ring that looked a little crusty—a faded black hoodie, combat boots. She was so tall and waiflike, with such a round face that she looked like a balloon on a string. She walked with a slight limp. She saw me looking at her and smirked, then went downstairs. She seemed used to people looking at her.

Everything hurt, but I felt overall mostly good. Kind of like I'd won the lottery, finding this place, these people.

Cory was back shortly with a big paper bag full of bagels. It smelled like heaven. Vero and Madhuri woke up when she came in, and she tossed each of them one. She passed me two, and a container of tofu cream cheese.

"No offense," I said, "but how did you afford all of this?"

She glanced at Vero. "Wealthy benefactor," she said.

He shrugged. "It's a long story."

I should have known something was up, but I was too hungry to care. When you're really hungry—not just having-a-late-lunch hungry, but truly starving—you can't think about anything else. That part of you that asks questions is eroded. There's no higher self when you're trying to survive.

"So, look," Vero was saying, when I stopped chewing long enough to catch bits of their conversation. "There's a press conference tomorrow. I think we should go, give 'em hell."

"Is that smart?" Madhuri said. "Security will be tight."

"And *he* will be there," said Cory.

"Well, exactly," Vero said. "We need to make a point."

"What's the press conference?" I asked, wiping tofu cream cheese from my chin. "Who will be there?"

"The mayor is going to announce the city's break with the national fossil fuel agreement."

"What does that mean?" I immediately felt stupid for asking.

Cory was nice about my ignorance. "So you know how all the major cities in the country have agreed to cut down on greenhouse gas emissions by seventy-five percent within the next five years?"

I nodded.

"The mayor of New York City has decided that he won't be doing that."

I was still shoveling the bagel into my face and assumed someone would explain later.

I knew a little bit about the mayor, the first Latine person to hold the office. He was the most right-wing politician ever to run New York City. He was outspoken, wealthy, terrifyingly appealing to certain people. And his platform rested largely on insisting that climate-change action came at the cost of American jobs. The inability to think long term stood out to me, even then, though in hindsight I shouldn't have underestimated him. He *was* thinking long term—because a changing climate would actually benefit him, and others like him. In fact, as it turned out, his platform was just a small piece of an international conspiracy already years in the making. (I'll get to it soon.) But I couldn't see any of that. Not yet.

"We'll need press passes to get in," Vero said. "From there we can let everyone else in through a side door, I'm sure."

"Where should we say we're from?" Cory asked. "The *Times* or some shit?"

"No, they won't believe that." He shook his head.

"They won't believe we work *anywhere* credible," said Madhuri. "Look at us."

I chimed in. "We might have to say we're interns. Sorry, but none of us look old enough to be reporters." I had already begun saying *us*.

"Sounds cool, but that doesn't solve our problem," Madhuri said. "We need those cards with the bar code to get through security."

I sat up taller, thrilled that I was about to be useful. "I can make those," I said.

Cory clapped. "I knew she'd come in handy."

"I just need to use a computer."

"How do you know how to do that?" Vero asked.

"I used to make up a lot of stuff to get out of doing schoolwork," I said, blushing. "Coding is easy if you know a few basics. I'm sure we can find out what information the QR code needs to have and just recreate it."

"What else do you know?" Vero said in wonder. I didn't know how to answer. "Do you know how to get through firewalls? How to get into password-protected accounts?"

"You mean do I know how to hack?"

Vero nodded. I felt all three pairs of eyes looking at me, but it was Vero's I felt the most keenly. The spark of something warm and exciting: his attention on me. I'd never felt anything quite like it and honestly haven't since. That first moment he really saw me. Like suddenly I was a real human girl, no longer made of wood.

"I mean, I've never really done it," I said, and then, sensing that I'd disappointed him, I said, "Other than breaking into my parents' bank accounts and rerouting their money."

"I don't know if that's technically hacking," Vero said, but he was smiling as though I'd tickled him.

"I can learn just about anything," I insisted.

I hoped this was the truth. I wanted him to look at me like this forever.

"I'm sure we can find someone to teach you," Vero said.

"I bet Arthur would," said Madhuri. "He's always up to no good down there."

"You'd owe him, though," said Cory.

"Nah." Vero shook his head. "He already owes me."

"What'd you do?" asked Madhuri.

"Oh, you know." He waved her off. "He owed money to some scary motherfuckers."

There it was again: the reminder that my new friends had access to funds. I wondered why they were homeless if they had money. It seemed like a choice, like a rejection of society, rather than tragic circumstances. I hadn't told them about the cash stashed in my backpack, but oddly, I hadn't yet needed it, beyond my trip to the bodega.

"Okay, kids," Cory said. "I'm going to go shower at the Y. Anyone coming?"

I stank. I followed Cory and Madhuri to the public locker rooms at the nearby Y, where we passed a bar of soap between the shower stalls and I watched the water run gray between my toes. Cory got out first and I looked over the dingy plastic curtain as she wrapped a small towel around her hips. The pandemic had robbed me of high school locker-room experiences and I didn't know I wasn't supposed to stare at her while she was wet and naked. She caught me looking at her and winked. I blushed and averted my gaze.

I'd replay that moment over and over throughout the day, even while we went to the library so I could use a computer. As I wrote a simple code and created some fake names that I hoped sounded believable, I stared straight ahead, afraid that I'd meet Cory's eyes again and everyone would see how flustered I was becoming. I wasn't used to that kind of attention, even as small as it was.

I wanted Vero to look at me, too. But he was so much more aloof, so much more focused on the plan.

They both watched over my shoulder as I created perfect replicas of *New York Times* badges saying we were interns. We paid ten cents a page to print them out. It was so easy it felt stupid. Like I shouldn't have been able to do it. But I was. Cory hugged me when I showed them all the final results, lingering for a second longer than she needed to. When she released me, Vero hugged me, too. Suddenly I had the confusing sense that they were competing for me, though that seemed like a crazy thing to think.

In hindsight, I think I was much prettier than I realized. Prettiness doesn't really matter in high school if you are also weird and shy—what matters more, I think, is the ability to be cool and funny and confident, as I can recall so many kids who were not necessarily attractive but simply behaved as though they were, and we all believed them. But out here, in the wild world, my quirkiness seemed to be attracting people. I tell you this not to sound vain but because I hope that you are aware of your powers *while* you have them. I had no idea that I could draw people to me if I wanted to. I thought I was just lucky to be included. Looking at old photos of myself, it's easy to see. My acne wasn't as bad as I thought. My freckles were cute. I was pretty short, but I had the body that women were told we were supposed to have, and although I covered my chest and my hips and my butt in loose layers of black, you could still tell. The streaks of blue in my hair made me look edgy. And I think, probably, my unawareness of my beauty added to my charm. Annoying but true.

I knew as soon as I saw you that you would also be beautiful, and it was confirmed as you became a child. You're beautiful in a different way, but it's still there. I hope you are careful with the hearts that you'll pull toward you. Just because they're easy to come by doesn't make them any less precious.

So. Back to the press conference.

We waited in line with the real reporters outside City Hall. Our passes were scanned; the light flashed green. It had worked. I knew it would, which helped my nerves. We joined the group of tense-looking reporters gathered around a microphone, clutching their phones and recorders. Cameras clicked and whirred around us. We tried not to giggle. Though we'd gotten in no problem, plenty of people were looking at us suspiciously. We stuck out, majorly. The press conference was surrounded by metal barricades and cops. There was electricity in the air, a sense of waiting for something. The sun beat down, reflecting on the concrete, and we were all sweating.

The mayor appeared, flanked by security. I'd never been this close to a famous person, and I was surprised at how normal he seemed, how *not* larger-than-life he was. He was just a man in a suit, his black hair in a military cut, not necessarily very tall or attractive, just kind of there, approachable and normal. While the applause distracted everyone, Vero snuck to the outside of the group of reporters, and shifted one of the barricades so that there was a gap between them. Before the mayor could say a word, we all heard chanting in the distance grow louder and louder: "You're killing us. You're killing us." Vero reappeared next to me and said, "It's go time."

A stream of people holding signs and megaphones and filming on their phones began pouring through the gap in the barricades. I had no idea we were bringing so many people in. It was a glorious sight to behold. The mayor seemed dumbstruck. His security detail surrounded him and guided him backward, toward the building he'd emerged from.

The cops started to close in. A few feet away, a girl was knocked to the ground. She was surrounded by phones, everyone scrambling to capture the moment while also trying to survive it.

"Let's go," Madhuri said. Cory grabbed my hand as we pushed our way through the throng of protestors. I wasn't sure why we were leaving. The excitement had only just started. Cory's hand was sweaty in mine, her grip so hard it hurt, but I didn't let go.

Then I heard it: "Vera!"

A voice coming closer and closer.

"Vera," a woman kept shouting at us. "Vera, wait."

"Who the fuck is Vera?" I asked, as we continued to make our way through the crowd.

"Me," Vero said, as he stopped and turned around.

I was shocked to see the mayor's wife facing us, her security detail rushing to get behind her. She was wearing a black suit and a pearl necklace, her hair in a perfect French twist.

"Hi, Mom," he said.

(We were still being filmed. This moment would later go viral on TikTok; would spark a conversation online about whether or not it was ethical to post Vero being deadnamed.)

My mouth fell open. I looked at Madhuri and Cory. They looked grim but unsurprised. Meaning: they already knew who Vero's mom was.

"Vera, you can still come home," she said, out of breath from chasing after us. "We miss you. We can work this out."

He folded his arms across his chest. In the distance, I saw the cops getting closer. "We should go," I whispered to Madhuri, the danger becoming clear to me now. She nodded.

Vero's mother said, "I see you have no problem still using our credit card."

Oh. There it was. We were being bankrolled by Vero's mom, and presumably his dad: the mayor.

For a moment, I wondered what it would be like to have parents who wanted me to come home. I felt sorry for myself watching his mother beg for him to return. I know now that it was more complicated than that—Vero's parents didn't want him to come home, they wanted him to be someone he wasn't. But my parents didn't want *any* version of me to come back.

"There is no Vera," Vero said. "And there won't be a Vero if you pull the city out of the climate deal."

As if on cue, Madhuri and Cory began to shout, "You're killing us! You're killing us!"

Vero took my arm as he turned. "Let's get the fuck out of here."

We tore down the street away from the crowds and the phones and through an alley, across a parking lot, over the bridge. We didn't stop running until we crossed the bridge.

"I know you have questions," Vero said, when we were almost back to the house.

"I'm not judging you," I said. I was out of breath.

"We only use the credit card for necessities."

"Why not use it for rent?" I asked. I was scared he would think I was mad at him. I wasn't. I was just confused and curious.

"Because then they'd know how to find me," he said. "Besides. We already have a place to live. And we can be there without lining another landlord's pockets."

I was quiet. I didn't know what else to say. He took out his phone and started scrolling through social media, looking at photos from the protest that were already being shared.

I fell into step with Cory.

"Don't think too hard about it," she said. "It'll make you crazy."

I laughed, relieved to be validated. "I already feel crazy," I said.

"Oh, join the club. I can't even imagine what it would be like to have a family who wanted me back."

"You read my mind," I said.

"Of course, I guess you and I can't imagine what it would be like to have a family who only wanted you back if you de-transitioned," she added.

I nodded. I was uncomfortable in how little I could relate to Vero's situation, crushed by self-pity.

"In case you were curious," Cory said, "Vero grew up like, country-club rich."

"Like skiing and sail-boating rich?"

She laughed. "Like oysters and caviar and plaid."

I tried to picture it and couldn't. "How did *you* grow up?" I asked her.

"Like food stamps and black eyes," she said. "You?"

"Oh, our two-bedroom walk-up was technically a penthouse," I joked. "No, I mean, we were pretty middle class. My parents fell down a QAnon rabbit hole, though. It was never going to work out between us after that."

"You were great back there," she said, changing the subject. "Fucking fearless."

"I was terrified," I admitted.

"Me, too." She smiled at me, and then she put her hand on my shoulder. I held my breath, scared she might move it if I had a reaction. Her cheeks turned pink. I was confused by how nervous I seemed to be able to make her.

Later, after everyone else had fallen asleep, Cory nudged me and whispered, "Let's go downstairs."

I followed her through the house and out the back window. I watched her smoke a cigarette and kick the dirt. We didn't speak. She flicked the cigarette onto the ground, stomped it out with her boot, and then took my face between her hands and kissed me, her silver rings digging into my cheeks. This was my first kiss. And then it was my first a lot of things.

I will spare you the details of what happened after that. I know there's nothing more disgusting than thinking about your mom being sexually active.

But regardless of the details, I felt far away. While Cory was kissing me, Vero's face kept flashing into my mind. I tried to ignore it, tried to focus on the feeling of her, not him. It's not that I didn't like what she was doing. It was just . . . complicated. If Vero had pursued me first, I would have gone out into the night with him instead. Cory had just been more aggressive, and I was impressionable enough that this mattered.

Eventually we went back inside, hand in hand. She motioned for me to share her sleeping bag. It was so warm and soft and I was thrilled to not be on the cold floor again. I tucked right in, the little spoon. Cory twisted herself around me like a pipe cleaner. Before I fell asleep, I realized that Vero's eyes were open, and he was looking at me with an expression I couldn't place. My heart sank. I couldn't meet his eyes.

When I woke up, everyone was gone except for Madhuri.

"Hey," she said, while I stretched my arms over my head and yawned. "Be careful with Coriander." I wondered how she knew, and then remembered I was in Cory's sleeping bag.

I rubbed my face. "What do you mean?"

She rolled her eyes impatiently. "Have you ever been in a relationship?"

I shook my head, but she already knew the answer. For some reason, I was angry. "You're just jealous," I said.

"Oh, please," she said. "If I wanted to be with Cory, I would be with Cory."

I contemplated that for a moment. Her confidence was annoying. But it did give me pause. Did *I* want to "be with" Cory? I liked kissing her, and I liked the feel of her hands on me, and I liked her attention. I'd liked sharing her sleeping bag, feeling her bones knocking into mine in the night. I didn't know what else I wanted beyond that. I didn't want Cory any more than I wanted Vero. And what did it mean to be careful with her? Was Madhuri looking out for me, or for Cory? What could I possibly do to hurt Cory, who was so cool and removed?

"Anyway, she's too old for you," Madhuri said.

"How old is she?"

"Twenty-two."

Was that too old for me? It didn't seem so. (It does now, of course. People in their twenties who date teenagers are surely lacking in some way. Please learn from my mistakes.)

"How old are *you*?" I asked.

"Nineteen," she said. "A lifetime older than you."

I laughed.

"Anyway," she continued, "Cory comes from a really fucked-up situation. Just . . . be gentle with her."

We were quiet. I said, "You know, Madhuri, you haven't told me about *your* family."

"There's not much to tell," she said. "My grandparents didn't come to this country so that their only granddaughter could be a degenerate, blah blah blah. You know. Same old story. I haven't seen them in years. That's old news, though." She clearly didn't want to talk about it, so I stopped pushing her for information.

Cory and Vero returned with a bag.

Cory pulled out a box and handed it to me. “Here you go,” she said. “A welcome present from us to you.”

It was a brand-new laptop.

I gasped as I pulled it out, and then felt a cold chill as I realized where it came from. I turned to Vero. “Did you charge this to your parents’ card?”

“Okay,” Vero said, sounding pissed off, “one more rule. If someone gives you something nice, just say thank you.” I think he was mad at me about the night before, though he’d never admit it. But there was nothing I could do about that.

Cory looked at me and shook her head, as if to say, *Let it go.* I said, “Thank you.”

I heard footsteps climbing the stairs to the attic and was surprised to see one of the guys I recognized from the first floor materialize in front of us.

“This is Arthur,” Vero said. “He’s going to teach you how to hack.”

Arthur saluted Vero and sat down beside me. He smelled like he was overdue for a shower, and his acne was worse than mine, which made me guess we were around the same age, our skin ruled by the hormones that ran through us like electricity. But he was nice; I felt this immediately.

“Okay, pal,” he said. “First I’m going to show you how cybersecurity works. Then I’m going to show you how to get around it.”

I didn’t even realize when everyone else vacated the room. I’d never been so thrilled to learn something in my life.

For the next few weeks, I spent every day with Arthur, sitting on the floor, peering over his shoulder and hardly even blinking. The others brought us food, I think, but I don’t remember eating.

Before bed each night, when my eyes were too bleary to keep staring at the screen, we’d all sit in a circle and talk about the state of the world. Vero had big, passionate ideas about climate change—like that it was still stoppable, even though we’d almost passed the tipping point. Beyond that, they were all interested in decolonizing the United States, in abolishing the prison system, in helping people get abortion pills, in getting trans kids out of states where their existence had been made illegal. I agreed with everything they said. I still do. But what could we—a group of unhoused, unloved young people—do about it? Their activism was centered around protest. They showed up around the city making trouble, mostly, coordinating with other groups from around the city and turning up in droves. I wasn't sure that was enough, but was too shy to say so, yet. Plus, Vero came from privilege. What did he really know about struggle?

I started dreaming in code.

Sometimes, in the middle of the night, I'd wake to Cory's hand on my arm, and follow her out into the moonlight, where she'd press me against the outside of the house. Even in those moments, though, I was thinking of firewalls, two-factor authentication, the dark web. Arthur must have owed Vero a lot of money for the amount of time he was putting in with me.

I knew Cory liked me more than I liked her—I could tell by how she noticed my every move, how her moods seemed to rest on how much attention I gave her in return—and I relished it. I liked to leave her wanting me, to be the one to pull away first.

Sometimes she asked me to tell her what I'd learned while she kissed my neck. I whispered to her about how to clear evidence of a breach in the warm night air. She'd laugh, amazed at how much I knew.

My brain was brimming with C++.

I bought my own sleeping bag from the dollar store. It was sweet to share Cory's, but also a little embarrassing to have our intimacy on display like that, especially when I still wasn't sure how to define what was happening between us, and I hated the thought of Vero witnessing it.

I eventually pieced together Cory's story based on little things she mentioned here and there. It was a rough one. Her childhood had been violent, thanks to her father's drinking and her mother's enabling. After the neighbors saw him kick her outside their trailer, she'd been removed from her home and placed in foster care, where she spent her adolescence bouncing from bad situation to worse situation, families who took fosters in for the money and then would neglect them, abuse them. When she was fifteen, she started trying to run away. She'd tried and failed several times. One time, she'd been so desperate to get away that she was careless and fell asleep on the subway, waking up to a group of men standing over her. They'd called her a dyke, a fag, not sure how to classify a butch teen and then beaten her so severely that later, in the hospital, she was told she'd needed to get a metal plate in her hip. (This explained the limp.) She was returned to her foster family when she could walk again, though the pain never fully let up. By the time she was eighteen, she was addicted to Oxy and on the street. Vero had found her, eventually, hanging around on the outskirts of a group of kids who lived beneath the underpass, and had taken her under his wing, taught her about activism. She felt she owed him her life.

He didn't know that she squirreled away change from cash he gave her for food to buy pills. Or at least, she didn't think he knew. She told me she needed them. She told me she was in chronic, debilitating pain. That when she didn't have them, everything felt impossible.

Her secret addiction meant she kept a part of herself separate from our group, and from me. I would never fully know her.

Her story made me anxious. She was clearly so traumatized.

They all seemed traumatized, though. It seemed like their trauma was what connected them. And the movement grounded them. I knew they believed in the cause, but it also seemed that they *needed* to have a cause, depended on the sense of belonging it gave them. Without it, they would be untethered and alone.

But there also wasn't a lot of time to dwell on it, because the rest of my waking moments were spent with Arthur.

Finally, one evening, Arthur took his hands off the keyboard and nodded at me. "Now you try," he said. He'd opened up the log-in page for the mayor's office.

I cracked my knuckles, not really because I needed to, but because I'd seen him do it, and it seemed like it brought him luck. And then, I was off to the races. I opened the tools he'd shown me. I ran the software that tried passwords. My fingers flew over the keys. The laptop's fan turned on, whirring as it grew hot on my legs. I was sweating, holding my breath. And then, I was in. The mayor's inbox glittered on the screen. Just like that.

Arthur high-fived me. "With great power comes great responsibility, yada yada," he said. "Be careful out in the ether."

I looked up and realized that the others were in the room. They began a slow clap.

"The student becomes the master," Vero said.

"Can you guys stop speaking in platitudes?" said Madhuri, rolling her eyes, but she was grinning at me. Cory laughed.

"Let's go get something to celebrate," Cory said. "Beer, maybe? Madly, come with?" They left, and Arthur followed. I was alone with Vero.

"I knew you could do it," he said.

"Thanks for believing in me."

"So what's going on with you and Cory?" he asked. There was a new sharpness to his voice. I tilted my head to look at him, wondering what he was thinking, feeling. He was biting his lip. I realized I was staring at his mouth, which was now starting to curl up into a smile. I forced myself to look instead at his big brown eyes. I gulped. He'd asked me a question, and now I was dumbstruck by his beauty.

"Oh," I said, searching for my voice. "Um. I'm not really sure."

"I'm not mad or anything," he said. "I just want to know what you're doing hooking up with her"—his voice cracked and he paused for what felt like a lifetime, and then he said—"and not with me."

I was stunned. When I could speak, I said, "I didn't realize that was an option." It was true: I figured he would have gone for me if he wanted me, and he hadn't. He'd just watched me from the sidelines. At least, until this moment. My thoughts were jumbled. What about Cory? But a louder roar in my heart said: *Isn't this what you wanted all along?*

"You don't see how special you are?" he said, coming toward me on his knees.

I put the laptop to the side. My heart was pounding.

Before I knew it, he was in front of me, so close I could touch him, and then his mouth was on mine. This didn't feel like kissing Cory. I was out of control, dizzy, like all the blood in my body had rushed to my . . . sorry. I'm sure you don't want to hear about that.

I heard a noise in the hall. I pulled back and opened my eyes, and there was Cory, her mouth hanging open.

"I forgot my wallet," she said finally.

"Oh, shit," Vero said.

"Fuck you," she said, and stormed out. I wasn't sure if she was talking to him or me.

I started to get up to go after her, but Vero stopped me. "This is my fault," he said. "Let me deal with it." And then I was alone again.

My first group of friends, and I had made a total mess of everything.

I was crying into Cory's sleeping bag when Madhuri got back.

"Oh, for the love of god," she said, and sat down beside me.

"Tell me what to do." I sniffled.

"For one thing, stop feeling sorry for yourself," she said. "Worse things have happened. This is not worse than your parents kicking you out. This isn't worse than like, climate change coming for our necks." Her directness was refreshing. She wasn't going to coddle me. I immediately sat up and stopped crying. She was right. I wiped the snot on my sleeve.

"Should I find somewhere else to crash?" I said. "I really don't want to cause drama."

"Don't be ridiculous," she said. "But what you need to know

is, Vero is probably totally fine with you doing whatever you want. He's been poly forever. Everyone has fucked Vero, is the truth. Not just the girls, either. But Cory . . . she's a little more traditional. She probably thinks you're in a relationship."

"*Am* I in a relationship with Cory? I don't know anything about dating," I said. "No one has ever liked me before."

"I doubt that," she said, but then assessed the look on my face and said, "Okay, maybe not that you've been aware of."

"What do I do? Do I have to choose between Vero and Cory?"

She shrugged. "Babe, it's your life. Do what you want."

"I guess I should go find Cory," I said. "And at least apologize."

Madhuri agreed that an apology was a good start, so I put my sneakers on and wandered downstairs. On the first floor of the house kids were lying around smoking weed or sleeping or talking quietly in corners. Another version of me, the me who hadn't gotten kicked out of her house, might have been afraid of them, but the person I'd become knew they were harmless. They were looking for safety and love like all of us.

I found Cory about a block away, leaning against the wall of a boarded-up restaurant, smoking. She looked like hell.

"Cory, I'm sorry," I said. "I don't know what I'm doing."

"He always fucking does this," she said.

"Does what?"

"Anytime I like someone. He just . . ." She trailed off.

I waited to feel jealous that Cory had liked other girls, but I didn't. I felt jealous that Vero had.

"Do you love him?" she said.

"*Love?*" I repeated. "I barely know him. We've only just kissed, once. I haven't had a minute to think about what it means."

Cory looked at me like I was the dumbest person in the world, which, I imagined, I was. At no point in my trysts with Cory had the idea of love occurred to me. It was physical attraction and nothing more. Did she love me? Was I supposed to love her? What did that even mean?

"If you love him, I'll leave you alone," she said. "But if you don't"—her face was open, her eyes wide and pleading—"if there's any chance of us, then I'm not going anywhere."

I'll be honest: this, to me, seemed pretty melodramatic. I didn't know what to say. I didn't want the burden of Cory waiting for me. It wasn't fair. Especially given the difference in intensity between my feelings for her and whatever had come over me the second Vero had kissed me. With Vero I was on fire. With Cory it felt more like getting into a warm bath. But I also couldn't let her go. Not yet. Maybe this was selfish. But I was so starved for love, I couldn't stand the idea of turning it away, in any form.

"I'll let you know if I decide I'm in love with him," I conceded.

That seemed to satisfy her. "Okay." She nodded.

"Should I talk to him?" I said. "I feel like I need to clear the air or something."

She laughed and shook her head at me. "Do whatever you want. Though I think this is on him. He knows you're just a kid."

If Cory thought I was just a kid, she had no business pursuing me. That didn't occur to me in the moment, though. All I felt was stinging shame as I realized that neither of them took me seriously. They were like dogs fighting over a chew toy.

It was August. Soon, my senior year would be starting. I had already decided that I was dropping out, but I wondered if anyone would notice, or try to find me. I hadn't responded to the automated email that directed me to a link to sign up for classes. I wasn't sure if you had to fill out any sort of official paperwork to drop out, or if you could just simply never show up again, so I chose the latter. I wanted to become a ghost.

I wanted to become a ghost in my new life, too. For the next few days I hid from both Cory and Vero. I volunteered to be the one to run errands; I posted up with my laptop in the corner and pretended to be busy for hours on end. Sometimes, in passing, Vero would graze the back of his hand against mine. Other times, Cory would leave little treats for me, cupcakes and soda, while I feigned absorption in the digital realm. They were both watching me, waiting for me to make a decision, but I was paralyzed.

I moved my sleeping bag so it was closest to Madhuri, where I felt safer. Instead of joining them for meals, I ate over my computer.

Choosing Vero would hurt Cory. Choosing Cory would mean walking away from the potential of Vero, which I couldn't bear. Looking back, it wasn't a fair comparison—I was trying to decide between a relationship I had stumbled into with someone I barely knew, and one that existed only in my imagination. It was like a competition where all the contestants were my own projections.

Sometimes Madhuri tried to pull me aside and talk to me, but I avoided her, too. The only person I talked to was Arthur, following him around like a sad kitten and making up questions to keep him engaged.

This went on for weeks. Meanwhile, the group continued to organize. We protested at the waterfront, where ships were dumping waste into the river. We covered an office building with posters depicting the rising cancer rates linked to the plastic they bottled water with. We set up bail donation funds for members of the group who were arrested on civil disobedience charges. We posted the personal cell phone number of a politician who gave a speech demonizing trans kids to TikTok. Despite the tension I'd caused—or maybe because of it, as though sowing seeds of romantic chaos had anchored me to them—I felt that I was part of something.

One night in the attic I noticed something weird was going on with Cory. She'd stumbled in after the rest of us were already settled, tripping over her feet. Her eyes looked glassy, and she was slurring her words. Her skin had an odd gray tint to it. Madhuri and Vero clearly noticed, too.

"Hey, are you okay?" I asked, after she collapsed into her sleeping bag.

"Oh, she speaks," she said.

I realized I hadn't uttered a word to her in days.

"Are you high?" Vero said.

"Are *you*?" she said. "I'm too tired for this shit." And then she appeared to fall asleep, mouth open.

"Fuck," Madhuri said.

I put my face in my hands.

"You're not responsible for Coriander," Vero said. "She's an adult."

"Counterpoint: you *are* responsible for how you treat people," Madhuri said.

We went to sleep with her words hanging in the air. I woke up a few times to check Cory's pulse. She lived through the night. I'd never seen someone so fucked up before. Vero brought her coffee in the morning. She didn't want to talk to anyone.

Over the next few weeks, as I continued to avoid making a decision, Cory seemed to be letting her addiction take the wheel. She reeked of alcohol, but her delirious affect hinted at the use of a heavier substance, too. She was getting so thin I imagined I could see through her. I was concerned about her, but also annoyed. She had been the one to pursue me. It didn't seem fair that she couldn't handle some bumps in the road. I should have been allowed to pause and consider my feelings without her falling apart. Vero stopped giving her the credit card, but it didn't seem to make a difference. Someone was supplying Cory with drugs in exchange for who knows what.

One morning Vero woke me up when it was still dark out. "Come watch the sunrise," he whispered.

We tiptoed up to the roof, which had a small area where you could sit. "She's a mess," he said.

"It's my fault."

"Nah," he said. "She was like this before you got here. I guess I'm just wondering . . . Why is that appealing to you?"

"It's not," I said. It was nice to admit that. Seeing how easily Cory had fallen apart had lifted any lingering attraction I had to her. "I think I just liked that she liked me."

"Look," he said. "I would never, ever tell you who to be with. If you want to be with both of us, that's cool. I'll take what I can get. I don't believe in monogamy and I certainly don't believe it's my place to tell a woman what to do with her body."

"Madhuri kind of told me that's how you felt," I said.

"Why didn't you just ask?"

I didn't have an answer.

He said, "Cory's pretty controlling."

In hindsight, it was odd for him to so readily drag his best friend through the mud like that. It was like he was saying whatever he needed to in order to get me to pick him, while also saying he didn't need me to decide either way. It's easy to understand you've been manipulated after the fact. But in the moment all I could think was that I loved him. Cory had been right about that.

I stared at the horizon, where the sun was starting to turn the skyline yellow. I shivered, and he put a warm arm around me, pulling me close. I was melting into him, and before I really knew what I was doing, I turned my face toward his and we kissed, at first tentatively and then desperately. I stopped thinking. Nothing had ever felt so right. I lost track of time, of place. If there were sounds, I couldn't hear them over the thudding of my heart.

When we finally went back inside, Cory was gone. I never saw her again.

That's all I have time to tell you now. More soon. I love you.

2

ORCHID
2078

JUST A FEW MILES AWAY FROM NEW YORK CITY—SO CLOSE she could see Inside's looming, lumpy form silhouetted against the reddish-gray sky—Orchid's front tire hit a hole in the road.

The sky appeared to flip upside down as she sailed through the air; her bike was below her, and then above her, and then below her again as she flew and then landed and then rolled, bouncing, like a stone skipping across the smooth surface of a pond, coming to a stop at the base of a rotted-out tree, where she looked up at the decaying black branches and the smoggy orange clouds and knew with absolute certainty that here was where she was going to die.

She'd been so good about the fucking potholes, too. Spent the entire ride down the endless highway watching out for them. There was only one highway left that went from the city to upstate, and then Canada. The road was corroded with decades of disasters and neglect. Ironic that the potholes were actually the least dangerous thing she'd swerved around. There'd been tree roots splitting through the pavement, sinkholes, places where the guardrails had decayed, leaving nothing standing between her and fatally steep drops. It was clear to Orchid that nature was taking this road back, as though the highway itself was a rotting corpse.

There was a part of her that knew that this decision to leave her small community in the wilderness of Canada in order to try to rescue Ava from whatever was happening Inside was nothing short of idiotic. She had left Ava over twenty years ago when Ava was accepted to the Inside Project and she wasn't; a decision she'd regretted almost immediately. Now, with news about the horrible things happening Inside and the knowledge that only she had about how to get in, she was determined to make it right.

The news had come from her friend Camilla's father. He had an old comms device that he used to talk to his oldest daughter, Shelby, who lived on the US space shuttle with her boss, Jacqueline Millender—also known as the woman running Inside. Orchid had never met nor spoken to Shelby, but given who she worked for, what she said had to be true.

Camilla and her father were the closest thing Orchid had to family, and the guilt she felt about leaving them was as heavy as a child strapped to her back. But staying wasn't an option, once she learned that Ava might need her. That maybe there was something she could do to fix what she'd broken so long ago.

Alone on the highway, she'd been careful, so very careful, for too many days to count. Past the empty towns and the signs for the US military base and the long stretches of nothing where once there was endless greenery and life. She was almost out of water when she finally reached the place from which she could see the shape of Inside. A few years ago she'd traded with someone for one of those old CamelBak water bottles, the ones with the long blue straw that you can wear on your back, and when she'd left she'd filled it to the brim, not imagining what might happen when she'd slurped the last of it. She'd rationed it well, anyway, along with the dried meat she'd stuffed in her pockets and fanny pack. Even though she was pretty hungry at all times, she at least wasn't starving. She had starved before. She knew what it felt like, the deep pit of emptiness that made it hard to focus on anything other than food and the lack of it. No, things had been going surprisingly well, really, on this journey.

That is, until they weren't.

It was only when Inside appeared over the horizon that she lost focus, her awe replacing her concentration. She forgot about the blisters on the bottoms of her feet and the burns on her skin everywhere the sun could get to; she forgot to worry about the thunder in the distance or the putrid, toxic smell of the air that had at times made her cough so hard she almost puked.

All she could think was: *Ava's been in there this whole time.* And then she'd failed to dodge a pothole. She became airborne, flipping over the front handles, leaving her bike behind.

Her helmet was still intact, still on. *Thank god for the helmet,* she thought, and then she thought: *But maybe without it I could have just died instantly.* Now, she wasn't sure how long it would take her to bleed out or starve or dehydrate. Which would come first? Which would hurt more? It was like a sinister game of Would You Rather. Only she had no one to play it with.

She was afraid to move, afraid of broken bones that maybe she just couldn't feel yet, and so she lay as still as possible, trying to calm her breathing. The loudest pain was in her hands, screaming and smarting and pulsing. Her palms were bleeding. Could that be the worst of it? It didn't seem possible. She breathed in and out, and in and out, slowly, deeply, until the thunderous roar of her heart felt more normal.

And because she was so tired from too many days of unending cycling, when her heart rate slowed and she let herself relax just a little bit, she fell asleep, sinking into nothingness.

Not exactly nothingness, though. Dreams like fun-house mirrors, her own face stretching and contorting, the faces of the people she'd left behind in Canada staring at her with disappointment and shame. Camilla telling her to come back. The monotony of building shelters repeated in a haunting carnivalesque loop: plan, gather, assemble, fortify, hope that a storm doesn't destroy it, rebuild. The queasy satisfaction of hunting: dead squirrels and birds and rats, peeling their skin, gutting them, cooking them so they were burnt to such a crisp that any lingering parasites would die, still feeling hungry after.

Her eyes flickered back and forth rapidly under her twitching eyelids, but none of these nightmares could possibly wake her from her badly needed slumber.

She awoke some time later, the rust-colored sky darker now, a light pattering of rain on her face. She had feeling in her toes, pins and needles that turned to sharp pain, but at least she wasn't numb. That was a good start. She shifted her legs. They still worked. So: her neck wasn't broken. The scrapes on her palms were starting to crust over. Her whole body hurt. The hurt gave her hope. Maybe she would live. Maybe she could walk. Maybe she'd still make it to Inside.

She hoisted herself up so that she was sitting, leaning against the base of the tree. In the distance she saw her bicycle, mangled on the ground. It looked as roughed up as she felt. She still wasn't sure how injured she was or how long she'd been lying there. She looked at the sky, thick and strange with pollution, and couldn't tell if the weak round glow behind the sickly clouds was the sun or the moon. If it was twilight or daylight. If she was brave or terribly stupid. (On that last point, of course, it was the latter. She knew it was the latter.)

She couldn't make out much around her. The smog blanketed the air, so thick that she could only see maybe a few hundred yards. She wondered if anyone else was alive out here, or if the air was too toxic, or the storms too frequent. It was at the very least too fucking hot out for anyone to *want* to be here.

She imagined she was somewhere near where Yonkers used to be. South of where she'd grown up. She could remember it so clearly, the perfect lawns and the quaint Craftsman houses and the cute little downtown areas with general stores that sold handmade soaps. Like another planet. Where had all those people gone? Was it possible, in the two decades since she'd left, a stubborn twentysomething with a chip on her shoulder, they'd all died?

She and Ava used to come here on weekends, sometimes, walking around laughing at how much those handmade soaps cost, eating farm-to-table organic gluten-free pastries and drinking whatever latest coffee trend was currently draining their bank accounts. She ached for the frivolousness, for how pretty Ava looked in a plaid shirt and hiking boots—Ava's country drag, though this had hardly been the country; more like a playground for the rich.

Orchid shifted uncomfortably, realizing her sweat had soaked through her jeans completely. Oh, the fucking heat. The feeling of her damp clothes on her body was making her claustrophobic. She took her helmet off.

Piercing pain, then, on the side of her head. She lifted a hand to it and touched wetness. She winced and forced herself to keep exploring, find the source. It seemed to be a gash in the cartilage of her left ear. She was bleeding like all get-out, but she sure as hell wasn't going to die from a cut on her ear. At least, she better not. Who dies of an ear wound? Not her. Not after everything she'd been through.

She ripped a long shred of material off the bottom of her T-shirt and wrapped it around her head, pressing into her ear. She drank some water from the CamelBak. At last, she tried to stand.

It was like she was looking at the world through a straw, and also like she was floating. She was no longer hot but cold, clammy. She realized she was about to pass out, and quickly sat back down.

She hung her head between her knees, still pressing the cotton to her gash, and wondered what in the world she was going to do now.

She was not going to actually reach Ava. This whole thing was just another dumb mistake.

Not only that, but she'd also never make it back north before her community left without her for greener pastures. She was all alone, and out of options.

And then she heard them.

First, the voice of a young girl: "Mom, there's someone over there."

And then, a voice she almost recognized: "Don't get too close."

Orchid blinked. She hadn't heard human voices in days. She strained to see the two strangers walking toward her through the smog, blurry figures clothed in strange pink outfits, and then suddenly they were clear and vivid: two women.

One of them was Ava.

Orchid wondered once again if she was dying. If her brain was shutting down, showing her random scenes from the past as it blinked off. She must have hit her head harder than she realized.

She knew it was a hallucination because the Ava walking toward her with a worried frown hadn't aged a day since the last time they'd seen each other. In fact, she looked younger; maybe the age that she'd been when they'd first met? This was the Ava of her memories, of her dreams. God, she was beautiful. Skin like a baby's. Curly brown hair that defied gravity. *Of course I'm seeing you right before I go,* she thought. In a way, she had almost expected this.

Something in this delusion didn't make sense, though. Why imagine an older woman walking alongside Ava? Who was that supposed to be? Who else could she possibly want to see in her final moments?

Her mom?

No. She couldn't even really remember what her mother looked like, but she did know she had been very young when she left Orchid, so who knew what the significance of this vision was. She was too tired to psychoanalyze herself. Surely this was just her brain saying goodbye to her, and soon, the abyss.

But the delirium wouldn't let her go, not yet. Ava was crouching down in front of her, saying, "Hey, are you all right?" and the older woman with her was saying, "Brook, don't touch her." Why did the older woman call Ava by that name? Did she know who Ava even was? Why did she think Ava's name was Brook? That was a funny name. She and Ava had lived in a place called Brook, the quaint seaside town that used to be Brooklyn, before all the floods. What a strange coincidence.

With all of her remaining strength, Orchid raised one hand to Ava's cheek. Ava jumped back when Orchid's finger made contact with her face, which was soft and warm. Meaning: she was real.

So, not a delusion, then. But something else very odd. Why hadn't she aged?

"It's me," Orchid wheezed at her. "Ava, it's me."

The older woman in front of her then. Pushing Ava out of the way.

Taking Orchid's hands. Looking deep into her eyes. Examining her face. And then saying, "Oh my god, oh my god, oh my god."

Orchid looked back and forth between the two women and at last she understood: Yes, *this* was Ava.

This beautiful, older person with wild hair and fine lines carved gently around her face, her cheeks a little more defined than they used to be, her jawline less sharp, her arms softer, a bit of silver around her temples glinting in the strange light—this was the Ava that Orchid had spent decades longing for. The other woman had to be her daughter.

Or—she thought, looking back and forth between the two with renewed focus—her clone.

"I was coming to save you," Orchid said.

Ava laughed then, a single gruff "*Ha!*," and the sound of it made all of Orchid's organs feel pulled like the tide toward Ava, the moon. Orchid promptly began to cry, though as was her habit, she was also laughing; at herself, for this embarrassing display of emotions, and at the situation, which was so unbelievable there was really nothing to do but find humor in it.

"Orchid, what the fuck? Is it really you? Why are you bleeding?" Ava asked. She touched Orchid's palms and her face and her legs softly, searching. "What in the world are you doing out here?"

But Orchid no longer felt any pain, not externally at least. She felt herself leaving her body and entering something more like shock. She wanted Ava to hold her in her arms. She wanted to rest her face on Ava's neck, a neck that used to be so smooth and was now decorated with beautiful, intricate lines like the rings of an old tree, and tell Ava the things she'd been thinking about for over twenty years. Things like, *I'm sorry I left you.* And *I was just so scared and so sad and didn't know what else to do. Can you forgive me for being young, for being closed off, for not knowing how to fight for us when it counted?*

As if by magic, Ava pulled out a first aid kit and began pouring something that stung sharply into the cuts on Orchid's hands. "Ow," Orchid said, and Ava said, "I know." She gently unwound the bandage around Orchid's head and swore when she saw her ear. *Of course you have a first aid kit,* Orchid thought. *Of course in the end, it is* you *saving* me.

But Orchid couldn't say any of that because she couldn't stop laughing and crying. More crying than laughing, now. She wept for the years they'd lost, for whatever had happened Inside that was so terrible it had made Ava leave of her own accord. She'd ask her about it, soon, when she could pull herself together, but in the meantime there was nothing she could do but fall apart.

"Oh, Orchid," Ava said. She didn't tell her to stop crying. She just sat there, watching her, creating a space for the enormous feelings that were crashing down on Orchid like a landslide. Ava's own eyes looked misty but she was composed. Grown. Maternal.

"Do you have any water?" Orchid asked when she could speak.

Ava nodded and pulled out her thermos. "Oh, that's all you have?" Orchid said, refusing it. "No, I can't take that from you."

"I have a water purifier," Ava said. "It's fine, really. We can just collect more." Ava placed it in her hands.

Orchid knew she didn't deserve such kindness. She was never able to do this for Ava, back when she could have; Ava's feelings had always scared Orchid, always made her shut down.

"How is this possible?" Orchid said. "How are you here? How are we here at the same time?" The happenstance of it all was making her head swim.

"I don't know," Ava said. "But if you were coming to save *me,* then that means you knew something. What did you hear?"

Orchid took a few sips of water, cleared her throat. "That Jacqueline Millender wants to start a war with the other Insides. That she lied to everyone about everything."

Ava looked confused. "That's it?"

Orchid smirked, despite herself. "What do you mean, *that's it*? Was there something more?"

Ava nodded, slowly.

"There were rumors," Orchid said. "But that's the first concrete information I got. I mean, I guess not exactly concrete. But from a reliable source."

"Who told you?"

Orchid grunted as she shifted her body, trying to find a position to sit in that didn't hurt so much. "A friend. Who told *you*?"

"A friend," Ava replied. So: communication was going to be hard. After all they'd been through, they were back at this impasse.

If she was ever going to change their story, it needed to start now. "Her name is Camilla," Orchid said. "She has a sister on the space shuttle. They talk."

At this, Ava froze. "How?"

"They have a thing," Orchid said. It was the best she could do. The pain in her ear was starting to scream, distorting her thoughts.

But Ava wouldn't let it go. "A *thing*? Like, a device? That we could use?"

"Sure," Orchid said. "If you feel like walking to Canada." She mustered her best half-smile.

"We might," Ava said, not smiling back. Orchid waited for her to elaborate, but she didn't.

"I guess we're lucky there's only one highway left in this godforsaken state," Orchid said. "And that I happened to be fucking dying on the side of it."

"You're not dying," Ava said. "And I haven't decided yet if we're lucky."

Orchid bristled. That was a cruel thing for Ava to say, when Orchid had risked her life to find her.

And then the younger woman said, in a voice that sounded so much like Ava's that Orchid had to smile: "Mom, what the fuck is going on?"

APRIL 6, 2041

Hi, baby,

Today I'm writing to you from the world's dingiest motel in South Dakota, and let me tell you, it's so damn hot here! The air-conditioning in this car sputtered until it stopped altogether. I thought I was going to drown in my own sweat on the highway. Then I heard the thunder, saw the lightning in the distance as the prairie stretched out endlessly around me on all sides. It was pouring rain before I even saw the clouds roll in. I had planned on sleeping in the car again, but this weather is ridiculous. And I am trying so hard to survive this journey. I am trying so hard to get back to you. Hence: motel.

I didn't get a good night's sleep. Every time I started to drift, I dreamt of merging onto highways. I'm worried about driving when I'm this tired, but I can't waste another day. I'm just waiting until after rush hour to get back on the road, which means it's the perfect time to get back to writing to you about what happened, why I left, and why I stayed away for so long.

So: back to the past. Cory had fled. She must have seen me and Vero kissing on the roof.

In a way I was relieved. This meant I wouldn't have to tell her. I was such a coward.

Madhuri was furious at us. Vero seemed sad, but that didn't

stop him from continuing to pursue a relationship with me. He held my hand. He brought me potato chips. He told me how pretty I looked, held doors for me, took me on little dates to different derelict parts of the city where we could be alone. He always made sure I was okay if I was being quiet. He asked what I thought. He took care of me. I know I said I wasn't going to go into the details of my sex life, and I promise I won't, but—I never knew how good I could feel until him.

It was a confusing time. I hated that following my heart meant losing people along the way. But I did, as Cory had feared, love him. I told him so one night when we decided to camp out under an overpass to get some privacy. He replied, "I loved you from the minute I saw you." I don't know if I can possibly convey what it felt like to hear those words after a lifetime of feeling unlovable, so maybe you can just imagine it.

I'm dragging my feet on telling you what happened next because it was so awful.

A little backstory: Vero's dad had announced a plan to not only *not* cut down on fossil fuels, but to partner with JM Inc., one of the largest oil companies in the world. JM Inc. was run by the granddaughter of its founder, a terrifying woman named Jacqueline Millender, who also had some sort of female-empowerment brand I never really bought into. Anyway, with JM Inc.'s help, they could begin fracking right off the coast of New York City. The deal was done. There was nothing anyone could do. Protests had happened, op-eds were written, but the proverbial ink was dry.

So naturally, we decided to chain our necks to City Hall.

It took weeks of planning. We'd need a way to distract security, a way to make sure the press would cover it, a way to get hundreds of other activists to come support us without accidentally alerting the powers that be to the protest. Luckily by this point, I had become something of an expert hacker. It came naturally to me. Vero told me it was a gift. I was no longer relying on Arthur for help, which was good, because nothing Arthur did came without a price.

After Vero decided Arthur had put in enough time with me to pay him back, he was out. So it was all me. I worked for free; just the price of being involved. Besides, I didn't think of it as work.

Vero and Madhuri made the plans. I implemented them.

We decided that Vero and I would be the ones in chains. Vero, because it was newsworthy, and me, because I didn't want to be separated from him.

As for Madhuri? Well. She wanted to start a fire. She'd earned the name Madly, I suppose.

We didn't want to hurt anyone. We just wanted to create a big enough scene that the men who stood at the doors of City Hall would leave their posts. There was a bank across the street. Madhuri and Vero liked the symbolism of setting a bank on fire; a *fuck you* to the capitalism that informed the mayor's decisions.

I hacked into the mayor's publicist's email and sent a note to the press announcing there'd be a meeting with the mayor and some celebrity that Madhuri suggested, a young woman who was big on social media for modeling, or acting, or brand deals, or some combination of the three that I couldn't really identify. It wasn't that out of the ordinary; the mayor was the type to constantly seek celebrity endorsements. And if this person was photographed walking into City Hall, it would immediately be news. So I sent the email out, and then deleted it from the outbox so no one would catch us, creating a filter for any replies to go straight to junk mail. It looked legit because it was legit, or at least as legit as a fake email could get.

The night before everything was set to go down, Vero, Madhuri, and I sat in a circle holding hands.

"We have to manifest a good day," Madhuri said, and then she made us go around and say what we were afraid of, and then let it go.

Vero said he was afraid we'd get arrested before completing the plan. Madhuri said she was afraid we'd get it done, but nothing would change, because nothing ever changes. I said I wasn't afraid of anything. Madhuri rolled her eyes, but Vero squeezed my hand. "That's my girl," he said.

Suffice to say, I didn't sleep one wink that night. The adrenaline was like gunpowder. I felt explosive.

It was a lie that I wasn't afraid of anything. I just wanted to look cool, to impress Vero. Oh, if you could have heard the fears that ping-ponged around in my skull! What if we got shot by the cops? What if we all went to jail? What if my parents saw me on TV? (That one was more of a wish. I wanted them to see me, to know I was alive and well without them.) What if Vero decided he didn't love me anymore? What if I wasn't exactly who he wanted me to be? It was horrible, being seventeen. I really can't recommend it to anyone. I'm glad I'll be there for you when you're that age. We'll get through it together, if you'll let me back into your life.

Anyway. When we got to City Hall at 8:00 a.m., there was already a crowd of paparazzi hovering around the steps. It had worked.

That was phase one.

Phase two: fire. The smell of smoke from across the street told us Madhuri had done it. But then we heard screaming.

The bank wasn't open yet. There wasn't supposed to be anyone inside. Flames billowed from the windows, and out of the corner of my eye I saw Madhuri dash out and away, down the street. Who was screaming? I didn't have time to think harder about it. No one chased her. She'd made it out. Phew.

Phase three: the guards at the doors of City Hall wandered out and toward the sidewalk like bored sheep, watching the spectacle of the building on fire. They were so predictable and stupid.

It was go time.

Vero held my hand as we ran up the steps. He pulled a bike chain from his backpack as we sat cross-legged on the ground in front of the door. He kissed me, and then wrapped the chain around our necks, and around the door handle. He locked it, and then with a wink he threw the key as far as he could. It landed on a subway grate, then disappeared.

Phase four: hundreds of activists appeared as if out of thin air on the steps in front of us. Vero's network of people, mostly. I was always so impressed by his ability to turn people out in droves. Their phones were held high as they documented every moment.

Vero and I were facing each other, still holding hands. Tears ran down my face. I was terrified, moved, inspired, alive. What a thing to be part of. History. We were powerful. For the first time in my life I was part of something that mattered, that meant something.

Phase five: the voices of the press in the crowd said, "Wait, is that the mayor's daughter? Hey, Vera! Look here, sweetie," followed by the flashing of cameras. Vero grimaced as they misgendered him. I couldn't believe that anyone could look at Vero with his short hair, boy's clothes, and fuzzy upper lip and think: *girl.* It was so disrespectful. I guess that was the point.

The fire department arrived across the street. The security guards pushed their way through the protestors and assessed us as if they weren't angry, just exhausted, which somehow felt worse.

Through the door to the side of us, politicians were being evacuated from City Hall. They gingerly stepped around us.

"Think your dad is coming out?" I asked, over the chaos.

"I bet he hides in his office," Vero said.

The protest was getting bigger. Someone approached us and said, "Hey, guys, the fire is getting out of control."

I couldn't see anything but smoke over the crowd, but my heart sank. It wasn't supposed to be a huge fire, just enough to create a diversion.

More fire trucks were coming. I heard police sirens.

"What if someone was in there?" I asked. "Did you hear the screams?"

Vero told me to be quiet. "We didn't set the fire," he said emphatically, loud enough for the guards to hear it.

More sirens, more fire trucks. The cops stood around us with their hands on their hips, talking into radios. Everything was going to plan. So why did I suddenly feel a sense of dread?

A couple of firemen appeared in front of us.

They used heavy-duty bolt cutters to break our chains, and within seconds, zip ties were tightened around my wrist. "Ow," I said. I didn't expect it to hurt so much. Someone was roughly lifting me by my armpits and I knew better than to fight. Vero was also being lifted and as our eyes met, I shouted, "I love you." He winked at me.

I started screaming: "You're killing us." Over and over while I made my body limp like Vero had taught me and allowed them to carry me through the protest and into a cop car. I could see them doing the same to Vero, but they were separating us, taking us to different places. "You're killing us, you're killing us, you're killing us." They drove me to a precinct and left me in a holding cell.

"You're killing us," I whispered over and over, rocking myself back and forth. "You're killing us." Finally, there was no one left to hear me.

I was shocked when, what felt like hours later, an FBI agent walked into the cell. She was wearing a jacket that said FBI just like in the movies.

"So, Kelly," she said. I didn't know how she knew my name.

I didn't say anything.

"Someone died. Because of you."

I had vowed silence, but at this, I couldn't stop myself. "*What*? Who?"

"The janitor at the bank you guys set on fire."

No, I thought. *No, no, no.*

"No," I said.

She smiled. I didn't trust her. "No, you're right. But he's in critical condition with third-degree burns covering seventy-five percent of his body."

I think I might have whispered "Fuck," but I'm not sure.

She was still talking. "Thanks to your boyfriend, we know who you are and what you've done," she said. "We've been tracking you online for months, of course, but up until today we didn't know that everXgreen was a teenage girl."

My username. Based on Vero's nickname for me. And: Vero had sold me out.

"He told you that?"

Should I have believed her? I had no idea.

"He struck a deal." She shrugged. "Perks of being a nepo baby. He'll get off with some community service. You are looking at something much more serious."

"Do I need a lawyer?"

"Do you?" She smiled. "We already know what you've done. The fire, the emails. And that's just about today. We also know about the doxing, the breaking and entering."

So Vero had put it all on me. No mention of Madhuri or Cory. I shook my head. "Lawyer."

She said: "What about parents, honey?"

I shook my head again.

She left, and to my embarrassment, I burst into tears. I looked at the camera in the corner. *Let them watch a little girl cry,* I thought.

No one came to pay my bail. I'll save you the boring details of my trial, of my long cold nights spent in the detention center.

What matters is the outcome. In the end, they couldn't pin the fire on me. Which was good, because I didn't do it. I never went into the bank, never put anything online about it. It was all Madhuri, by design, but who knew where she was. And, of course, I still shared some of the responsibility. After all, I didn't speak out against this plan, didn't do anything when I heard screams.

I was charged with disorderly conduct for the protest, which was a misdemeanor, and phishing, for sending the email from the mayor's office . . . which was a felony.

My lawyer, a public defender—a balding white man with stains on his khakis—told me I was lucky it wasn't arson. And doubly lucky that I was being tried as a minor.

When the judge announced I'd be sentenced to a year in a juvenile detention facility, my knees nearly buckled.

There was no one in the courthouse for me. The lawyer had tried to reach my parents, but they clearly weren't interested in what had become of me. I hadn't heard anything from Vero or Madhuri. I was completely on my own. Everyone had abandoned me.

Exactly as I abandoned you, I suppose. I'm so sorry.

I don't really want to write about the year I spent locked up. It was scary, but mostly boring, and I did my best to keep to myself. I read a lot of books. I cleaned the toilets. I avoided eye contact. I handed my white bread sandwiches over to girls who were bigger than me when they asked for them. I never got into fights. I never made friends. I got by however I could. I'm nothing if not a survivor.

I did write my parents a few letters asking them to come see me. You probably could have guessed that they never did. I don't even know why I tried. I've always been a letter writer, I guess.

I passed the time by developing crushes on some of the other girls, but I was also terrified of flirting with the wrong person. There were a lot of gay girls around but also a lot of violently homophobic ones who would kick you in the shins if you looked at them the wrong way. I lived in my fantasies.

I got my GED. It was a good distraction from my reality, studying and reading and taking tests. (As though any of the subjects taught to high schoolers would be helpful in the real world—still, it was a good way to make the time go by.)

And then, speaking of the real world, it was time to return to it. I won't say *suddenly* because it wasn't. It was a fucking eternity.

I'd lost everything. And the worst part—as the conditions of my release dictated, I was assigned a guardian. It was a full guardianship, meaning I'd never be allowed to have my own bank account or make major travel decisions without someone else approving them. Because no family showed up for me, the court approved a public one.

The day I was released, a van full of other scared-looking girls took me to a halfway house for women getting out of juvenile detention. We were too old for foster care but too dysfunctional to simply be released into the wild. The woman assigned to be my guardian was waiting for me in the lobby. I had no belongings but the clothes I'd worn to the protest a year ago and my phone.

She was an older Black woman in a gray pantsuit. She gave me a hug.

"You can call me Brianna," she said. "I'll be helping you get back on your feet."

My arms were limp at my sides. I wasn't going to be distracted by kindness.

"You'll have to find a job," she said. "I'll manage your money with you."

"What does that mean?" I asked, flatly.

"I'll supervise your use of what you make."

"So I can't make my own financial decisions?"

"Not exactly," she said with a sigh. I could tell she was just trying to protect me from the truth of my situation. "I'll help you decide how much to use and for what. No major travel for now, as you get used to your life. You and I will meet twice a week but you can call me as often as you need to. No associating with other felons. And Kelly"—at this, she placed her hands on my shoulders—"no more activism, or whatever you want to call it."

I nodded, crestfallen. Defeated.

"I'll pay your phone bill until you find work," Brianna said. "After that, you can pay me back. I know how important a phone will be in finding a job, in getting your footing."

"Thank you," I said. It came out as a whisper.

The phone thing was nice of her, but again, I wasn't willing to let myself trust anyone. Not after everything that had happened.

When she left, the person who ran the facility took me to a room I'd share with three other women. This was not so different from juvie.

The other girls in the room didn't look up when I came in. "Hi," I said. One of them grunted something I couldn't hear. They seemed set on pretending I wasn't there, and I decided not to push it.

This was somewhat of a relief. I had nothing left to give anyone, especially not friendship. The twin-sized bed at least had a proper pillow and blanket.

When I woke up, it was hardly dawn, and everyone was still sleeping. I put my hoodie on and tiptoed out of the house. Before I realized where I was going, I found myself walking to the edge of Queens.

I didn't know what I was looking for, or what I'd find, but I definitely did not expect what was there in place of our old, abandoned house: a construction zone. They were building condos. The house was totally bulldozed.

Even the previously shuttered businesses in the surrounding blocks were being reopened; coffee shops and a dry cleaner and a ramen place. Incredible, given the state of the world. I guessed the mayor's new fracking situation was working. People were making money again. (Though in a few years that whole part of the island would be underwater, so . . .)

I pulled out my phone and texted Vero, even though I hated him. Where the fuck are you, I sent. It didn't go through.

I sat down on the curb across the street from the construction. My next text was to Madhuri. Hey girl.

It was early, and I didn't really expect a response, but my phone immediately started buzzing. She had called me.

"Oh my god," I said when I picked up.

"You got out," she said. "You're alive. Holy fucking shit." Her voice on the other line sounded like a miracle.

"Did you know they bulldozed our house?" I said. "Where is everyone?"

"Oh, honey," she said.

"Did you know Vero threw me under the bus?"

"No, but . . ." She trailed off. "No one has heard from him."

"What?"

"The working theory is that he moved back in with his family."

I wanted to cry, but was too angry. "I guess that makes sense."

I told her about my situation: the halfway house, the guardianship, how I needed to get a real job.

"You know someone got really hurt, right?" I said. "At the protest? In the fire?"

"What the fuck is wrong with you?" she hissed. "Don't say shit like that. Not over the phone."

I clamped my hand over my mouth. "Sorry," I said.

Her voice softened. "It's okay. I know you're just getting used to real life again."

"How's Cory?" I asked. "Have you heard anything from her?"

Madhuri had still been keeping tabs on her before all the shit went down at the protest, so I figured they were still in touch.

"Oh," Madhuri gasped. "You don't know. Fuck." She was stalling.

My heart sank, listening to her silence.

"She died," Madhuri said.

It's an odd thing, to lose someone you've already lost. I thought of everything Cory and I had been through, and at the same time, everything we didn't go through together. I thought of how I'd hurt her. How scared I was of her. I had the impulse, strangely, to call her, to tell her that she'd died. To ask her what I should do with this feeling of grief that was perhaps not unlike what she'd felt about me. We hadn't spoken since she left our house that day.

Madhuri was crying. "She overdosed," she said. "I mean, that's what we think. She was found in a subway station. Cops thought she was asleep on a bench. They've been kicking everyone out of the stations. You can't even sleep on a bench anymore. But she wasn't asleep."

"Shit," I said. "I feel so awful. How'd you find out?"

"Someone who saw it go down told me," she said. "Don't blame yourself. Coriander was messed up long before you."

I didn't know what to say. I wanted to cry with her, but couldn't.

"What about the others? What about Arthur?"

"Oh, poor Arthur landed himself in jail," she said. "He got caught trying to hack the FBI. I don't think we'll be seeing him for a long, long time, if ever again."

"Tell me more about you," I said, desperate for good news.

She told me how she'd spent the past year looking over her shoulder, waiting for the cops to find her, but they never did.

She'd been crashing on couches, mostly, until she landed a gig as a bartender, and eventually got her own place, a shitty little studio in the projects that she loved because it was all hers.

"Madly, that's awesome," I said. "You really turned things around."

"I could probably hook you up, if you want," she said. "You could start as a barback. I can't pay you hourly unless you're official, which would mean getting your food handlers license. You should do that eventually. In the meantime you can work for tips. See how it goes."

I'd never been behind a bar in my life, but I accepted her help quickly. My only hesitation was whether or not my guardian would deem this appropriate work.

I got off the phone with Madhuri and called the guardian next. "Good morning, uh, ma'am," I said. "I think I've found a job." I told her what Madhuri had proposed.

She said, "You know, I'm impressed that you moved on this so quickly, but I hardly think working for tips will be enough to get you back on your feet."

She had a point. I would need to be able to pay rent, bills. Buy my own food. Things I'd never had to do.

"Usually I set my girls up with highway cleanup work," she offered.

"You mean like picking up garbage on the side of the road?"

"It pays fifteen dollars an hour," she said. "A steady, regular paycheck."

"Great," I said, feeling tired just thinking about it. "I'm in. Send me the information."

Within a few days, the bones of my new life were in place. In the mornings at eight a.m. I'd report for duty at a trailer on the side of a major freeway to grab my orange vest, gloves, and trash bags, and then I'd set out collecting discarded bottles, condoms, and fast-food wrappers while the sun beat down.

On Friday and Saturday nights, I met Madhuri around six p.m. when she opened the gate of a dive bar on the water's edge in Brooklyn. I washed glasses, handed people cans of beer, kept Madhuri's well full while she shook cocktails. Avoided having my ass grabbed by regulars. Kept my head down, in general.

I wondered, often, if Madhuri felt guilty for the man she'd hurt, but she acted like it had never happened, and I was too afraid to bring it up. Afraid she'd get mad, but more than that, afraid I'd lose her, like I'd lost everyone else.

All my paychecks went through Brianna, but I started keeping tips for myself. She didn't ask about it. I assume she knew, but she was nice like that. I used the cash to buy new clothes, to get a haircut, to start to make myself look more like a human who participated in society. I didn't have enough to get my own place yet, but that was okay. I kind of liked the idea of living with all those other women. In some ways it reminded me of the abandoned house. We were all so lost.

Sometimes Madhuri and I talked about Vero. We wondered where he went.

"I know it's dumb, but I miss him so much," I said.

"How about I teach you how to make a margarita? Would that help?" Madhuri said. The bar was starting to fill up. I nodded.

Wait. Sorry.

Baby, I'm going to take a break from writing to you not because I want to stop but because I heard some strange noises outside my motel room. It almost sounded like someone was listening at the door. I'm trying not to be paranoid, but—I don't know. Something feels off. When I looked, there was nobody there. I've decided to check out early and drive through the night. I'll write to you from where I end up next.

I love you.

Mom

3

CAMILLA

2078

CAMILLA WOKE UP SLOWLY, HER EYELIDS HEAVY AND HER body too warm, drifting in and out of a delirious dream state. It had been another wretchedly hot night, but the swarms of bugs had been too dense to leave the door flap open, which meant it was even hotter inside her hut. Her raggedy clothes smelled of a sweaty, unsatisfying sleep, clinging unpleasantly to the salty puddles on her skin.

Still half-dreaming, Camilla conjured up the feel of her childhood bed. It had been decades, but she could still feel it clearly: the twin-sized thrift-store mattress with its stained floral sheets and Pesto vibrating gently on top of her head, sounds of her parents in the kitchen, and the reassurance of her sister Shelby still asleep in the next room. But she couldn't hold on to the vision for long. Her bed of animal furs and soft garbage from a nearby landfill was too uncomfortable. And Pesto, her lifelong companion, her purring sleep hat, was dead, though he'd hung on to life until he was frail—feather-light and crusty. He rested in a grave just outside her door, dug as deep in the ground as she could for fear that an impending flood might resurface him if the grave was too shallow.

Camilla and her family had fled New York City with millions of other climate refugees after most of Manhattan was zoned for the Inside Project, which Camilla always thought was just a government euphemism for *evicted.* Other people would be chosen to live on the island her family had called home in what was essentially a climate-safe bubble, and then those lucky chosen ones would be kept safe in perpetuity. She'd been hardly a teenager when her world turned upside-down, when her sister left for the space shuttle with her billionaire boss, when they left New York City and then her mother died on the side of the road of a mysterious stomach flu that ripped through the waves of migrants like a strong wind. Camilla was lucky to be alive. She was lucky her father had lived, too.

She was just a kid when she realized how fragile the line between life and death is, when she learned all the dangers the world held and the fact that her safety could not be guaranteed by anyone. It meant she had to grow up quickly. As a result, when she did open her heart to people, she was all in, fiercely protective because she knew that at any moment, they could be ripped from her forever.

That was how she felt about Orchid, her dearest friend in the world. For a moment, she wondered if Orchid was up yet, and opened her eyes a sliver to check. But the bed was empty. Still fighting her way out of the soupy darkness of her waking mind, she couldn't remember where her friend had gone. Perhaps Orchid had simply risen before her and had gotten a head start on the day.

But then it all came rushing back, and she forced herself to look across their shared cabin at the empty bed.

You really did it, she thought. *You left me here.* Camilla had fought the urge to tie Orchid to a tree when she informed Camilla she was leaving. Out of respect for Orchid, she let her go.

Orchid didn't have many things, and she'd taken all of them. There was no trace of her left in the hut, other than the hut itself, which Orchid had built for Camilla.

Thinking about it as she lay in bed made her stomach twist. She was worried. She was also a little mad. Camilla thought it was a ridiculous plan; a non-plan, really. Orchid had always seemed a little bit impulsive, but this was something else.

She hoped that Orchid would be successful, that she'd be able to get Inside and convince the woman named Ava to leave, but it sounded so far-fetched. At the same time, Camilla knew it wasn't her place to judge; she'd never been in love with anyone and didn't know what she would have done in the same situation. She hoped, at least, that Orchid would return before they were due to head north, as planned.

And if Camilla did take issue with Orchid's decision—well, she had only herself to blame. It was Camilla's intel that sparked Orchid's departure. Well, her father's, really, but Camilla had been the one to insist that they tell everyone what Shelby had told him about what was happening Inside, the way its director was maybe plotting the mass murder of the other Inside populations. In a way, she figured that if anything bad were to happen to Orchid on her journey, it would be Camilla's fault. She already felt guilty.

More than anything else in the world, Camilla wanted the people she loved to be in the same place so that she could watch them, make sure they were safe. Her dad once jokingly referred to her as the family's herding dog. It wasn't untrue. She hated when she didn't know where someone was. She'd always been like this.

She forced herself to get up. Her shoulders were sore from hauling firewood yesterday, and she stretched her arms up to the ceiling, trying to relieve the tension. Everything hurt, but that was nothing new. There were blisters on her feet from her ancient sneakers. Her stomach ached from going to bed hungry. And then there was the deeper, more endemic hurt; the pain of everyone she'd lost along the way. Her mother. Shelby, her sister. Every friend she'd grown up with. Would she really be adding Orchid to that list?

She ran a hand through her short brown hair, which she cut at the base of her neck with a pair of dull scissors every time it became long enough to put into a low ponytail. She'd once seen a photograph of a woman with a blunt bob while peering over Shelby's shoulder as her sister scrolled through her phone, and the image had stuck with her, perhaps because she knew Shelby was so drawn to it.

She was still trying to impress Shelby with things Shelby would never see or know. You never stop being someone's sister, even when your sister is gone.

Camilla was in her mid-thirties but the pain she carried in her body made her feel much older than that, and she knew she looked it, too. The elements had been hard on her. Being outside in the sun and the wind and the storms meant she was scarred and discolored, her once-even skin tone now more like puzzle pieces of pink and beige from the sunburns that peeled again and again. Not that it mattered how she looked. From the moment they'd had to flee New York City, the only thing that mattered was staying alive.

She opened the cabin's front flap and poked her head out. Her dad was already up, sitting in front of his hut in a plastic folding chair she and Orchid had found at the nearest garbage dump, drinking coffee from a chipped mug.

As was her tradition, she quietly greeted the little grave between their huts. "Hi, Pesto," she whispered. That damn little cat. Even his memory brought out her tenderness the way few living people could.

Then she called, "Hey, Dad."

"Oh, hi, honey," her dad called after a few moments, a delayed reaction that was more than a little worrisome. "Rough night."

"Awful," she said. "Still can't believe how quickly the heat caught up to us."

When Camilla was a child, her dad had been larger than life. Broad-shouldered, tall. But these days he was almost the same height as her, curling in on himself like a shrimp cocktail (what she wouldn't do for a shrimp cocktail), his arms and legs becoming skinny as his skin sagged off his bones.

A woman named Parker, who had become something of a leader in the group, walked by. "Hey, Camilla," she said with a friendly wink. Parker reminded Camilla of an old sea witch.

"Morning," Camilla said. "Hot as fuck, huh?"

"Girl, you're telling me," Parker said, not stopping for a longer conversation but still being nice enough. "Just wait until you start having hot flashes."

Camilla laughed politely, swatting gnats away from her face. Menopause was an abstract idea to her. The truth was she hardly got her period at all anymore; the combination of malnutrition and the stress of fighting to survive, she assumed.

"See you at the meeting later," Parker said, and Camilla nodded.

She'd need to get her shit done before it got too warm out, but without Orchid there to share the burden, she was struggling to get started. Instead she turned her face toward the sun and felt its dangerous warm caress on her skin as she closed her eyes.

She was thirsty. The sweat on her upper lip was making her cracked mouth burn. It hadn't rained for weeks.

"This drought is crazy," she said in the direction of her dad.

"It's no good," he agreed. "Think we need to start worrying about fires?"

"We should always be worried about fire," she said. She wondered when the script had flipped; when he started asking her things, instead of the other way around. She couldn't remember. In some ways it felt like it had always been like this.

"I'll get us water," she said.

She grabbed her water pot from inside the hut and began the trek to what was left of the nearest stream, where she'd collect as much water as she could and then boil it for thirty minutes over the fire. As she knelt in the mud, she wondered what this water had looked like when it had been a river. White, frothy, rushing madly. Parker once told her the rivers and lakes in Canada used to be as clear and turquoise as the Caribbean Sea, not that Camilla had seen that, either, but she remembered a screen saver at school that showed teal water and one single palm tree, and that's what she pictured. Except this water used to be cold, probably. God, it must have felt good. Now, the stream's weak, hot trickle of water around her ankles was making her have to pee. It smelled like sulfur. She wondered what (or who) might be decaying upstream.

Camilla had never actually expected to become a climate refugee—the thing of her own childhood nightmares. She remembered the notification from Inside that flashed on her parents' phones with the utmost clarity. Those words still had the power to make her blood run cold. Her mom and dad had been at the sink, washing and drying dishes together, their phones on the table, where Camilla was doing homework, so she had seen it first. Their screens had turned red, revealing the words:

> We regret to inform you that your application to Inside has been rejected.

It had made a horrible and sudden buzzing sound when the message came through, and her mom had dropped a glass onto the floor. It shattered, but Camilla couldn't take her eyes off the phones, which continued to flash.

> Over the next two months, every power grid in the country will be shut off.
>
> Please be advised that it is no longer recommended to live near the ocean, in a fire zone, or in any area designated as a tornado risk.
>
> The United World Government wishes you the best of luck.

"What now?" her mom said.

"I have to make some calls," her dad said. "I bet there's going to be a protest."

"There's no point in protesting this," her mom said, getting angry. "We need to figure out what's best for our family."

Camilla had started to cry. "We have to leave, don't we?" Her parents stopped arguing and turned to her. They simply nodded, unable to repackage the truth as something more pleasant. She knew at that moment her life would never be the same.

Camilla had begged Shelby to stay with them, to leave New York City as a family, but Shelby was Jacqueline Millender's assistant, which meant she was given a spot on the space shuttle, where she'd be guaranteed survival. Camilla couldn't fault Shelby for going to space instead of signing up for a life in the wilderness, though it had been the first heartbreak of her life. Shelby was just trying to live.

Shelby's parting gift to her bereft family was an off-grid, which they could use to call her. Camilla hated the damn thing, resented how far away and different Shelby sounded through its speakers, but without it, there was no other way they could communicate. Camilla had called her on it when their mom died.

Over twenty years had gone by since she and her sister parted.

Camilla was glad, in the end, that she hadn't been accepted Inside, though it took her a long time to reach that conclusion. Fleeing New York City with her parents when she was thirteen had been as bad, worse maybe, as her fears. The constant threat of natural disaster combined with an ongoing uncertainty of where they'd sleep, what they'd eat, how long they'd be roaming for. The goddamn inescapable heat. But she'd survived. So many others hadn't.

Most days she tried to be grateful. On a day like this one, though, she just felt old and sad; mourning the life she didn't get to live. Who would she have been if she'd been born a few decades earlier? Who would have loved her? Married her, even?

This was a pointless line of thinking. She only had this one life, and she'd been born into turmoil, danger. Her memories of pleasure were few and far between, though she treasured them: once, when she was in middle school, before the collapse, she'd kissed a boy in the darkness of a movie theater, his hands on her legs and his tongue in her mouth the most exciting thing that had ever happened to her. But then, before she had a chance to really experience being a normal teenager, they were without a home, without safety. There were no more movie theaters.

Before she died, Camilla's mom had explained sex to her, but it had felt largely abstract at that point. She had questions as she got older and no one to ask. Her mother would have talked to her about it, had she been there. Shelby, too. But her dad was awkward around the subject of Camilla's body and what it wanted, and she hated making him uncomfortable.

Later, when she and her dad were moving from settlement to settlement, there'd been a girl around her age who taught her how to spark a fire from two rocks, and then kissed her over the roaring flames. The moment was full of promise and magic. But the girl and her family had been gone the next day.

There were a few other chance encounters. The first time she had sex was with a much-older man while she and her dad stayed with cousin Harriett, but it had been deeply disappointing, rushed and painful, and it was not something she sought to recreate.

As she got older, she got so used to being undesired that the heat that used to flare between her legs at the thought of being kissed and touched dimmed over the years until it was hardly there at all, which in a way was a relief. It was easier this way, wanting nothing except survival.

Until Max showed up.

Max was younger and prettier than Camilla, with light brown skin and long black hair that hung loosely around their freckled, bony shoulders, and a quiet grimness that showed itself in subtle details: a jaw that was always clenched, thick eyebrows stuck in a straight line.

Camilla's interactions with Max had been limited. All she knew was that they had appeared a few weeks ago alone, carrying only a small backpack and wearing a strange sort of gas mask. Max seemed wounded, nervous, flighty. They had eventually taken off the gas mask, stashed it somewhere, and their face was almost too beautiful to stare at directly. It was odd for Camilla to be so intrigued by a stranger. Usually she was just wary. But there was something about Max. Something different that she couldn't ignore.

Max was reigniting that feeling in her. She wondered what to do with these urges that had roared back into her life after so many years of dormancy. Especially given how closed-off Max seemed, how unapproachable.

"Where did Max come from, anyway?" she'd asked Parker a few days after it became clear that Max was going to stay with them.

Parker lifted an eyebrow. "Ran away from a cult."

"Oh, shit," Camilla said, surprised. "Which one?"

Parker shrugged. "Winter Liberation Army. I don't know that much about it. They were born into it. They left their family behind and showed up here." Camilla must have been making a shocked face because Parker added, "This world is full of unimaginable horrors. We're the fortunate ones."

Now, Camilla pondered the idea of her life being fortunate while she tried to fill her bucket with water from the stream's weak trickle. To be alive was a sort of fortune, she supposed.

That night, a man who was friendly with her father was stirring a large pot of something brown and chunky over the communal fire while a line formed. The sun was starting to set and the light was turning pink, the hum of the night bugs beginning to pulse.

When it was Camilla's turn, she said, "Do I want to know what's in that?"

The man smiled. "Nope," he said, and dumped some of the slop into her bowl.

The air pressure felt low and too heavy as Camilla took her seat next to her dad in the large circle. A strong wind blew, and Camilla coughed, the dust and dirt filling her mouth. It was starting to feel muggy out, a far cry from the dry heat that had plagued them for so long. Camilla forced herself to take a bite of mystery stew. It wasn't awful. A little chewy, but it would do.

It was time for the meeting to start, and the group quieted as Parker rose and cleared her throat.

"It saddens me to say we'll need to begin making plans to head northwest," she said. "I know we've all grown to love this place, but given the heat, it won't be safe much longer. I'd like to put together a committee to draw up a route."

"We should go to Alaska," a younger woman wearing overalls said.

"No," a man across the fire chimed in. "Too far. And too many sides of it touch the water. Better to try the Northwest Territories first."

"Where exactly are we right now?" Max asked, and someone laughed.

"Sorry," they said, looking a little bit embarrassed to have everyone's eyes on them. "I kind of lost track."

Even the sound of Max's voice made Camilla flush. They caught her staring, and held her gaze until she looked away.

"It's a good question," Parker was saying. "We've estimated we are somewhere close to the border between Ontario and Quebec. Beyond that, it's anybody's guess."

Max nodded, and the conversation moved on, with some people nominating themselves to join the committee and others, like Camilla and her father, remaining quiet. She had no desire to help lead this journey; on the contrary, what she wanted was to stall it, at least until Orchid came back. She couldn't imagine leaving before Orchid returned.

In the distance, there was a low rumbling sound. The conversation stopped. Though the sun had only just set, the sky turned black as midnight.

There was a loud crack. Thunder? Camilla glanced at her father nervously. She held her breath. The wind picked up.

Then, rain. Hot, heavy, thick. Fat droplets stung her face with their velocity.

There was confusion and chaos as the group scrambled to their feet. Someone yelped with joy. *The rain is good,* Camilla told herself, trying to calm the panicked other voice in her head that was saying, *This feels wrong.* It was too much rain, too soon.

"Everyone back to your huts," Parker yelled.

Camilla tried to take a step, but her foot got stuck in the mud.

That's when she realized water was coming up from the ground.

"It's the permafrost," someone shouted above the rain. "It must have melted. We have to get to higher ground."

Her clothes were already drenched. They needed to get the fuck out of there, and fast. She grabbed her dad by the wrist and began tugging. When he didn't come quickly enough, she threw an arm around his waist and used all her strength to half-carry, half-drag him toward the hill, where the rest of the group was already starting to scramble their way up. The forest shuddered with thunder.

A flash of lightning illuminated her dad's face, highlighting his terror. Camilla doubled down on her efforts to get him up the hill. *We're going to be okay.* She gritted her teeth and plodded on. The ground was still muddy and uncertain beneath their feet, but after what seemed like an eternity it began to feel more solid, and soon they joined the others under a canopy of trees.

A baby was crying. Someone started praying.

They stayed like that, huddled together and shivering, for the rest of the night, waiting for the storm to pass. They bowed their heads together in a tight, impenetrable circle. The storm was so loud that if anyone was trying to talk, Camilla couldn't hear it.

She wondered if a tree would fall on them, if their homes would be destroyed, if they'd get struck by lightning, if this storm would be the first of many. She missed a younger version of her father, who could have comforted her instead of the other way around.

Hours passed before the rain let up, but eventually it came to a stop. Weak light from dawn started to sparkle on the wet surfaces all around them. On the ground in front of her, a potato bug wriggled desperately on its back, and Camilla flipped it over with a pine needle.

Parker stood up. "Is everyone okay?"

Camilla looked around. They were sodden, scared, but alive.

"I think we're going to have to adjust our timeline," Parker said, stating the obvious.

"Over here," a voice called.

Everyone turned to look.

It was Max. They were on the ground outside of the circle with a large branch pinning them down.

It took several people to lift the branch, Max's face clenched tight in pain. They let out one single animalistic cry the moment it was cleared, and then fell silent.

The person who functioned as the community doctor rushed over to look. "Their leg is broken," she said.

A few people surrounded Max to carry them down the hill. Camilla trailed behind, making sure there were no stragglers.

They reached the bottom and the group let out a collective gasp.

The huts were destroyed, shattered and strewn about the clearing so chaotically that it was impossible to tell they'd ever been homes at all.

It was a crushing loss after a lifetime of crushing losses, and Camilla wondered if maybe she should be used to this feeling by now, to the impermanence. But she wasn't. She let the grief wash over her. She'd been with these people for seven years, longer than she'd been anywhere else. She'd helped Orchid build many of the homes that lay in tatters on the ground.

"We need to make a new plan," she heard Parker say. The group gathered in a circle, and Camilla joined them.

"I think we need to leave, today," Parker said. "There's no point in rebuilding. It would take too long."

"Let's vote on it," someone else said.

"All in favor of leaving," Parker said.

Camilla looked around the circle of people who had become her community. They were dirty, exhausted. Terrified.

No one moved. Parker said, "This isn't our home anymore. We don't even have a place to sleep safely tonight. There might be more storms. There might be more flooding. It'll be safer up north. We can't waste any more time."

One by one they raised their hands, except Camilla, whose arms were suddenly frozen, pinned at her sides, and Max.

"Max," Parker said. "Oh, fuck."

Max had quietly observed the voting process with their leg elevated. It was clear that this journey would be too hard for them, at least until their leg healed.

"It's okay," Max said. "I've been alone before." Max was sweaty and pale. Camilla could tell they were in an incredible amount of pain. It made her feel ill, watching Max clench their jaw like that.

"We're not going to leave you," Parker said. "We could carry you. We could make some sort of gurney to put you on."

This suggestion seemed to horrify Max. "I'll just slow you down."

It occurred to Camilla that the length of time it would take Max's leg to heal might—if everything worked out—be approximately the same amount of time it would take Orchid to reach Inside and return, with or without Ava (and, Camilla suspected, without was more likely).

Max aside, Camilla couldn't imagine leaving before Orchid returned.

When Camilla and her father had stumbled across this place so many years ago, Orchid had taught them everything she knew about how to live off the land, and then, instead of leaving, they'd stayed, falling in love with these people and the place they'd chosen to settle. Orchid and Camilla were soon inseparable; Orchid was a replacement big sister, but also something more. A dear friend. They took care of each other—they'd even moved in together. Camilla's life just didn't make sense without Orchid anymore.

"I'll stay with Max," Camilla interjected, and everyone turned to stare at her.

"Camilla, what are you talking about?" her father said.

"It's not right to leave Max alone. And besides, who is going to tell Orchid where we went? She built this entire community. We can't just leave it while she's gone. You can make a plan for where you'll go, and then I'll just be a few weeks behind you."

Even while she felt a bright flash of excitement at declaring her plan, Camilla also had a sickly, sinking feeling in her stomach: dread. There were a lot of variables, a lot that could go wrong. But she'd made up her mind. She was staying, risks be damned.

"Thank you," Max said, "but no. Please don't sacrifice yourself for me. I've been on my own plenty."

"Not like this, you haven't," Camilla said, which was more of a guess than anything; she had no idea what Max's life on their own had been like. But it seemed she was right, because they nodded and didn't speak up again.

"But how will I look out for you?" her father said. "I promised your mom."

"Dad," she said, overcome with a sadness so deep she wasn't sure she could finish the sentence.

"I'm staying with you," he said. "We stick together."

"Dad, no," she said. "It's safer for you in the group. I'll catch up in a few weeks."

He shook his head.

"Can we talk in private?" Camilla said. She took him by the elbow and they walked to the edge of the clearing, underneath the trees that were still dripping wet. The group turned their backs to give them privacy.

"It's a nonstarter, Cam," he said. She looked into his eyes. They were paler than they used to be, more rimmed in red. A skin tag hung from his left eyelid. "We've made it this far and this long because we have each other. I'm not going to let you risk that. If you stay, I stay."

"I'll catch up to you," she said. "Don't you think someone needs to wait for Orchid? After everything she did for us?"

"Orchid is an adult. She made her choice." Camilla heard the resentment in his voice.

"I'm an adult, too. I can make my own choice. And she's going to come back. Besides, what about Max?"

"I just don't think these people are your responsibility," he said. His voice was shaking now. "Especially Max. We don't even know them." He was starting to cry. Camilla fought against the urge to comfort him, to go along with what he wanted just to make him feel better. "Our only responsibility is to each other," he added. "You and me, kid."

"Dad," she said. "I'm thirty-five. I love you. But it's good for me to have other people I care about, you know?"

For a moment he looked confused. "Last time I counted, you were twenty-five," he said.

"If only." She managed a smile.

The conversation went on like this for a while. He protested, she held fast. The sun was rising higher, the puddles starting to sizzle into steam. Drops from the leaves fell onto her head. The mud at their feet was hardening. Her dad clenched his jaw, his fist. His eyes filled with tears; his brows lowered. But Camilla remained calm. She explained herself again and again. Her resolve was unbreakable, though she remained open to his anguish, tried to contain it even as she knew she was causing it. She wondered how long it would take him to give in.

Eventually, they heard footsteps, and then Parker approached them, putting her hands on their arms so they formed a semicircle. She smiled sadly in a way that said he was being overruled by everyone, not just Camilla.

"We'll take care of him," Parker said to Camilla. "I think it's right that someone stays behind with Max and to wait for Orchid."

Camilla nodded. "Thank you for understanding," she said.

"I see no one is going to listen to me," her dad said.

"I'm sorry, Dad. I love you. I'm listening to myself this time."

And so, despite her father's pleading, Camilla decided to wait.

APRIL 9, 2041

Hi. Me again.

I've decided no more motels. I don't know, it just doesn't feel safe. I've learned to trust my gut. I can feel people watching me, keeping track of me. I don't like it. There are a number of different people who might be following me, for varying reasons, as I'm sure you've started to gather.

I drove as far south as I could in one go, to the middle of the country, so that at night I could sleep in my car again, like how I started this journey. It's warm enough so that I don't need shelter but not so hot that I die of goddamn heat stroke. I'm going to make my way east toward you from this part of the US. When I hit the East Coast, I'll head north. For now, I'm in Oklahoma, a few hours outside Tulsa. It's beautiful here. Rolling hills, quaint pastures. There are plenty of places to hide in plain sight. It's dry as well—too dry, really, it's a huge problem—but that makes it the perfect weather for me to camp out. I just wish all these bottles of water weren't so expensive.

I wonder if these letters are getting to you. Each time I drop one in a mailbox I wonder about the people whose job it is to get it where it needs to go. Perhaps I should have just sent them all at once. I was too impatient, though. I wanted to send each as soon as

I finished it. I wonder what you think as you read them, what your face does. If you still have those cheeks.

I promise this long, rambling story has a point. So: let me get back to it.

I was living in the halfway house, working two jobs. In my free time I hung out with Madhuri, met with my guardian, Brianna, or lay in my bed and searched for news of Verò on my phone. There was still nothing. I'd started reaching out to old activist contacts, but no one had heard a thing. All of his social media had been deleted.

I didn't know what I'd do if I found him. Slap him, probably. Demand to know why he'd betrayed me. Ask if he still loved me. Forgive him, if he asked me to. Take him back, if he wanted. My daydreams were intense and intensely pathetic.

Madhuri became my best (okay, my only) friend. Despite what I knew about her violent streak, I trusted her completely. She was everything. My family, my mentor, my sister. I think she felt the same way about me.

My guardian still hadn't said anything about the tips I was squirreling away. She *had* started to ask me when I was going to get my own place, but she seemed to understand the hand I'd been dealt. No one had taught me how to be an adult. She was patient with me.

I wish I'd appreciated her more.

Then one night at the bar, I poured a whiskey shot for a man who said, "And one for you, too?"

I wasn't supposed to drink on the job. Or at all—I had just turned twenty. I was terrified of getting in trouble. I knew what it felt like to have the law come down on you.

"No," I said. "Thanks."

"Come on," he said.

I tilted my head to the side and examined him. This wasn't the first time a patron had tried to get me to drink with them. Usually I said no and laughed it off.

I'd never had much interest in men, except for Vero. But there was something about him.

I can see from this vantage point that sometimes falling in love isn't about finding the right person, but about who shows up when the protections you've built around your heart are wearing thin. And mine were so thin that night. Despite my anger, I missed Vero so much. I was exhausted from my two jobs, from working so hard and still not making ends meet. It made me vulnerable.

Plus, he was very handsome, with thick dark hair and an easy smile. I liked the look of him as much as I liked the feel of him looking at me.

He left his phone number on a napkin with his name: Rick. I was texting him before he was out the door: Come back soon.

Madhuri watched all this unfold with a raised eyebrow. "Too old for you," she said.

"You always say that," I said.

"I mean it this time."

It was true: he was at least thirty. In hindsight, he was basically a father figure. For reasons I'm sure you can guess, this held appeal.

I don't know how much you remember about this story. I'm sure we told it to you. For our first date he took me to the nicest restaurant I'd ever been in, a steakhouse in Williamsburg. I borrowed some of Madhuri's clothes, a black dress and boots. He held the door for me as we walked in, which is silly but made me feel special. When we settled into the table and looked at the menus I immediately realized there was nothing for me to eat.

"Are the fries cooked in animal fat?" I asked, when the waiter came.

"I'll double-check with the kitchen," he said.

"I'm so sorry," Rick said. "I should have asked you where you wanted to go."

"It's fine," I lied. "I don't eat that much."

"You must be vegan," he said.

"How could you tell?"

He smirked. "Give me a little more credit," he said. "I'm a good reader of people."

"Not so good that you didn't consider this in advance," I said, and then quickly apologized when I saw his cheeks redden. I was surprised that he was sensitive. "No, this is great, really," I assured him. "I love French fries."

Rick, as you know, was a construction worker. He didn't seem to care that I had no real home. He told me his dreams: he wanted to buy a house upstate and have a family. I was honest with him about who I was, because I didn't have anything left to lose. I told him about getting kicked out, being on the street, trying to get my life together. We agreed on a lot, maybe not 100 percent politically (I didn't expect him to be as much of an anarchist as me), but we felt the same way about climate change and women's rights, which was surprising. He surprised me in a lot of ways. He was funny. At least, he had a good sense of humor. Meaning he laughed at my jokes.

We started seeing each other regularly. He visited me at work a lot. Madhuri hated when he did this because he'd distract me, but I loved him watching me behind the bar. It made me feel like I was on a stage, and he was my adoring audience. He took me to dinners where he would say things like, "Order anything you want," followed by nights in his bed spent staying up until dawn. I was surprised that I enjoyed having sex that was so heteronormative. Again, I won't go into details, but sometimes it seemed like we were following a script for men and women in the bedroom. There was something comforting about this—the dependability of what he'd want from me. The predictability of it. I liked knowing what I was going to get. It was safe.

Despite all this, it also didn't seem like it was a relationship built to last. Soon, I thought, we'd grow tired of each other; he, of someone whose life was such a mess, and me, of a man who existed so far outside of my world. We didn't know any of the same people, hadn't had any of the same experiences. There was a generational divide, too; he didn't get any of my pop culture references. He didn't even use social media. He sometimes went to bed before I was even done with work. He had a 401(k). A savings account. Parents who loved him. A brother he was close with. Friends who had jobs. Work parties. We might as well have been from different planets.

But I also couldn't help the feelings that were growing.

I liked him so much that I often got mad at him. I was extremely sensitive to the things he thought and said, and wound so tight that we had explosive fights those first few weeks anytime he said something that hurt my feelings, even though he never meant to. But even my temper didn't seem to bother him. "You're my feisty little gingersnap," he'd say, which was annoying but kind of sweet.

Falling in love makes everything feel like magic. I caught myself smiling as I picked up trash during the day. At night at the bar, I thought every man who walked in might be him. I could hardly pay attention to the things Madhuri said to me. All I could think about was when I'd get to see Rick next.

He lived in Astoria, not far from where I was staying, in a one-bedroom apartment that I immediately loved. It was simple and messy—but very him. The natural light in the morning was beautiful, dancing on his white walls. I loved waking up in his bed to the smell of coffee.

My guardian was hesitantly supportive. She tried to give me vague warnings about what an older man's interest in me might mean, but I brushed her off.

"Maybe you should try being on your own for a while," she suggested.

"I'm really not sure what's supposed to be so great about being on your own," I replied. (I still think this. Life is better shared.)

Besides: Rick looked out for me. He kept other guys off me at the bar. He texted me to make sure I got home okay. He opened doors and paid for dinner and just generally treated me like a princess, sweeping me off my feet. How could I not be falling for him? I was being cared for. I felt like a fat, happy baby.

But in my world outside of the light Rick provided, things were pretty dark. The circumstances at the halfway house had become rough; I should have made friends when I first arrived, but instead had no allies. I hadn't done anything nice for anyone in the house, and didn't have anyone I counted on, either. This—and, I think, honestly, my prettiness—made me a target, left me vulnerable. One night I came home to find my mattress turned upside down and my meager things spilled all over the floor. With a gasp I fell to my knees and began searching for the pouch I kept my tips in. I had accumulated so much cash that it had become impractical to carry it around with me, as I'd done in the beginning.

It was gone. One of the other women had robbed me blind. I couldn't tell anyone about it, because that would mean admitting to my guardian that I had had cash she didn't know about. It had been my emergency fund, and now all I had was the account controlled by a woman who worked for the state.

As if things could get any worse: a few days later, I missed my period.

I threw up in the toilet while I brushed my teeth, and I just knew, in my bones, I *knew.* (At first, the potential for pregnancy struck me as almost funny. Until Rick, I'd never had to worry that there might be such consequences to intercourse.) But then there was the less funny fact that—thanks to Vero's dad—New York had gone red, which meant I couldn't have gotten an abortion even if I wanted to.

I texted Madhuri: SOS.

She met me at CVS and held my hand while I bought a test and then peed on a stick in the bathroom.

"What the fuck am I going to do?" I sobbed when the two pink lines appeared. We were still in the CVS bathroom.

"Keep it down," she whispered. And then she said: "I know people who can help. It's not going to be cheap, though."

"All my cash is gone," I cried, hiccupping with the effort of keeping my voice down. "I got robbed. I have nothing."

She squeezed the bridge of her nose as though I was giving her a migraine. “I’ll spot you,” she said.

I stood up and hugged her, crying into her shoulder. She held me tightly. “We’re going to get through this,” she said.

It took Madhuri a few days to pull whatever strings she had to get me an abortion pill. In the meantime, I was puking my guts out every day. One afternoon picking up trash I nearly fainted from the nausea and the heat. I was avoiding Rick, too, which made me feel sad and alone. Responding to his texts hours after he sent them, flaking on plans. I couldn’t bear to tell him. I was afraid of his reaction. I figured he’d get angry. We hadn’t talked at all about a future together, not to mention a future with a child. I thought if he knew, it would ruin his life.

Finally, in the middle of our Friday-night shift, Madhuri pulled me into the bathroom and pressed a pill bottle into my hands. “Take it when you get home.”

“Thank you,” I said. “You’re my best friend in the whole world and I literally don’t know what I’d do without you.”

“I know,” she said. “I love you, too.”

I slipped the pill bottle into my pocket.

I do want to pause here, because I know this is a complicated thing for me to tell you about. I did not know that the baby was *you.* I love you and I have no regrets about the choices I made. But in the moment? I was so fucking young. I had nothing. I could not fathom how I was supposed to raise you. It had nothing to do with my feelings about being your mom, and everything to do with what I was capable of, on my own. I didn’t think I could give you the life you deserved with things as they were.

When we emerged from the bathroom, Rick was sitting at the bar.

“Hi, stranger,” he said, looking sheepish. “I’m sorry to just show up like this, I just . . .” He paused. “I was worried about you.”

I glanced at Madhuri.

“Go,” she sighed. “I’ll close up.”

We went outside and he pulled me into a hug. My head fit under his chin. He said, "If you're going to dump me, I just need to know. I can't stand the uncertainty." He was clutching me as though at any moment I might vaporize.

"I'm not going to dump you," I said.

"What, then? Did I do something?"

He ran his hands down my waist and collided with the pill bottle in my pocket. "What's that?" he asked.

Was this a red flag? Should I have thought it was weird that Rick felt entitled to know what was in my pocket? I don't know. All I know is I told him the truth: I was pregnant, and it was his, and the pills in my pocket were going to take care of it, so he didn't have to worry.

He took a step back. "Worry? Kelly!" He was smiling. "This is amazing."

"It's what?" Never in a million years could I have predicted this reaction.

"Marry me," he said. "Have the baby."

I laughed.

He got down on one knee. What an idiot. The memory still makes me smile, even after everything that's happened.

"Kelly, I want to spend the rest of my life with you. I know we don't know each other that well, but we do, don't we? I want us to be parents."

"This is insane," I said. "Stand up."

He took my left hand between his huge palms. "I'll get you a ring."

"Do I look like the kind of girl who wants a ring?"

"I'll get you a house, then," he pleaded.

"Rick, you know my situation. I can't do anything without my guardian's approval. And I really don't think she'd approve of me marrying a man I've only known for three months."

He stood up. He was still smiling. "It's all going to be okay," he said. "I have an idea."

He kissed me hard on the mouth and then said, "Just wait to make any major decisions about the baby, okay? Give me forty-eight hours."

"Okay," I said, because I felt that our relationship was hanging in the balance, and I couldn't lose it.

I went back inside. Madhuri was standing with her hands on her hips. The bar had emptied out.

"Let me guess," she said. "Rick wants you to have the baby."

I nodded, and then sank down straight to the floor.

"No!" Madhuri cried. "We are *not* sitting on the floor about this. You know what you want to do. You know what you *have* to do. Don't let those pretty eyes make you think you actually want to have a child right now. You've just gotten out of prison, for fuck's sake. It's time to run your own life."

I put my face in my hands. I couldn't speak. It was awkward when we parted for the night. I felt I had already let her down.

Right on schedule, two days later, Rick called me and said, "Marry me."

I groaned. "This again?" The abortion pill was on my bedside table, mocking me for not taking it yet.

"I can become your guardian," he said. "The only reason you were assigned a public one is because you didn't have any family to speak up for you. But if we were married, I would be your family, and then guardianship could transfer to me."

"And then you'd be in charge of me."

"No!" he said. "I could take care of you. You wouldn't have to work two jobs. You could be happy."

"As your wife and the mother of your child."

"Is that so bad? We could leave the city and go somewhere nice."

"I love the city," I said.

"Kelly," he said.

Why was I having such an adverse reaction to this? Did it really sound so bad? I walked to the window, where the chaotic bustle of the city was humming. I put my hand on my belly, which was still flat.

I thought of my parents, kicking me out on my birthday, dooming me to a life of pain and struggle. I thought of Vero, and how he'd abandoned me. I thought of Cory, and how I'd abandoned *her*, and then she'd abandoned all of us by dying. I thought of all the people we used to squat with and how they lived: off the grid, not knowing where their next meal was coming from. It felt like everyone I'd known was dead or in jail, except Madly, who was working so hard to make a meager living, pretending not to be guilty of nearly killing someone. I thought of the cash that had been taken from me, my guardian who controlled my bank account, the court that was dictating the shape of my life.

It's possible that if any of those things hadn't happened—if Vero hadn't turned on me, if Cory was still alive—that I wouldn't have felt as bereft as I did. I was sad and scared for all of us, but more than that, I was exhausted. Like I had nothing left. What if I could be taken care of? What if I didn't have to worry? What if my life was normal? Could I allow that? Could I trust someone enough to let something nice happen for me?

"Okay," I said, finally. "This is fucking insane, but fine."

The truth was, I didn't think it was insane at all. I felt like I was being saved from myself. Like this might finally be a situation where I'd be safe. Rick would be bound to me in three ways: marriage, the guardianship, and our child. He would never be able to leave me. I craved the feeling of waking up in the morning confident that my life was what it was, that there wouldn't be any unknowns to fear.

I could hear him smiling at the other end of the line. "Can I come pick you up now?"

I never went back to the halfway house.

I took Madhuri out for lunch to tell her my decision, a few days later. Rick had given me money to cover it. She said, "You have no idea the lengths I had to go to get you an abortion pill."

She whispered the word *abortion.* I looked around, anxious someone would hear.

"I'm sorry," I said meekly. I was always disappointing Madhuri, from the moment we'd met. "You can have it back. Or I'll pay you back for it. Rick will, at least."

She said, "I never pegged you for someone who wanted to be a trad wife."

"I'm just so tired," I said, my eyes filling with tears. The waiter had started to approach our table but turned on his heel seeing me cry. "And I'm scared. Dude, I'm scared all the fucking time. I just want something nice for myself. I think this could be it."

"I get it," she said. "So I guess you're quitting, huh?"

I nodded. Rick had asked me to stop working at the bar and in the cleanup crew, for the baby's sake. "Sorry to leave you hanging. I'm going to live my housewife fantasy, I guess."

"Is that your fantasy, or his?" she asked. I didn't know how to answer.

Rick's brother was our witness when we got married at City Hall, where, just a few years before, I'd sat with my neck chained to the front door. I tried not to think about Vero as we said our vows. Rick promised to always love me and take care of me. He was weeping, which I found moving and sweet. When we kissed, instead of feeling the earth tilt like I used to with Vero, it was almost like I felt the ground steadying.

We didn't take a honeymoon. Rick couldn't get the days off work. Instead, one night he came home to the apartment and said, "Babe, I bought us a house."

He showed me pictures on his phone of a little blue cottage upstate, in the Hudson Valley. It looked like something out of a fairy-tale book. It had an arched doorway and a manicured lawn and hedges, an A-frame roof and pristine shingles. It even had a white picket fence. He said, "The neighborhood is perfect for young families."

"Did you buy it without seeing it?" I asked, confused at how all this had happened so quickly.

"No," he said. "I saw it."

"Without me?"

"Can we please not have a fight?" he said.

I stormed out of the bedroom and locked myself in the bathroom. He started banging on the door. "Kelly, I bought you a fucking house," he shouted. "You're the only woman on earth who would be mad about that. Now we can raise our kid like humans, not like animals cooped up in a cage."

I shouted back, "I think you're the human and I'm the animal in this situation."

He was quiet. I opened the door. I felt guilty for my reaction. Surely he was right; a normal person would be thrilled. So I apologized, and thanked him, and we made up.

With Rick, I was more like how I'd been with my parents. Quick to anger, reactions larger than the situation called for. I didn't realize I was so triggered by him in the moment, but in hindsight it's clear. He was so paternalistic. I don't know how else I could have possibly reacted to that sort of energy.

Before I knew it, we were moving out of the city and into a new life. I quit my jobs. Rick started commuting an hour on the train every day to work, which he swore he didn't mind. While he was gone I cooked and cleaned, neither of which I was very good at, but it was fun to play house, and nice to be appreciated. Sometimes, I turned the music all the way up and danced around, just because I could.

He'd come home and throw his arms around me, kiss my face all over. We'd laugh through my attempts at soups, stews, pasta. I tried to get him to eat seitan and tofu. He was a good sport.

He taught me how to drive in the library parking lot when it was empty, laughing as I accidentally accelerated when I meant to brake. He was patient, all things considered. I knew he'd be a good father. As he showed me how to merge into traffic on the highway, all I could think about was him eventually doing this with our child. With you.

In time, I got my driver's license. When he was at work I'd take myself to the grocery store, to the drugstore, to the mall, to the rapidly evaporating lake at the edge of town. Rick had gotten me a debit card and would put some money on it every month. The bank would text him if I purchased something out of the ordinary, but I rarely did that. I was a good girl. I did what he wanted me to. Sometimes Rick tried to suggest that I make some friends, but I knew I wouldn't have anything in common with the middle-aged parents who lived around us. I was so much younger than them, I could have been *their* child. Plus I still dressed like someone with no money. I stuck out like a sore thumb, so I did a lot of hiding.

The initial joy I'd felt upon moving upstate was evaporating like the water in the lake where I'd sit and stare into the void.

I started to feel like something was wrong with me. Like I could no longer see the world in full color. Everything became muted, neutral; perhaps it was because of the lack of danger, or the adherence to routine, or the isolation of living in a single-family house. I had a role to play, and I played it, because the alternative was what, exactly? Life back on the streets?

Rick convinced me I should start seeing a therapist. He said I needed to confront my trauma before raising a kid. He had a point. I didn't want to put my abandonment issues on you. We found someone in town and I started going weekly. I actually really liked therapy. It was luxurious to have an hour each week where I could just talk about myself. So indulgent and gratifying. My therapist was a kind older woman who listened with tears in her eyes as I told her my story. We tried to unpack my feelings about my parents. She tried to help me with my temper. She gave me tools. She taught me how to hum to myself when I felt like I was about to lose control. She called it self-soothing. I liked the idea of it.

I avoided computers. I didn't trust myself not to hack into Rick's accounts just to see if I could. I wanted to be the New Kelly, the Kelly who was fully committed to being Rick's wife and not much else. (The joke was on me. You are always yourself, no matter who you are with.)

Meanwhile, I was starting to show. The morning sickness was over. My hair was getting thick. I wanted to eat bacon, but followed a recipe for fried mushrooms instead. It was almost satisfying enough. I was lonely, but I also was at peace knowing you were with me. I started talking to you, singing to you, reading books to you. I felt you flutter and kick in response. The doctors said you were perfect, but I already knew that. Oh, the bliss of having doctors! On Rick's union health insurance we had everything taken care of. It was a dream not to worry. We even had dental insurance. I got my teeth fixed—they'd been yellow and chipped for so many years. Now they were blinding white, my cavities filled in, my gums no longer bleeding when I brushed. I didn't think I'd ever looked better. The blue in my hair was gone. I hardly recognized myself.

I was getting ready for you, on every level. Trying to become a woman worthy of being your mom. I did the best I could.

I love you. I'll write to you more tomorrow.

Mom

4

AVA
2078

IT HAD TAKEN AVA AN EMBARRASSING AMOUNT OF TIME to realize it was Orchid; this dirty, bleeding figure curled up against a burned-out tree.

She looked like she'd been put through a garbage disposal.

If Brook hadn't been so insistent that they check on this person on the side of the road, they would have kept walking. They weren't out there to save strangers. They had left their home—the only home Brook had ever known—to find July, the girl Ava always thought of as Brook's best friend, but who turned out to be so much more. And because staying, after learning what they had learned about the darkness that was built into Inside's very foundation, would be impossible. No: they were out here to save themselves, not whoever this was.

But Brook had never seen a homeless person before, had never known what it meant to compartmentalize your empathy in order to go about your day. She'd pulled Ava over by the hand, saying, "Mom, we just have to see if they're all right."

It was so hot out. The heat on her skin felt like reaching into an oven without mitts, which she'd done a few times by accident when she had an apartment on Brook—the small island that once contained Brooklyn and Queens. She'd always managed to pull her hands back out quickly, her reflexes saving her from burns. But now? There was no reflex that could spare her skin from singeing in the sun. She couldn't pull her hands out. There was nowhere to go.

Her lips were cracked. Her thoughts were swampy. They'd been walking for days, and she was having trouble keeping track of time. They'd spent terrifying nights in abandoned cars, taking turns keeping watch, but no one came. As far as Ava could tell, the country was a graveyard.

And then—there she was. Orchid. Her reddish-brown hair was now long and graying, and her skin looked worn in, like an old leather jacket, but it was without a doubt *her.* Ava hadn't even realized she'd fallen to her knees, only returning to herself when Orchid began to sob hysterically.

"Mom, what the fuck is going on?"

Both Orchid and Ava turned to Brook at the same time.

"Baby, this is . . ." She paused. *What are you to me?* "This is a very old friend."

Orchid didn't correct her.

"And Orchid, this is Brook. My daughter." Pride swelled in her then. She'd created something out of the heartbreak Orchid had left her with, something beautiful and pure.

"Nice to meet you," Orchid said. Her voice was hoarser than Ava remembered. "Sorry it has to be under these circumstances."

Orchid and Brook studied each other. "How old are you?" Orchid asked.

"I'm twenty-two," Brook said. "How old are *you*?"

Orchid laughed but didn't answer. She was looking at Ava then, and Ava knew she was trying to calculate the years. As far as Orchid knew, Ava hadn't wanted kids at all. She'd always thought it was unethical, given the state of the world. She watched these thoughts play out across Orchid's furrowed brows, but before she could address them, Brook said, "What are you doing out here?"

"I could ask the same of you," Orchid said, hoisting herself up to a more fully seated position. "How did you get out?"

It had been many, many years since Ava had dared to dream of seeing Orchid again, and she found herself very disoriented by the physical fact of her, the flesh and blood and stink. (Oh—the stink. As though Orchid hadn't had a proper shower since the last time they'd seen each other.)

Orchid had lived in her mind for so long, and then not at all. Her children had taken her place in Ava's heart, and then of course there was Olympia. But now she would probably never see Olympia again, and here Orchid was, looking at her with these pleading eyes.

How in the world? She couldn't even begin to parse out the tornado of feelings overtaking her. Anger. Relief. Confusion. Worry. Would finding Orchid here be a distraction from their purpose? Or could she somehow help them find July, out here in this unfamiliar wasteland?

"How do you feel now?" Ava asked, after she cleaned the wounds she could see. It was impossible to tell how hurt she was; Orchid was covered in dirt.

"I think I'm okay," she said. "Just a little scraped up. I had a stupid fall."

"Can you stand?" Ava's knees cracked as she stood up and extended a hand.

Orchid looked up at it and then shook her head. "Actually, maybe I need to sit here for a while."

"That's fine," Ava said. "We could use a rest, too."

They didn't need to rest; they needed to keep going. They hadn't been prepared for the heat, not really, and they should press on until they were safely past it. But Ava was already bending the truth to fit Orchid's needs. She hesitated, wondering if she could correct herself, but Orchid looked so pathetic that she couldn't bring herself to be that brutal. She could be kind.

Brook was sitting quietly a few feet away, picking at the dirt.

"So what have you guys been up to?" Orchid said. She said it as though she was joking, but her face gave away a more intense question.

Ava wasn't sure how to summarize the events of the past twenty or so years: the shock of learning what Inside really was, and how she'd made it work for her anyway. What she'd learned about it that had made her leave.

July, and how much Ava and Brook loved her. Where they were going and why. Olympia. Her greatest love, left behind.

So instead of trying to explain, she said, "Why don't you go first?"

"I lived in Canada, like I told you I would," Orchid said. It was hard to miss the sadness in her voice. The regret. "It's okay up there. I found a community. We were like . . . I don't know. Like early settlers. A simpler life. I had people. A couple of really close friends. But then I heard what might be happening Inside and I knew I had to try to convince you to leave."

The sun had started to set, turning the brownish sky to neon pink and orange; foreboding in its beauty, the toxic clouds more vibrant than Ava remembered.

"Mom, I'm starving," Brook interrupted.

"So eat, honey," Ava said. Brook pulled out some bread and a jar of peanut butter from her tote bag.

"No way," Orchid said, staring at the jar. "Is that really . . . ?"

"Do you want some?" Brook said.

Ava sighed. They certainly did not have enough food for three.

"If it's okay," Orchid said, looking back and forth between them. "Actually, you know what, no, it's fine."

"Oh, come on." Ava dismissed this. "We're not going to just sit here and eat in front of you."

Brook divided the bread into three equal pieces, spread a perfectly even amount of peanut butter on each, and handed them out.

Ava watched Orchid's eyes roll back into her head as she took a bite. "Fuck," she groaned. "I literally can't remember the last time I had peanut butter."

Brook laughed, confused.

"I guess we'll have to sleep here and get a head start tomorrow," Ava said. "I can take the first watch."

"What are you watching for?" Orchid said. "There's no one coming down this way anymore. Just harmless idiots like me. Trust me. I haven't seen anyone for days."

"Still. I'll feel better."

"Well, I'm going to sleep," Brook announced, going to the other side of the tree and curling up on the ground. Ava heard the sound of her snores begin quickly; Brook was already exhausted from what was only the very, very beginning of their journey.

"Hi," Orchid whispered.

"Hi."

"Ava, is it true?" she asked.

"Is what true?"

"That they didn't let any men Inside?"

Ava was surprised to hear the secrets of her home had escaped into the world. "Yeah," she said. "I didn't know word had gotten out."

"Come on, give me a little more credit," Orchid said lightly, but then her tone shifted and she grew serious. "Everyone I've met knew or heard of a woman who got accepted. We all started to put the pieces together, eventually. What was it like?"

"It was amazing." Ava stretched her arms above her head. She was so sore from walking. "Until, you know, it wasn't."

"Yeah?"

"Yeah." She couldn't bring herself to go on.

"Ava, I . . ." Orchid started to say.

Ava watched her, waiting. She was not going to help Orchid fill in her own blanks. The time for that had long passed.

"You're still wearing the bracelet I gave you," Orchid said hopefully.

Ava looked at it, the unfamiliar feel of metal on her wrist after so many decades spent unadorned. "Don't read too much into it," she warned.

Still, Orchid looked pleased. That maddening little smirk.

Ava said, "I'll wake you up in a few hours to take the second watch."

"Okay," Orchid said, nodding, lying down on her side. She grinned, and for a second, she looked as young as the day she'd left. "I love you."

Something inside Ava defrosted, a little. She laughed, despite herself; it startled her as it came out of her mouth. "Okay," she said. "I'm sure you do."

So it was going to be like that, then. Well, it didn't matter. The only things Ava could focus on was finding July and keeping Brook safe.

She watched Orchid's eyelids flutter into sleep, and then studied her face and her body. She looked weathered, but strong. Unfortunately for the resentment in Ava's stomach, she still found Orchid irresistibly attractive. It was shameful to feel this way. How could she be attracted to someone who had abandoned her like that? Was it possible that she was attracted not in spite of but *because* of the abandonment?

And was it a betrayal of Olympia, this stirring deep inside of her? Was it cruel, how soon she was capable of feeling this?

At any rate, perhaps Orchid could make herself useful and come with them, teach them how to survive in this strange new land. Or not. Ava wouldn't force her. She could barely even imagine asking Orchid to go with them. Asking Orchid for anything, really. The thought of needing Orchid again made her flush with humiliation.

There was a rustling sound on the other side of the tree and then Brook appeared, tiptoeing back to where Ava sat.

"Mom," she whispered.

"Yeah?"

"Is this the woman?"

Ava raised her eyebrows. Brook's memory was too sharp for her own good.

"The woman you loved?" she pressed.

Ava nodded.

"I like her," Brook said.

"Everyone always does." Ava sighed. "Try to get some sleep."

In the morning, Ava helped Orchid change the bandage around her ear.

It was disorienting to be outside and not hear any birds. To not hear anything, really, except the wind rustling the charred branches and the sound of garbage rolling down the highway like great tumbleweeds of plastic. She wasn't sure they'd be able to survive out here. Why should they, when no one else had?

"Yikes," Ava whispered as she unwrapped the cotton and inspected the gash. It looked like it was getting infected, pus coming out of the wound and the flesh inflamed. Orchid recoiled when she tried to touch it.

"Sorry." Ava gritted her teeth to keep the nausea at bay. It was a disgusting sight. "Hold still." She put a few drops of hydrogen peroxide on it, watching it sizzle.

"Are you trying to kill me?" Orchid said.

"Yes," Ava said.

Brook was waking from where she'd curled up in the tree's roots. "What did I miss?" she said as she stretched.

"Your mother is inflicting bodily harm on me," Orchid said.

"She loves to do that," Brook said.

Orchid and Brook were smiling at each other. A knot of something old, familiar, and jagged formed in Ava's throat.

"All right, enough making fun of me," she said. "I think we need to keep moving."

"Where are we going?" Orchid said.

"You didn't tell her?" Brook asked. "Mom!"

"Well!" Ava said. But she had nothing else to say. She knew Brook had expected her to fill Orchid in on everything after she'd gone to sleep, but she hadn't been able to bring herself to. She was worried she'd come undone, and so she'd said practically nothing of the past twenty-some years.

"Why don't *you* tell me," Orchid said to Brook gently, letting Ava off the hook.

"My sister was taken."

"You've got a sister?"

"Well, sort of."

Ava couldn't stand to hear the story of July come out of Brook's mouth. It hurt too much. So as Brook began talking, Ava wandered back to the road, examined what was clearly the remains of Orchid's bike. The same bike she'd had when they loved each other. The same bike she'd left on.

As she crouched beside the bicycle, inspecting it, trying to see if it was salvageable, the memories fought to come back.

She saw their highlight reel, as if she were watching an old film montage: Orchid riding this bike down the street, grinning over her shoulder at Ava. Orchid in bed, running her hands along Ava's legs, making her laugh so hard her stomach hurt. Meeting for a drink, feeling Orchid's eyes on her and only her as she walked across a crowded bar. Holding hands as they walked down the street, not caring who stared at them. Moving in together, the bike leaning against the living room wall like a spindly roommate.

Their first fight. Oh, god, she smiled at how dumb it had been. Red meat had become illegal and Ava couldn't stop complaining about how much she missed hamburgers. Orchid, trying to be romantic, had tracked down someone at work who claimed to have a black-market hookup to a cattle farm. She'd come home with a pound of red meat wrapped in brown paper. They'd grilled it on the roof of her apartment building and eaten every last crumb. The next day Orchid came home and told her what she'd found out: it wasn't cow meat, it was dog. They'd taken turns gagging into the toilet while Ava yelled at Orchid: *You didn't think to clarify what you were buying?*

And then, their last fight. This one Ava couldn't laugh about. Orchid abandoning her the night her Inside acceptance came through, insisting she was doing it for Ava's own good, that Ava should just go without her even though they had long ago decided to only go in if they could go together. It had been so clear to Ava that Orchid had just been looking for an excuse to bail.

It still stung, even though she felt she'd healed, even though she'd found other, better love with Olympia.

She rocked back onto the seat of her butt, giving in to how overwhelmed she was. The sky was a putrid brown color, and so was the ground below her. The trees that remained on the sides of the highway were mostly black and burned, or fallen and rotting. It was an alien landscape. It wasn't home. But what was?

She thought of Olympia. Inside, they'd spent years falling in love with each other, an excruciating buildup that was absolutely worth the wait. Olympia had been her family's doctor, had known everything there was to know about Ava, and loved her anyway. Loved her because of who she was, not in spite of it.

And then, the ultimate betrayal. Olympia didn't tell her the most important thing: Ava had been chosen to be Jacqueline Millender's surrogate, though she hadn't consented. Instead, she was just lied to; told she was carrying one baby when in fact there were two, one hers, and one made from Jacqueline's egg.

During Ava's pregnancy, she remained isolated, too depressed to want to be around anyone else, so she couldn't see how much bigger she was than the other pregnant people, and her own medical information was concealed from her. She had an emergency C-section, was put under anesthesia. July was whisked away and Ava awoke to just Brook in her arms, no reason to think anything was off.

Despite being separated at birth, Brook and July had found each other, become best friends, inseparable for their whole lives. Until July vanished.

After twenty-two years of allowing other people to care for her biological daughter, Jacqueline had sent for July, taken her to the US space shuttle. It was more like a kidnapping, really. And it was only when July was gone that Olympia told Ava the truth about who July really was: Jacqueline Millender's daughter, yes, but also Ava's.

Now, Ava and Brook were determined to find July and get her back.

The space shuttle would have to land. After all, the wealthy on board had been forcing the people of Inside to grow their food, and Ava herself had sealed off the one entrance to Inside that allowed them access to it. Which meant the space shuttle would run out of food soon—Ava just didn't know how soon.

It was as good a guess as any that it would land at the base it took off from, on the border of the US and Canada.

This was the story she couldn't stand to tell Orchid.

She'd forgiven Olympia, once she realized she had to leave Inside. There was no use being angry with someone who you're never going to see again. But the hurt was still there, walking beside her on this journey, clutching her heart in a viselike grip that every now and then made her wonder if she had the strength to go on, after everything that had been taken from her.

She could hear Orchid and Brook still talking, not what they were saying but the sounds of their voices. They sounded chummy, happy, excited to get to know each other.

Brook was never supposed to meet Orchid. This part of her life should have been long over.

It clearly wasn't, though.

"Mom," Brook called. "Mom, come back."

She hauled herself up and walked back to where they sat under the tree. "So, are you up to speed?" she asked. She knew she sounded callous, but she didn't know what else to say, how else to be.

"Yes," Orchid said, her face crumpling with concern. "Ava, I'm so sorry."

"What do you want to do?" Ava said, dismissing the apology, bristling at the pity. "*We* have to keep going north."

"Mom," Brook said. "Obviously she's coming with us."

"I didn't want to assume."

"I don't have to, if you don't want me to," Orchid said. "But honestly, I came all this way to find you. I'd like to stick with you for as long as you'll let me."

Ava hung her head and rolled her neck back and forth, trying to loosen the tension. She was conflicted. Orchid might be helpful. But she could also be a burden. In the end, though, she couldn't imagine parting ways now that they'd found each other, no matter how much anger she held on to. "Okay. Come."

"Yay!" Brook squealed.

"Thank you," said Orchid. "I promise to make myself useful. I think I have an idea of where the space shuttle landing site is. I rode past signs for it on my way south. It's on the military base, right? And I think I'm good to walk now. I feel much better."

Ava and Brook had just been heading up the highway with no real plan. "Lead the way," Ava said.

"And if she's not there," Orchid said, "you could come back north with me and maybe you could reach her on Camilla's comms device."

"She'll be there," Ava said, unwilling to admit that they needed a backup plan.

"I'm sure she will be," Orchid said, thankfully not pressing it. Ava wasn't prepared to truly consider what it might mean if July—and the space shuttle she was on—didn't land where it was supposed to. She didn't want to simply talk to July. She wanted July *with* her.

And so they began walking. And walking, and walking.

"What is all this shit?" Ava said, stepping around piles of debris that decorated the pavement.

"Have you ever seen a town flattened by a tornado?" Orchid replied.

"No," Ava said. "Not in person. Have you?"

"Tons," Orchid said. "If I had to guess, I'd say that's what happened, probably nearby. The wind must have brought the remains here. The path of a tornado is actually usually just fifty yards wide, give or take."

"There's so much of it," Brook said, wrinkling her nose at the mess.

"I didn't realize tornados reached this area," Ava said.

"Oh, this is nothing," Orchid said. "Pretty standard, really. I bet when it first happened there was some salvageable stuff, but it's probably all been picked over by now. Migrants pass through here every now and then. If we do see anybody, they'll be on their way to somewhere else. No one is really trying to live this far south anymore."

They continued on, walking down the middle where it was clearest. "Don't look at the sides of the road," Orchid said at one point.

"Why?" Brook said.

"Some things you can't unsee."

Ava felt her stomach twist. She guessed there were bodies all around them, hiding just underneath the debris.

She was starting to get hungry. Not even the dead could suppress the appetite that had gone unsatiated since they left Inside; every time they ate, she tried to only take a few bites, in order to save more for later. She wondered if they'd find July at all, or if they'd join the bodies on the side of the highway first.

"We should probably talk basic survival skills," Orchid said, reading her mind.

Ava nodded. It was true. They didn't know the first thing about being out here.

"So obviously it's quite warm out," Orchid said, which made Brook laugh. "Even though it's cloudy, the UV is still dangerous, so make sure your skin is covered, no matter how hot you are. And keep an eye on your hydration. If you start to feel dizzy, drink water. If you get tunnel vision, drink water. If you think you're going to pass out, find shade and drink water."

"Okay, we get it," Ava said. "Water."

"But it's also possible to drink too much water," Orchid said. "You can drown yourself from the inside. So no chugging, even if you think you need to."

"No chugging," Ava repeated. "What else?"

"Don't eat anything that's already dead, because you don't know if it's diseased. Don't eat anything without cooking it completely, for that matter."

"We have food," Brook said.

"Yeah, same, but we're going to run out," Orchid said. "And when we do, we can find things. Rats. Squirrels. I can catch and cook them for us, and dry the meat so we can travel with it. I'll show you how to do it in case . . ." She trailed off. "In case you need to do it without me."

Ava nodded, but didn't say anything. *Without me* could mean lots of different things.

"We'll hang the food from the trees at night so critters can't get to it. Also, be careful of insects. The wasps love the heat, so they're worse in the afternoon. So do the ticks. Always check yourself. Don't leave skin exposed if we're walking through grass."

"Got it," Ava said.

"And, you know, the thing that really fucked people in the end was the storms," Orchid said, gesturing to the debris around them. "There's bound to be some weather event while we're out here."

"And then what?" Brook asked.

"Right," Orchid smiled weakly. "That's the question. Taking cover is usually your best bet. But not under the tallest thing around—that's how you'll get struck by lightning. And not under something that's not sturdy. It'll just blow away, maybe take you with it."

"So what you're saying is, if we get caught in a storm, we're screwed," Ava said.

"You had to know that before you left Inside," Orchid replied with a shrug. "It's a big risk being out here at all. But I think we'll be okay as long as there are no tornadoes."

"What do we do if there's a tornado?" Brook said.

"Get the fuck out of its way," Orchid said. "However you can."

Ava clenched her teeth.

"One more thing," she said. "The biggest danger is going to be other people. Heat can make people go crazy. I doubt there's anyone dangerous around here, but hopefully we won't have to find out."

This was a terrifying thought, and Ava tried not to dwell on it.

Brook was moving her lips, mouthing words to herself, and Ava could tell this meant she was counting: their steps, cars, trees, the debris. Categorizing everything they saw. Trying to understand it.

There was a lot of new information to take in. But Ava was concerned that Brook was spending so much time trying to find invisible patterns in the world around her that she was going to miss what was real. Several times she saw her trip over branches while her mouth was moving.

At one point, after Brook stumbled over a large crack in the ground, Ava said, "Baby, can you take a break from the counting? Can you just try and be present?"

Brook looked ashamed, but she pushed back: "Can't you just let me have this one thing?"

Ava dropped it. Orchid tilted her head and mouthed to Ava, *Counting?* But Ava shook her head. She didn't need to tell Orchid about Brook's demons. That was up to Brook.

"How far is it, anyway?" Brook asked Orchid.

"Depends on how slow you are," Orchid said.

Brook laughed. "I'm not slow," she said.

"Well, you sure are whiny," Orchid replied, grinning. Brook laughed again. If Ava had said that, Brook would have given her the silent treatment.

"I already don't like this friendship," Ava said. They ignored her.

"It'll take a week or two, maybe more," Orchid said. "It was faster on the bike."

Brook groaned.

"You got this," Ava said.

"Thanks, Mom." Brook rolled her eyes, and Orchid chuckled.

What was happening? Why were Brook and Orchid so drawn to each other?

They kept walking.

"Do you ever get used to the heat out here?" Ava asked Orchid as the sun pierced through the smog, sizzling the puddles on the ground into steam, making Ava feel lightheaded and heavy at the same time.

"It's cooler where I settled," Orchid said. "I mean, it's still warm, but it's not like this. This is next-level insanity."

"It's a sauna," Ava said.

"I hate it," Brook muttered.

The two of them were both slower than Orchid, despite the state they'd found her in. Orchid was used to the heat. Ava had never felt anything like it. She was sure her organs would boil.

Along the way, Ava kept an eye out for pools of water that had collected on the tops of busted cars so she could collect it and purify it. They'd be dead without the water purifier that came in the emergency kit they'd taken with them.

One afternoon it got so hot that the bottoms of Ava's shoes started sticking to the concrete.

"I think my shoes are melting," she said with alarm. "Brook?"

"Mine, too," Brook cried.

Orchid grabbed her arm. "Get to the median," she said, and the three of them ran to the overgrown center of the highway, where Ava ripped her shoes off just as the liquifying soles were about to touch her skin.

"Take mine," Orchid said, starting to unlace her boots.

Ava refused, unwilling to accept this kindness. "I'll put them back on when they dry."

She didn't say anything when the shape the soles hardened into was disfigured and uncomfortable, and neither did Brook. Complaining would have only slowed them down.

They spent the afternoon in the grass, waiting for the sun to set and the air to cool. At dusk, they resumed walking. Within a few hours the bottoms of Ava's feet were ripped to shreds. It took a lot of effort not to limp. She wished she could do something for Brook's feet, which were surely smarting just as much as hers were, but all she could do was plod onward. However much it hurt.

She stayed on the dirt as much as possible after that, tucking her pants into her socks to avoid the insects Orchid had warned her about.

They made it two more days together before they got caught in a bad storm.

There were a few moments when the sudden gust of wind actually felt good on her sweaty, sunburned skin. But she knew better than to enjoy it. Plus, Orchid immediately started screaming: "Let's go, let's go."

Ava wasn't sure where they were going, until she saw in the distance there was a semitrailer truck on its side.

They reached it just as a crack of thunder did.

Orchid pried the doors open and leapt inside, then extended her hand out to pull Ava and Brook up into it with her. They crawled into the back of the truck, which looked like it had been raided for supplies long ago, and watched as branches and garbage blew by.

Orchid closed the doors and flicked on a flashlight. The truck shuddered in the wind.

They sat in a circle, listening to the sounds of garbage hitting the metal walls. It was dark but cool inside. Brook rested her head on Ava's shoulder and Ava felt her shivering.

"Just pray for no tornadoes," Orchid said.

"You pray now?" Ava said, untangling a dried leaf from her hair.

"Sometimes, yeah, I do," Orchid said, sounding surprisingly earnest.

"Mom," Brook said. "This seems bad."

"It's okay, honey," Ava said. "We're safe here."

She wasn't sure if she was right, but it was what Brook needed to hear.

Orchid was exploring the rest of the truck, disappearing into the shadows, and then she said, "Oh, shit!"

She returned with a small bag of potato chips. "Oh my god," Ava said. "You better check the expiration date on those."

"Potato chips don't go bad," Orchid said, grinning. "Thank you, preservatives."

"I want one," Brook said, as Orchid popped the bag open and the salty smell hit them.

"Oh," Orchid said, peering inside. "Actually, these don't look so good." She looked sheepishly at Ava, who raised her eyebrows. *Told you.*

They decided to spend the night in the back of the truck. They didn't really have another option; it was raining too hard, and the wind seemed strong enough to lift them off their feet. But that was okay, because inside the truck it was dry, though it was creaking and swaying.

When Brook fell asleep, Orchid crawled over to the corner where Ava was trying to get comfortable, and stared at her.

"Yes?" Ava said.

"Nothing," Orchid said. "Just missed looking at you. Sorry."

They were both quiet then, the sound of Brook's snoring audible even over the roar of thunder outside. Eventually the solar-powered flashlight flickered off. It was too dark for Ava's eyes to adjust; they were sealed in, no light getting through the truck's doors.

They fell asleep sitting next to each other. Ava woke a few times, confused about where she was, trying to make out the face of the stranger next to her in the darkness.

In the morning, the storm was over, and they continued on, Ava's disfigured shoes squelching as they sank into the newly wet mud.

There would be time, later, to think about what Orchid had said. For now, all she could think about was putting one foot in front of the other, each painful step taking her deeper into the unknown, where the changed world held dangers she couldn't yet fathom.

APRIL 11, 2041

Hi, my love,

I'm sorry that it's been a few days since I last wrote to you.

After I sent my last letter, I got pulled over on the freeway. I hadn't realized I was speeding; something about the high of getting closer to you made me feel invincible. I wanted the wind in my hair. And then I saw flashing lights behind me.

Luckily, they accepted my license and registration without question. I started to cry—a trick I picked up—and said my husband would kill me if I got a ticket. They let me go.

But it's made me feel paranoid. I can't have a record of my whereabouts.

So I drove and drove and drove and now I'm somewhere in Alabama, where the air is hot and thick as soup, and all through the state I see neighborhoods that have been destroyed by floods and hurricanes. It's a sad place. Lots of unhoused people. They need to migrate somewhere safer. I'm not sure what anyone is still doing here. Sometimes I feel like stubbornness is going to be the death of our species.

I'm writing from a diner. Sorry for the greasy fingerprints.

Okay, back to you, back to us. I was nearing the end of my pregnancy.

With so much time on my hands, I decided to take up gardening;

inside, mostly, because it was getting so hot outside. This seemed to please Rick. He liked that I was making our home beautiful and that I had something productive to do.

Our living room slowly turned into my personal little jungle.

One day Rick came home with a potted orchid for me as a gift. It was purple and black, spotted, and looked like it had a face. It proved to be a finicky, tricky thing to keep healthy, and I began organizing my time around caring for it; spritzing it with water and gently turning it so that it caught the right amount of light.

I decided that when you were born, I would name you after that weird little plant, because surely if I could keep this ugly-beautiful purple bloom alive, I could keep Orchid the human girl alive, too.

I wanted to have a natural birth at home with a doula, but Rick said no.

In case you've forgotten, I wasn't legally allowed to make any of my own decisions. It was all up to him. And he was scared. He loved me, he already loved you. He wanted to take every precaution. I took this to mean he didn't think I could do it. I knew I could. I was young and brave. But he'd made his mind up.

The day I went into labor, we drove to the hospital, and I shook the whole way there. It was a pain like I've never felt since, like I never knew existed. Worth it, of course, but I thought I was going to be torn in two. I didn't cry. I didn't scream. The pain sealed my lips, paralyzed my tongue. It felt like all I knew, all I'd ever known.

Rick, on the other hand, couldn't shut the fuck up. "Are you okay? What do you need? What does it feel like? Kelly? Kelly? *Kelly*?"

I could have murdered him.

When we got to the hospital, they told us something was wrong. Before I knew what was happening, your father consented to a C-section.

He was, after all, my guardian.

"I want to keep pushing," I said. "I think I can do this."

"You can't," Rick said.

"You can't," the doctor agreed.

"I can. I *can.* It's my body. It's my decision," I said.

But it wasn't. It was Rick's.

So you were sliced out of me while I lay there weeping, not from the pain anymore (I couldn't feel a damn thing) but from the loss of control. I'd had no say in this most personal decision. The doctor lifted you up and you waited a beat before you started to scream. You were screaming for both of us, I thought. My emotional spokesperson.

"Give her to me," I said.

They laid you on my chest, and for the first time but certainly not the last, you and I cried together. You were pink, splotchy, and perfect, totally singular. An orchid. Now that I'd met you, I knew for sure that I chose the right name.

Then your father held you while they sewed me back up.

When we took you home, your father was terrified. He drove at a snail's pace the whole way back to the house. I was touched by this. He wanted to protect us. I forgave him for what he'd done. I was always forgiving him easily, even when he didn't apologize. I just wanted it to work, this new life.

Those first few months with you were bliss. We felt like a real family. Your father really rose to the occasion. He took care of everything so you and I could just relax into each other. I'd never been so loved, so nurtured. I was young enough that even the lack of sleep didn't really bother me. I could have stayed up with you all night forever. Every week brought new wonders. You were slowly waking up, noticing more and more.

I allowed myself to admit that I had always wanted to be a mother. I just never thought it would be possible. I couldn't imagine the part where someone would love me enough to want a family with me.

It got so fun when you could hold your own head up, when I wasn't afraid I'd accidentally break your neck, and you could perch on my hip. The three of us would dance around together, singing songs. You made a lot of cute little noises, trying to speak, trying to tell us things. I made the noises back to you. So did your dad, sometimes. It was harder for him to be silly, but he was a good sport. You'd kick your legs and squeal while he tickled you. God, if I could go back to any time in my life, it would be that one.

Things got harder when Rick went back to work, though I knew his four-month paternity leave was much more than most fathers got.

You wanted to be held at all times, but without an extra set of hands, I was struggling to do the basic things; shower, for example. I was anxious about how much you needed me, though of course that's natural for a baby. But I didn't want to make you dependent on me. A girl should know how to stand on her own. Even then, I think, I wanted you to be prepared in case you were ever without me.

So I left you in the room alone while I did the things I needed to do. I put in my EarPods so I wouldn't hear your cries. You were perhaps too young when I started doing this. But no one was telling me the right way to raise you, so I made it up as we went along.

Eventually, you needed me less, and this I felt was a positive thing.

When you were old enough for toys, you wanted to play with cars, trucks, trains. I liked that we were raising a girl in a nontraditional way. It was so fun to dress you up however I wanted and watch strangers try to categorize you while we went to the playground. It provided me with endless entertainment. They'd call you a handsome little dude if you were wearing blue. Which was true; you *were* handsome and you were a little dude. You were also my perfect baby girl.

You were good at playing by yourself. Sometimes I worried that you preferred it. Maybe I had broken you. I was constantly worrying that I ruined you.

Sometimes I hired a babysitter to stay with you when I went on errands. You had no stranger anxiety, even though the books

I'd read said you should. You liked everyone. You wanted everyone to like you, too. You were such a little crowd-pleaser. Eventually you stopped crying when I left. The flip side of this was that you stopped looking happy to see me when I got back. You were fine either way.

At night I'd put you to bed—a long ritual involving a bath, a bottle, and books—and then I'd watch TV until your dad came home.

Sometimes I'd fall asleep on the couch before he showed up. Instead of waking me up he'd lay a blanket over me and turn all the lights off. I'd wake in the morning confused and stiff.

I didn't realize, at first, that your dad had started coming home from work later and later.

We were always happy to see him. You in particular were always thrilled, which hurt my feelings. I was the one home with you. That meant I was the one who got your temper tantrums. He only got you screaming *DADDA!* and throwing yourself at his legs, if you were still awake when he showed up. That was starting to happen less often, though. Most of the time you'd be asleep for hours by the time he walked through the door.

It wasn't really until you started preschool—leaving me home alone for the first time since you were born—that it hit me. Where had my husband gone?

I started to keep track of his comings and goings, noticing the time, whether or not he'd claim to have already eaten dinner when he got home. How quickly he showered after walking through the door.

I asked him about it. I don't want you to think I was afraid of confronting him. But he just lied to my face, made up stories about working late hours that I knew were bullshit because the union didn't let them work overtime.

He told me I was crazy, that I needed to get out of the house more. He started taking his phone with him everywhere he went, including the bathroom. He used to just plug it in and forget about it. But now he was clearly hiding something.

I begged him not to call me crazy. It's what my parents had called me.

Even my therapist said I was overreacting. That you being at preschool probably made me feel like he was gone more. In all likelihood, she said, he was probably not away any more than he ever was.

I started to wonder if she was in cahoots with him, if they talked behind my back and planned out their lies together. I felt paranoid. Gaslit. I had no one I could trust. Madhuri and I had lost touch; she had no interest in being part of my life now that it looked as it did. And I thought if I reached out she'd just yell at me for staying, given the circumstances. That she'd say she told me so. (I should have given Madhuri more credit.)

This went on for longer than I'd like to admit; me in the dark, Rick avoiding me. You were growing faster than I could believe. Soon it was time for kindergarten. You made little friends. God, you were so freaking cute.

I was terrified when you went to school. It seemed like a horrible time to be a child. I remembered my own experiences with active shooter drills and was paralyzed with the thought that soon you'd learn about people who took guns to schools to shoot kids. I just prayed that you wouldn't have to learn it from firsthand experience. Had it been selfish to bring a child into a world like this? A world of mass shootings and climate breakdown?

These thoughts kept me up at night. The lack of sleep was making me feel unhinged.

One night Rick forgot to take his phone with him into the bathroom when he went to take his nightly shower. I lunged for it as soon as the door closed, typed in the password I'd figured out after years of watching him, and opened his messages.

It was all right there. He hadn't hidden anything. There were so many women he was talking to, so many pictures they'd sent him. It turns out, it doesn't feel good to find what you're looking for. I think part of me had hoped I was wrong.

They were all so young, too. Younger even than me. I guess it was nice to not be crazy. They were pretty and thin.

I wondered if Rick had always been a cheater or if I'd done something to drive him away. I supposed I had; I'd loved you more than I could ever love anyone else, including him. Was it possible I pushed him away? Maybe. But what seemed more likely was that I didn't need him like I used to, which meant he was no longer my savior, and that made me less appealing.

I wondered if he had ever really loved me or if he'd just wanted to control me. My whole life felt like it was a joke. Madhuri was right. I didn't regret having you, but I did regret trying to become a traditional wife. I was a round peg, bruised and bloodied from being violently crammed into a square hole. I was never meant for this. Maybe that's why he found solace in other women: because I was so bad at being his wife.

In hindsight, all that was bullshit. I was never anything but myself. I was a fine wife. His decisions were his own.

I was afraid to tell my therapist what I'd found on his phone; she would just tell him, I figured. So I said I was ready to stop seeing her. I said I was happy and healed and felt like I had all the tools I needed. Everyone bought my story.

I became more isolated than ever.

I hadn't worked a day since getting pregnant with you. I had no money to my name other than the allowance he gave me, and all of that usually just went to groceries. I'm not sure he would have given me a divorce even if I'd asked for one. I think he liked the idea of a family even if he didn't want to participate in it; he'd always take me to the union holiday party, me in a red dress on his arm, receiving compliments like a well-groomed pet, while the other wives asked me about you and told me about their own children. He liked to show me off. I was so much younger than the other women and I think this was a source of pride for him. As were you. He kept a photo of you as the background on his phone, flashing it for all to see. But when it came to his private life, his real life outside of work, I didn't matter at all.

But I didn't want to fuck you up more than I worried I already had. I wanted you to have two parents. I wanted you to grow up in a stable home. I wanted you to have a better life than I did.

So I stayed. I stayed and said nothing while he cheated on me with god knows how many women. I poured myself into raising you. You and I were a team. It was us against the world.

And it wasn't all bad with Rick. When you started showing an interest in sports, he'd take you to the park to throw a ball back and forth. He still wanted to be your dad. And sometimes in the night, he'd still reach for me. I rebuffed him, but it was nice to be wanted.

I still had needs, though. One night when he was "at a conference" (please—what kind of conference could Rick possibly need to go to?), I hired a sitter and drove two hours to the nearest small-town gay bar, where I drank a beer so slowly it got warm and waited for an older butch to notice me. She did, eventually. We hooked up in the bathroom. I came home feeling calmer, if not sadder. If Rick suspected anything when he got home the next day, he didn't say anything. I don't think he was paying close enough attention to notice a difference in me.

I'm telling you this because I don't want you to think I was a total victim. I acted out, too.

"I never asked you to live this life," I said one night while we lay as far away from each other in the bed as possible.

"I know," he said.

"Why are you punishing me?"

"I'm not," he said. "Kelly, remember when we met? Remember how I took care of you, made everything okay? I'm still that guy."

We had a thousand variations of this conversation. He couldn't admit that our marriage was falling apart. Instead, he repeated his savior narrative. He seemed almost afraid to sit in the discomfort of his own actions.

I also didn't bring it up directly, so it's partially on me that we grew further and further apart. I could have confronted him more plainly. But I didn't. I just stopped trying. Instead I did everything I could to make your life as positive as possible. I powered through it, for you.

I imagine I'm getting to the point in your life that you remember, so I won't go too far into recounting it for you.

I believe you had a happy childhood. You were decent enough in school. You had friends. You had things you liked to do. I hope you remember it as being full of light.

Rick was a good father, despite everything; at least, when he was home. He had endless patience for you. These moments gave me hope that maybe we would make it after all. Maybe he'd come around; maybe if he slept with enough other women, he'd get it out of his system.

I know what you're thinking: Why hang on so tight to our family if I was just going to leave you? But like I said when I first started writing to you, I didn't mean to leave *you.* It was only supposed to be for a couple of days.

You were seven when it started—the chain of events that led to my departure.

I remember that day very clearly, because I've thought about it a million times since.

I have this feeling now that if I could just recreate the details perfectly, I could transport back there. Maybe choose something different. I don't know. I know that sounds crazy.

So let me walk you through everything I remember. I kissed you goodbye in the morning and watched you walk down the driveway to the school bus, your little red backpack bouncing as you caught up to your friend from down the street. You were crunching leaves under your muddy sneakers, your tiny, high-pitched voices not dissimilar from the birds chirping in the trees above.

I was wearing my mom uniform: high-waisted vintage jeans and a faded, oversized men's shirt, my hair in a bun at the top of my head. Fleece slippers. A painful row of pimples outlined my jaw. I was twenty-seven—still young enough to have out-of-control hormonal acne. In the afternoons I'd hide the pustules beneath a gleam of drugstore concealer, which I knew on some level was only making them worse.

I put on a happy, excited face for you that morning just like every morning because, I thought, that's just what you did. And I had a lot to do that day—well, every day—to maintain that nice, normal life. For one, the house was a mess. We were out of toilet paper. And I didn't have a plan for dinner.

The neighbor called out good morning to me as he walked down his driveway in a robe to get the newspaper. His dense green lawn sparkled with dew and I heard the click of his sprinklers turning on.

Imagine: maintaining grass, at a time like that! Elsewhere, droughts were causing entire species to go extinct. I waved, quickly retreating into the safety and privacy of our house. It was best that I not have a conversation with him, that I pretend not to notice the way the neighbors took our resources for granted.

Not so far away, on Long Island, whole neighborhoods were under two feet of water, their evacuated residents moving closer and closer to the boroughs of a city that could already barely contain its population. There was no such threat up where we were, and I think this made it easy for people to forget the stakes. I wondered, more often than I'd like to admit, how my parents were doing, if they were safe from the flooding or what their old age looked like or if they were even alive at this point, when the natural disasters were starting to exact a mounting human toll all along the coast. I was sad for myself that I couldn't show you off to your grandparents. But they'd made their choice.

Anyway, back to that day. I went back inside, kicked my slippers off, and began cleaning the kitchen. Your father had left his dirty cereal bowl on the table, coffee dribbled on the counter. You had left a nest of toast crumbs on the linoleum floor, which was more forgivable. I hummed as I worked, the self-soothing habit the therapist had encouraged. I hummed louder as I wiped away Rick's mess.

My cell phone rang, a number I didn't recognize.

"Yeah?" I said when I picked up, balancing the phone between my shoulder and my face as I swept the floor.

"Kelly?" a man's voice said after a few seconds.

"Uh-huh," I said, wary.

There was another long pause. "Hello?" I said. And then, getting a little spooked, I snapped, "I don't know how you got this number, but don't call again." I blocked the caller and then tossed the phone onto the counter.

I was always careful with giving my info out, which meant I rarely got the automated messages that plagued everyone else. Still, I supposed, I wasn't immune to them. I started humming again.

It was November, already eighty degrees outside though the trees were almost bare. Such hot days this time of year meant that along the coast there'd be worsening hurricanes, tornadoes, even monsoons in some places. It was like that every fall now that the climate-change tipping point had passed.

Crescent moons of sweat were blossoming under my arms. A wild and uneven beating in my chest, as though my heart was unsure what its own rhythm should be (this was nothing new—I functioned best when I ignored it).

I retrieved my phone from where I'd thrown it so I could start making a grocery list. Being vegan was tricky in the town center where I did my grocery shopping, so I had long since given up on trying to get you or Rick to eat like me; there simply weren't enough options to keep you happy. I existed mostly on beans and vegetables and green juice, whereas I made you roast chicken, cringing at the feel of the raw meat in my hands but also becoming ravenously hungry the minute the smell of it cooking filled the kitchen.

I checked the fridge to see what we were running low on, pulling the garbage can over to start getting rid of the food that had turned. A bag of grated cheese with blue fuzz, lettuces that were wet and wilted. A Tupperware of spaghetti leftovers from last week that Rick had promised to take for lunch and forgotten.

Of course, as you know now, there was a time when I would have balked to see myself living this sort of existence. A time of tattered clothes and dumpster diving and protests, welts on my wrist from plastic zip-tie handcuffs. At that point, I never could have predicted this life I found myself in, cleaning out the fridge so I could restock it with newer, fresher things. I tried to be grateful for it.

I backed out of the driveway and began the ten-minute trip to the small grocery at the center of town. I turned on NPR and caught the tail end of a sentence, a man's voice saying, ". . . and that's how we plan to begin to address the global crisis of the attack on masculinity."

I scoffed. There was no crisis, as far as I was concerned. Just some whiny dudes getting their feelings hurt.

"But will a gender-based affirmative action program really do anything?" the interviewer asked. "Won't that just re-center straight cis men after so many movements have fought for—and in many ways, won—equality?"

"Well, it's not equality if men don't benefit from it, too," the man said.

"Not to play devil's advocate, but perhaps men just need to work as hard as everyone else," the interviewer suggested.

"I didn't realize I was coming on your show to be attacked," the man said, and the interviewer laughed and apologized.

Too soft, as always. I'd been reading about the proposed affirmative action program, which would mandate universities to admit 50 percent men; a legislative attempt to fix the lopsided demographics of the present, when women were finally dominating in all academic and professional fields—both in numbers and achievements. Backlash always follows progress.

I promise I'm telling you these details for a reason. The context is important.

Back on the radio, the interviewer was saying, "So how do you think gender nonconforming people fit into the gender-based affirmative action proposal?"

"Well, they'd be grouped in with women," the man said, as though it were obvious, and I groaned.

"So, you're saying a college, for example, should be fifty percent cis men, and fifty percent everybody else?"

"You know," the man said, "this business about *cis men* is a recent invention. We used to just be called men. Simpler times, don't you think?"

I rolled my eyes. Men falling behind was hardly an issue compared to the racism and classism that still ran through the fabric of the country. Not to mention the climate disaster. Besides, as I knew from my own marriage, men were still very much in control of things. But these were no longer my issues to fight. The responsibilities of adulthood in America had eclipsed the panic that used to drive me. I told myself there was really nothing I could do about the state of the earth but go about my business as best I could; make the best of my life while I still had it. My cell phone rang again from a private number. I turned the radio off and pulled over to answer, with my car at a sharp angle at the curb.

"Stop fucking calling me," I said, assuming correctly that it was the same person.

A voice on the other end started to say, "Kelly—"

Before the voice could say anything else, I hung up, with shaking hands. Perhaps someone else would have been curious about who was calling and what they wanted, but I just wanted to be left alone. I had things to do. People to take care of. A neutral mental state to maintain. That the voice sounded familiar was not something I had the capacity to consider. There was no one I wanted to hear from.

And then, a few days later, the van showed up outside our house.

All right, baby, I think I need to take a break. It is upsetting me more than I thought it would, revisiting the lead-up to when I left you. Sorry for the cliff-hanger. It'll all make sense soon.

I've got to hit the road, anyway. My eyes are crossing from writing so quickly. I need to down some coffee and buck up for the drive.

Love,
Mom

5

MAX
2078

MAX WAS SHIVERING VIOLENTLY IN THE RAIN THAT hammered down on them as they scrambled up the hill. The wind lifted their black hair off their neck and whipped dirt into their eyes, momentarily blinding them.

To distract themself, they tried to think about the best parts of what they'd left behind on the Winter Liberation Army compound. The cool, clean air that would fill the room after someone opened a window when the morning bell rang. And Sterrett's face. Always, in these awful moments, Sterrett's voice and eyes and mouth and neck and hands came to Max with blinding clarity, as though it had only been moments and not months since they went their separate ways.

And then—so quickly they couldn't move out of the way—they heard the unmistakable sound of bark being split, a whoosh of leaves and twigs followed by a crack from within their own body, and excruciating, blinding pain. They were pinned to the muddy earth.

Max screamed, but it was drowned out by the storm. The ground spun, and they turned their head to throw up, the vomit quickly washed away by the rivulets of water.

Their leg was broken. In how many places, they couldn't be sure. They tried a few times to push the branch off, but the effort made the pain worse.

Lying there in the mud, Max watched the back of Camilla's head as she put her arms around her father.

Camilla was older than them—they guessed maybe by ten years or so. That didn't bother Max. After a lifetime of enforced reclusiveness with the same group of people, they were attracted to newness. There was something so compelling about her; her toughness, how capable she was. A real salt-of-the-earth quality. Max had been watching her for weeks, drawn to her but unsure how to approach her. It was unlike how Max had ever felt about Sterrett. With Sterrett, everything was easy; they'd known each other for too long for Max to feel nervous. Camilla was different. They didn't have a shared history. In a way, this was what attracted Max to her, or at least, to the idea of her; Max didn't really know anything about Camilla, other than what they saw her say to other people, what they watched her do for her community.

Now, though, lying in the dirt, even thoughts of Camilla couldn't break through the pain.

There was only one thing to do as they lay there waiting for the rain to stop, and that was to relive the past few months. They'd been trying so hard to keep the memories at bay, but here, held hostage by this branch, there was nowhere to hide.

Max had convinced Sterrett to leave the WLA. It hadn't been a hard conversation. One night at their secret place in the trees, just a few days after they'd overheard Max's mother and the doctors, Max simply said, "I'm leaving. Will you come?"

Sterrett first said, "No, that's crazy," but then when Max listed all the reasons—the way Len was permitted to abuse children, that Max's mother might be allowed to keep her baby if they weren't there, the fact that they were now second-guessing every detail of everything they'd ever been told—Sterrett sighed and said, "Fine. But only because I can't imagine being here without you."

It wasn't a good reason. Max should have known that immediately. But they were so glad to not be leaving alone that they accepted it.

Max and Sterrett stuffed their backpacks full of as much B3k and water as they could hold, as well as gas masks, a couple changes of underwear, a knife, and a keychain that held some flint and steel for starting fires. At the last minute Sterrett had grabbed a B3k sprig for good luck. They left notes for their parents.

They waited until everyone else was busy working. They climbed the gate that surrounded the land they grew up on, and then the forest became dense, alive, full of unknowns.

And then—it was kind of blissful. Arduous and exhausting, but romantic, full of adventure. They slept on the ground with their shoulders touching. They pointed out birds to each other. They ate their B3k, trying to save as much as possible.

It took a few days to start noticing signs of other people. The first time they saw a campfire in the distance, they walked right up to it, brazen and curious. There were tents and signs of community everywhere, but it all seemed primitive. No evidence of the technology that Max couldn't separate from the culture of the WLA, and they felt a heady rush of optimism. They'd been hoping to find something like this; a people whose culture wasn't poisoned by the science they hoarded. Max couldn't think of another reason why so much abuse simmered in the WLA.

But the first person who appeared in front of them was a man brandishing an ax, waving it in their faces and shouting at them to get away, get away.

They ran and ran. When they stopped running they decided it was better with just the two of them, and they had more than enough supplies to get to the north without having to find other people.

They passed through a few abandoned suburbs on the way. They broke the windows of houses that looked appealing and searched for food. They ate from old dusty cans of peaches, peas, olives. They slept in strange beds. They used toilets that no longer flushed.

It was too hot to stay in these towns, though, which was presumably why they were all empty except for the occasional slumped figure of a corpse in a doorway or on the side of a road. They couldn't really even walk during the day, the heat felt so dangerous. The concrete—which they had never encountered before—made it worse.

So they went north until there were no more towns; only them, the mountains, the trees, the sky. Just as Max had imagined it.

But after a few more days, Sterrett woke up and looked tired, hungry, pale. They complained that their feet hurt, that they couldn't sleep on the ground. They missed home.

"I miss home, too," Max had said. "We knew this wouldn't be easy."

But there was something in Sterrett's face that let Max know Sterrett was homesick in a different way. They were quiet for a few minutes. Max dug a stick into the ground, waiting for Sterrett to talk.

"I just think we'd be safer if we went back," they said at last. "I feel like maybe this was a mistake."

Max was shocked. "After everything we've been through, you just want to turn around and go *back*?"

"I just think maybe it wasn't so bad. I mean, I was living with it just fine until you found out. I think we can go back and forget about all of this."

"I think you need to drink some water," Max said. They'd argued some more until Sterrett dropped it, but they brought it up a couple days later, and Max could tell by the resigned look on Sterrett's face that a decision had been made.

"I can't do this, Max."

The terror of being outside alone was starting to set in. Their stomach felt like they had eaten rocks. But Max would not tell Sterrett how badly they needed them to stay. It was against their nature. Instead they said, simply, "Are you sure?"

"I'm sorry," Sterrett said. "I'm not cut out for life on the run. You can come with me. I know they'll take us back."

"I can't," Max said. "You know I can't. My mom. It's me or her."

"I'll look out for her," Sterrett said. "I promise."

They hugged tightly. "Don't let anyone fuck with you," Max said into

Sterrett's neck. "Promise me." Sterrett only nodded. They were never going to see each other again, and there weren't words for that.

Max felt Sterrett's skinny rib cage digging into theirs. There had been a time when a hug between them was their full stomachs pressed into each other. Now it was just bones.

Sterrett pulled away, pressing their B3k sprig into Max's hand.

Max said, "I don't want this," but Sterrett wouldn't take it back.

"It's good luck. Something to remember me by," Sterrett said, and the last words Max said to them were, "Why do you think I'll need help remembering you?" Sterrett smiled sadly and shrugged.

And then, just like that, Sterrett left—turned and walked out of Max's life, back the way they came. Max was too sad to be angry. They understood the decision, even while it felt like a betrayal. It was an awful thing, to have no home. They wouldn't wish it on anyone. But was it worse than returning to a community who worshiped your abuser? Max would not have made the same decision in Sterrett's shoes, but Max was not Sterrett, and it was not their decision to make.

After that, Max was alone. Would Sterrett have stayed if they'd begged? If they had been able to say they needed help? They'd never know. They kept the sprig, though it felt more like a curse than a sign of luck.

In their despair, Max scrapped the plan to head straight north. Instead, they began heading northeast, trying to get as far away from the WLA as possible. Max had the urge to put the whole continent between them. And they had.

It was pure chance that they'd come across this group of people, where Camilla lived. When Max had stumbled into the clearing, exhausted and hungry, so thin their clothes barely stayed up, they weren't sure what would happen next. It was a gamble. They'd been avoiding the other humans they'd seen in the woods so far, but they were fairly certain they were close to death and figured that their choices were either starving or being killed by strangers. If they were going to die either way, might as well take a chance.

They'd called, "Help," their voice hoarse and strained, and a group of people had rushed toward them and then given them food, water, shelter, care. They didn't judge Max when they told these people where they'd come from, and the people didn't ask why they'd left.

The only thing the woman named Parker, who had taken them under her wing, had said was: "Isn't that a cult? I remember it from the news. From a million years ago."

Max had shrugged. "Depends on how you define cult, I guess."

"How do *you* define it?" Parker had asked, but Max had no answer.

Now, in the pouring rain, the rest of the group remained in their protective huddle, heads down, unaware that Max was being held by this rogue branch as the storm raged on. That was fine. They didn't need witnesses to the agony painted plainly on their face or the tears that mixed with the rain and the mud. Max would wait to ask for help when everyone else was okay.

In time the rain let up. Max watched as the community took stock of everyone, and then called out, "Over here." After that, the humiliating walk down the hill helped by several people, followed by the shocking meeting in which Camilla announced she'd stay behind with Max while everyone else left.

While Camilla and her dad argued at the edge of the clearing, Parker used a long straight stick to create a makeshift splint for Max's leg, wrapping it tightly in what looked like the remains of an old sheet. "Don't walk on it," she said. "Promise me."

Max had only nodded. As if they could have.

Camilla came back and said, "I'm staying with you."

They didn't want Camilla to sacrifice herself for them, but what was the alternative? They'd die here without help. And wasn't it also true that part of Max was a little bit glad that it had all worked out like this—the two of them stranded alone together? Max couldn't help but feel an immense sense of relief. Camilla would take care of them.

Max and Camilla watched as the community foraged what they could from their destroyed huts. Then one by one they disappeared into the small winding path that led into the forest and beyond that, the great unknown.

Parker was the last to say goodbye, holding up a handful of red T-shirts. "See these?" she said. "I'll shred them up and tie the pieces to trees to mark out the path. If we turn, I'll carve an arrow to show you which direction. I'll make sure you have a way to catch up to us." Parker put both her hands on Camilla's shoulders. "And don't worry about your dad, honey. I got him."

"I know," Camilla whispered. "Thank you." And then Parker, and everyone else, was gone, and it was just the two of them. Max felt awkward, embarrassed by Camilla's kindness.

"You really didn't have to stay with me," Max said, though what they wanted to say was: *Thank you.*

Camilla turned away from them, her shoulders rising toward her ears, as though she was folding in on herself.

"I mean, I'm grateful," Max said. "I just . . . I feel bad."

"Don't," Camilla said. "I wanted to. I have to wait for my friend."

"So it wasn't about me at all?" Max asked, trying to get her to smile.

She didn't. "Nope."

"Oh," Max said. They didn't believe her, but they'd clearly struck a nerve. "Sorry. Okay."

"I'm going to start rebuilding one of these houses," she said. "So we at least can sleep somewhere."

"I'm sorry I can't help," Max said.

"Who said I needed help?" Finally, she turned back to them and smiled. Max's chest unclenched and they smiled back.

Camilla took stock of the damage and began to gather materials. She was good at this, Max could tell. She knew what she was doing out here.

It took her the rest of the day to build a structure that would be safe for them to spend the night in. Max watched as she dug holes deep into the ground for the support beams.

"It won't go anywhere this time," she grunted as she dug. "Thank you, melted permafrost."

"You couldn't get the beams that deep before?" Max asked, just to make conversation.

"Nah," she said, pausing to wipe the sweat from her face on her T-shirt. "Ground was too hard. Not this time, though. For better or worse, I guess."

Max watched with quiet admiration as Camilla put their new shelter together. It was basic; it had four walls, a roof, a door. But it would keep them safe. Though last night's storm had left a sunny, perfect day in its wake, there was no way to know when another one might come.

Someday, when their leg had healed, Max might show Camilla how to collect the materials to build a magnetized platform for the house to levitate above. It would be safer from floods that way. But for now, all they could do was watch.

A small ant crawled across Max's foot, but they couldn't reach to brush it off. It was nearly sunset; Max's shadow stretched long on the ground. Their stomach growled and Camilla, a few feet away putting the final details on the door, laughed and said, "Oh, shit, I heard that. I'm hungry, too."

Max pressed on their stomach, felt its hollowness.

"If you grab my bag, I have something we can eat," they said, pointing to their backpack on the ground.

Camilla unzipped it, pulling out the containers that held Max's last supply of white B3k bricks.

"What in the world is this?" she asked. "It looks like . . . oh god, what was it called? Tofu!"

"I don't know what that is. This is what we used to eat at home. I filled my bag with it before I left. I guess I've been saving the last of it for a rainy day. What a coincidence."

"I love coincidences," Camilla said. "And puns."

Max smiled. "You won't be making fun of me once you've eaten one."

"Do we need to cook it or anything? I can start a fire."

"Nah," Max said. "Just split one in half and give me some."

Camilla sat on the ground next to Max's chair and handed them a piece of the squishy brick.

"Mmmm," she said sarcastically as she took a bite. "I've never tasted something that tastes like my own saliva before."

"Besides your own saliva," they said, taking a bite, "it's not so bad, right?"

"No, I guess there is a taste," she conceded. After a few moments, she said, "Wait, why is this so filling?"

"Told you," Max said.

"Is this how you survived, before you got here?"

Max had been waiting for her to ask, and sighed. "It's complicated."

"Try me."

"I lived in a self-sustaining community. We had all this technology that the elders had stolen from the government, back before the collapse. So we had everything we needed. Stuff that seems miraculous, now that I know how everyone else lives out here. We had rules. It was strict."

"Will you tell me what happened to you? Why you left?"

"Soon," they said. "I don't know if I'm ready to tell you everything just yet. I'm sorry."

"It's okay," she said, and Max felt grateful that she wasn't pressing.

"Why don't you tell me *your* story?" Max said.

"Sure," she said, with a sigh that sounded so sad, Max almost grimaced. "I was born in Ohio. We moved to New York when I was little, because my sister needed to transition and there wasn't any healthcare for her in the Midwest. You probably weren't born yet."

Max reflected on their age difference with a flash of embarrassment, but they didn't want to make her feel uncomfortable. "Probably not," they said. "But please, keep going."

"Shelby, my sister, ended up going to work for Jacqueline Millender. Do you know who that is?"

"Of course," Max said. "We had access to information about what the world once was."

Camilla nodded. "Well, Shelby's on the space shuttle with Jacqueline now. Pretty soon after she left, we had to leave the city. The block next to our apartment was already underwater, and we knew we only had so much time. Plus, our building was zoned for Inside, so we were about to be evicted anyway. It was such bullshit. So we started driving, my parents and me, toward my mother's cousin's house in New Hampshire. But then the car broke down and we had to try to walk the rest of the way. There were thousands of other people walking north. My mom caught a virus." Camilla paused, looking at her hands. "She got so sick. I've never seen someone vomit that much. And then one day she died on the side of the road, just like that."

"I'm really sorry, Camilla," Max said. "That sounds hard."

Camilla's eyes filled with tears. Max knew how she felt: recounting something meant reliving it. Camilla wasn't going to cry, though. Max could tell this, too—she wouldn't let herself. Instead she kept talking.

"My dad and I continued on without her. It took us months to reach cousin Harriet. We got there, eventually, and she let us live with her, even though she was my mom's cousin and my mom was dead. The house was big enough, an old mansion, basically. There was a small town. It was in the mountains so the weather was good. We spent years there with her. It was an elderly community, so my dad and I helped some of the neighbors a lot. We were the youngest people for miles."

"That doesn't sound so bad," Max said.

"It wasn't. I mean, it was sad. We missed my mom and my sister so much. And Harriet was ancient, like everyone else there. I was lonely. There was nothing to do but go into town to trade stuff and then come back and cook dinner. We grew a little garden, and she had some chickens, so I kept busy with that. She had a lot of books that I read. My dad tried to teach me things I should have learned in school. There was obviously no school system anymore, not by that point, after everything shut down. It was a quiet life. And then, you know, the storms started again."

"Shit."

"Yeah. Hurricanes, tornadoes, heat waves. Floods. The same insanity we thought we'd left behind in New York City finally caught up to us. That's how Harriet died—in a heat wave. We found her in her bed. We assumed heat stroke. Lots of elderly people couldn't survive the heat. Anyway, things got a little nuts after that. There were raiders that came through the town. They showed up with guns, knives. They broke into the house in the middle of the night and forced us to leave. We barely had a chance to take anything. I thought for sure they were going to kill us. It obviously wouldn't have made a difference to them either way. Suddenly we were back in the wilderness again. There was nothing we could do about it. The time we spent at Harriet's felt like a dream that ended too quickly."

Max was overcome with empathy. "Then what?"

"We headed north. We met people on the way that told us about Orchid, that there was a woman in the Canadian mountains who could teach us everything we needed to know to survive out here, so we were kind of on a quest to find her. It took a really long time. When we actually got here I couldn't believe she was real. Sometimes I still can't."

"And then you stayed."

"Yeah. We loved it here. We loved the people, we loved her. It was like we finally belonged somewhere. She's like a prophet. All of us, journeying to find her."

The word *prophet* made Max flinch. Camilla said quickly, "I don't mean that literally."

"No, I know," they said. "I guess that word is just kind of a trigger when you come from a place everyone calls a cult."

"Did you have a prophet?" she asked.

"In theory, we had a committee. But a prophet . . . yeah, kind of. Originally."

"What happened to him?"

"He died, a long time ago. Then someone replaced him. Someone much worse."

They were quiet, then, watching the lightning bugs flicker into view. Max knew Camilla wanted to ask for more details, and appreciated when she didn't.

"How's the leg?"

"Amazing." Max frowned.

The truth was, Max was still in excruciating pain. Even talking made it hurt. But they felt that it was implied. Camilla could obviously tell they were suffering. She was just trying to be nice.

The pine trees were silhouetted in the twilight; the rocky mountains in the distance had turned pink and now blue. There were no sounds but the gentle pulsing of nighttime bugs in the forest, a song that was getting fainter and fainter each season as the bugs faced their own apocalypse.

"Want to try to get some sleep?" Camilla said.

"You got a bed in there?"

"I found a mattress, but actually I think you should sleep in that chair, so you can keep your leg up," Camilla said. "That is, if you think you can sleep in that position."

"One thing about me, I'm a really good sleeper."

"Lucky you," Camilla said. She stood up and extended her hands to Max, who gripped them as they stood on one foot, wincing. "Stay right there," she said, and ran the chair into the hut, then returned. Max put an arm around her shoulder and she took all their weight as they hopped, tentatively, into the little home she'd rebuilt, and then collapsed back into the plastic lawn chair.

Camilla lay down on the dirty mattress on the ground a few feet away. For a moment Max thought she was sleeping, and then she said, softly, "I'm glad it's you."

"What?" Max said, because it was hard to hear her, and because they weren't sure what she was trying to say.

"I mean, I'm not glad you got hurt. I'm really sorry for that. But if I had to be stuck here waiting for Orchid with anyone . . ." She trailed off. "Sorry."

"Don't be," Max said. "I'm glad I can keep you company, even in my current state."

They didn't look at each other. It felt too intense. Max reflected on the fact of the one mattress, and what it might mean for the weeks ahead. After a few minutes, Camilla started to snore.

Max tilted their head back so that it was resting on the hard plastic of the lawn chair, and their mind drifted elsewhere: home. Earth-colored sheets billowing as they dried in the wind. Their mother's face, looking happy. The sound of the community singing together in the evening, Max hovering at the periphery of the group. The men getting drunk and rowdy. The women putting the children to bed. Crumbs of memories, these were, half-baked together to make a loaf that was almost whole, memories of a place that Max would never return to, colored by the sadness of this fact, but also by the relief of it. Freedom was a terrifying, dangerous thing, but it was all they had now.

They thought of Sterrett again. They could almost feel Sterrett's hand in theirs, just like they could still feel the coldness of Sterrett pulling away, the finality of the back of Sterrett's head disappearing into the trees. The void of solitude that settled around them, a black hole that threatened to pull them into oblivion. Everywhere they went after that was just another place without their friend. Until they came here.

Memories swirled with made-up stories pulled from the depths of Max's unconscious mind as they slipped away into a dream.

Now, so far from home and struggling to wake up, Max heard the sounds of Camilla returning, and smelled the campfire as it began to crackle.

Camilla poked her head into the hut. "I'm boiling water," she said. "Also, hi. Good morning."

"Hey." Max started to stretch but was interrupted by the splitting pain in their leg. "Shit."

Camilla lowered her brow in concern. "I wish there was something I could do for you."

"Are you kidding? You've already done so much."

"Still." She chewed her lip.

She went back outside and Max heard the water sloshing as she stirred the fire. She was singing to herself. The sound of her voice, sweet and slightly off tune, made Max smile.

"Oh!" they heard Camilla cry. "Wait. Fuck."

Max laughed, charmed by the way Camilla talked to herself. "What is it?" they called.

Camilla said, "I can see a squirrel."

"I swear on the earth," Max said, their mouth already beginning to water. They had tasted meat for the first time when they found this group of people, and they had the feeling that they'd never be able to eat enough of it. It was so rich, so fatty, the texture so incredibly new and different. Sweet and salty and addictive. It gave them more energy than they thought possible. It also gave them a near-permanent stomachache and unspeakable digestive issues that they were committed to just powering through. Surely they'd get used to it.

"Shh," Camilla said, and Max wasn't sure if she was talking to them or to the squirrel. All went quiet for a few moments. Max held their breath, afraid to make a sound.

And then, farther away, they heard: "Got you."

Camilla appeared in the doorway clutching a large, squirming rodent. "This'll do for today," she said.

Max looked at its scared eyes and twitching mouth. "It's cute," they said.

Camilla shook her head. "It's breakfast, lunch, and dinner," she said. "Don't look at her face too closely. You'll never unsee it."

Camilla was tougher than Max, this had been immediately clear. It was, they thought as Camilla left to slaughter the animal, pretty hot.

Apparently the pain in their leg was not going to detract from the sudden pulse of want, a yearning that was, in itself, a kind of torturous pleasure. It was a relief that Camilla was not there to see them blush.

APRIL 13, 2041

Dear Orchid,

I made it to the Appalachian Mountains this morning. There's nothing like the beauty of this country to really break a girl's heart. I still can't believe how careless people have been with the planet. I don't think I'll ever get over it, frankly.

I've driven past roaring streams and fields of the sweetest, palest green leaves. I've driven so far up into the clouds that I can see the gentle rolling hills and sharp blue peaks for miles in every direction.

I thought it would be empty out here. Instead, the mountains seem more populated than other areas I've driven through. I didn't realize people would want to gentrify Appalachia. It seems insane. I asked a gas station attendant about it. He told me that it turns out this is one of the safest places in the country right now. The climate here has remained stable. He said there's some drought expected in the south, but for the most part, the mountains seem to be a protected place.

He also told me the locals aren't thrilled with the influx of people buying up land and building their bunkers. Where there used to be nothing but nature, there's now millionaires and their coffee shops and private schools.

That means there's also a lot of traffic on these winding mountain roads. All the cars have made it hard to confirm a growing suspicion: I swear I'm being followed.

All my life people have told me I was crazy about things that I ended up being right about. So, I ditched my phone. I probably shouldn't have had it for this long. I left it on the side of the road about a hundred miles back. I felt like it was watching me, following me, leaking my location to whoever I keep catching glimpses of in the rearview.

Anyway. Each day brings me closer to you. Which means I have to hurry up and tell you what happened. And I have to make sure I'm not caught along the way.

So: the van.

I was folding laundry when I saw it out the window: a dilapidated gray vehicle that simply appeared outside, parked at the curb. Just sitting there, engine off. I couldn't see the driver's face. No one got out. No one got in. It was two p.m.

I folded the rest of the laundry, tidied up, read articles on my phone, keeping one eye on the van at all times. It stayed put until exactly three p.m., and then it drove away. It was an odd thing. If it had been there to, say, service someone's house, maybe hook up their Refillables line—a trendy new thing from JM Inc. that allowed household products to be automatically refilled by drones—the van would have been labeled. Someone would have at least gotten out of the vehicle.

Plus, the hour between two and three p.m. was specific; it was a time when the neighbors were at work, and before the kids who lived on the block (including you) came home from school, which meant I was fairly certain I was the only witness to this strange event. Because of that, it seemed intentional. It seemed like it was there specifically for me.

I tried telling Rick about the van when he got home from work, but he dismissed me.

"That's crazy," he said, tossing his keys on the table and kicking his dirty boots off. "Maybe you imagined it." *Crazy* made my eye twitch. He sounded just like my father sometimes.

"Please don't use that word," I said.

"Kelly, I'm tired. I had the world's longest day. Client wanted us to knock down a wall to make her bathroom bigger and it made the ceiling cave in. Total fucking mess. She wants to hold payment now."

"I'm going to sleep," I said. I didn't care about Rick's complaints from his day. He always had so many. I often thought, while he rambled on: *If I allowed myself to get upset about every little thing the way you do, I would never make it through the day.*

When he got into bed a couple hours later, I felt him inching toward me, and I scooted as far away as I could.

In the morning, I didn't say goodbye when he left for work. I was done pretending to be happy.

While I tidied up, I put the news on, half-listening to something about a tropical storm headed for Long Island. Thanks to the coastal flooding of the past few years, entire towns had been cleared of residents and still the policies didn't change. There was nothing in place to protect the people who still lived there, and it seemed obvious to me that the problems were just going to get worse. But I'd also found that if I got upset about the things I heard on the news I'd become paralyzed with fear. And I couldn't afford to become overwhelmed, not with a little girl depending on me. I hummed over the anchor's voice.

At two p.m., the van was back. I peered at it through the blinds, and then, thinking of Rick calling me crazy, I took a picture of it.

"Look," I said, shoving my phone in his face the moment he walked through the door a little after eight p.m. "It came back."

"Hmm," he said, before wandering off into the other room, clearly more bothered by me pestering him than by the thought of a strange van stalking me.

Rick wasn't always impatient with me. But recently he seemed to have no capacity for me, as though any deviation from my role as the housewife was intolerable. I knew he was stressed about work. But still. He should have been able to be kinder toward me.

The next day, I called the town helpline and explained the situation.

"Ma'am, there are no laws about parking at the curb in your neighborhood," the person on the other end of the line said, as though I was just another suburban white woman complaining about nothing, which maybe I was.

But then the van continued to show up at the exact same time, day after day, parked in the shade of a sycamore tree, as though waiting.

Meanwhile, the news I caught was getting increasingly urgent. Long Island, Queens, and parts of Brooklyn were being evacuated. Because so much of the island was already flooded, the reporters said, the land was that much more vulnerable to damage from a storm. I tried not to think about it. I was safe upstate. I had to be. Because *you* had to be.

One afternoon after a few days of watching the van appear and then drive off, I decided to wait for it in its usual spot with a Tupperware container of homemade chocolate chip cookies.

The van pulled up and the window rolled down. "Those for me?" the driver asked. He was missing a few teeth.

I nodded, tried to smile. "I figured we're neighbors now," I said.

"I'm vegan," he said. The first clue, though I didn't catch it.

"Oh, me too," I said, nodding at the cookies. "Them, also."

He reached a tattooed hand out to take the offering from me and in exchange, gave me a flier. It read simply "WINTER LIBERATION." He rolled the window back up. I went inside.

There was something familiar about the man. Not him as an individual, but the type of guy. He reminded me of the kids I used to squat with.

I smoothed the flier on the table, inspected it for secrets. It was blue. It looked photocopied. But it held no information other than those two words.

When Rick came home that night I was still sitting at the kitchen table staring at it. I handed it to him and he sighed as he put his bag down to examine it.

"I've heard about these guys," he said.

"They're the people who have been sitting outside the house," I said. "They gave me this today."

"You've been talking to them? Kelly!"

"Well, I just figured . . ."

"You don't want to get mixed up with these guys." He shook his head. "These guys . . ." He trailed off, always unable to express himself fully.

"I was just trying to be friendly," I interrupted him. "Kill 'em with kindness, you know?"

"They're climate-change deniers, Kell," he said.

"Oh, please." I rolled my eyes. "No one denies climate change anymore. The change has happened. Have you heard about the storm that's gonna hit Long Island this week? Besides, why would they want to *liberate winter* if they're deniers?"

"I heard about it on the news." Rick abruptly balled the flier up and tossed it into the trash. "They call them WinLibs for short. I'm not trying to be mean," he said, assessing the look on my face. "I'm just worried about you. I'm allowed to worry, right?"

"Sure," I said.

"Forget about it," he said. "What's for dinner?"

I saw you peeking your little head around the corner. "Climate-change deniers," you repeated in a small voice, though because of your speech impediment it came out as "cwy-mut change deni-aws." Do you remember this moment? I often wonder about it.

"Don't worry, hon," I said. "Come help me make dinner."

That night, when I went to sleep, I dreamt of mudslides.

The van was back the next day at the same time.

I went outside and knocked on its window. "Can I have my Tupperware back?"

The window rolled down, but the driver was different.

Here was a man wearing a light blue button-down shirt, with round sunglasses, and—unlike the other driver—he had all of his teeth, and they were gleaming white. Something pinged in my brain. Something . . . familiar.

"Oh," I said. "Sorry, I thought you might be someone else."

He smiled, the disarming, easy grin of someone used to getting his way. "Hi, Kelly," he said, his voice deep and warm, like something from a distant dream. "I don't have your container, but I think I might have something else you need."

"How do you know my name?" I asked, but at this point I was not surprised. This felt inevitable. They *had* been waiting for me. "What do you think I need?"

He got out of the van and took his sunglasses off. Familiar dark brown eyes blinked at me. I gasped.

It was Vero.

"It's nice to see you," he said.

I hadn't seen Vero since we'd tied ourselves together by the neck to the doors of City Hall. Nearly a decade ago.

"You can't just show up like this," I said.

"Well, to be fair, I called first." He smiled, and I felt myself begin to unravel.

Vero was older now, his charm sharpened as though from practice. This was not the crust punk activist I'd made love to beneath the overpass after hacking into the mainframe of the city's power grid. This was a man in charge of something.

"You ratted on me," I said.

"Kelly, I would never do that," he said. "Please."

"You cut a deal with the cops," I said. "They told me everything."

"And you believed them?"

I had.

"My parents pulled strings to get me out. Anything the cops said to you, they were making up. I'm sorry you believed them. You must hate me."

"I could never hate you," I said. It was the truth, despite my anger.

Impulsively, I threw my arms around his torso, pressing myself into the stiff linen of his button-down. He felt different. He hadn't had the money for gender-affirmation surgery when I'd known him, loved him. Well—technically he could have charged it to his parents, but I doubted they would have allowed it.

He looked great.

I was glad for him, even though he'd broken my heart, and the sight of him—the warm feel and musky smell of him, too—stung. He hugged me back, and then I pulled away, remembering I was supposed to hate him.

"You got married," he observed.

"You disappeared on me," I said.

"And you had a baby," he said.

"You've been watching me?"

"I had to see what your life was like before inserting myself into it again," he said.

"You made me feel like I was going crazy," I said.

"I'm sorry. For what it's worth, you seem less crazy than I've ever seen you."

I laughed. Vero was always the only person on earth allowed to use that word with me. "Yeah," I said. "I grew up. Decided to just go with it. And you? What happened to you? And why are you back now?"

I put my hands in my pockets and looked around. The street was empty. No one was watching. He didn't answer me.

"Are you real?" I asked.

Vero laughed. "I hope so."

"Sorry," I said, "just had to check." I sat down on the curb and he sat down next to me, barely an inch between us.

"Kelly Green, I want you to come back."

"To you?" I couldn't hide the hope in my voice.

"To the movement. I would never presume you'd want *me* back."

"Winter Liberation? That's what you're calling it now?"

"Don't you miss snow?" he asked. "We thought it was a good reference point for people. Remind them what we've lost in a way that doesn't hit them over the head with something as hard as the truth, which is that an ongoing absence of winter means hundreds of millions of people are dying."

"Babe," I said, and then blushed. I hadn't meant to call him that, but now it was out and I couldn't take it back. "I have a family."

"None of us are going to have *anything* unless we change things," he said.

I looked back at our little house. You were in there playing with trucks.

"Think about it," he said. "We're much more organized now. You could help us do something that matters. But it's your choice. Obviously."

"And what are you doing?"

"The only people who can do anything are the ones in office," he said. "Not the activists, not the cops, not the teachers. The government controls the resources. They can still turn this thing around. They just don't want to, because it wouldn't benefit them."

"What's your point?"

"The wrong people are in office."

"So you want me to help you with what? Election campaigns?"

"No."

I sighed. "Election tampering, then." I wasn't above it.

He held a finger to his lips. "The results of our work might influence the elections, but that's not the point. I really can't tell you any more unless you agree to help us."

And then he got up and walked back to the van, not looking behind him as he drove off.

I was shook. Vero, after all this time.

After he drove away, I went back to the house to wait for Rick to get home.

I couldn't believe Vero had just shown up like this. I was feeling everything, like a chef's tasting menu of every possible emotion. Rage, relief, fear, curiosity. What on earth could he want with me? And did I have the guts to do it?

When your dad got home, I couldn't bring myself to tell him about the man from my past and what he'd said to me. He would have just gotten upset, probably. *Worried* about me. So I said nothing, watched TV next to him on the couch until he went to bed, and then lay awake until the wee hours of the morning, thinking of nothing but Vero.

The van came back at its usual time. I waited for it on the curb, dark circles under my eyes and a tremble in my lower lip.

Vero got out and sat beside me. He smelled nice, like expensive soap; like someone with money. I took in his white-gold cuff links and spotless brown loafers. Suddenly it occurred to me: maybe Vero's money would be our way out—you and me.

"I couldn't sleep," I said.

"Honestly, Kelly, me either." He was looking straight ahead. "It's good to see you. It makes me feel . . . a lot of things."

"Tell me how you went from the Vero I knew to whoever this is," I said, gesturing at his outfit. "You look like your dad."

He laughed. "It's a long story."

"I think I liked you better with your rattail." His hair was short now, almost like a military cut.

"And I liked you better as a hacker," he said.

"I'm retired from all that," I said.

"Permanently?"

I raised an eyebrow.

Finally, he turned to face me. His brown eyes were wide and unblinking. "The people in power," he said. "You have to know that this"—he gestured at our surroundings, which were ironically peaceful and quaint—"all the destruction and pain, it's all intentional. They could stop it. But they've chosen not to."

"Have you not become someone with power?" I asked, skeptical. Even the way he spoke sounded like wealth.

He smiled and said nothing.

"This is all so weird," I said. "You're like, a different person. And you're showing up out of the blue after how many years? I had to get over you, Vero. I had to survive without you. I built a whole life."

He stood up, abruptly. "I'm sorry, Kelly, I really don't mean to upset you," he said. "Come to me when you're ready. But in the meantime, a word of advice. Your tap water is basically poison. Don't drink it, don't shower in it."

He got back in the van and drove off, leaving me speechless under the sycamore.

Was the water poison? It seemed unlikely, but when I got back inside I did a deep dive into the internet and began printing out everything I could find on the local water-filtration system, and the rising cancer rates, making a map of information on the wall of the room that served as my office, just like I'd seen people on TV do.

Before going to bed, I ordered several cases of bottled water, and in the morning when I woke up I couldn't bring myself to get into the shower. I bought baby wipes for you and me to use. For as long as I lived in that blue house, Vero's words rang in my ears, and I never showered again.

Two weeks later, while Rick was at work and you were at school, I called the number he'd given me.

"Thirty thousand," I said, when he answered.

"What?"

"That's how much I want to do whatever it is you need. And this is a one-time thing. I have a kid to take care of. I can't be gone for more than a few days. A week, tops."

"Done," he said. "We'll pick you up tomorrow."

How quickly he agreed to my terms made me wonder if I should have asked for more; made me question the real value of what I was giving him in return.

"Wanna tell me what you're hiring me for?"

"Mmm," he said. "Let's just say I need you to set up some servers."

"You don't need me for that," I said. I realized he wasn't going to say the real reason over the phone. I agreed anyway.

I want to pause here and tell you about why I made the decision I did.

First, as I said, I thought I'd only be gone for a few days.

Second, though, and just as important, was the cash. Because by that point—perhaps you have guessed this—I had decided to leave your father. I needed money to do that, especially if I was to take you with me, which was the plan. I figured I'd go work with Vero for a couple of days, get paid a huge chunk of change, and then whisk you off somewhere nice. You were always the center of my plan, of my reason for leaving. I didn't want you to grow up with parents who didn't love each other. I thought it would be better for you to see me stand up for myself than see a loveless marriage. I'm sure that all feels backward now, since I've been gone for so long. I will make it up to you.

So: the time had come.

I scribbled a note on the table for Rick and hired a babysitter to stay until he came home. I promised you I'd be back soon, just as soon as the project was finished.

As I left, I glanced anxiously back at you, barefoot and bewildered in the overgrown front yard of our tiny blue house, the babysitter watching from the porch, before stepping into the graffiti-covered van and buckling myself into a sticky seat that smelled of cigarettes and body odor.

The van's door slid shut after me, but I could still hear the lovely summer sounds of our neighborhood—children playing and dogs barking—and from the dark muffled inside of the vehicle the noise sounded surreal. Like the soundtrack to someone else's life.

The driver grinned at me, revealing several missing teeth.

"I'm Len. You made the right choice," he said with a lisp.

The sunlight glinted off his bald head as he shifted gears and peeled out of the driveway. At the last minute, I turned my head to look out the window, a final glimpse of you in the yard, dumbfounded, mouth hanging open, your rumpled kitchen-scissor haircut making you look like a lost baby bird.

I'll never forgive myself for this moment.

"She'll understand when she's older," Len said.

"What? I'll just explain it to her when I come back later," I said, and from the row behind me I heard a woman's voice.

"Oh, sweetheart," she said.

I recognized the voice immediately. "Madly," I said, turning toward her. The thrill of her presence distracted me from those words. In hindsight, she was already trying to tell me something.

She put a hand on my shoulder. She looked almost exactly the same, just with some smile lines around her eyes. She'd cut her hair short, around her chin. She looked beautiful.

"It's so good to see you," she said.

"I've missed you," I said. She squeezed my shoulder. "Where are we going? Do you know?"

Before she could answer, Len said, "Hang on," and reached for the radio, turning the volume all the way up. "We're about to go live."

The sounds of a news broadcast filled the van as it bumped and shuddered along the highway.

"Today we're taking a deep dive into one group unlike any other," a radio voice said.

Behind me, Madhuri cheered. "Here we go," she said. "The big time, baby."

The broadcaster said, "The domestic terrorist group known as the Winter Liberation Army believes that climate change is an elaborate hoax created by the government to distract people from the effects of late-stage capitalism. But is it just a political belief, or something more dangerous? Last week, their headquarters were raided by the FBI, resulting in twelve people arrested and up to a million dollars in property damage. Several missing are believed to be dead. The leaders of the group are still at large. So why was the

FBI interested in this fringe collective at all? Are they a cult? Or are they simply misguided? And should anyone care?"

Len banged on the steering wheel. "They always get it wrong," he said.

"Why do you let them think that's who you are?" I asked. "That that's what this group stands for?"

He shrugged. "Doesn't matter what they say about us. All that matters is what we do."

"And what's your interpretation of what you do?" I wasn't sure who was in on what plan.

"Listen," he said. "I don't know why this concept is too complicated for the media to grasp. It's not that we believe climate change is a *hoax*. It's that we believe it's *not an inevitability*. Once upon a time this was not a radical opinion. The change can still be stopped. Or we can at least live with it. The government just doesn't want to, because then people would remain free."

"Remain free?" I repeated.

"I'm sure Vero will fill you in on the rest," Len said.

The radio shifted to coverage of a men's rights protest at the White House. I couldn't hide my sigh, and Len smirked at me, briefly glancing up from the road. "Bunch of bullshit, huh?" he said.

"It's just funny to me that men think equality means that they're being oppressed," I said.

"Well," he said, "not all men, blah blah blah. Right?"

"Right," I said, though something in the way he said this made my chest tighten.

Madhuri said, "She doesn't mean you, Len. Don't be such a pussy."

Len turned around and gave her a look that made my stomach curdle; it was full of venom. She shrank back, something I'd never seen her do.

"I just think this whole ordeal is a little beside the point," Len said. "There will be no one left to care about which gender has the most power if we all die in a heat wave."

"You don't think it's all connected?" I asked. "That if there were more equality, we wouldn't be in this mess?"

"You're talking about ecofeminism?" Len asked. I nodded. "The theory that the forces of oppression against women are the same forces that have ruined the earth, right? But now women aren't being held back, and still the earth burns." There was something odd about his tone of voice. Like he was preaching from a pulpit, not talking to me in the front seat.

"Well, I don't know about that," I said. "*Some* women are in *some* positions of power, but we don't really have equal rights. And anyway, I don't think it's an issue of men versus women anymore."

"So what do you think?" Len said. "It's about all marginalized people versus the *patriarchy*?" He seemed to be teasing me. There was a mean edge to it that I couldn't quite put my finger on. Like at any minute it would turn into a fight.

Madhuri came to my rescue. "Leave her alone," she said. "She's been in suburbia just a little too long."

"Are we not saying the word *patriarchy* anymore?" I asked, genuinely confused.

Len shrugged. "Like I said. It just seems a little beside the point to me."

"And coming up," the radio broadcast continued, "we'll go live from what's now the beachfront in Brooklyn."

"Damn fucking shame," Len said.

I was surprised to feel tears spring to my eyes. The tropical storm had done more damage than anyone had predicted, sinking all of Long Island and Queens into the ocean. Bridges, homes, businesses, schools—vanished into the sea. What remained of Brooklyn was a sliver of land. They were even talking about renaming it. The authorities were still counting bodies, searching for the missing. The death toll climbed every day.

"Do you guys really think there's anything we can do at this point that'll make a difference?" I asked.

"Oh, absolutely," he said. "You have no idea how bad this shit is about to get."

"That sounds like something Vero would say."

Len grinned. "I love that guy," he said.

"I used to love him," I said, more to myself than the others in the car, though they heard me.

"I'm glad he convinced you to come back," Madhuri said. "We need you. None of us are good with computers. At least, none of us who are left. That last raid really fucked us."

"Yeah, he mentioned that," I said. "So, where exactly are these so-called servers he wants me to set up?"

"I can't tell you," Len said. "But buckle in for a long drive."

I settled into the seat. To calm myself, I thought of the money that Vero had promised me. It would be enough money to take you away from Rick and start a new life.

I looked out the window again, but the house had long since faded from view.

Never in a million years could I have guessed how long I'd be gone for. How far we were about to go. The insanity that would ensue once we got there.

I have to get some sleep. I'll write you more tomorrow.

X,
Mom

6

BROOK
2078

THERE WERE FOUR HUNDRED AND TWENTY-THREE FALLEN trees strewn about the highway between the entrance of the tunnel that led to Inside and the place where Brook, Ava, and Orchid stood.

There were also one hundred and three abandoned vehicles, sixty-two sinkholes of varying sizes, and as for steps, Brook's favorite metric? Well, she had given up at five hundred thousand, which was the highest number she'd ever counted to, and it felt like a success and a failure at the same time.

"How many miles do you think it is, total?" she asked Orchid. "Like how far are we really walking?"

"Five, six hundred miles, I think," Orchid said. "From where you found me to where we're going."

"That's so many," Brook said, in awe. "Could that be right?"

"Not that you care what I think, but it does sound right," Ava said.

"I care what you think," Brook said, bristling at her mother's tone. She knew Ava was uncomfortable with how close she and Orchid were getting, but she couldn't help it. She liked Orchid. Plus she hadn't met someone new in . . . well, forever, since her whole life had been spent within Inside's walls. The only new people she'd ever met were babies. Orchid was funny and cool and, most compellingly, she was so competent out here in the wild. She knew what she was doing. Brook felt admiration that bordered on jealousy. She wanted to learn the secrets of the outside world, too.

They were almost there, at the space shuttle landing site. Orchid had said she recognized where they were, and that it should be a day, maybe less if they made good time.

As they walked, Brook's counting distracted her from thoughts of July, mostly. Sometimes those thoughts intruded anyway, making her briefly forget what number she was up to. She'd picture July's face, hear her laugh, and then just as quickly she'd worry about her, trying to imagine where she was, if she was okay, if she was missing Brook as much as Brook was missing her. And then she'd realize she missed a hundred steps or more and become flustered, her eyes filling with tears and her heart in her throat as she tried to backtrack, tried to return to the dulled calm she felt when she knew exactly how much of everything was around her.

Ava and Orchid didn't notice these moments, no matter how loud they felt in Brook's mind. They were too busy engaged in some sort of complicated emotional dance that Brook couldn't really keep track of or relate to.

The outside world was nothing like Brook had imagined. She'd known, objectively, that climate change had altered the landscape she saw in photos and textbooks, but there'd been no one around to document the worst of the worst after it had happened.

It was a hellscape of garbage and plastic and burnt trees and rotting infrastructure, a gray-orange sky and a smell that she never got used to, a kind of sour fecal scent that was surely being made worse by how incredibly hot it was. Inside, they'd learned about wildlife, and also how much of it had been wiped out. She was prepared but disappointed that the only animals seemed to be rats and squirrels and snakes, though she found them interesting.

She missed her soft pink linens and warm showers and fresh fruits and vegetables.

Most of all, she missed July.

She wondered, often, as they walked, if she and July never should have wanted to leave Inside. If only they could have appreciated what they had, maybe they wouldn't be in this mess at all. She would have done anything to go back in time. It was a maddening paradox. She could only appreciate what she had Inside by knowing for sure what was beyond it. But once she knew what she missed, she couldn't return.

And then, after days and days of walking, one morning when she woke up from an unsatisfying sleep in the back of a car with broken windows, Orchid said, "The gate is off the next exit. Look, you can almost make out the sign for it."

Brook stretched, squinted. In the weak hazy morning light she could, indeed, almost make out a weathered sign that hung, swinging haphazardly over the highway, reading in faded white letters on a green background: US/JM INC. SPACE BASE, EXIT 89, 3 MILES.

She scrambled out of the car and onto her feet. "Mom!" she shouted. "Mom, we're almost there!"

"Please don't scream," Ava said, trailing behind her. "I see it."

Ava did not sound as excited as she should have been, but Brook was used to that by now. She understood her mom's hesitance to feel hope. Hope was a dangerous thing. It could let you down harder than anything (or anyone) else.

In a quieter voice, Brook said, "We'll be there in an hour or two. Do you think she's there?"

"We're about to find out," Ava replied.

Brook had to stop herself from running and skipping down the road into the fog. The excitement replaced the sharp pinch of hunger in her belly and the soreness in her feet. All she could think was: *July. July. July.* That, and the number of steps, of course.

Seven thousand and forty-three steps later, they reached the exit. The highway diverged, a smaller road peeling off to the side at a sharp angle and disappearing into the smog ahead.

"You ready?" Orchid said to Ava, who nodded.

"Come *on*," Brook said.

"Just . . . ," Orchid said. "Be careful, okay? I didn't leave the highway at all when I came down this way and I'm not sure what's beyond it."

"There's nothing," Brook said, growing impatient. "There's never anything out here."

"Just humor me," Orchid said.

"We'll be careful," Ava said. "Right, Brook?"

Brook was sulking as they veered off the highway and began walking around the U-shaped exit ramp, but she wasn't sure why she felt so annoyed. Objectively, they were just looking out for her. Her bad mood was a storm rolling in. There was nothing to do but wait for it to pass.

Luckily everyone seemed to want to walk in silence.

As she'd guessed, for a few miles it was more of the same, this time just up close. The exit ramp took them out into a wide-open space, where evidence of buildings lay in piles here and there. She knew by now what hurricane and tornado damage looked like, and she wondered how long their luck would hold out; how long before they got stuck in one or the other.

There were no more signs, out here off the highway on the flat ground—nothing to indicate if they were going in the right direction. Three thousand steps later Brook started to suspect that they were lost.

She looked sideways at her mother, who was walking with her head down, and Orchid, who was walking with her head up, as though there might be a map in the clouds. Neither was looking where they were going.

Which meant a few minutes later, Brook was the first to see the huge metal gate and barbed-wire fence in the distance.

It rendered her speechless, and she grabbed onto Ava's arm, pointing. They all stopped walking to gape.

"That's gotta be it, right?" Orchid said, wiping the sweat from her face.

"Your guess is as good as mine," Ava said.

"I mean, what else could it possibly be?" Brook asked. "Let's go. Can you guys hurry?"

"Can you be nicer?" Ava said.

"Sorry, I just—" But instead of finishing, she decided to sprint ahead.

If her mother didn't understand her urgency, she had no words left to explain it.

She reached the gate just as an alarm, the loudest sound she'd ever heard in her life, started blaring.

It was an excruciating beep, over and over and over. She put her hands over her ears and dropped to a crouch.

The sound was slamming into her, the beeps too overwhelming to count. Ava and Orchid caught up to her. Ava was shouting something, but Brook couldn't hear it over the beeping. Orchid started pulling on her arm. They were trying to get her to do something, but she wasn't sure what. All she could do was press her hands harder into her ears.

When the alarm finally stopped, the silence was almost as deafening as the noise had been. She'd been so excited to reach this place. But now she was just scared.

The gate made an ancient creaking sound, metal on metal, and then began to open.

"Get back," Orchid said.

Despite the terror coursing through her blood like lightning, Brook remained planted in place. Why would she get back, when the whole point was that they were there to get *in*?

When the gate had opened wide enough for her to see past it, she realized why Orchid had wanted her to move. Standing before them was an old white man. He stood with his legs apart, his hands on his hips.

"Don't move," Orchid whispered. As if she could. She was too startled.

The man had wiry gray hair that was densest around his ears, and he was wearing a faded green uniform. He was mostly gaunt but had a round belly, giving him a kind of sickly, alien look.

Orchid put her hands up. "Hey, man," she said, her voice suddenly calm and friendly, placating. *A magic trick*, Brook thought, *to be able to change your tone like that.*

"What do you want?" he said, his voice rough and phlegmy. "What are you doing out here?"

"We're looking for someone," Ava said. Brook noticed the shake in her voice.

"Ain't nobody left," he croaked. "My name's Abel. Who the hell are you three?" He squinted, sizing them up, examining them perhaps a little too closely.

But now that Brook could see him, she was no longer afraid. There was a smallness to him. He was just a little old man. Besides, there were three of them, and one of him.

Abel looked back and forth from Orchid to Ava to Brook. "What are you wearing?"

Brook looked down at her mauve tunic, which was covered in dirt and sweat stains.

"We were Inside," Brook said, though Orchid was shaking her head at her not to.

"Jesus," he said. "Don't know why you'd leave. Well, look. I don't know who you could possibly be looking for. It's been just me and my family here for a very, very long time."

"My daughter," Ava said, as though the mention of his family meant he might care about theirs. "We're looking for my daughter."

Brook noticed that though they were now having a full conversation with Abel, he hadn't moved aside to let them in. But at this, he seemed to soften.

"Why would your daughter be *here*?" he asked.

"It's a really long story," Ava said. "And, sir, we're honestly starving and exhausted. If you have a safe place for us in there, even for just a few hours, I'd love to tell you everything."

Brook caught a glance that passed between Ava and Orchid; a shake of Orchid's head indicating trepidation, while Ava lifted her jaw in return, signaling she was overruling Orchid's warning. Brook tried to chime in with her own nonverbal cues, smiling at Orchid, nodding at her mother, showing them that she was fine, she had no reason not to trust Abel, and anyway, nothing was more important than getting past that gate.

"You'd better come in," he said.

The gate creaked closed behind them. As Brook got closer to the man, she couldn't stop staring at his cracked, graying face.

"Help you?" he asked, catching her examining him.

"Sorry," she said. "I've just never seen a man before. I mean a man who isn't young. Not that you're old. I mean . . ."

"So it is true," he said.

"*Brook,*" Orchid whispered. She was still trying to warn both of them, Brook assumed, but they were ignoring her. Any danger this man posed would be worth the risk if he could take them to July.

"Let's go," he said.

They fell into step behind him. Ava grabbed her hand and didn't let go.

Brook looked around. They were in a large field, surrounded by nothingness.

Then she saw it, in the distance: a large concrete pad surrounded by all sorts of machinery that she had no name for. She squeezed Ava's hand and pointed. Ava squeezed back. "Mom, do you think . . . ?" Brook whispered, and Ava was nodding, whispering back, "Maybe, yes, oh god, that has to be it."

Orchid shot them a look. As though she knew something they didn't. Brook raised her eyebrows. *What?*, she mouthed, but Orchid just shook her head.

If that was the landing pad, where was the space shuttle? The concrete surface was empty. Surely with their access to Inside's resources cut off, they would have run out of food by now and needed to return.

They were walking toward it. As they approached, Brook could see it more clearly: The machinery was all twisted and broken, rusting in some places. A huge crack split the concrete pad in two. Something that looked like a huge metal ladder was folded over on itself. She didn't need to know exactly what she was looking at to know it was destroyed.

"No," she whispered.

"Oh, that godforsaken mess?" the man said, hearing her shock. "Tornadoes, couple years back."

Ava was squeezing her hand harder.

"Is it usable?" Orchid asked, the only one of them still able to speak.

"Nah," he said.

Brook felt Ava sway a little and she threw an arm around her waist, steadying her.

"You're looking for someone on the space shuttle?" the man asked. "We've been listening to all that drama on the radios."

"But they have to land, right?" Ava asked.

He nodded, chuckled as he said, "Seems kind of preordained, if you ask me. Don't know why they thought they could force all those people on the ground to farm for them indefinitely."

Brook's voice shook as she asked, "Do you know where it's going to land instead?"

"Auckland. New Zealand," he said, glancing behind him. "With the rest of 'em. At least that's what the chatter on the radios has been saying."

"New Zealand," she repeated. The other side of the world. A place they could never get to, by any means. She wished the earth would open and swallow her. Anything but feel this grief, the magnitude of this loss.

The man was still talking. "Damn shame, what's happened. Don't really understand what all that's got to do with you three, though. Can't imagine how your daughter could've ended up there."

"Told you it was a long story," Ava said, finally finding her voice. Brook felt her heart sink into her stomach. *That was it*, she thought. They weren't going to find July here.

Later, Brook sat at a long table in a cavernous bunker shoveling spoonfuls of beans into her mouth so rapidly that a few times she almost choked.

The beans were chunky and brown and hot. Brook couldn't decide if they were the most delicious thing she'd ever tasted or the most disgusting; they were bland but satisfying, slimy but rich. At least they were definitely better than the tough strips of squirrel meat they'd been subsisting on for the past two days, after their supply from Inside's surplus food had run out.

If she ate fast enough, she didn't have room in her brain to think about July. So she continued to force the beans down her throat, long after the hunger was replaced with nausea.

Abel's family was in a silent row across from the three of them: his wife, their two sons and their wives, several babies, and some toddlers who were running around so chaotically that Brook couldn't count how many there were. Instead she counted the mounds of beans that she shoved into her mouth. *Ten, eleven, twelve.* She alternated counting sips of water. *Six, seven, eight.*

"Easy," Abel's wife said. "There's plenty. You don't have to rush it."

"Sorry," Brook said, coughing into a cloth napkin.

Brook had been relieved to meet the women of Abel's family. They provided some balance to what was otherwise an overwhelmingly masculine scene. But now that she was facing them, they were too quiet, too orderly. Watching her a little too closely.

It had been a strange experience, descending into a hole in the ground down several flights of stairs and into what Brook felt was another universe. Orchid had been the last to enter, looking around wildly in a way that gave Brook pause, but not enough pause to convince her not to go.

"It'll be okay," Ava had whispered to her, pulling her hand, but Orchid hadn't replied. She'd looked too troubled. Still, she'd given in. She did everything Ava said, Brook noticed.

The military bunker was clearly designed for an entire army, but the only people here seemed to be this man and his family.

Brook recognized the solar lightbulbs that illuminated the brick-lined space, with their tiny JM Inc. logos. So, not another universe. A different planet within the same one.

Each woman had a sleeping baby bound to her chest, including the oldest wife.

When they had eaten as much as they could, Ava and Orchid began speaking to the other adults in low tones. Brook could hardly pay attention to what they were saying. She was so overcome with tiredness that she was tempted to hold her heavy eyelids open with her fingers.

They'd come all this way for nothing.

She wondered what July was doing at this moment. If she was eating food that was better than this, if she'd found people who were more normal than this family to be with. If anyone was looking out for her the way they'd always looked out for each other.

She realized if they'd made introductions, she'd missed them. She assessed the people across the table, naming them in her head. Abel, Abel's wife. Son 1, Son 2. Wife 1, Wife 2. It was easier to number them anyway. She studied Wife 1 and 2. They were homely; they looked kind of sallow and sad, as though their diet lacked nutrients and their days lacked joy, which accentuated the hollows of their cheeks and the strange twisted curves of their noses.

They looked a lot alike.

It wasn't just the women who looked alike, she realized. They all did. They all had that crooked nose. All four of them could have been siblings. She looked at the man's wife. She, too, had the same nose, as though she was the mother of all of them.

It was too weird to think about. She put it out of her mind.

She tuned back in to the conversation just in time to hear the man's wife say, "I'm so sorry for all that has happened to you."

Unable to stand the sound of pity, Brook said, "Can I ask you guys a question?"

"Go ahead," Abel said.

"Where *is* everyone?"

"You mean on the base, or in general?"

"Both, I guess. You're the first people we've seen in like, weeks."

"I'm going to put the kids to bed," one of the son's wives said. The other wives got up as well, gathering the children and leaving the men, none of whom lifted a finger to help.

Abel rested his elbows on the table and peered at her. "They're all dead, honey," he said.

"But surely not all of them," Ava said, making it clear she had been wondering this as well. "Humans have become migratory, no? The people who didn't go Inside must have learned to adapt. Orchid here did."

"This far south had some unforeseen dangers," he said. "Hurricanes. Floods. Tornadoes. Fire. It got fucking biblical."

"This far south?" Ava repeated. "Aren't we basically in Canada?"

"After all the disasters, the thing that killed everyone off was mostly disease," he said, not really answering her question but instead seeming lost in his own thoughts. "Plague."

Brook wondered if she should add disease to her list of worries. She hated the idea of germs; organisms too small and numerous to count.

"First was the bird flu," Abel said, beginning to tick things off on his gnarled, hairy fingers. "All these wannabe survivalists thinking they could just hunt what they saw and then eat it. It spread from bird to person and then from person to population. After that, I think, Ebola. Malaria. And then—West Nile. We had an influx of mosquitos after so many years of flooding. Then, of course, the mosquitos went away. Probably a virus of their own. Or maybe they got cooked in the heat. Just like the humans. You know, the wet-bulb temperatures the human body can survive—well, let's just say I'm surprised you made it this far."

"Shit," Orchid exhaled.

"Where'd *you* settle?" the man asked her.

"Way north, in the mountains," Orchid said. "I don't know, we must have just gotten lucky where we ended up. There were maybe fifty of us by the time I left. It was pretty safe, all things considered. There were a few other communities nearby, too."

"That's the most people I've heard of in decades," he said.

"What about everyone here?" Brook asked. "Is it just you?"

"There were others," he said, "but not anymore."

She was going to press him for more information, but Ava put a hand on her knee and squeezed. "What are the chances we could stay here? Just for the night."

Brook noticed a vein pulsing in Orchid's forehead as she said, "We should probably go, Ava. They've been kind enough to us."

"What? Why?" Ava said. "We're exhausted."

"We certainly have room," he said. "My wife will show you where the extra beds are." And then he added, "Stay awhile."

Brook couldn't be sure, but she felt almost certain she saw Orchid shudder.

Abel's wife, who wore her greasy brown hair in a low bun and had a dirty apron tied tight around her frail waist, guided them down a tunnel into a deeper, darker part of the bunker. It reminded Brook of Inside in a strange way, like a distorted version of her home, and she felt a pang of homesickness, followed by a queasy twist of sadness. Inside was no longer her home, now that it didn't have July in it.

She realized she'd missed a conversation that was happening between Abel's wife and Ava. "But you chose to be here?" Ava was saying. "You wanted to stay with him?"

"I chose my family," the woman said. She had an odd way of speaking, like her words were being clipped as they left her mouth.

Orchid's arms were folded across her chest, but she was quiet, letting Ava take the lead.

"What's up with you?" Brook whispered to her, as they fell a few steps behind Ava and Abel's wife.

"Got a bad feeling about this place. These people give me the creeps," she whispered back. "Just keep your guard up, okay?"

"I think it's fine," Brook dismissed her. "So, they're a little weird. They live in a hole in the ground. You'd be weird, too."

Orchid managed a weak smile. "They really did teach you to accept everyone, huh?"

Brook smiled at her, trying to get her to loosen up. "You should try it," she said.

They reached a room lined with twin-sized beds. Abel's wife showed them where the light switch was and then left.

Brook chose the bed closest to the wall from a row of maybe fifty other beds. Orchid and Ava spread out, choosing beds on other sides of the room. They'd all slept so close to one another for countless nights and Brook was glad for a little bit of privacy.

"See?" Ava said to Orchid. "This is fine. We could use the rest."

Orchid didn't say anything, just wordlessly got into her own bed.

When Orchid turned the lights out, Brook was far enough away from both of them that she couldn't hear them breathing, a sound that had kept her awake many nights on the highway. Actually, she couldn't hear anything. She couldn't see anything, either. She didn't even realize when her eyes closed and sleep came.

* * *

In the morning, Brook woke to Ava gently shaking her.

"Get up, honey."

She hadn't slept so hard since leaving Inside. She hadn't even been dreaming. As soon as she pulled the blankets up and nestled her head into the pillow—a real pillow!—in the hard bed, it was just blackness.

She rubbed her eyes. "Are we leaving?"

"Not yet," Ava said. "First, breakfast."

On the other side of the room, Orchid was getting out of bed. "We could still leave," she said, as she approached them.

"I think we need a break," Ava said. "Just a little while longer."

The three of them walked down the tunnel, following the sounds of talking and pans clattering. They found an industrial-looking kitchen, with a metal table and walls of ovens.

"We're making bread," Wife 1 said when she saw them. Her hands were deep in dough while the children ran around her ankles. "Want to help?"

"I've never made bread before," Brook said.

"I'll teach you," Wife 1 said with a smile.

Brook turned to Ava, seeking her approval, but Ava seemed lost in thought.

"Okay," Brook said.

She stood next to Wife 1 at the metal table and watched as she combined flour, water, salt, yeast, and then kneaded them together. She broke off a piece and handed it to Brook. "Just work it until it's bouncy and smooth," she said.

"How do you have all these ingredients?" Brook said. Unlike Inside, there didn't seem to be any crops growing here.

"This place was stocked for a whole army," Wife 1 said. "I doubt we'll run out any time soon."

Brook was surprised at how much she liked to work the dough. She counted each time she folded it, pressed into it. The world around her started to melt away. There was just this sticky dough in her hands, the flour on the table. When it seemed done, Wife 1 took it from her and put it on a metal tray that went into the oven. A few minutes later the smell of baking bread filled the kitchen and Brook wanted to weep for the simple pleasure of it.

Ava and Orchid had wandered away, at some point, but that was okay. For now Brook was content to stay here with Wife 1 and the children and eat the bread she'd made with her own hands.

"Now the children will bring it to the fathers," Wife 2 said. "And you and I will clean up."

Brook was content to do this, too. Anything to distract her from the fact that July wasn't here.

When the kitchen was clean, Ava and Orchid returned. "Where'd you go?" Brook asked.

"Yes, do tell us," Wife 2 said.

"We were just exploring the place," Orchid said.

"I'm happy to give you a tour," Wife 1 said.

"That's okay," Ava said. "We got the gist. I think we'll stay one more night, if that's okay with you. And then be out of your hair in the morning."

"Like we said, stay as long as you like."

Brook felt torn. She liked it here, even if it was a little strange. But she also knew that July's absence meant they had to keep searching. Just because she wasn't here didn't mean she wasn't anywhere.

They spent the day helping the wives with the rest of their chores; more food to be cooked, rooms to be cleaned, children to be bathed. They stayed largely out of sight of the men, who seemed to have their own responsibilities elsewhere.

At one point in the afternoon, Wife 2 said, "Brook, would you like to join us for Bible study?"

Brook raised her eyebrows questioningly at Ava, who shook her head, and then at Orchid, who folded her arms across her chest, but neither of them said anything and she couldn't help but be curious. "Sure," she said.

Wife 2 produced an old dusty book and sat cross-legged on the floor. The children gathered around her in a circle. She opened to the middle and began reading. "Bless the Lord," she said. The words after that didn't make any sense to Brook, and she stopped paying attention.

Instead, she assessed the rapt toddlers with a renewed, if morbid, curiosity. They were definitely odd-looking. A few were cross-eyed, with faces that looked squished.

The babies Inside had all been gorgeous, perfectly shaped, adorable. These kids were different. They were hard to look at.

From somewhere deep in her brain she located the word: *inbred.* Her stomach twisted at the thought and she shook it off, not wanting to throw up the beans she'd had for lunch. It was a crazy thing to suspect, anyway. Just her imagination running wild again. The delirium of sleep deprivation and hunger and sadness.

"Brook, do you have any questions about the Bible?" Wife 2 asked.

"Um," Brook said. "No, thank you." The book and the wife's reverence for it gave her an uneasy feeling.

Ava and Orchid were hovering in the doorway. "Maybe we could just eat dinner and go to bed," Ava interjected.

Dinner with the whole family was bread and beans and quiet; they had nothing left to talk about. Even Abel was silent, which was a relief to Brook. She didn't have it in her to make more conversation. By the time they'd eaten and cleaned up and gotten back into bed, Brook was as exhausted as if they'd walked the whole day, and immediately fell asleep again.

She awoke to a hand over her mouth.

Son 1 was hissing at her as he held her down, "*Stop. Fighting.*"

He pressed on her face so hard that her head sank all the way down into the pillow. With his other hand, he was pulling the blankets off her, and then grasping at the waistband of her pants.

She could barely breathe, but her arms and legs were free. She began kicking and scratching, trying to scream, though the sound was trapped in her mouth by his huge, rough hand. She could reach the wall with her left hand and so she began to bang on it as hard as she could.

And then, the lights flicked on.

The hand was abruptly lifted from her mouth and she let out all the screams that had been building. Over and over and over she screamed, until she saw why he'd let her go.

Orchid was behind him, with a knife pressed into his throat and an arm holding him around his middle. He looked puny in her arms, worm-like.

He was breathing heavily, and every time he exhaled, the knife got tighter on his throat.

Ava reached her then. Jumped on the bed and wrapped her arms tightly around her, saying, "Are you okay, fuck, oh my god, are you okay?"

Brook pushed Ava off. She couldn't stand to be pinned down again.

Ava turned to Son 1 with a murderous glare on her face. "You motherfucker," she said.

"Get your things," Orchid said to Brook.

Brook was trembling violently as she and Ava walked behind Orchid, who forced Son 1 out of the room with the beds and into the main cavern of the bunker, where the rest of the family was emerging, rubbing their eyes with sleepiness and confusion.

"What the fuck do you think you're doing?" Abel asked.

"That's a better question for your son," Orchid said.

"Dad," Son 1 said meekly.

"What do you want?" Abel's wife said.

Wife 1 said, "Please. There are children."

In the distance, as if on cue, Brook heard the sound of a baby begin to wail.

"Well, we just wanted to get a good night's sleep, but your inbreeding rapist of a son had other ideas," Orchid snapped.

So: Orchid had noticed it, too. Brook hadn't been imagining the similarities between the sons and their wives.

Abel held his hands up. "Listen, we can explain all that," he said. "Humans are animals. The singular drive of all animals on this earth is to reproduce. To keep the species going. We did what we had to. There's nothing to be afraid of. You would have done the same thing."

"I'd rather die," Orchid spat.

"Can you please take the knife off my son's throat?" Abel pleaded.

"Here's what's going to happen," Ava said. "We're going to leave, and you're going to let us."

"Fine with me," Son 1 said. Orchid tightened her grip on him and he let out a pathetic little cry.

"Wait, wait," Abel said. "Maybe you should consider staying. We could work this out, whatever this is. I'm sure it's just a misunderstanding. And we have plenty of space for you."

"And what, it would be good to mix up the gene pool?" Ava said.

"Well, sure," he said.

"In your dreams," Orchid said. "We're getting the fuck out of here."

"First, you have to give us food," Brook said. Ava and Orchid looked startled to see her talk, but she ignored them. "Here's our bags. We'll wait here while she fills them with provisions that won't go bad."

Brook handed their empty tote bags to Wife 1, who nodded and then vanished down a corridor.

There was no more talking as they waited for her to return.

Wife 1 reappeared with the bags brimming with cans. Brook and Ava took them. They were heavy, which was good; heavy meant the supply would last longer.

The family watched as they began climbing the stairs to get out of the hellhole they'd found themselves in. Orchid followed behind them, backward, dragging Son 1 up the stairs with her.

When they reached the top, Abel said, "Are you going to let my child go?"

Brook scoffed. *Child.*

"Sure," Orchid said. She released the knife from Son 1's neck just as they got to the door at the top of the stairs. As quickly as she let him go, he whirled around and lunged at her.

As if acting on pure instinct, Orchid kicked him in the stomach.

Brook saw it in slow motion, his wild, terrified face as he realized he was about to fall backward down the stairs.

Below, his wife let out a horrible scream.

Before his body hit the ground, Orchid said, "Run," and they burst through the door into the humid night air and the weak purple light of dawn and didn't stop running until they reached the gate, which, to Brook's relief, opened with a push of a large red button and then creaked closed behind them.

They ran until they reached the highway's on-ramp. Adrenaline was coursing through her blood as they finally stopped to catch their breath. She felt she could have run forever, if it meant getting away from what they'd just experienced.

"Are you mad at us?" Brook said to Orchid, when she could breathe.

"Oh, honey," Orchid said. "Why would I be mad?"

"Because you knew something would happen. You tried to tell us and we ignored you."

"I didn't *want* to be right," Orchid said.

Ava tried to hug Brook again but Brook shook her off. "Please," Brook said. "Don't touch me. Not yet."

Ava nodded, wounded but understanding. Instead, Ava reached for Orchid, and Brook watched as Orchid wrapped her arms around her mother and clutched her tightly while Ava's knees softened and she leaned her whole body weight into Orchid, who buried her face in Ava's hair.

"This is why," she heard Ava say, her voice muffled in Orchid's neck.

"Why what?" Orchid said, so gently that Brook blushed.

"Why they didn't let any men Inside."

Orchid laughed. "That's kind of an oversimplified take on sexual violence," Orchid said. "Especially coming from you." The way she said it was soft and tender, not a criticism but a gentle push.

Ava groaned. "I know," she said. "Sorry, I guess I'm still deprogramming."

Brook, embarrassed by this display, turned away from it.

The tears came then, Brook facing the muddy sunrise as she allowed the experience she'd just lived through to fully sink in. The violation of it. The invasion of her space, her body. No one had ever touched her like that.

Brook usually felt as though her *self,* whatever that was, occupied a small corner of her mind, her soul disconnected from the rest of her, kept safe and precious. But now she felt, for the first time, as though she was living in her entire body. The feeling of embodiment spread from her fingertips to her toes, filling her skin. There was nowhere he could have touched her that wasn't *her.* He'd covered her mouth, but she'd felt it everywhere, inside and out.

There wasn't really a difference between her exterior and the inner landscape where she hid, and she was surprised by how powerful this realization felt, despite the pain it came with.

The tears fell faster as she also realized she'd never see her best friend, her soulmate, ever again. She'd be alone, without July, forever. July would never know this version of her that was rising from the ashes.

Unless Brook were to estimate the amount of years she'd be alive for and then count the minutes therein, forever was a terribly unquantifiable amount of time.

APRIL 14, 2041

Dear Orchid,

The day I left you, Madhuri, Len, and I drove for ten hours. Mostly in silence. We were heading across the country to the Winter Liberation Army's compound, which is somewhere in the Pacific Northwest, but for reasons that will soon become clear, I am not going to write down exactly where it is.

Now, writing this, I'm still in the mountains of the south. I'm trying to avoid the major highways because I don't want anyone to spot me. So the drive is taking longer than I thought it would. All these back-country roads that end up leading nowhere, winding around the mountain. It's so pretty here, though. I wish you could see it.

I can't believe I've made it this far alive. It feels like a miracle.

I sent you my last letter from a mailbox in a one-stoplight town. I got some weird looks as I filled up my tank. I stick out here. It's like they can smell my politics. I got back on the road as soon as I could.

I'm pulled over off the road now, hidden by some trees. It seems like as good a place as any to get some sleep. But first, I still have so much to tell you.

So, the first day I was gone. When Rick got home from work and found you with the babysitter, and the note on the counter, he started calling my cell phone. I didn't want to talk to him in front of Madhuri and Len, so I let it go to voicemail while my stomach turned over. He texted a series of question marks. I wrote back, hang on.

He replied: are you kidding me?

We stopped when we crossed into Ohio and pulled into the lot of an old motel, its vacancy light flickering and buzzing.

"Kelly, do you need your own room, or are you good to crash with us?" Madhuri said.

"What do you mean *us*?" I asked, realizing as I said it that I'd missed what was right in front of me. They were dating. She put her hands on her hips, annoyed at my obliviousness. It was a comforting gesture. We were still ourselves, after all this time.

"Uh, yeah. I need my own room," I said, horrified by the idea of having to see her and Len in a bed together. I forgot how few boundaries we used to have. She and I used to sleep one foot away from each other on the ground. I wondered how she lived these days.

She rolled her eyes at me. "Well, who do you expect to pay for that?"

"Vero," I said. "Duh. Speaking of which. Where is he?"

"He's meeting us in the morning," Len said. "But yeah, you're right, I'm sure he'll pay for you."

I already didn't like the way Len seemed to have a direct line to Vero while Madhuri and I were in the dark, but I didn't say anything.

I got the room next to them. It was pretty abysmal—there were weird stains on the sheets—but it would do. I could hear Madhuri and Len's voices through the thin wall. When they quieted, going to bed, I called Rick.

He picked up on the first ring. "Where the fuck are you?" he hissed into the phone.

I could hear you crying in the background. You were too old to cry like that. I must have really scared you. I felt something break inside me. I was a monster to leave you.

"Orchid said you left in a bus?" he was yelling now. "Kelly, did you leave with those people?"

You and your big imagination. I wondered what you thought you'd seen. "It's just a *van,* not a bus," I said. "And yeah, I did, but I'm coming back. They hired me onto a project. It's just for a few days."

"A van? The one you were complaining about? And what's this about a project?" His voice got louder with each question. "They *hired* you? Why do you need work? Have I not given you everything you've ever wanted?"

My heart started to pound. "Everything except your loyalty," I said.

He was quiet.

"Rick," I said.

"So you're doing this to punish me? You left with no notice and now I have to figure out what to do with the kid while I'm at work?"

"She goes to school, Rick," I said. "She's not an infant. You can have the babysitter stay with her in the afternoons. It'll be affordable if you don't stay out late like you usually do."

"Fuck you," he said.

"Can I talk to her?" I was getting desperate to hear your voice, to tell you everything was okay.

"Absolutely not," he said. "You can talk to her when you get back. And the first words out of your mouth better be 'I'm sorry.'" He hung up.

This was the moment it dawned on me that perhaps I had made a terrible mistake. I was hit with waves of regret. Not for leaving, but for not taking you with me. I should have just carried you into the van with us and never looked back. Though I suppose that Rick probably would have called the police, tried to have me arrested for kidnapping. So. I don't know what I could have done differently, is the truth.

Also, the money. The money was still the problem. I ran through every possible scenario, every way out I could have taken, and money was the wall I kept running into. We'd have no life without it. I didn't want to be homeless again. I didn't want you to ever be homeless, more importantly.

I lay back and tried to sleep. Every time I started to drift I'd wake suddenly from a too-vivid dream that you were screaming for me.

I woke to a hard, quick knock on the door. The sunlight was trickling through the dirty white curtain.

I was still wearing my clothes from yesterday when I opened the door. It was Vero.

He placed a cup of coffee in my hands. "Let's talk," he said. "Come on, it's nice out. Bring your phone."

I rubbed my eyes. While I followed him to a nearby bench in the sun, I wondered if Rick had remembered to wake you up for school. The school bus comes at 7:15, I texted him quickly. He didn't write back.

"I need you to be honest with me," I said. "Where are we going, and what are we doing?"

"Give me your phone," he said. I handed it to him. He took the SIM card out and started to fold it in half. It broke. He tossed it into the grass. I wasn't shocked, but it was still annoying. He should have asked first.

"Sorry," he said. "Necessary safety precautions. I'll buy you a burner."

"I need that to call my daughter," I said.

"I know. I said I'd get you another one."

He looked around, checking for people. We were alone.

"We're going to __________," he said.

"That's really fucking far away," I snapped. "You told me this would just be a few days."

"I said whatever I could to get you to come," he admitted. "I'm sorry. But I'm hoping that now you're on the road anyway, I can convince you to make the rest of the trip."

"Tell me," I said. "It better be good." I started thinking of ways I could get home alone if I needed to. I wondered if Rick had frozen my credit card yet, or if he'd let me charge a bus fare back.

"When I said that the government could stop climate change, but are choosing not to, I meant it," he began.

"Wait," I said. "Before you tell me what you know, tell me how you know it."

He looked embarrassed. Or maybe I was putting that on him. Maybe he didn't feel any shame about it. "After we got arrested, I moved back in with my parents."

"I figured," I said. "Did they make you go by your deadname? What kind of deal with the devil did you have to make?"

"The thing is," he said. He fidgeted with the edge of his black button-down. "They decided to accept me."

"Oh," I said, shocked. "That's amazing."

"Thanks. Yeah. I guess they realized they could have me on my terms or not at all."

I felt that old familiar pang of jealousy.

"So," he said, "it worked, me living there. We figured out how to get along. They even—well, you probably read about this—my dad is the reason why New York became a safe haven state for trans people."

In the years since we'd seen each other, Vero's dad had become a senator.

I shook my head. "No, I didn't know that was him," I said. "Honestly, I stopped following the news as closely as I used to. It was making it hard to get through the day. I mean, I listened to the radio, but I didn't make it my business to know every little thing that was happening."

He raised his eyebrows at me. "You really have changed," he said.

We were quiet. I was feeling too many things to articulate any of them. Finally, realizing he hadn't even told me anything useful, I said, "Keep going. Please."

"My parents put me through college. Yale."

"Wow," I said. "So you were playing Frisbee on the quad while I was in juvie."

"I'm sorry, Kelly," he said.

"It's fine," I said, though we both knew it wasn't. "Then what?"

"After I graduated, I . . . I ended up working for my dad."

"You did not," I said, laughing. I couldn't believe it. But also I could. "They let you into government buildings with your record?"

"Records can be wiped clean if you're related to someone important enough," he said.

"Okay," I said. "So you're lurking in all these top-secret meetings, right? Getting info?"

"Basically," he said. "Can I tell you the rest now?"

I nodded. "You better."

"There are countless people working on real-time solutions for climate change. Even knowing that we didn't stop using fossil fuels in time, there's still stuff that can be done. Ways we can slow the earth's warming, ways we can adapt to it, technologies that will start to undo the damage. You would not believe some of the shit people are coming up with. It would blow your mind. But every time someone is about to publish their findings, they . . ." He paused and stared at the sky for a while. "They disappear," he said. "I mean, they *are disappeared.* Along with their work. I don't know what exact branch of the government is doing it. It might even be coordinated globally."

"But why?" I said. "Who does it serve to allow climate change to progress?"

"So, here's where it gets really insane," he said. "It's estimated that, what, seventy percent of the population will die in climate-related disasters if nothing changes? That's a serious culling of the population. The thing is, they want it to happen. The world has gotten too big to control."

I was speechless.

He went on. "It's a Malthusian trap." When I stared blankly, he said, "The theory that population growth is exponential while resources increase linearly? And that means standards of living decrease as the population increases, until some sort of disaster naturally reduces the population?" I shook my head. I had no idea what he was talking about. I resented his college education, his new big words. "It means there's an inevitability to the catastrophe we're in. That there was always going to be something that came along to course correct, to rightsize the amount of people on earth with the resources available to us. It could be stopped, but then the rich would have to start sharing. They don't want to."

"Okay," I said, hesitantly, "I think I'm following. So they want climate change to take most of us out so that they don't have to give anything up, materially."

He nodded. "They're going to decide who gets to survive. And then, I guess, kind of start over."

"This is a nightmare," I said, putting it mildly. I tried to swallow. My mouth was suddenly so dry. "And why do you think it's being coordinated globally?"

"Things I heard. There are whispers that some sort of united global governing body is going to form soon. But they'll only have power if the world is at the brink of collapse. And then they can swoop in with a solution. It's going to seem like salvation. But really it'll be the result of decades of planning and manipulation."

"What's their solution going to be?" I asked.

"They're calling it the Inside Project," he said. "It's pretty much what it sounds like. They'll select groups of people to live in these crazy new weatherproof structures. They'll be the size of small cities. My guess is it'll happen in ten years, fifteen years, based on how fast things fall apart. And everyone else will be shut out. Fucked."

I believed him. I wanted to cry, scream, break things.

Instead I said: "What do you need me to do?"

"I need you to get to the information before they make it disappear. The scientists, their research, the things we could use to stop things from getting out of control. I want to get to it before the government does."

"What makes you think I can do that?" I asked.

"Not *think*, Kelly," he said. "I know you can."

Maybe it was his belief in me that made me agree—I was, shamefully, a little bit starving for someone to validate what I was capable of—or maybe it was just the way he was looking at me, his eyes full of uncomplicated desire. Either way he could tell when he'd won me over. He always could.

"So you'll stay?" He took my hands in his.

"Obviously," I whispered.

How could I not try to save a world that had you in it?

"Do your parents know?" I asked.

"Know what?"

"What you just told me?"

He nodded.

"Do they know what you're planning?"

He shrugged. "I don't care if they do. As long as they don't try to stop me."

"What about the raid? I heard about it on the radio."

He squeezed my hands. "The raid happened because we didn't have someone like you with us. We didn't know how to cover our tracks. If everything works out, it'll never happen again."

"Arthur is still in jail?" I asked. He nodded, looking regretful.

I squeezed his hands back.

"We need to get moving," he said. "I'm going to drive with you guys the rest of the way."

"Yay," I said, but couldn't muster any enthusiasm in my voice. I was too overwhelmed, too scared. The world was way more evil than I had thought. And that was really saying something.

The next time we stopped, Vero bought me that burner phone he'd promised.

It took us a little over a week to get to where we were going. I called Rick every night and every morning. I wished we had a landline so there'd be a chance you'd answer. Instead I had to call his cell.

Every time we spoke, he screamed at me while I begged him to put you on the phone. He wouldn't. Sometimes I'd hear you in the background, saying, "Daddy, who is it? Is it Mom?" And he'd lie to you. He'd say, "It's work," or, worse, "It's no one."

"Just come home," he'd say, alternating between yelling at me and pleading with me. "We can fix this."

"I *will*," I'd say. "I just have to see this through."

"See what through?" He'd start to yell again. "Are you sure you haven't just lost it?"

I'd hang up and sob.

Sometimes I'd seek out Madhuri and we'd go buy a six-pack of beer and blow through the whole thing, sitting in our hotel rooms talking about the good old days.

Sometimes Madhuri and I talked about Cory. She told me stories from before I met them.

"Do you blame me for her death?" I asked on one of those nights. We were in the Midwest, at a hotel on the side of the highway, in a town I'd never heard of.

She took a big gulp of beer. "Sometimes," she said.

It was the answer I was expecting. "I blame myself, too," I said.

She ran a hand through her hair, which was greasy and flat after so many days using motel shampoo. "No, dude," she said. "I didn't really mean that. It wasn't your fault. You were allowed to not want to be with her."

"I could have handled it better."

"You were just a kid. We all were."

My heart swelled with love for Madhuri and everything she'd ever done for me, how much she loved me despite seeing me at my worst so many times.

Vero knocked on the door. "Can I join you?"

Madhuri passed him a beer. We were sitting on my bed facing each other and he sat down next to me so our shoulders were touching. I was drunk, dizzy with the happy-sadness of being with my friends but missing you. I leaned into him. His shoulder felt thicker than I remembered, strong and warm through his shirt. He put his arm around me.

"This again, huh?" Madhuri said, never one to not comment on the obvious.

Since it's probably obvious to you, too, I'll just say that after a few days, Vero started booking himself and me in the same room.

It was so easy to let him back into my heart. As though he'd never left it.

At each new location we stopped in, we'd lay in bed whispering to each other for hours.

"Tell me how you went from finding out what was happening to starting a movement," I said. "Winter Liberation Army. It sounds so hardcore."

"It is hardcore." I could hear the smile on his face in the darkness. "Well, as you can imagine, a lot of people were really pissed at me. They felt I'd betrayed them by moving back in with my parents, going to college, working at the White House."

"Yeah," I said. "I mean, same."

"I won people back one by one. Once I realized what was happening, I couldn't do nothing. I reached out to old friends. I gained their trust back slowly. I told them what I knew. They told their people. It happened organically. We started planning actions. We wanted to reveal what was being done. But we didn't really get to do much before the smear campaign started."

"I heard about you on the news. I mean, I didn't realize it was you at the time. They called you a domestic terrorist organization."

"Yes. It made me realize that people in the media might be in on all this. That the CEOs of certain networks have perhaps been promised survival in exchange for a certain spin on current events."

"That's why they call you climate-change deniers." Things were starting to fall into place. I could see the fuller picture.

"Yeah. When really we're the opposite of that."

"This is so fucked up!" I said. I was saying that a lot those days.

One night when we were eating Chinese takeout from a strip

mall somewhere in the middle of who knows where, all four of us in a faded orange booth, Vero said, "I bought us a piece of land."

"You didn't," Madhuri gasped. "That's where we're going?"

I hadn't realized that Madhuri didn't know where we were going, either.

He smirked, nodded. Looked pleased with himself. "Fifty acres in a protected forest," he said. "Nothing and no one will ever find us. Not the authorities. It's not a fire zone. It's the safest place in the country."

"Why the fuck do we need fifty acres?" I said.

They were quiet. "It'll be nice to belong somewhere," Len said.

It seems like a good time to tell you that by this point, I'd decided I really hated Len.

It wasn't just his stupid laugh or his condescending tone of voice or the way I found I couldn't really believe anything he said. I mean, who cared how he treated *me.* It was the way he treated Madhuri, who adored him, for reasons I'll never comprehend.

I watched him push her away so many times when she tried to be tender. He laughed at her when she was clumsy, he talked over her when it was the four of us. He was grabby with her; he'd pull her into his lap and force her to stay there, even if he'd just been making fun of her.

For the life of me I couldn't understand why she was going along with it. She seemed desperate for his love. Perhaps I related. Rick was never exactly cruel to me outright. But he left me hungry in the same way Madhuri seemed hungry.

We didn't talk about it. I was afraid of offending her. I watched silently, taking it all in.

I did try to ask Vero about it one morning as we got ready to hit the road again. "Of all the people in the world, why'd you bring Len in?" I was buttoning up my shirt while he flossed.

"Len's a good guy," he said. "I'd trust him with my life."

"You don't see the way he treats Madly?"

He spit into the sink and fixed his hair in the mirror. "I've learned you never really know what happens between two people. Best not to judge, you know?"

"I'm not judging," I insisted. "I'm concerned for her."

"Kelly, I don't mean to be an asshole, but it seems like you should worry about your own house."

He'd heard me crying after talking to Rick day after day through different burner phones that we'd then throw out. I'd told him about you. He knew how much I missed you, how guilty I felt. Was he using all that against me?

I didn't say anything. We got back in the car.

We were doing the reverse of my current journey back to you, though on the way there it was much easier. We took turns driving, for one. And we knew where we were going. We had GPS. All I have now are some maps and a vague sense of cardinal directions.

So we got there much faster than I'll be getting to you. It was maybe ten days, then.

The drive through the last state was unlike anything I'd ever seen before. Roads lined with pines, boulders covered in moss, snowcapped mountains looming in the distance, fog that rolled in like a cashmere blanket and rolled out just as quickly, giving way to the bluest skies, the freshest air. Everything smelled like sweet fern and untouched dirt. We were quiet—feeling, I think, a sense of almost religious reverence for the exquisiteness of this world. This world that we had nearly succeeded in destroying, but hadn't, because we were about to destroy ourselves first.

At some point we turned off the main road and onto a dirt path. Vero was driving. He stopped at a gate and got out, unlocking it, swinging it open, and then got back in the car to drive through. Len hopped out to close it behind us.

It was another hour's drive down that dirt road. We passed a lake so clean and clear it looked like a crystal. The treetops leaned toward one another like they were making a tunnel over the road, protecting us. Vero put his hand on mine.

And then we were there. A simple, windowless brick building with an iron door.

"Base camp," Vero said.

Madhuri and Len were making whooping noises as they got out of the car and whirled around. I sat quietly. "Vero, what is this place?"

"It's where we're going to save the world."

"Is there anyone else here?"

"Yes."

"Who?" I hated that he made everything such a damn mystery, while also knowing that his mysteriousness was what attracted me to him.

"Come inside and meet them," he said, smiling at me in that way I couldn't argue with.

I unbuckled my seatbelt and we went into the building.

Madhuri and Len were ahead of us. I heard them react before I saw it for myself. "Whoa, dude," Madhuri said, while Len laughed with glee.

It looked like how a TV show would portray a NASA control room. Endless rows of desks with computers facing one huge screen, and a few people who looked up and waved at us as we walked in.

"Come," Vero said. He introduced us and then took us up a flight of stairs, where we found ourselves in a long hallway with doors all along it.

"Pick a bedroom," he said to Madhuri. "They're all the same." He turned to me. "You can have your own, or you can share mine."

I immediately understood that Vero's room was not the same as everyone else's. "I'm with you," I said.

I was right. While everyone else had a simple bedroom and bathroom, Vero had the corner suite. And now so did I. Sleeping with the leader had its perks.

I asked him to leave the room while I called your dad. By this point he knew to give me space for these awful conversations.

He produced a laptop from under the bed. "Use this," he said. "It can make untraceable calls."

"Nice," I said weakly, loading the program that would scramble the signal while Vero backed out of the room.

"Kelly." Rick picked up.

"Please let me talk to her," I said, as I always did. "I need to tell her I love her and that I'm going to come home soon."

"No, actually, you're not," he said.

"What?"

"I'm out of patience with this bullshit. You know how long two weeks is to a seven-year-old? You've been gone an eternity. You can't come back. That's it. I'm done."

I nearly choked on my own spit.

"She's my daughter."

"You're the one who left her," he said.

"Just for a little while! I'm coming back!"

"Don't call again," he said. "If you do, I'll get a restraining order. Don't push me, Kel. I'm at the end of my rope."

"No," I begged. "Please don't do this. Please. You don't understand."

"No, *you* don't understand," he said. And then he hung up.

I put my face in a pillow and sobbed so hard I thought I might die.

How could he do this to me? To you?

This story is upsetting for me to revisit. I feel like I'm right back there, in Vero's room, crying my guts out, thinking I'd never see you again. You, the only person who has ever really mattered to me.

I'm going to take a break and try to get some sleep. I'll write you more tomorrow.

Love,
Mom

7

CAMILLA
2078

"I WANT TO CHANGE YOUR BANDAGES," CAMILLA SAID. IT was morning. She had woken up and immediately noticed a kind of sour odor coming from Max, though she would never say that. She didn't want to embarrass them. And she didn't mind the smell. She was just concerned about what it might mean.

"My skin thanks you," Max said. "It's so itchy."

Camilla helped Max out of the hut, from one chair to another. Mosquitos were swarming around her ankles, though less densely than they had been since the storm. There were only a few puddles that remained from the flood.

They didn't look at each other as Camilla gently unwrapped Max's leg. She swore under her breath when she saw what was underneath the fabric; their skin was nearly black where the tree had hit it. It was irritated in places from the bandages and the stick. She inspected further and found a few sores starting to form. Hence the smell, she supposed.

But the swelling had gone down from the first time she'd looked. So that was something.

"Let me clean these," she said. They still had some water left over from yesterday and she poured it over the sores. Max flinched.

"Sorry," she whispered. "Sorry, sorry, sorry." She washed the dirt, blood, and crust away.

Max gritted their teeth and closed their eyes as she rearranged the splint.

"Do you still feel like you need this?" she asked. She wasn't sure how good it was to have this piece of wood digging into them day after day.

"I have no idea," Max said. "Maybe."

"Okay," she said. "But I want to check on it more frequently."

"Okay," Max said. "Thank you."

Max's tofu, or whatever it was, had long run out.

Camilla hunted for squirrels, chipmunks, field mice, anything she could find, really, that was living. But the meat was always tough, never filling. Even the animals seemed to be starving. Max and Camilla were growing weaker. Max didn't complain, but Camilla could tell. They were both deteriorating. It was hard to sleep when she was so hungry, and then being more tired during the day made it harder to look for food.

Finally, sick of feeling so unsatisfied, Camilla decided it was time for something else.

It took her the better part of a day to weave a net out of soft, bendable birch branches and discarded clothes the way Orchid had shown her.

"How does fish for dinner sound?" she asked while she worked on it, but Max didn't answer. They were staring out at the mountains. "Did you hear me?" she asked, and Max startled, as though they'd been deep in a daydream.

"Yes, I'm sorry. Fish. Sounds great."

She sighed. If Max wasn't going to be excited about eating something different, she'd be excited for both of them. "I'll be back later today. Don't go anywhere."

At this, Max managed a laugh.

She fastened the net to her back and began the trek down the mountain to where the stream let out into a lake. It was a few hours away. This was why she hadn't done it yet; she hadn't wanted to be away from Max for that long. What if they needed her? But now, she thought, things were dire enough that it was worth the risk. The lake had been pretty dry for as long as she could remember, but after the huge storm, she had a feeling it might be in better shape.

She was right; when she reached the water's edge she was delighted to find that it was much deeper. She pulled her clothes off and left them in a pile on a rock. She waded in up to her hips. There was a raft in the middle of it that Orchid had built, and she swam out to it, pulling herself up and then letting her legs dangle over the edge into the tepid water.

She sank the net into the water and waited.

She was going to get a sunburn, she knew, but the warmth felt so good as it evaporated the droplets from her skin. She arched her head back and closed her eyes, letting herself enjoy this feeling, her hair dripping onto the wooden planks.

She held still for a long time, resisting the urge to kick her legs in the water. She was good at this, at making herself blend into her surroundings.

She thought of Max. How compelled she was by their mystery, their woundedness—the wounds she knew about, and the ones she didn't.

Finally, she felt something bump her foot. She tried not to flinch. A catfish, hideous and fat, swam over the net, and she pulled the whole thing up and around the fish before the poor sucker even knew what was happening.

Without hesitation she slammed the fish onto the raft once, twice, at the perfect angle so that its body didn't crack open, and then she wrapped it up tightly in the net and clutched it to her chest while she swam back to shore.

She put her clothes on and ran back to the campsite.

"Catfish!" she called as she got close.

Max shook their head in disbelief. "You're amazing," they said. They touched her arm.

Other than when they'd gripped her arms for support, this was the first time Max had touched her—the first time they'd done it because they wanted to, not because they needed to.

She tried not to react to the feeling of Max's hand on her skin. "Oh, it's nothing," she said. "I should have done it sooner."

"It's not nothing," they said. "Thank you." They squeezed her arm before letting go. For a long time after, she could still feel the pressure of their fingers.

Camilla caught a fish the next day, and the day after that, and so on.

For the first time since they'd been alone together, she and Max had enough to eat. It made everything easier between them. They were becoming comfortable, used to each other's rhythms.

It made everything easier for Camilla, too. With a belly full of fish she could wake in the morning with enough strength to catch a rabbit. With rabbit for breakfast she had the strength to get more water. Each day brought more and more. They could live like this forever, she thought.

She cleaned the sores on Max's legs until they were healed. The black splotch was getting smaller and smaller every day.

She started combing through the debris from the other huts. There, buried in the destruction, she found a knife, a pot, some clothes, blankets.

Eventually she found the rest of the materials she needed to make their own hut sturdier, restoring it to almost its former shabby glory, back when Orchid had been the one in charge of building things. She felt Max watching her while she hammered a stronger roof into place.

Days and nights were blending together. Camilla lost track of time. How long it had been since Orchid left, she couldn't be sure.

It hadn't rained since the terrible storm that caused everyone to leave, but because that one storm had dumped so much water on the parched land, there was an influx of neon-yellow wildflowers. In truth they were weeds, but they were pretty; they illuminated the hillsides and made everything appear to glow, especially since it was so hot that the air seemed to bend and swirl. The hills were otherwise verdant and lush, thick with grass.

The grass and the wildflowers wouldn't have a long life, Camilla knew.

They would flower and then wilt in the heat like everything else, and then become straw, dry and dangerous. But for now, everything was alive. She was alive, too. Perhaps more alive than ever before.

One day she decided to fashion crutches for Max out of the branches that had fallen in the storm. She spent all afternoon on them, wrapping old towels around the tops so they wouldn't chafe.

She presented the crutches to Max shyly. "I made these for you. You don't have to use them, I just thought . . ."

Max's face lit up. "Thank you," they said.

She helped them up and tucked one makeshift crutch under each arm. It took a few tries but they got the hang of it quickly, and soon they were crutching all around the clearing. To Camilla's delight, they started to laugh. "Look at me go," they said.

"Look at you go." She smiled.

One afternoon when she came back with another lumpy catfish, the fire was already going, crackling in the fading light.

"Oh my god," she said. "Thank you. How did you manage?"

"You gave me the gift of being able to hobble around," they said.

"This is wonderful," she said. She felt relieved, suddenly, to not be responsible for every little thing.

Now that Max could get around, they were more helpful in general. They kept the fire going, at any rate. Camilla taught them how to prep and cook the fish, and Max turned out to be good at it, dexterous and nimble. It was something they could do while sitting.

One day she came back from the pond and Max had picked a cluster of yellow wildflowers and left them by the campfire. "For you," they said, a little sheepishly, and she felt her heart swell to twice its size.

After that Max started doing little things for her when she went off to find food. She'd come back to find her spare clothes folded, her tools cleaned. She worried that Max was putting too much pressure on their leg in order to make these gestures, but she was also grateful—for the acts, but mostly for the fact that it meant while she was off thinking of Max, Max was thinking of her, too.

* * *

One evening sometime later, Max said, "Let me show you something." Max balanced on their good leg and, with a small groan, stood.

"Max, don't," she said. "It's too soon."

Max took a wobbly step forward. They winced, but they were able to put weight on it. They limped another step toward her. The splint was making it so they couldn't bend their leg.

"It's not," they said. "It's been over a month."

Had it? Had she really been so focused on the daily tasks that she'd let weeks go by? Apparently so.

"Still," she said. "That looks really painful. I think you should . . ."

Max cut her off. "Camilla, let me do this." Their voice was firm but not mean. They wanted to show her.

"Okay," she said. "I'll shut up."

She hadn't seen Max stand on their own since they got hurt. Every time they'd gotten up, they'd needed Camilla's help, including, to both of their embarrassment, relieving themself over a hole in the ground.

"It's really feeling so much better," they insisted. "I think we should take the stick out of my bandages." They were an arm's length away now. She didn't believe them; the grimace on their face gave them away. But they were determined, and that made her soften. She understood that kind of drive. It makes you push through the pain.

One more step and they were inches from her.

Without thinking twice, Camilla flung her arms around Max's shoulders and hugged them, hard. Max wrapped an arm around her waist and squeezed her back.

Something delicate passed between them, a tenderness greater than the fact that Camilla had kept them both alive for the past few weeks, and she needed a way to express it. Words wouldn't do. She wanted to feel them. She wanted it so badly that she hadn't stopped to think if Max wanted it, too.

And then, before she could stop herself, she kissed their neck, her lips parted so she could taste their sweat.

They pulled away. "Camilla, I . . ."

She couldn't bear to hear what she was sure was going to be a kind but firm rejection.

"Sorry," she said. She couldn't look at them. Instead she turned toward the fire and said, "I'm starving."

Generously, Max let it go. "Let's eat this thing," they said.

Camilla tried not to look at them while she prepared the fish for dinner.

They picked the flesh from the bones with their fingers, grease on their chins and bellies getting full.

They finished their fish in silence, and then Camilla stomped out the fire. "Sleep?" she said, extending a hand. Max ignored her outstretched hand and stood up without her help, and she lowered her arm. It felt like a slight. "Okay, then," she said, turning away.

"Wait," Max said, and clutched her arm, pulling her back. "Just because I can stand up on my own now doesn't mean I don't need you."

"Oh," she said. "Okay." She already knew Max needed her, but hearing them say it out loud made her pulse quicken.

"And I don't think I've properly thanked you for all you've done for me these past few weeks," they said. "I'm so grateful to you. It's almost embarrassing how indebted I feel."

"I don't want you to feel indebted," she said. "A thank-you is plenty."

"Well, then, thank you," Max said, but still holding her arm, as though there was something more they needed to say.

"Yeah?" Camilla asked, nervous, feeling stripped naked by Max's intense gaze.

"Nothing," Max said, and released her.

"If your leg is a little better, maybe you can sleep on the mattress instead of the chair," she offered. "We probably don't need to keep elevating it at night."

Max nodded. "I'd like that."

They went into the hut and lay down, facing away from each other. Camilla's heart was pounding. It took her a long time to fall asleep. Instead she lay there wondering what Max was thinking, over on their side of the bed.

They slept together on the mattress a few feet apart every night now.

Sometimes she'd wake in the night to Max muttering in their sleep. Other times she'd sleep so hard that it was like being dead.

Mornings were a little awkward. Usually she got up first, taking the time to study Max's face, those long dark lashes twitching in a dream. But sometimes she'd awaken to Max already up, staring at her. She wasn't sure what to make of these moments. They would smile nervously at each other until someone broke the silence. It was usually her. She'd say, "I'll get us some water," or "I'll start the fire," and the spell would be broken.

She worried about her father. She wondered if the journey north was hard on his brittle bones, if the group would go slow enough for him. But she was also completely occupied with what she had to do in the immediate future. Keeping herself and Max alive, for one. That was the main thing she had to focus on. She had to figure out how much they needed each day and how to get it. Not just food but water—she had to get twice as much water as she used to get for herself. Sometimes she felt that all she did was walk back and forth to that damn stream.

Figuring out what was happening between them, if it was anything at all, came in second. It was probably nothing, she told herself over and over.

But still. Sometimes in the night Max would press their foot into hers. She was never sure if they were doing it on purpose, but she didn't move away. Other times, during the day, Max held her gaze for a few seconds longer than necessary. In those few seconds she felt certain something was burning between them.

Finally, after countless days and nights of this unnameable dance between them, one evening, as they finished eating a particularly fat fish and the sun was starting to set, Max said, "Camilla?"

She turned to look at them. There was an expression on their face she hadn't seen before, something more open, their eyes wide and unblinking.

Each meal they'd eaten together they sat closer and closer to each other. Now, they were mere inches apart, and the hairs on Camilla's arm were standing up.

Max put a warm hand on her shoulder. "Can I kiss you?" they asked.

Because she was so surprised, all she could do was say, "Because of all the fish?"

Max laughed, the skin around their eyes crinkling. "No, not because of the fish. Camilla, you've kept us alive while my leg heals. Yes, the fish is awesome. But so is everything else you've done for me."

"Okay," she said, and opened herself up to the desire between them. Max put an arm around her waist and pulled her close.

Max tasted like dinner, but Camilla imagined that she did, too. She knew she at least probably had a few fish scales on her clothes from carrying it home. But she didn't have time to worry because their tongue in her mouth was forceful, a little too aggressive, their teeth bumping painfully. She kept her eyes open, curious to observe what Max would look like while kissing her. Her hands were clutching at their ribs and she could feel them breathing in and out and in and out, and she was glad their arm was around her because she was certain that the world was spinning off its axis.

She pulled away, needing to breathe. "I thought you didn't want me," she said. "That one time I tried to kiss you. And then . . ."

"You mean when I froze that time you licked my neck?" Max laughed, and she blushed. "Sorry. I was just caught off guard."

"I'm sorry," she said, smiling, her shame replaced with want. "Couldn't control myself."

"Let's go inside."

Max led Camilla into their hut by the hand. "This is going to take me a minute," they said, before gingerly lowering themself onto the dirty mattress on the ground. Camilla couldn't believe it was finally happening, after all this time spent wondering if Max returned her feelings.

"Tell me how to do this without hurting you," she said. She was still standing. She didn't know what to do with herself.

She hoped she wouldn't have to explain that it wasn't so much about Max's healing leg but about the fact that she didn't even know where to begin.

But Max didn't seem bothered by this request. Instead, they said, "You'll have to teach me what you want, too, you know."

Camilla didn't know what she wanted. Her own body was as foreign to her as Max's. What would she even say, and how would she say it?

Suddenly, Camilla was overwhelmed with too many feelings at once. Excitement but also anxiety; fear that she wouldn't be a good lover, or that it wouldn't live up to her expectations. That she'd fuck it all up somehow. It was getting hard to breathe. She turned away.

"Hey," Max said, reaching for her. "Hey." Like they were soothing a wild animal. "What's wrong?"

There was a ringing in her ears.

"We don't have to do this," Max said, taking her hand.

"I want to," she whispered, and then to her absolute embarrassment, she realized she was trembling.

"Sit down next to me," Max said, and she did.

"This is humiliating," she said.

"You can tell me," they said.

But she couldn't. She didn't know how to put it into words: Her lack of experience. Max's beauty. The fact that she'd never been naked with someone she truly cared for. The way opening herself up to Max meant that it might destroy her if she lost them. And there were so many ways she could lose them, in this changed and dangerous world.

"It's okay," Max said, and they sounded like they really meant it. Hearing their words, she almost believed them. "We can take it slow."

"Okay," she said.

She wanted to weep for how sweet they were being, but she didn't. Instead she thought about how much she missed her family; how desperately she wished she could tell her mom or Shelby about Max. The past few weeks had depleted her. She had never felt more exhausted, being in charge of finding food for both of them.

They were quiet for a while. Camilla's shame hung in the air. Eventually Max lay back and she tentatively lay beside them, scooting close so that their skin was touching. She fell asleep listening to them breathing.

When Camilla woke up, she and Max were back-to-back, a film of sweat sticking their skin together. She shifted, peeling herself off them, the humidity a heavy blanket. The morning light was playing across Max's face like ribbons through the branches that made up their roof, illuminating bits of dirt and dust.

Max opened their eyes. "Hi."

"Hi. I'm sorry about last night."

They sat up. "It's really okay." Max paused. "There's something else we need to talk about."

"Uh-oh."

"Now that I can walk . . ."

Camilla sat up next to them, so they were shoulder to shoulder. She knew where this was going, and she didn't want to be lying down and vulnerable for it. "I mean, you can *barely* walk, but go on."

"How long do you want to wait for her?"

"As long as it takes."

"Camilla," Max said gently but not without urgency. "We can't stay here forever. What if there's another storm? It would take us out."

She sighed. She hung her head between her knees. She knew Max was right. But how could she abandon Orchid? After everything Orchid had done for her and her father?

"What if she gets here and we're gone and she has no way to find us?" she said.

"I know," Max said. "I'm not saying we need to leave right now. But it's almost summer. Soon everything will die and, I don't know, potentially catch fire? I would love for us to be north before that happens."

Us. The word hung in the heavy air, pulling Camilla to change her mind. It wasn't just her waiting for Orchid anymore. They were a unit, of some sort.

She was torn between wanting to wait for Orchid and wanting to make Max happy. She had the odd feeling she'd say just about anything to keep Max saying things like *us.* "Can we just give it a few more weeks?" She turned to face them, looking at them with pleading eyes. "I'd never forgive myself if we left too soon."

"Yes," Max said. "Absolutely. I'll be in better shape by then anyway."

"I think you're in pretty good shape now," Camilla said, shocking herself with her own forwardness.

Max laughed. "You must like me," they said.

Time was passing strangely now.

During the day, Camilla would fish and then Max would prepare it. They'd spend their free time talking, or mostly just sitting quietly together, taking in the vulnerable beauty of the natural world around them, the mountains and the fir trees and the evergreens and the birches.

Max was patient and gentle with her. At night they slept holding each other, clothes on.

Though this liminal period of time was marked by waiting—for Orchid to get back, or for the time to come to head north without her—Camilla found herself wishing they could be suspended in this in-between space of anticipation forever.

In the mornings, Camilla would walk into the thick tree line and fields of yellow, returning with her catch.

This morning, though, Camilla came back to the campsite empty-handed.

"The hotter it gets, the less I'm finding," she said, lowering herself down on the ground next to Max.

"I know," they said. Their stomach growled.

"I know what you're thinking," Camilla said.

"Can you blame me?" Max asked. "We've been waiting a long time."

"But what if she gets here and we're gone? We'd never see her again."

Even as she said these words, she felt a sinking feeling that told her she was being overly optimistic. If Orchid hadn't returned by now, she probably wasn't going to. But she couldn't let her go, not yet. "Let's give it a few more days. One week, maybe," she said. "Deal?"

"Deal." Camilla was surprised at Max's willingness to compromise.

Camilla put her hand over Max's, feeling how warm their skin was.

"We do need food and water for this week, though," they said.

Camilla sighed. "I'll find us something."

"I can help."

"No offense, but that's not really your strength," she said, affectionately. "You and your tofu bricks. Did you ever have to find your own food growing up?"

"No," Max admitted. "But speaking of which, I wanted to tell you. Why I left." Max wiped the sweat from their upper lip on the back of their hand. "I didn't mean to keep it a secret for so long. I just didn't know how to bring it up."

Camilla waited for Max to go on.

"The main thing was that everyone was only allowed to have one kid."

"Oh," Camilla said. "That's . . . definitely a stance to take."

"Yeah. Population control. They didn't want us to get bigger than we had resources for. They basically thought population growth was part of the reason everything collapsed. So they kept our numbers tight."

"How did they enforce it?"

"Most people got preventative surgeries. Like, had their tubes tied, after they had their first child."

"Not everyone?"

"No. Some people didn't want to. But then they'd be compelled to get abortions, basically, which was a best-case scenario. Or . . ."

Max trailed off. Camilla stared at them.

"So, sometimes, people tried to keep their pregnancies a secret. Then of course they wouldn't be able to hide it once they did have a baby, and the committee would make them choose."

"Make them choose what?"

"If they had the baby, one of them—like, the parent or the baby—would have to leave."

"You mean they'd have to give up their infants? What would they do with them?" Camilla's voice was rising in panic.

"I overheard doctors talking about leaving the babies in the woods. I never found out if it was true."

"What?" Camilla said, startled by the violence of this.

"But people didn't usually choose themselves. They usually opted for their babies to stay, and then they'd just kind of vanish. Leave or, I used to suspect, be killed."

"Be killed?" Camilla repeated. "Max, that's . . . a wild thing to accuse your own community of."

"No, I know," Max said. "Maybe I'm making that up."

"But you believe it," she said. She already knew them so well.

"Yeah. I mean, people would just disappear. Where did they go, if not to die?"

Camilla's head was swimming.

"I'm sorry," Max said. "I know that's a lot. I know it sounds totally fucking crazy. But it's just how things were."

"Keep going," Camilla said. "Did something happen that made you leave?"

"My mom got pregnant," they said quietly now, sounding very sad.

"How old was she?" Camilla said.

"She was in her forties," they said. "Old enough for it to be a surprise, but not too old for it to be impossible. I think maybe she thought those days were behind her and wasn't careful."

"Who got her pregnant?"

"I don't know." This question clearly annoyed Max, and they weren't trying to hide it. "I don't know who my father was, either. I don't really think it matters, do you?"

"I guess not," Camilla said, flushing. "I never really thought about it like that. I'm sorry I keep interrupting you. Please go on. So, your mom was pregnant. But she already had you . . . Oh god." She started to fill in the blanks. "How did you find out?"

"I overheard some stuff. I didn't want her to have to choose between herself and the baby. So I left."

"Why couldn't she just have an abortion?" Camilla couldn't help but ask.

Max was quiet for a moment. "It's a good question," they said.

"I don't mean to pry," she said. "It just seems like . . ."

"It's okay," Max said. "Honestly I think I was looking for an excuse to leave."

They were silent for a few moments. Camilla held her tongue. She had interrupted enough already.

Finally Max said, "She would have just had the abortion, probably, if I'd stayed. And it would have been fine. Not a big deal. We would have moved on. I didn't give her that choice, though. This isn't as valiant as it sounds. It was maybe selfish. Maybe I used her pregnancy as an excuse to do what I wanted to do regardless."

"I don't think that's true," Camilla said. "You're very brave to leave by yourself."

"I didn't leave by myself."

"Oh," Camilla said, backtracking. "Sorry, I . . ."

"No, it's okay. I left with someone. Sterrett."

"Did she die?" she whispered.

"They," Max said. "And no, not that I know of. They just decided it was too hard out here. They went back."

"They went *back*? Did they know all the things you did?"

Max nodded. "That and worse. The devil you know, I guess."

It was painful to hear this story, but it was also a relief. These secrets had been heavy between them. Camilla needed to know everything about Max, even the darkness.

"Were you in love?" Camilla asked, addressing the sudden pang of jealousy. "With Sterrett? Did they break your heart?"

"I loved them a lot," Max said. "But we were more friends than anything else. It's not like with you, if that's what you were wondering."

It was, but she wasn't going to admit it. It was beside the point of this story. Instead she said, "I still don't feel like I have a good sense of what your life was like."

"What else do you want to know?"

"If you were home, what would you be doing now?"

"Depends on the day," they said. "But . . . maybe going to the nearest landfill and scrounging for metal."

"What would you do with the metal?"

"Melt it down. Build solar panels. Build magnets. Build anything, really. Or if I wasn't on metal duty I'd be helping make clothes. Or cooking. I don't know."

"It sounds busy," she said.

"There was always so much work to do," they said. "It was an exhausting life, but we didn't really question it. It was how we survived."

"I certainly get that," she said. "Though your way sounds much more organized than what we do."

"It was organized by design," Max said. "Rigid, even. They kept us in line. Kept us distracted from the bad things."

"Worse than the one-child policy?"

"Sterrett had been sexually abused. By our leader."

"Oh my god," Camilla said.

"And I'm sure others were, too. I think it was an open secret. We weren't really allowed to make complaints about anything because we were told over and over that the only thing that mattered was saving the planet, living in harmony with it. Our individual grievances didn't matter. Who we were didn't really matter, either. We were a collective."

"There's something so cynical about that," Camilla said.

"I agree," Max said.

"Why tell me now?"

"Because I love you," Max said, simply. "And I'm so fucking hungry that maybe my judgment is clouded."

Camilla laughed and put her hands on either side of their face. Her palms were cold and sweaty even though it was hot out, as though Max's story had drained her of blood.

"I love you, too," she said. "I'll find us something to eat."

"I would eat the grass," Max said.

"You might have to," she replied.

Perhaps it was the fact that she finally knew the truth about where Max had come from, or maybe it was just that she needed to be touched so badly it overrode her fear, but the next day she woke up and felt ready for more.

Max opened their eyes and smiled.

She placed a hand on their sharp hip bone.

"I want to try again," Camilla said.

"Are you sure?" Max said, their eyes opening wider. They were awake now. "We really don't have to. I don't want you to do anything you don't want to do."

"I know," she said.

She sat up, pulling her shirt off, wiggling out of her pants.

"You're really beautiful," Max said, gazing at her naked body.

Camilla had not really considered her own beauty before. Her life had been about the basics of survival for so long that she had never developed any sort of vanity. If she was muscular it was because of all the physical labor she did. If her hair shone, it meant she was eating well. If her skin was tan it was because there was nowhere to hide from the sun. There certainly weren't any mirrors in the wilderness.

Maybe she didn't feel beautiful, but she did feel strong and, if not young anymore, confident in what her body could do, in how it had kept her alive, and finally ready for someone to appreciate it.

"Now you," she said, and then knelt beside them on the mattress and helped them undress.

Max was skinny from going so long without enough to eat. Too skinny, but gorgeous anyway, light brown skin and tufts of black hair that gathered in soft, scraggly patches. A fernlike smell was wafting off them, sweet and earthy, kind of like the B3k bricks they'd kept in their bag for so long. Camilla felt drunk off it. She wanted to press her nose to their collarbone and huff their skin.

Then, going on instinct, Camilla climbed on top of them, lowering her chest to theirs, gently avoiding putting any weight on their bad leg by straddling them as wide as she could.

"Wait," Max said. "Kiss me."

She pressed her mouth to theirs, drinking them in.

Max placed their hands on either side of her hips and maneuvered her until her pelvis hovered directly above theirs. "Is it okay?" Camilla asked, balancing on one elbow while she took them into her hand.

Max nodded. "I want to be against you," they said. "Just not inside you, okay? That's not how I think about my body."

"Of course," she said, thrilled. This was how she wanted them, too, she realized, opening herself up to what her body was telling her. She didn't want to be penetrated by Max, she wanted to envelop them.

She kept her mouth on theirs and moved their hands to her chest. They didn't need to continue guiding her hips; she wanted to set the pace. She felt powerful, being in charge like this. Max seemed pleased, too. She could tell by their breathing, their noises. They were letting her take the lead, much as she had been for the past few weeks. This was exactly how Camilla had imagined it; her on top, Max overcome with pleasure below her, *because* of her. She was still taking care of them, in this way.

Max sat up and Camilla wrapped her arms and legs fully around them. They pressed their forehead into her chest, snug below her chin. As they moved together she remembered the fact that Max hadn't even wanted Camilla to stay with them at all, but had eventually softened to her help, her nurturing. She felt certain that because of this she was seeing a side of Max no one else had ever known; the side who accepted help and care. Who received pleasure. Who wasn't alone.

Max came with a shudder against her, and she rolled off them and to the side. She knew enough to know she hadn't had an orgasm, but she was okay with that. One thing at a time.

Max propped themself up on an elbow and then kissed her. She was thirsty; the inside of her mouth was like sandpaper and her teeth felt like they were wearing sweaters. But she forgot to feel self-conscious.

The sunlight was turning Max's sweat into golden nectar as it dripped down the sides of their face. Camilla wanted to become a hummingbird and sip it.

Max kissed her once on each cheek, then her forehead, her chin, and finally her mouth. It was such a strange and wonderful thing, this mutual adoration. She wasn't sure she'd ever get used to it. And then, because she couldn't help it, she bit their cheek.

APRIL 15, 2041

Hi, baby,

I think maybe it was a mistake to try to drive up the East Coast. Have you read about what's happened down here, in North Carolina? I've never seen destruction like it. The roads are barely usable. It's going to take me for-freaking-ever to get north.

But I do feel a little safer in terms of people. I don't know. I don't think anyone would follow me here; I don't think they'd want to risk it.

I never got to see the Carolina coastline before it started disappearing. I haven't traveled much at all, except my one trip across the country and now my journey back. Here, the sea level is rising *while* the coastline is sinking. A killer combo. Anyway, the highway on my map no longer exists, so that's going to be fun.

I'll figure out how to get north without it. Don't worry.

I found an abandoned garage to pull the car into for the night. So I'll write to you as long as I have daylight, which won't be long, but I'll get as much down as I can. I've gotten pretty good at scribbling quickly, over the past couple of weeks of this.

Back to where I left off.

For the next few weeks, though he'd told me not to, I kept calling your father.

Sometimes he'd pick up. Usually he'd let it go to voicemail.

Sometimes he'd answer just to say, "Kelly, stop," or, "Kelly, I'm getting a restraining order."

Once I heard you singing in the background and I felt my heart shattering.

"Kelly, you no longer have custody," he'd say. "Kelly, if you ever want to see Orchid again, just come home and we'll figure it out." He was making me hate my own name. Kelly this, Kelly that, Kelly, I hate you.

Finally he changed his number, and I had no way to reach him. Or you, for that matter.

I tried calling the cell phone company to get them to tell me what his new number was, but every time I did that, they notified him that someone was trying to access his account, and gave me nothing. I emailed him over and over until I got a bounceback saying the email address didn't exist.

I was bereft.

And I was also distracting myself with work. And with Vero.

I'm not sure which to tell you about first. I guess they're not so separate.

The team Vero had assembled was good—hackers and engineers and activists—but not as good as me. They'd gotten as far as they could go breaking into the government databases where the scientists were being tracked. It was clear that I was needed, and I liked that feeling.

Each morning I'd talk to the group about what we were going to do, and then I'd help them do it. I liked being in charge. I even liked that behind my back they'd started to call me Mom, and Vero Dad. It was sweet, even if the word *mom* made my stomach hurt with missing you.

I was more in love with Vero than I ever had been. He'd really become an adult. He was totally self-assured, so brilliant and brave. I loved how everyone else looked up to him and how I was the only one who got to sleep in his bed at night. I was so attracted to him I thought I might lose my mind. Or maybe I already had. I know you don't want to hear about that. But sex is important. It's part of how we love each other. You'll learn that someday.

Our group was growing. Vero kept inviting people to come live with us. Some of the people were starting to build a new compound where more of us could live. There were a lot of newcomers.

I noticed the way they looked at Vero.

One day I found him having a close, intimate conversation with one of the new women at a picnic table outside. His hands were on her knees and she was whispering in his ear. I couldn't handle it, seeing him so focused on someone else like that. I could tell he wanted her. He was making the same face he'd make at me.

I'd never been the jealous type, but I think your father broke something in me. I started becoming paranoid, obsessively needing to know every time Vero talked to a woman without me there. Technically it wasn't just the women who were a threat, but for some reason that's who my jealousy landed on. I felt I couldn't compete with people who were different from me, but I wanted to be the only woman who got to have him. Vero was still poly, of course, so it was more complicated than other people being a threat. In his mind, he could be committed to me *and* interested in other people. For me, that was a betrayal.

Finally one night in bed I said: "I need you to commit to me, or I can't do this."

At first he laughed.

"We haven't even talked about what we're doing together," I said, trying not to cry. "Do you love me? Do you want to be with me and only me?"

I'd told him about Rick's cheating. He knew how triggered I was.

And he said all the right things. He always did. "Of course I love you," he said, reaching for me and pulling me close. "I've always loved you. I will always love you."

"But?" I said.

"You know I don't believe that people own each other."

I let myself cry, then. He held me, despite the fact that he was causing my anguish.

"You can sleep with whoever you want, too," he pleaded. "I just want us to be free and happy."

"I don't want anyone but you," I said.

"Maybe right now, but that won't always be true," he said. "I'll always be here for you. Can't that be enough?"

"Can you just not sleep with *everyone*?" I tried.

He laughed again. "Kelly."

"Please."

"Don't make me change who I am," he said. "You love me. If I was monogamous, I wouldn't be me."

"I do love you," I said. "I also hate you."

"I understand your anger," he said. "And I can take it."

"How about this," I said. "Just don't do it in front of me."

"Deal," he said, and I think we were actually both happy with this arrangement. If not happy, then at least content.

As long as I could pretend that I was the only person he was intimate with, things were okay. He made me laugh, he listened to me, he made me feel strong and capable and good.

I hope that you know a love like this. Even if it doesn't last. My nights, when I had him to myself, were filled with magic. I woke up smiling, confident, calm. It does change you, to be treasured. It makes things possible in a way you can't imagine before you've felt it.

And I needed to be my best self. During the day, we were getting closer and closer to finding what we needed.

There were setbacks, of course. Sometimes I wondered if the government was on to us, if they were leading us on wild goose chases down into the depths of empty servers. We made a lot of wrong turns. We fell into traps set for us. But it wasn't anything we couldn't recover from.

I was careful about covering our tracks. We were virtually untraceable.

Vero was losing patience. He never said so, but I could tell. A few times he came into the room where we worked and wordlessly looked over everyone's shoulders. He made people nervous. He was also lighting a fire under them. Everyone longed for his approval. We didn't have it yet.

After we worked, we ate communally. One of the floors of the building housed an indoor garden, a sort of greenhouse. We grew all kinds of veggies and beans and fruit. It wasn't a ton of food—enough to keep the hunger at bay and no more—but it was fresh and delicious. I hadn't had access to fresh vegetables probably ever. By the time produce hit the grocery store it was usually wilting and sad. I missed eating with you, but it was such a relief to no longer have to prepare meat. I hoped to never touch it again.

I hung out with Madhuri as often as I could, but she was usually with Len, and I still hated his guts. I think he knew how much I hated him and fed off it. He liked to fuck with me. He liked to say nasty things to Madhuri in my presence and then watch me struggle not to react. He interrupted both of us, me and Madly, constantly. It was like our words, our opinions just didn't mean anything.

One night I said to Vero, "I know you love Len, but he's seriously a misogynist."

He groaned.

We were lying in bed. I was facing him, but he was on his back, looking up.

"Do you really want someone who hates women so much to be part of the movement?" I asked.

"We agree on the things that matter," he said.

"Like?"

"Like how important the work you're doing is."

"Ah," I said. "So we're a one-issue party. Got it."

He groaned again. "Kelly Green."

"Yes?"

"I love you."

I said, "Stop. Talk to me about this. I don't want to compromise my feminism because you've chosen to befriend a men's rights-er."

"Technically, Madhuri chose him."

"Okay, but . . ."

He said, "You don't think I know how fucked up the men's rights movement is? You don't think being raised as a girl showed me what it's like to be a woman in America?"

"Being raised as a girl isn't the same thing as being one," I said.

"I'm not saying it is."

"I just wish you'd admit how loaded the concept is. How problematic it is for Len to be here at all."

"I'm trying to tell *you* that it's loaded," he said. "You're the one who isn't listening. My allegiance to Len isn't because he's a man. It's because he's more devoted to the climate cause than anyone I've ever met. More than you, more than Madhuri. He knows it's the only thing that matters. There are no gray areas for Len, and there aren't for me. Not when it comes to the mission."

"But what about how he treats her?" I said.

"Maybe we should avoid talking about this," he said, not willing to criticize his friend. "I have a bad feeling about where it's going."

"Fine," I said.

I didn't bring it up again. Not for a while, at least.

And then one morning in the computer bay, everything changed.

One of the engineers shouted, "I'm in." We all rushed to his computer. He'd accessed the desktop of some high-ranking employee. There, we found folders keeping track of scientists around the world who were researching practical climate-change solutions.

From there, we found it all.

There was a man in Maine who was working on a new way to build houses and their foundations out of super-powerful magnets. The houses *floated* two to three feet off the ground. It meant they were safe from flash floods and earthquakes.

A woman in Texas was using solar power for desalination.

A team in Ghana had figured out how to grow rice—which typically releases more methane than the cattle industry—in a way that was actually *reducing* the amount of methane in the air.

A PhD candidate in Montreal was making cheap gas masks for civilians to wear in areas where the air pollution was at carcinogenic levels.

A team in Arkansas had discovered how to use solar-radiation modification to block the sun, which would, if used correctly, refreeze the poles.

A college student in Toronto had successfully achieved nuclear fusion, and was able to recreate it. That would mean no more need for fossil fuels.

But they were all being watched, their every movement documented and saved to the portal we hacked into. There were spies planted in labs around the world, pretending to be students and researchers, all the while reporting back to the government, making sure no one got too close to publishing their findings. The minute they did—if they even so much as mentioned taking their results to the public—a SWAT team would take them in the night.

Their families were told they died, but they were rotting in top-secret prisons.

This was like something out of a nightmare.

We found their work, though. We saved it. We replicated it.

At one point it occurred to me that we should try to find someone who was engineering a sustainable food source. Something with minimal damage to the environment that could grow easily regardless of the weather and provide maximum nutrition. That's when we sought out the scientist in London who was trying to genetically modify a fast-growing wild bean. Though she wasn't on the government's list, we started saving her work, too.

And—not to give myself too much credit here, but—I read about a woman who had found a way to pull carbon from the air and put it back in the earth. Kind of a reverse fracking. I started looking into whether or not we could do that on the land where we were. If we could drill deep enough to reach the place in the earth's crust where we could safely tuck away the emissions we collected.

It was just a hunch, but I turned out to be right. We could do it. Vero got to work recruiting people who could drill the hole, and I started keeping track of the woman whose research had inspired me. She was remarkable. It was such a simple solution, but I felt it had great symbolism. There were few other people thinking about how to undo climate change in the way she was.

I wanted to start releasing everything we found to the public immediately, but everyone else thought we should wait, release it all at once. Make a bigger splash. I was overruled, but that was okay. I saw their point. It wouldn't get any attention to publish small solutions. It never had.

I could be patient. I could wait for more information so we could release it all at once.

Except, of course, that meant I'd be gone longer. Away from you while we waited for more information to collect.

Months had already passed.

"I can't just sit here and wait while we collect data," I said to Madhuri one morning over coffee, looking out into the expansive pine forest that protected us.

"You can't leave," she said. "We need you."

"What if there was something more we could be doing?" I said.

"Like?"

"What if we brought the scientists here, instead of just watching them work from afar? What if we made them part of our community?" I was thinking of my carbon scientist.

She was shaking her head at me and smiling. "You're too brilliant for this world," she said.

Vero liked the plan, too. Before I knew it, we were sending people out into the world, recruiting scientists to come live and work alongside us. They wouldn't know we'd already hacked into their work until they were here.

That was fine with most of them, once they understood what we were doing. Once they understood the risks they'd unknowingly been taking. Once we showed them where their colleagues were.

We did convince my carbon scientist to come, too. She helped us set up the machines that began pulling carbon from the air, worked with the engineers to drill into the ground without causing too much damage to the surrounding ecosystem.

All the scientists we brought in worked well among us. We supported their creativity and their hard work. It was in our labs that the scientist from London finally cracked the genetic code of the super bean. We started cooking it into squares, making something that was not quite loaves of bread and not quite blocks of tofu but some indescribable texture in between. It tasted like nothing, but also like everything. It's what saved us. I was no longer hungry all the time. I didn't realize how much the deprivation had been putting me on edge.

The compound grew and grew. We built houses using the technology they were developing. We were making the world's first totally climate-safe community. It was so beautiful to watch it unfold. It gives me the chills just thinking about it. I was still waiting for the go-ahead to release the data, but in the meantime, bringing in the scientists was scratching my save-the-world itch.

It wasn't just the science that allowed us to blossom. Relationships started to form between our original group and the newcomers. It was all so beautiful and inspiring.

And then: a year had gone by.

I'd tried every way I could think of to reach you. But I was starting to get worried that if I contacted you, my location could be traced. What we were creating needed to be protected just as much as you did. I was in an impossible situation. But I also felt I was doing this work for you; so that you could have a chance to grow up, be safe. The future was so bleak otherwise. As your mom, I do think I had an obligation to make the world safer for you. Even if it meant being apart. I imagined that as soon as we were done, I'd come get you.

Anyway. It was around this time that Madhuri and Len got married.

There were over a hundred of us by then. Madhuri wore a white T-shirt and white jeans and Len wore the same disgusting sweats he was always in, but they were both radiant, and I put on a happy face for her, even while thinking about what a mistake she was making.

Vero married them. I was the maid of honor. I toasted their love, even though I didn't believe it, and our friendship. We danced until morning.

It was important that we maintained traditions like this. Otherwise, what were we fighting for?

I was even managing to overlook my feelings about Len. He was still a loser—he wasn't funny, handsome, or interesting—but Madhuri loved him and that counted for a lot. He made her happy, somehow. She didn't seem to mind that he pinched her ass in front of everyone else or that his temper had a hair trigger. So who was I to judge him for her? I was learning to be accepting, forgiving.

The only thing missing was you.

Vero knew the toll it was taking on me, to not have you there. "Soon," he'd promise me. "We'll be done so soon."

"You owe me thirty grand," I said.

Every day we found more people all over the world who were creating technologies that amazed me. And every day I wondered: Would we save them before it was too late? The government was moving so quickly. People would be there one day and gone the next, their offices burned to the ground, their labs destroyed, their identities erased. It was terrifying to watch it unfold, even though we were so removed.

The government, of course, had noticed that we were disappearing the scientists they were trying to take out, which meant we were more vulnerable than ever. They'd begun to look for us. They figured out who we were. Our faces were on the news, spun with stories about eco-terrorism. My face. I wondered if you'd seen it.

Vero assured me they had no way to find us. I made sure of it on the backend.

Soon, sooner than I'd expected, we got news that the governments of the world were uniting. Just as Vero had foretold.

I had believed Vero when he told me this would happen, but it's always nice to have proof that someone is right—especially when you've put all your trust in them.

Vero had predicted this wouldn't happen for another decade, though. Which meant that the climate emergency was, perhaps, more immediate than we'd realized. If the United World Government was going to be the public's salvation, then there was something imminent we'd need saving from.

We found it quickly, in emails: a secret deal was being struck with various big players in the oil industry to ramp up fracking. But if there was a global increase in drilling, that would mean the world was going to heat up faster than anyone had calculated. They were manufacturing a crisis. We knew there was more to it, but couldn't figure it out yet.

Do you remember when they first announced the United World Government? You were probably old enough to pay attention to the news. It was presented as such a good thing. Finally, world peace in the face of climate change, the common enemy.

But we knew what the public didn't: they were only uniting so they could save themselves. Class loyalty trumps everything. It's bigger than borders, than nationalism. This was wealthy people reaching across continents and pulling themselves together into one irrefutable power. It wasn't something to be celebrated. It was fucking terrifying.

Vero again promised me we were safe. We weren't in a place that appeared on the map.

I wondered if you were safe, in our little blue house with the man I used to love so much. Not a second went by that I wasn't thinking of you.

One morning one of the engineers let out a little scream from her computer. "Oh my god," she said, her face turning white.

We all rushed over.

"What?" I demanded. "Did you find something?"

"They're building these huge fucking space shuttles," she said, pulling up plans. "Designed for people to live on."

We watched as the news over the next few months shared what we already knew. The UWG announced what, to the public, would seem like a revelation: civilian space travel. For the first time, space tourism was possible. Instead of taking airplanes around the world, people were taking rocket ships. It was insane to me. The amount of fuel needed for this new vanity industry was speeding up global warming faster than anything before it. And at a time when natural disasters were eclipsing everything else? It was pure evil.

It sounded insane, but it also made perfect sense to me. Of course they were doing that. They *wanted* to speed it up.

Vero didn't seem surprised, either, just sort of grim and determined.

"We'll stop them," he said. "What we're doing now—it has to work."

I wasn't so sure. "What good are all these climate-change solutions if they're about to increase the damage by tenfold? None of this holds up. It's all based on calculations that are no longer accurate."

He put his hands on my shoulders and looked me deep in the eyes. As always I felt the room spin, butterflies in my stomach, a melty feeling in my hips. He had such power over me.

"Trust me," he said, and so I did.

Okay, that's it, babe. I'm out of light. I can barely see this. I'll send this first thing in the morning and then continue onward. I'm getting so close. I can almost feel you.

Love,
Mom

8

AVA
2078

"WE HAVE TO DECIDE WHERE TO GO FROM HERE," AVA said to Brook when they were back on the highway, the military base and all its horrors safely in the distance.

"You mean we *get* to decide," Brook corrected her. "We're free. We've never had choices before." She paused. "Well, maybe you have, but I haven't."

This stung, but Ava let it go.

Orchid said, "I was hoping you'd come back north with me. Not for my sake, but because there's still a chance Camilla could help us call July."

"Or we could go back to Inside and break down the door," Ava said, cutting her off before she could argue this point further.

Brook looked crestfallen. "Mom, after all this, you'd want to go *back*?"

"I mean," she said. She didn't know what she meant, though. Or what she wanted, other than things that were impossible. Continuing north with Orchid meant putting an incredible amount of trust in her, and she wasn't sure she was ready to do that.

Orchid said, "I'll let you two discuss it," and backed off, pretending to look busy examining something on the side of the road.

"Mom, we should stay with Orchid," Brook said, firmly. "This was our backup plan, remember?"

"That's really what you want?"

"What I want is to find July."

Ava suddenly felt that she didn't know what to do with her arms. They hung awkwardly at her sides. She wanted to use them to hug Brook, but Brook hadn't allowed anyone to touch her since the assault. She folded them across her chest, but that felt too closed off, and she dropped them again.

"Mom, why are you so fidgety?" Brook asked, sounding more annoyed than concerned.

"Because I'm anxious that you don't know what you're signing up for." She sighed. "Orchid lives in a shack in the woods with a bunch of random people. They hunt for food and they risk their lives every time there's a storm. They don't have running water or air-conditioning. They shit in a hole. Is that really a life you want?"

"Yeah, it is. We've been shitting in holes for weeks. I don't care. And anyway, I don't think you're being serious about going back Inside. We literally sealed the door shut. We made it so the UWG couldn't get in anymore. Which means no one can get in. Including us. This is kind of our only option left. And besides, Orchid said we might be able to talk to July through her friend. Isn't that worth trying?"

Ava was too tired to argue, to explain to Brook that just because Orchid was likable and funny didn't mean she was always the best person to put your faith in. She called Orchid back over.

"We'll go with you," Ava said.

Orchid lit up. She started to say something excitedly, and then stopped, calming herself. "I'm so glad," she said. "I'm so, so glad."

"How do you know how to do all this?" said Brook, as Orchid tied their food into a bundle and then strung it up in the branches of a pine tree before they tucked in for the night.

They were far enough north now that there was evidence of creatures running around, squirrels and chipmunks and rats and even deer, and the food needed to be protected.

"My dad taught me," she said. "One night when I was like, fourteen or fifteen, or maybe even thirteen, I can't remember. He woke me up in the middle of the night and said, *Today's the day I teach you to become a man.*"

Brook giggled.

"He did not," Ava said, rolling her eyes.

"True," Orchid conceded. "But that's what he meant. Anyway, we spent basically the whole summer outside. He taught me how to hunt and fish and prep what we caught and cook it. How to build a shelter. What to do in a storm. What plants are safe to eat."

"That's awesome," Brook said, her eyes wide. Ava felt a surge of resentment. Brook never thought *she* was awesome, or at least hadn't thought so since she had been a little girl.

"How did *he* know how to do everything?" Brook asked.

"He took out a bunch of library books," Orchid said with a shrug. "I didn't really ask. I was just relieved he seemed set on teaching me himself, versus making me read all that."

"You're lucky," Brook said.

Orchid gave a sheepish smile. "I really didn't think it would ever come in handy, but"—she gestured around them—"maybe he knew something we didn't. It was like a switch got flipped. He had this sudden urgency about it."

"He probably just watched the news like everyone else," Ava said.

"I don't know," Orchid said. "It was like something changed in him overnight. Like he suddenly realized something. Or someone said something."

"Like who?" Ava pressed.

"I don't know," she said, looking embarrassed. "Never mind."

"Sorry, I'm just curious."

"No, it's fine. I forgot how you like to poke holes in my logic and make me feel like an idiot."

Ava felt her cheeks redden. "Oh god," she said. "Do I do that?"

"You totally do that," Brook chimed in.

"I'm horrible," she said, and then, correcting herself, said, "For what it's worth, I never mean to make anyone feel like an idiot. I'm sorry."

"The plight of being the smartest," Orchid said with a wink, letting her off the hook. "We're getting close to where I settled. Soon you'll meet my friends and you'll have other people to talk to, not just boring old me."

"You're not boring," Brook said.

Ava chimed in, "You've never been boring." She hadn't meant to say something so nice, but now that it had left her mouth, she couldn't take it back. Orchid beamed.

Later, when Brook was asleep and a hearty fire was warming a small circle of tepid night air, Orchid whispered, "Do you ever think about the fact that it's not really a matter of *if* there is life on other planets, but whether or not those civilizations exist at the same time as ours?"

Ava tilted her head, surprised. "Do *you* ever think about that?"

Orchid nodded, looking a little shy. "Constantly," she said.

"Timing really does count for a lot, huh?" Ava said, and as the words left her mouth she realized she wasn't sure if they were still talking about aliens.

She stared at the campfire's dancing flames, watched the sparks lift into the air and then blink out. Her mauve uniform reeked of smoke and sweat. A few feet away, Brook was on the ground, curled onto her side. She looked peaceful. The only thing missing from her position on the ground was July, who in another life would be curled toward her. Ava wondered what July was doing right now, if she was somewhere asleep on her side, too, facing nothing but the memory of what she'd lost. There was a lump in her throat. She tried to think of something else. She was worried that if she started to cry about July, she'd never stop.

Orchid turned to her and placed a hand on her arm, at first lightly and then she tightened her grip. Their eyes met and Ava's heart rate quickened like it used to when she was young and Orchid looked at her like this.

"Ava, I can't stand it," Orchid said. "I've missed you so much. I feel it in my whole body."

Ava pulled her arm away, though it pained her to. She wanted Orchid as badly as Orchid seemed to want her, but she couldn't bring herself to allow it. It was too scary. She knew what it would lead to. It might feel good in the moment. But what good was a moment? Orchid was destined to disappoint her again. She couldn't imagine any other outcome.

"I can't," she said.

"Can't I just hold you?" Orchid said. "We don't have to do anything but lay here."

Ava shook her head. "We won't be able to just lay here."

Orchid looked bereft.

Ava searched for the words to describe how she was feeling. "There was a time when I could be reckless," she said.

"Me, too," Orchid nodded. "I was a reckless piece of shit."

"No, not like how you were," Ava said. "You might have been careless with who you hurt, but you were always very guarded with yourself. You never let me in, not really. I have to imagine you were like that with everyone before me, too."

"I didn't know how to be open," Orchid said.

"I know. I understand. But I became the opposite of that, after you. I was reckless with my body. I slept with everyone." Orchid's eyebrows rose, and her mouth fell open just a little, registering shock that she was trying to control. Ava kept talking. "None of it mattered. Nothing was sacred. No one could hurt me because you'd already hurt me the most. I was immune. But I'm older now, Orchid. The last person I was with, I knew her for twenty-two years before she touched me. Can you even imagine what that felt like, to know someone so well, and then have a sexual relationship?"

Orchid was quiet, crestfallen.

"I can't just jump back into something with you because you want it. Or even because I might want it, on some level." Orchid raised her eyebrows again. "Don't get any ideas," she said. "What I'm trying to say is that I'm different. Love is something different to me now. And I can't separate sex from love. I don't want to try to."

"I wasn't asking you to do that."

"What were you asking me to do, then?"

"I was hoping you could still love me." Tears were running down Orchid's face, and she made no attempt to wipe them away.

"But I don't even know you," Ava said. "And you don't know me. We've been apart for a lifetime."

"I do know you," Orchid whispered.

"You know an idea of me. You know the person you left. That girl is long gone. She became a mother. She lost a daughter. She had her life turned upside down in ways you'll never understand."

"Help me understand," Orchid said.

Ava sighed. "I feel like you're not hearing me."

"But I am," Orchid insisted. "I get it, okay? I don't know you. We're strangers. But now we get a chance to start over." She held a hand out. "Hi, I'm Orchid. It's nice to meet you."

Despite herself, Ava laughed and squeezed Orchid's calloused hand. "Hi."

"Would you like to get a drink sometime?" Orchid asked.

"Maybe," Ava said. Their hands were still clasped.

"I can work with maybe." Orchid smiled. Her front tooth was chipped and graying. "Maybe it's the start of yes."

Ava rolled her eyes. "You sound like a greeting card."

"Oh my god. Remember greeting cards? Remember fortune cookies?" Orchid was brightening, talking faster and faster, and louder. Ava motioned for her to keep quiet, but she ignored her. "Remember restaurants? Remember takeout? Remember when we met?"

"Remember when you left me?" Ava interrupted her. "Remember when we had this whole plan that we'd only go Inside if we could go together, and then at the last minute you jumped ship?"

"Remember when I was a fucking idiot?"

"Was?" Ava shot back.

There was a tense moment, and then they both erupted into laughter. Ava was laughing so hard she had to put her face in her hands. Tears leaked from her eyes as she tried to be quiet.

When they both calmed down, Orchid said, "I think we're going to figure this out."

"I think it's not going to look like how you want it to," she said.

"You know what," Orchid said, her face softening, "I'll take what I can get."

Ava reached over and touched her rough, strong hand. "Thank you," she said.

The next day, in the afternoon, when the sun was just a little too warm on their skin and the pine trees whispered in the wind, they reached the beginning of a path that had obviously been cleared with human hands.

Orchid turned around, grinning. "We're here," she said. Brook squealed.

The path was lined with luminous yellow wildflowers and sweet-smelling pines. It was protected overhead by branches that curved around it, making a tunnel, and footprints were visible in the dry dirt. Brook and Orchid began to skip ahead, but Ava was taking her time. Something rustled in the underbrush: a small brown lizard.

Ava worried about what this new community would be like, if they'd accept her and her daughter even after they knew what Inside had become. If maybe instead they'd resent her for the privileges they'd had while the rest of humanity was struggling to survive. She wondered what Orchid had told them about her, and what they'd expect their relationship to be. She felt self-conscious after the last few conversations with Brook and Orchid where they'd both called her out for being a know-it-all. What if she didn't know how to get along with people? What if she was truly unlikable?

But when the path opened up to a large clearing, there was no one there. Just mounds of debris where, she guessed, their homes had been. One structure looked like it had been shoddily re-erected, but otherwise there was silence.

"What the fuck," Orchid said.

"Where is everyone?" Brook asked.

Orchid ignored her and started screaming, "Hello?" She bellowed into the stillness. In response, a group of birds flew off a tree, the rustling of the leaves and their chirps the only sounds.

Finally Orchid turned and faced Ava and Brook with her hands on her hips and her brow furrowed. "Well, shit," she said. "It seems they left without me."

"What do you mean, left without you?" Ava asked. "Where did they go?"

"Well . . . ," Orchid started to say.

Ava felt an old familiar fury. "What are you not telling us?"

"They wanted to go north," Orchid admitted. "They said it was getting too dangerous here."

"And you knew they were leaving when you went to find me?" This was exactly what Ava had been afraid of; that Orchid would omit something important, that it would turn out to be a mistake to follow her all this way. She should have trusted her gut.

"Well, no," Orchid protested. "I didn't know *when* they were going. I thought maybe I'd be back in time."

"You thought, or you hoped?"

"Is there a difference?"

"Guys," Brook interrupted. "Can you please stop yelling at each other?"

Ava and Orchid stared at her. "Sorry," Ava said. "I'm allowed to be angry."

"She's right," Orchid said. "I should have told you everything. I was just afraid of losing you again."

"You don't get to create a version of the truth that best suits your needs," Ava said.

"I know," Orchid said, hanging her head. "I *know*."

There was nothing left to say. Orchid walked toward the one remaining hut and disappeared inside it. Brook simply sat on the ground and began digging into it with a stick. Ava was left alone with her anger and disappointment. Orchid had led them here under false pretenses, had given her hope when there wasn't anything to hope for. Had let her down once again.

There were things scattered around the outside of the hut; something that resembled a burlap sack, the remains of what looked like a fishing net. As far as Ava could tell it was all garbage.

She began rummaging through it, trying to find anything useful.

"I can go try to catch a fish before sundown," Orchid called from the hut, after some time.

"Whatever you want," Ava said, depleted. Her bones were tired. They'd come all this way for nothing. She began looking for dry twigs to start a fire, gathering them in her arms.

Orchid was so close to being the person Ava needed her to be and, like always, had fallen short.

Then, suddenly, she heard the sound of someone running, and a woman burst through the trees into the clearing, wielding a stick sharpened to a point, looking wild and dangerous.

"Get behind me," Ava whispered to Brook.

"Hey!" the woman screamed across the clearing at Ava. She looked feral. Behind her, another figure appeared. Ava dropped the kindling to the ground, worried it looked like she was stealing this wilderness woman's things.

"Hi there," Ava called, trying to sound friendly and not terrified. "We don't mean you any harm." Her heart was thudding in her chest. So this was how they were going to die: murdered by a deranged woods person.

"Get away from my house," the woman called.

"We didn't realize it was yours," Ava said. "I swear."

"What did you take?"

"Nothing," Ava said. "Really."

Orchid emerged from the hut. "Camilla," she cried.

Camilla? Ava looked more closely at the people at the edge of the woods. The woman was still clutching her sharp stick. Could this really be Orchid's friend? She looked dangerous.

"*Camilla,*" Orchid said again. "It's me."

"Oh my god," the woman exclaimed, and began to walk toward them, as though she was seeing a ghost. "I was so sure you were dead." She tossed her weapon to the ground.

Orchid held her arms out and Ava watched curiously as the woman stepped into them, clutching Orchid tightly.

"Jesus fucking Christ, Camilla," Orchid said. "I'm not dead, but you are trying to kill me."

"You came back," the woman said.

Orchid was hugging her back, tightly, lovingly. "Of course I did."

The other person was limping across the clearing now, with long black hair and wide eyes.

"We waited for you," they said.

Orchid said, incredulously, "Max? What happened?"

Brook and Ava hung back, watching the three unite.

"You okay?" Ava whispered to Brook, who seemed shy.

Brook nodded. "Just a little overwhelmed, I guess. I thought she was going to . . ." She trailed off.

Ava took her hand. "I know."

The woman finally seemed to notice Ava and Brook. "Holy shit," she said to Orchid. "You got her out."

"Not exactly," Ava said.

So Camilla *was* actually here, after all that. Ava wondered what that meant for the resentment that was still burning inside her.

The woman approached Ava and then, without hesitating, threw her arms around her. "I'm sorry," she said, squeezing her so hard that Ava had no choice but to hug her back. "I didn't realize it was you. You're not what I pictured."

When Ava was able to detangle herself from Camilla's startling embrace, she said, "This is my daughter, Brook."

"Brook," Camilla repeated. "Like the island. I used to live in Manhattan."

Brook nodded, still seeming shy but starting to warm up. "Hi," she said. "I guess technically I did, too."

"Inside," Camilla said. "I heard all about it."

"Wait," Brook said. "Are you the one with the sister? The sister we can call?"

"The one and only," Camilla said. "Though my father took the off-grid when they all left."

Ava's heart sank. Anytime she got her hopes up about July, those hopes were crushed. She was right not to trust Orchid's promise of a way to call July. It had always been too good to be true.

"Your dad left you behind?" Orchid said, raising her eyebrows.

"Someone didn't give him much of a choice," Max said, side-eyeing Camilla.

She crossed her arms over her chest. "Well?" she said. "I needed to wait for you. And I had to babysit the injured."

Orchid was looking back and forth between the two of them as though there was more to the story. "I'm so glad you waited for me," she said, finally. "Even though it was a dumb move." Ava liked that Orchid was being hard on these people. Showed she still had a backbone in there, underneath all the remorse.

"We'll catch up to them," Camilla said. "We have to."

"We really, really do," Orchid said, looking sidewise at Ava.

She felt the tightness in her chest start to loosen. It was always so hard to stay mad at Orchid. Despite everything, Ava was already forgiving her.

Later, Orchid was racing against the sun to set up a place for them to sleep, even though they'd spent so long sleeping on the ground, and while she worked, Ava and Brook explored the edges of the campsite.

"I'm sad we missed everyone," Brook said. "It seemed like it would have been a nice place to live."

Ava agreed. It was beautiful here, on the side of a mountain. Peaceful.

"We'll find them soon," Ava said. "We can't stay here forever."

"So this is just what our lives are now?" Brook asked. "We wander from place to place, looking for people?"

Ava frowned. She wanted, badly, to fix the world for Brook, to make it a place Brook could enjoy living in.

"I do think our lives will be pretty migratory," she said.

"Don't use science words," Brook said. "It makes it sound like it's not real."

Ava sighed. Brook had a point. She was distancing herself from the reality of their situation by intellectualizing it, not feeling it.

"If I let myself actually acknowledge my feelings about this, I don't think I'll be able to hold it together," she admitted.

"You don't have to hold it together for me," Brook said. "I would rather you experience it with me."

A few feet away, a chipmunk darted out from underneath the brush, pausing in front of them before taking off again. Brook made a sound of pure delight. "That was the cutest thing I've ever seen," she whispered.

"Right?" Ava said. "They are pretty damn cute."

"I'm scared we won't survive more walking," Brook said.

"I know," Ava said. "Me, too. But we're with people who have been doing this for a long time now. If they've survived this long, it only means good things for us."

In the distance she could hear Orchid and Camilla talking, catching each other up on the events they'd missed.

"It must be nice to have friends," she said, more to herself than to Brook.

"I'm your friend," Brook said.

"You're my daughter," Ava corrected. "You don't have to be anything else."

She couldn't be sure, but she could have sworn that when she said this, Brook relaxed a little bit. As though a worry had been crossed off a list.

When the sun had set and a few stars began to twinkle above the horizon, the five of them sat in a circle around the fire and Ava dumped their last cans of beans into a pot, making a slimy pile.

"Oh, red beans," Max said, examining the contents of the can. "We had something like this where I come from."

"Oh, yeah?" Ava replied, absentmindedly, as she moved the pot over the fire.

"Well, sort of. It was a super bean. Genetically modified. It had all the amino acids you need in a day, or whatever. It was the only thing we ate."

Orchid had been gathering twigs to keep the fire going, but at this, she stopped what she was doing. "Your entire community lived off one plant?"

Max nodded. "It was the best thing for the environment."

Ava felt queasy. "What if something had happened to it?"

"What do you mean?"

"Have you heard of the potato famine?" Ava asked, trying not to sound condescending.

"Ava was a plant professor," Orchid explained to Max. Their eyes met, and Orchid nodded at Ava to go on. For a brief moment Ava felt them becoming a united front; like they were parents together, a team. She appreciated the support, the vote of confidence.

"Plants get diseases just like people," Ava said. "Crops can get taken out by viruses, bacteria, fungus. It's why it's not a good idea to rely on just one thing. In case something happens to it."

"Well, I guess it's good that nothing happened to it," Max said, sounding defensive.

"Mom," Brook whispered. "Be nice."

Ava pretended not to hear her. *Nice* was beside the point.

Ava woke in the night to ecstatic groans: the unmistakable sound of Camilla and Max fucking.

She rolled over. Enough moonlight was coming through the branches of their roof that she could see Orchid's eyes open, too, an amused little smirk on her face.

Brook, Ava, and Orchid were in a small hut that Orchid had quickly fashioned, sharing a dirty mattress that Camilla had somehow salvaged from the piles of debris that littered the campsite. Camilla and Max were in the adjacent hut, clearly thinking that having walls to separate them meant soundproof privacy.

"How long do you think this is going to go on for?" Ava whispered, as Camilla let out what seemed like an unnecessarily loud moan.

"I'm impressed it's lasted as long as it has," Orchid whispered back. "Oh, to be young."

"We were young once," Ava said, and she could almost hear Orchid's smile in the darkness.

"I can hear you," Brook said, and Ava stifled a laugh.

"Sorry, Brook," Orchid said. "Someday I'll build you your own house."

In the morning, after Ava got up and peed behind a tree, she joined the others in the main clearing just as Camilla was saying, "And she said she'd tie bits of a red shirt on the trees to mark their path. We'll definitely be able to follow it. I'm not worried."

"What are you not worried about?" Ava said, sitting next to Brook.

"Finding our people," Orchid said. "Up north, or wherever they went."

Ava stretched her arms up toward the sky. Her whole body felt stiff, as though the softness of the disgusting old mattress was foreign to her spine now that she was used to sleeping on the hard ground. The thought of walking again for weeks on end was not appealing, but she knew they couldn't stay. Finding this group of strangers aside, it was too hot here.

"Did you know the poles used to be tropical?" she asked.

They stared at her, waiting for her to continue.

"Millions and millions of years ago. Some people believe it'll go back to being that way soon. If there's any safe ground to get to, it's either very, very north, like Greenland, or very, very south, the Arctic. Of course, we don't know what has been laid bare by the melting ice. The Arctic sea ice was already completely melted by what, 2035? That's plenty of time to thaw out the corpses of extinct animals and the viruses that killed them. It might sound like paradise but it could also be more like a disease-riddled hell. There's no way to know, not now."

She was rambling, she knew.

"That's where they're going," Camilla interjected. "I mean, not Greenland, obviously, but up there. Northern Quebec, I guess."

"Great." Ava nodded. She could feel Orchid watching her. She knew how important it was to Orchid that she get along with her people. And she wanted to find a way to be Orchid's friend again.

Ava went on, trying to keep the conversation going, "I read a theory that said if we'd refrozen the poles, we could have reversed climate change. And that it wouldn't have been that hard to do."

Max spoke up. "There are lots of things that could have been done to stop or reverse it."

"How did they survive where you came from, Max?" Ava asked.

Camilla and Max exchanged glances, as though this was something she should not have asked.

"Sorry," she said. "Just making conversation."

"No, it's okay. It's kind of a long story. Decades ago, they stole technology from the government that could have been used to stop climate change, that makes it easier to live. With the weather and temperatures how they are."

Ava laughed, but stopped when she realized Max was being serious. "That's insane," she said.

"Yes," Max said. "I'm aware."

"What sort of technology are we talking about?" Orchid asked. "You got any of it with you?"

"Not really, but . . ." Max paused. "I knew how it all worked. I could recreate it, if I needed to. They trained us."

"Can you give us an example?" said Orchid.

"I mean . . . sure. One cool thing was, if you blast a certain kind of particle into the atmosphere, it reflects the sun and makes the temperature cooler."

"And you know how to do that?" Ava said.

Max nodded, weakly. "But you don't understand. All that stuff, it's evil."

"It's *evil,*" Ava repeated. "The things that could help us survive?"

She knew they were ganging up on Max, but she couldn't help it.

"It's cursed. It ruins people, when they have that kind of power," Max said, suddenly sounding small, yet defiant, like a child. "I don't want to recreate what happened there. So yeah, I didn't tell you. I'm not sorry."

Ava sighed, impatient. "We wouldn't become fascists," she said. "We would become people who didn't have to struggle every day for the rest of our lives. Why do you sound so superstitious? This wasn't a religious sort of thing, was it?"

"We had our own religion, in a way. We worshiped the earth. And the technology we used. It was all part of the belief system."

"So like, some sort of futuristic paganism?" Ava said, thinking with a pang how similar it sounded to Inside. "That sounds okay."

"Yeah, but . . ." Max looked at the ground. Ava knew she was making them uncomfortable, but she couldn't stop pushing. "There was other stuff, too. Bad stuff. I can't help but feel like it's all connected, you know? Maybe that's stupid. I've never really said it out loud before. But I can't separate the technology from how they treated us. It's all the same thing." They coughed. "Sorry, this is hard to talk about."

"You don't have to," Camilla said, rushing to their defense, which made Ava even more mad. "Go easy on them, okay?"

"Whatever," Ava said. "But if we get to where we're going and you know things that could make my daughter's life easier, you better share it."

Brook hadn't said anything since this argument started, but at this she said, "Mom. Please."

"What?"

"Just . . . don't bring me into this."

"Oh my god," Ava cried. She was at a loss. Everyone was being irrational.

She got up and stormed to the tree line, where she put her hands on her hips and tried to calm down. She was exhausted and hungry. She knew that was making everything feel worse.

After a few moments Orchid joined her. "I understand why you're upset," Orchid said.

"I don't get why no one else is as upset as me," Ava replied.

"There's something else," Orchid said, and Ava turned to her. "The group that Max was in. It sounds really familiar. The Winter Liberation Army. I swear I've heard that name before. Not from the news. I remember my dad muttering about it. They were domestic terrorists. I think . . . I think that's what my mom was involved with. I think that's what she joined when she left us."

"Your *mom*?" Ava said. She would not have admitted it, but it was hard for her to remember what Orchid had told her about her mother, other than her absence. It was so long ago that they'd discussed their parents.

Orchid shuffled her feet and nodded. "Pretty fucking weird, right?"

"Weird doesn't cover it," Ava said. "But if that's true, then we *really* need to get the full story from Max."

"Well, who knows how long we'll be walking for," Orchid said. "My guess is we'll have plenty of time to hear all about it."

"You don't want to ask now? If I were you, I'd be dying to know."

"Nah," Orchid said. "I'm sure I'll just be disappointed by the answer. You ready to hit the road again?"

"No, but yes," Ava said. "All I really want to do is lie down on the ground and never get up."

"Get used to it," Orchid said, and then smiled. For a moment, Ava let herself feel how she used to feel when Orchid smiled at her: disarmed and vulnerable.

As quickly as she let the wall down, she brought it back up. "I will," she said. "I always do."

APRIL 20, 2041

Hi, my sweet baby girl,

This is the home stretch. The last letter I'll write to you. I'll be there in a couple of days. I'm going to overnight this one to make sure it gets to you on time. At least, on time in terms of my arrival; I mean, I want it to get there before I do. Sorry. I'm feeling nervous, the closer I get. It's making it hard to write clearly.

Do you understand my nervousness? I bet it's annoying. I'd hate me, if I were you. That's what I'm nervous about, mostly. I know I've been writing as though I expect you to spend the time reading my words. That might feel like too much to ask. I'm the fucking worst. I'm not rallying for a pity party. I just . . .

God, I'm scared of how angry you might be at me, because I know I deserve it.

By tomorrow I imagine I'll make it to DC. There's supposed to be a stupid amount of traffic after that—that hurricane last year caused so much damage to the area that it's nearly impossible to drive through. So my guess is two days, maybe three, tops. Before you know it I'll be crossing the border into New Jersey, flying through the city, and heading upstate toward our little blue house, toward you.

I wonder what you think at this point. I hope you'll tell me soon.

I do want to finish this story. The end of it is important.

A lot happened that I'm not going to get into. Years had passed. I liked to pretend that time was passing differently for you, but I know it wasn't. You weren't in suspended animation. I know you were getting older. The older you got, the further away from me you became. I was probably fading in your memory. But you were always vivid in mine.

As I've explained, we were waiting on our scientists to finish their work before sharing it with the world all at once. We wanted to make a big splash. A huge statement that no one would be able to deny or look away from. We wanted to say: *Not only can we stop this, we can do it now. We have all the tools. Look, look. There's hope. Listen.*

There were a few people who were taking longer with their research than others, but they were of course working on the things that were the most complicated and important and would be just totally game-changing for the planet. So we waited for them.

Days, weeks, months, years flew by. I was thinking of you the whole time.

I still tried to call you. I searched for you online. It was like your father had hidden you away, out of sight, or maybe he hired someone to erase your digital footprint. The only information I could find was your school records, but of course that didn't include a way to contact you, since you were a child. At least he kept you enrolled in school. I saw my own name listed in your file as a known danger. If I were to contact them, they were instructed to alert the authorities.

Meanwhile, our community was still growing. New people came to us, built homes on the land.

Something strange had started to happen, now that our numbers were growing. People were becoming . . . I don't want to say religious, but that's what it felt like. The way our science was talked about, it was like it was being revered. Worshiped. I noticed people started drying B3k twigs and leaving them in windowsills, like odd little voodoo dolls. Sometimes before meals I'd see them clasping their hands in prayer.

I was also starting to wonder how large Vero was going to let the group get. I didn't really have a good sense of how big fifty acres was; sometimes we went on hikes, but more often than not we stayed put in the little clearing where the buildings were. It was hard to gauge how many we could actually contain comfortably.

So, never one to keep my mouth shut, one night over dinner, I asked him. We were sitting with Madhuri and Len eating our soft bland bricks of nutrients. Though I was still grateful for the steady supply of food, by this point I would have done anything for a French fry.

"What are you going to do about the amount of people here?" I asked. "We're going to run out of room at some point."

"What am *I* going to do about it?" His eyes twinkled at me. He loved to pretend he wasn't in charge.

"Actually, yeah," Madhuri said. "We can't just keep growing. You didn't buy the whole state."

Len said with his mouth full, "Population control, dude."

"What was that?" I said.

He swallowed. "Look, if it were up to me, no one would have kids."

"It's a good thing it's not up to you," Madhuri said, and he looked like he wanted to hit her. She even flinched as though he might.

Over the years I'd watched their relationship become . . . darker. He had no patience for her. She seemed afraid of him. It was upsetting to me to see my friend—who used to be so wildly brave we literally called her Madly—cowering in front of that dingus.

It had become a weird time for gender issues. The men's rights movement had actually gained traction, which meant the strides women had made in the fight for equality were being slowly pushed back. It was kind of crazy-making to watch. For my whole life men had been acting all pathetic and sad while women finally caught up to them in terms of pay and power. And then the scales shifted again and they had their power back, and now they seemed to be out for revenge. Even progressive lefty climate-change activists like Len. I mean, maybe especially guys like Len. Guys that felt they were owed something by feminism.

"Hey," I said to him. "What's your fucking problem?"

Madhuri looked down at her food.

"You better stay out of it," Len said to me.

Vero, ever the peacekeeper, said, "What sort of population control were you thinking, Len?"

"I mean, at a certain point you're going to have to stop letting people in," Len said.

"And?" Vero said, prompting him.

"And realistically I don't think anybody should be allowed to have more than one kid," Len said.

I just about choked on my food. "Are you kidding?" I said. "You want to have a birth-control policy?"

Vero put a cold hand on mine. "It makes sense," he said. "We don't want to be hypocritical here. We all know the best thing for the planet is *less* people, not more."

"No," I said, pulling my hand away. "That's what the *government* thinks. That's why we're doing all this!"

"I mean, they're not wrong about that part, though, don't you think?" Vero said. He was still speaking in that infuriating, gentle voice, like I was a child. "Fewer people means less damage. It's a simple formula."

Len looked like he was going to jump out of his skin with excitement. "I've been saying this for years, man."

"You have?" I asked. "You've talked about this before?"

Vero looked like he felt guilty, but maybe I was just projecting that onto him. He pushed his plate to the side. He hadn't taken a single bite.

"I think you guys are a bunch of misogynists," I said.

They laughed, but I wasn't kidding.

"This isn't about population control," I said. "This is about you controlling women."

"Easy," Vero said. "No one said that."

"You didn't have to," Madhuri said.

"I'm too tired for this," Vero said. He rubbed his temples.

I jumped back in, not wanting him to have an easy out. We were all tired. "What are you going to do? Arrest people who won't comply? Set up a jail here, just for pregnant people?"

"Of course not," Vero said, but he had no explanation for how they'd enforce it otherwise.

"Is this going to be part of the religion you're starting?"

Now they looked at me like I was crazy. "Don't act like you don't know what I'm talking about," I said. "We are two seconds away from one of you wearing ceremonial robes and giving blessings."

"Kelly!" Vero said. "You're taking it too far. This is a community founded in the name of science."

"Oh, please," I said. "As if people can't worship science." But then I couldn't think of what else to say, so I stormed off.

Later, Madhuri found me at my computer, doomscrolling. She pulled up a chair.

"What are we going to do?" she said.

We were alone in the room and so I put my face in my hands, let myself fall apart a little. "This is so fucked," I wailed.

"I think we should get the women together," she said. "Tell them what Vero and Len think about population control."

"You'd really turn on Len like that?" I lifted my face.

"You'd turn on Vero?"

"Hell yeah, I'd turn on Vero," I said, so forcefully that she laughed. "Like he turned on us," I added. "Now, and a decade ago." She stopped laughing.

And there it was—my old anger. I had never really resolved it, just buried it under layers of hero worship and physical chemistry and a desperate need for somebody, anybody, to call my family.

"Okay, okay," she said. "I don't think we are actually *turning* on anybody. We just need more numbers to make a point."

But a few nights later, Madhuri showed up to dinner with her lip cut and swollen.

Len was following her around like a sad dog. The guilt was written all over his face.

I took her aside the moment I could. "What the fuck did he do?" I hissed. I didn't mean to sound angry with her. But that's how it came out.

She recoiled from me. "I provoked him," she said.

"I'm worried about your safety," I said.

"If you're so worried about me, then I think we should reconsider organizing against the men," she whispered. "I got backhanded for bringing it up, okay? I don't know what would happen to me if he knew we were plotting something."

My heart sank. I wasn't going to do anything that would put her in more danger than she already was. "Okay," I said. "We can drop it for now."

She hugged me. I wanted to cry while she thanked me for understanding.

Over the next few days, the work was escalating, and it was hard to focus on anything else. Soon I was letting Vero hold me in bed again. Maybe I had been crazy, making a big thing out of nothing, like I always do, I thought.

It was an exciting time. In our research, we finally had everything we needed. One of the women I worked with had developed a way to send a push notification to everyone with a cell phone that was connected to Wi-Fi (it had taken her months—she was brilliant and thorough). We were going to send out a massive report detailing everything we'd found and everything our scientists had discovered. Vero had recorded a video to go with it; we knew it would be more compelling if it arrived with his face attached, the famous son of the senator.

But the night before it was supposed to be sent, something changed. I'm still not sure what.

Vero called a meeting. I assumed it was to congratulate us, give us a pep talk for what might be ahead. I was even looking forward to it.

It was the last week of March, warm enough to be outside in the evening without our jackets, so we met in the garden where a bunch of picnic tables were arranged under some solar-powered string lights. Sometimes a warmed earth felt nice. Silly to enjoy it, I know.

I planted myself on the edge of the group, alone. Madhuri and Len weren't there yet. And Vero was leading the meeting, so he couldn't sit with me. From afar I noticed he was dressed somewhat oddly; wrapped in several layers of clothing, though it was perfectly nice outside. It made him look older, somehow, and smaller, all swaddled like that.

When Madhuri finally arrived, Len trailing behind her, she had a black eye, and his hand was bandaged.

I scrambled to my feet, started to race toward them, but the look on Madhuri's face told me to stay away and I froze in place. They settled into a corner. I sat back down, but couldn't take my eyes off her.

Everyone else arrived and took their seats, and when it was finally quiet, Vero cleared his throat a few times. He held one finger up and began to cough, hacking so hard I had the urge to get him a glass of water, but I didn't. I stayed where I was. When he finally stopped coughing, he said: "It's come to my attention that some of you have different ideas for how to move forward with our information."

I was stunned. Who? What? I looked around. A few people shifted in their seats. Why hadn't he said anything to me?

Len stood up. Of course, fucking Len.

"Listen," he said, his voice booming. "We have a choice to make. We could do what we planned and send out our findings to the whole world and try to just trust that people will do the right thing."

My heart was pounding.

"Or," he said.

Vero glanced at me. I raised my eyebrows.

"Or," Len said, "we keep it for ourselves."

I jumped to my feet. "Wait, wait, wait," I said. "You've got to be kidding me. What good would that do?"

Vero cleared his throat again. I wondered if he had a cold. "We could control this one little corner of the world," he said. "We could protect our people and start anew."

My jaw literally dropped. They were in on this together. I found Madhuri's face. She looked just as shocked as I felt. Plus—the irony of the word *protect* while she sat there with a black eye.

I realized she and I—two people who used to be Vero's right and left hands—were now on the outside. I hadn't even realized when it happened. Maybe slowly over time. He had a new alliance, and it was with Len. They were just two men trying to save the world, and we were the women getting in the way.

"We know everything is about to collapse," Vero said. "The government wants to wash their hands of everyone but a select few. Who is to say that our findings would make a dent in what they've been planning for decades? And who is to say that the population would care enough to try to fix the problems? It's not like they've cared so far—they all knew what fossil fuels were doing, and kept using them anyway. So why wouldn't we do everything we can to protect ourselves and what we've built here?"

One of the scientists stood up. "It's not a bad call," he said. "We have everything we need to get through the dangerous years to come. We can use what we've invented right here. We don't have to wait to find out if the rest of the world will follow. Plus, it puts us at risk—contacting everyone like that. It would make us vulnerable to retaliation from the government."

Vero said, "I chose this part of the country for a reason. We're safe here, especially if we implement our new technologies. We could be okay, when everywhere else isn't. As long as we remain under the radar."

Other people stood up and spoke. There were a couple of people who expressed hesitation, but the majority of folks agreed with them. It seemed they'd all been thinking this for a long time. I'd been totally in the dark.

Madhuri was looking at me. *What the fuck?* I mouthed at her, and she shook her head at me as if to say, *I know.*

Vero said, "Let's take a vote," but I already knew how the vote would turn out. I could tell by looking at the faces around me.

"Wait," I said, scrambling to my feet.

"Yeah?" Vero said.

All eyes were on me. "Before we vote on this, we need to have a frank conversation about reproductive rights moving forward," I said, as loudly and bravely as I could.

Vero looked annoyed.

Len looked like he was going to punch me next.

"I just think if we're about to like, cut ourselves off from society forever, that everyone needs to know about your one-child-per-family plan," I said. There were confused murmurs. "Oh, you all didn't know, either? Well, Vero and Len think anything more than one baby is unethical, and they're going to enforce their beliefs."

Madhuri was nodding, urging me silently to go on, even though I could tell how scared she was.

"I'm not calling anyone out," I clarified. "I'm calling you *in.* Let's have a dialogue." I was doing my best to speak in their social justice language, praying it would subdue them. It didn't.

Len stood up. "You guys," he said. "This is ridiculous. We have one focus here, and it's the climate."

"Is that why you get to hit your wife?" I shot back. "Because nothing matters but the climate?" Lord, I could never keep my mouth shut.

There were murmurs in the group as everyone stretched to get a look at Madhuri, who was covering her face. I felt bad for putting her on the spot like that. But not bad for letting everyone know who Len was.

"Listen, whatever you think of me, *feminism* is not more important than the planet," he said. "How dare you try to weaponize it."

If feminism was my weapon, I wanted to murder him with it.

Vero stood then. "Listen," he said. "I think there's been some confusion. The women—and everyone with the capacity to give birth, Kelly—have full reproductive rights here."

He was reminding me that he was in the category I was trying to claim oppression for. This made things complicated. I knew that. I knew that he was a man who would also be impacted by reproductive restrictions. But then why wasn't he siding with me? Why was he trying to make me look like an idiot in front of everyone?

"That's not what you said," I cried. "You said you wanted to limit . . ."

Len cut me off. "Maybe you don't know what you're talking about," he said.

They were gaslighting me. I knew it while it was happening. But no one came to my rescue.

"Then why don't you tell me," I said.

Vero sat down heavily, as though standing was draining him. He said, "At some point we do need to be honest about the growth of this community versus our resources. But that point does not have to be now. Right now, we have a more important choice to make. Do we share what we know, or do we use it to make sure this group survives?"

It was clear what would be decided, and I couldn't bear to see it play out. So I stormed back to our room, pacing in circles and fuming until Vero came back.

"Please don't criticize me in public like that," he said. *He* had the audacity to be mad at *me.*

He took me by the arms and made me sit on the bed.

I had to keep myself from screaming. "What about my fucking daughter?"

He looked stricken, then. I think he'd forgotten, somehow. I'd basically talked about nothing but you for years. He must have just tuned me out after a certain point.

"All this time, I've been waiting to do this one thing so that I could go back to her," I hissed. "And now we're not even doing it?"

"Kelly, I'm sorry," he said. "It's for the greater good."

"No, it's not," I said. "If it was for the greater good you wouldn't be hoarding intelligence. You'd be sharing it like we planned. This is about running your little fucking cult."

I'd never called it a cult before. I'm not sure I really thought it was, but I wanted to get him where it hurt.

"I'm going to just send it out myself," I declared. "You can't stop me."

I saw rage register on his face. "You think you can go up against this entire community?" he said, almost laughing at me. "No one agrees with you. We would all come together to stop you. Physically. I'm sorry, Kelly, but you're not that powerful. You'd never even make it to the lab before we stopped you."

"I'm going to leave," I said.

"No," he said. "Kelly, you can't."

"I can't, or you won't let me?"

He stared at me as though he felt very sorry for me. "It's not safe. The second you're trackable—if your face is caught by a security camera or you activate any of your accounts on the grid—they'll come for you."

I laughed. There was really nothing else to do. He was going to try to hold me hostage? *Me?* Based on vague ideas about how surveillance worked? After everything?

He smiled back, uncertainly. "I'm not kidding," he said.

"Me, either," I said.

"Kelly Green, seriously," he said. "You'd put us all in jeopardy." He looked at the clock. It was almost midnight. "I'm exhausted. I'm going to sleep." He yawned. "Let's talk about it in the morning, okay? I love you."

"Okay," I said. "Whatever."

"There's something else I need to talk to you about," he said. All the anger had been sapped from his voice. He sounded . . . worried. "But this is not how I'd like to tell you."

I looked at him more closely. He really did look exhausted. But I was so angry that I couldn't bear to press it. I'd had enough for one night.

We went to sleep in silence, as far away from each other on the bed as we could get. I was surprised I fell asleep. I was so angry I felt like I could levitate.

I woke a few hours later in the darkness to Madhuri's hand on my arm, her finger over her mouth urging me to be quiet. I got out of bed as quietly as I could. Vero was snoring loudly on the other side of the bed, dead to the world. I followed her out into the hallway on my tiptoes, closing the door behind us.

She pressed a set of car keys into my hand. "Go to her," she whispered.

I clutched them to my chest. "Come with me," I said.

She shook her head. "I can't."

"Why?" I said, too loudly, and then again softly, "Madly, *why*?"

"Would you believe," she said, her eyelid twitching, "I love him."

"Motherfucker," I said, in disbelief.

"I love him," she said. "I want to have a baby with him." I couldn't believe she was saying those words with her face in its current state, bruised and swollen. I touched a hand to her cheek and she flinched.

"What are you going to do if you want more than one kid?" I said. "What if he keeps hitting you? What if he hits the kid?"

She shrugged. "Cross those bridges when I come to them?"

I was speechless. I took her hands in mine and squeezed.

"I know it's hard to understand," she said, "but you don't know him like I do."

Tears were running down my face.

"Be careful," she said.

I knew leaving was beyond risky. But if it meant getting back to you? Well, I would have risked anything.

I should have done it sooner. That's my only real regret.

"Vero can't know I'm leaving," I said. "He'd never be okay with it."

"Hence me sneaking into your room in the middle of the night."

"He mentioned there was something important he had to tell me. Do you know what it could be?"

She shook her head. We heard a creaking sound from the floor above. It occurred to me that someone could be listening; that we couldn't trust anyone but each other.

"Oh, I brought your bag," she said. I don't know how she grabbed my things without me realizing. She's good like that. "I put some cash in it. A few changes of clothes. Your toothbrush. Some of those disgusting bean bricks. Three thousandth time is a charm, right?"

"Madhuri," I started to say, wanting to thank her, to tell her I loved her, to tell her she was my guardian angel and I didn't know why she kept saving me again and again, but she interrupted me.

"Go now," she said, and so I did.

Madhuri's car, this old pickup truck that I've been in for so many weeks, was parked at the edge of the land and I ran as fast as I could in the darkness toward it, toward you.

I drove as fast as I could and I didn't look back.

When morning came, I stopped at a store to buy paper, pens, envelopes, stamps. And then I started writing to you.

And then, when I felt like I was a safe distance away, I bought a temporary phone and I called Vero's secure line. I couldn't help it. After everything, I felt I owed it to him to properly close the door on us, not leave it swinging open behind me.

But that's not what happened when I called.

He picked up on the first ring. "You actually left me," he said.

"You didn't give me a choice," I said.

"I understand," he said. "And I'm sorry it came to this. Please be careful. Please make sure no one is following you."

"I'm being careful," I said, not mentioning the fact that I already suspected I was being followed. "For what it's worth, I think you and stupid fucking Len are making a huge mistake. You could choose to save the whole entire planet."

"No," he said. "It was never going to be that simple. The thing is, people have accepted that we're in a doom spiral. No one wants to put in the work to stop it. It's too late. The only thing we can do is protect our own people."

I hated that I could see his point. The climate-change doomers were more dangerous than the deniers. They'd leaned so hard into complacency that they probably wouldn't care when we provided them with solutions.

And then he said, "Kelly, there's something else." My heart caught in my throat as I waited for him to go on. The thing he'd wanted to tell me before I left. "I'm sick."

My mouth was dry. "How sick?"

"I have cancer." He sounded so matter-of-fact. He was always proud like that.

"Oh, Vero," I said, my heart breaking. I pressed the phone into my ear as though it might transport me to him. "What can we do?" I thought of how tired he had been lately, his terrible cough. How had I not realized there was something wrong? Was I that wrapped up in my own shit?

"I don't think there's anything anyone can do for me at this point," he said. "Except be there. I want you to be there for me, Kel. To be *here* for me."

"We brought the best scientists in the world to live with us, and you're telling me there's nothing anyone can do?" It didn't make sense. There was still something he wasn't telling me. Then it hit me like a ton of bricks. "You don't think there's anything anyone can do, or you're not going to try?"

He chuckled. "You know me so well." We were silent for a long time. I listened to the sound of my heart pounding. Finally he said,

"I don't want to be a hypocrite. I can't fight for the survival of one when each and every human taking up space on this earth is contributing to its decline. It would be a misappropriation of our resources."

"You're such a fucking martyr," I all but shouted. "You're going to die to prove a point?" This didn't feel real.

"I've accepted it," he said. "Statistically, it was bound to happen to someone from our group, given where we lived for so long. I'm glad it's me. I couldn't live with myself if it was you or Madly. You know the cancer rates spiked after the fracking. Ironic, isn't it? All roads seem to lead back to my father, even after everything we've accomplished." He sounded far away and wistful, like he was talking to himself. "The fewer of us there are, the better chance we all have," he said. "Besides, the group doesn't need me anymore. It's up and running. I did my part."

"But Vero," I said, "don't you *want* to live? You can intellectualize death all you want, but what about the basic human desire to be alive?"

"Of course I want to live," he said. "But not if my death can mean something more than my life would."

I started to sob. "I hate you," I said.

"I know that you also love me," he replied. "And I will always love you, too, no matter what."

I told him I loved him and got off the phone. He didn't need to hear me crying for him. Or maybe I just couldn't stand for him to hear how much he was hurting me.

How could I leave him when he was going to let himself die?

But without you, how could I go back?

I felt pulled in a million different directions, as each day brought me farther and farther away from him, but closer to you.

Which brings us full circle.

So, my love, now you know the story of why I am heading to you now. You know what I've left behind.

When I reach you, we have a choice to make. Or rather, you do.

When I left, all I thought about was figuring out a way to be in your life again. But if Vero is dying, it changes things, and I had a new thought: What if we go back to the Winter Liberation Army together?

We'd be safe, and you could grow up in a special community of people who think differently. I don't think what they're doing is right, but that doesn't make it less safe of an option, you know? We were in a terrible position and there were probably no right or wrong choices. Just choices. Vero made the one he felt was best for us. I can't fault him for that. I would like to go back with you at my side, but you don't have to do what I want.

I also, of course, would like to be there for Vero. He's the second love of my life, after you. Death is funny like that; it makes you see all the bullshit for what it is. I can see him so clearly now. I can't imagine a world without him in it. I wonder if I was there, if maybe I could convince him to try to survive this. If our love could be greater than his martyrdom.

I know I've also told you about the sexism problem there. That was on purpose. I wanted you to have all the info before you commit either way. It's definitely not a perfect place to live. As a girl you might have trouble there. But we'd be protected physically, from the elements at least, and that does count for a lot. Perhaps you and I could fight the good fight together. We could help the women there find their voices again. I don't know. A girl can dream.

Perhaps, though, you want to stay near your dad? That's okay, too. I would understand that. The WLA is far and foreign. You might want to stick with what you know. We could do that. I could get an apartment close to the house and see you as often as he'll let me. I won't go back to the WLA unless you come with me. Once I'm back in your life, I'll be back. Don't worry about losing me again. We can live wherever you want. I don't want my love for Vero, my concern for his health, to cloud this decision. That's why I'm leaving it up to you.

That's the other reason I'm sending you these letters in advance of my arrival. So you can think about what you want to do with all this information.

Please don't tell your dad any of this. I don't want him getting between us again. This is your decision, not his. He's controlled us for too long.

You let me know what you've decided when I get there.

I'll see you so soon.

I love you.

Mom

9

ORCHID
2078

ORCHID WAS DREAMING OF A SUBURBAN SUMMER barbecue—her mom marinating mushrooms in the kitchen and her dad by the grill holding a spatula, birds chirping and Top 40 radio playing from somewhere—when she snapped awake to the sound of Camilla screaming: "*Fire.*"

She was on her feet before she could think. "Wake up, wake up, wake up," she shouted at Ava and Brook, who were getting up too slowly, as though they'd never experienced a natural disaster before, which was true for Brook, but Ava should have known better than to allow herself the luxury of hesitation.

The trees were smoking. The neon-yellow wildflowers that had spread and bloomed and then died and dried out in Orchid's absence were the perfect tinder, and it was alive with orange flames, the sparks flying in all directions as the sky was starting to darken with smoke.

It would only be a matter of time before the piles of debris that used to be houses caught fire, and then everything else.

How quiet the fire was surprised Orchid. Just the sound of sparks crackling, but the flames were dead silent as they licked up the trees. It was hypnotizing. She hadn't seen a wildfire up close in some time. She'd been safe in this part of the world for so long. She'd never taken one moment for granted, but still, she found herself wishing she'd appreciated the calm more. The safe monotony.

The sight before her sparked nothing but terror. Black, billowing smoke clouds that signaled death.

Orchid started coughing. Her lungs felt like they were closing up. She doubled over, hacking so hard the earth began to spin. Perhaps she'd throw up her lungs, she thought, wondering if it was possible.

Someone was pulling on her arm. "Time to go, my friend," Camilla said. "Stop coughing and grab your shit."

Orchid managed a smile as she coughed a few more times and then focused on steadying her breathing. Camilla was a pain in the ass, just like her.

Orchid licked her finger and held it up to the wind. "It's gonna blow south," she wheezed.

"Yeah," Camilla said. "Opposite of us. Thank fuck."

Finally, Ava and Brook emerged from the hut, looked tired and confused, but luckily already holding their things. Ava tossed Orchid's backpack to her and muttered wearily, "We're ready."

Max produced a black gas mask from their backpack and handed it to Camilla. "Wear it, please," they said. Camilla took it, but she put it over Brook's face, tightening the straps around her head. Max didn't protest. Everyone seemed to agree: the youngest among them was the one worth saving.

For the second time since Orchid had found them on the highway, she told them to run.

It took what felt like forever to outrun the smoke, though even as the sky cleared Orchid swore she could still smell it. The fire hadn't followed them, though. It had indeed blown south.

Max seemed like they were in a great deal of pain, limping alongside them, but didn't complain.

When they reached a high peak, following the red scraps Parker had faithfully tied to trees, they turned around and looked. The fire was clearing everything in its path. The evergreens and the firs and the birches and the fields of flowers were being decimated. The chipmunks and the birds and the squirrels were hopefully fleeing, but Orchid doubted most of them would get out in time.

"Can I take this off now?" Brook said, her voice muffled by the mask that encompassed her whole head.

"Let me help," Max said. "I think it should be okay now."

"We're good," Camilla said. "It's going the other way."

"It still fucking sucks," Orchid said. "This whole part of the country is about to be ash."

"It was inevitable," Max said. "I'm surprised it didn't happen sooner."

They rested there, in a small clearing on top of the mountain, for the night.

Orchid stayed awake for a while, after everyone else was snoring under the trees. The sky appeared bifurcated. To the south was a layer of dense smoke. To the north, though, it was clear. The stars were so densely packed in the sky it was like a vial of glitter had exploded. It would have blown her mind to see such a sight back when she lived on Brook, when the only things they could see were a few faded, dim stars, JM Inc. satellites, airplanes, and maybe, if they were lucky, Saturn.

She tried to remember which one was Saturn, if it should be visible or if it was blanketed by the smoke. She couldn't. She wanted to wake Ava up and ask her, but knew Ava would not be receptive to this sort of intrusion.

She wondered if any other planets were also on fire thanks to the beings who lived there. If any aliens were as dumb as humans had been, or as wasteful.

The next day, they found a red scrap tied on a branch down the hill, and continued onward.

They all stank of smoke. They were mostly quiet, rendered mute by their tiredness and hunger. Brook, in particular, had been silent for a long time. Orchid was worried about her, but she also knew it wasn't really her business. She wasn't Brook's mother. She wasn't even her stepmother.

Thinking about it made her chest hurt, so she switched gears.

"Hey," Orchid said, slowing her pace to match Max's. "Did you ever meet a woman named Kelly?"

Max tilted their head. "You don't mean Kelly *Green*, do you?"

"No," Orchid said. "Kelly Turner. Or maybe she was going by her maiden name—Hayes?"

Max shook their head. "No. The only Kelly I know of went by Green."

Ava, listening, said, "But that was obviously a nickname, right? No one would actually name their child Kelly Green. That's ridiculous."

"True," Max said. "All the elders had nicknames for one another. No idea what her real name was. And anyway, I never met her."

"What happened to her?" Orchid asked.

"She vanished," Max said. "But not before hacking into top secret government stuff and getting all the information we used to survive. She was a fucking legend."

"What do you mean, vanished?" Ava said.

"It was one of the mysteries of the community," Max said. "There one day, gone the next. Before my time."

Orchid looked at Ava. "That certainly sounds like my mother," she said, trying to smile, but found her mouth had started to twitch.

"Kelly Green was your mother?" Max repeated.

"I don't know," Orchid said. "She left when I was seven."

"Well, if it was her"—Max stopped walking and took Orchid's hand—"then I feel like I need to pay my respects to you. She was a really big deal." Max bowed their head.

Orchid pulled away, uncomfortable. "Okay," she said. "Cool."

The chances of Orchid's mother and Kelly Green being the same person were slim to none, she knew. The world was big. There were a lot of women named Kelly. Probably a lot of women named Kelly who liked to up and leave the people who were counting on them. But still. She liked the idea that her mom had not left her for something nefarious but for something noble. It was a large change to her personal narrative. She could make room for it, this new perspective. She wanted to. It was time.

"Was she crazy?" Orchid asked. "I mean, this Kelly Green woman."

"Only in the way that all the elders were crazy," Max replied. "Like, it took guts to do what they did. They had to really believe in the cause. Which I think is a kind of insanity."

"My dad told me that my mom left us to join a climate-change-denial cult. That she had lost her mind. I have all these memories of her and I'm not sure how real they are. I remember that she stopped showering. I remember she would print articles out and hang them all over the walls."

"Climate-change *denial*?" Max said. "No way. The elders were like, the only people who believed it could be stopped. But they never denied it was happening."

"What do *you* think?" Ava asked Max. "Do you think it could have been stopped with the information that they stole?"

"Yeah," Max says. "I do. I think they sacrificed the entire world for themselves."

"No wonder you left," Ava said, the tension between her and Max starting to dissipate.

"There were other reasons," Max said, but didn't elaborate. And then, after a few moments of quiet, they said, "Maybe there are *some* things we could recreate. Maybe it doesn't have to ruin us."

"We wouldn't let it," Ava said. "We could promise each other to always share the information with other people who need it. We could end the secrecy."

Max only nodded, deep in thought. Ava, to her credit, didn't press it further. Max would come around, Orchid thought. They just needed time. They needed to feel like they had a choice in the matter.

As they walked, Orchid tried to remember what she could of her mother, but it was like trying to remember an old dream.

She could recall certain details. That when her mother laughed, like really lost it, it was silent; she'd put her hands over her face and shake while tears poured out of her eyes. Orchid used to love being able to get a good silent laugh out of her mom. Now that she thought of it, she realized something uncanny: Ava laughed like that, too. Orchid tried not to dwell on it. It was too painful to think of the ways in which Ava and her mother were similar. *Goddamn mommy issues,* she thought.

She remembered that her mom didn't have friends, that the other moms were weird to her. In hindsight she realized it was probably because her mother was so much younger and prettier than the rounding, middle-aged moms of her friends. Orchid was now so much older than her mom had been when she'd left her. She felt a pang of sadness, having never gotten to see her mother age.

It was hard for her to remember her mom's face at all. There was a blur where it should have been, just an idea, a smudge with red hair wearing a flannel shirt. She could remember her smell, though: her patchouli-scented natural deodorant, her green-juice breath.

What Orchid remembered more vividly was her mother's absence. How one day she said she'd be right back and then never came home. She remembered her father's rage, and then his sadness, and then his never-ending stream of replacements. She remembered her own frustration that she couldn't bring her mother home just by virtue of wanting to, that she couldn't stomp her feet loud enough or wail for long enough for her mom to hear her. That she couldn't turn back the clock to the moment just before her mother walked out the door. That it was too late, would forever be too late, to grab her hand and say something like, "But I still need you."

Ten years after her mom left, her dad had a heart attack on the job, died in the ambulance before he got to the hospital. One of his coworkers had called Orchid to tell her. It was late fall during her senior year of high school, still hot as summer, no air-conditioning in her overcrowded, underfunded public school. She remembered thinking she might suffocate. When she left school that day, jaw clenched tight as though that would hold her grief in, she never went back. There was no point, she felt. There was nothing she'd gain in the final months of high school that would help her face the world alone.

She'd gone through his things by herself, after the funeral. She wanted to respect his privacy as much as possible. In his closet, she'd found boxes and boxes of paperwork and letters. She couldn't believe he'd kept so many hard copies of things, when the whole world had become digital. The letters in particular seemed ridiculous. Who sends letters? Who *keeps* letters? She was too heartbroken to actually read through any of it. Once she found the important stuff—the deed to the house, his will, his credit card info—she threw the rest out without opening it, filling the recycling bin to the brim. He'd always been kind of a hoarder, especially after her mom left.

When she cleared the rest of the house out, she listed it for rent online and quickly found tenants, a young family who seemed responsible enough, who were willing to pay the jacked-up price she'd arbitrarily picked. She used their rent money to move to Brook, living for free for a brief, wild period of time and spending the extra cash on stupid things: expensive dates with older women she never saw again, the latest phones and televisions and tablets, club drugs, booze.

She rarely told anyone she was still a teenager, and no one asked. Sadness makes you seem older. Makes you feel older, too.

When a flash flood hit the town she'd grown up in, turning the road into a river, it filled the little blue house with four feet of brown water, and the tenants fled. Orchid didn't bother trying to repair it. In fact she couldn't even bear to go see it; the photos they sent her were enough. She didn't know if her dad had gotten flood insurance. If there was paperwork documenting it, she'd thrown it away.

Soon her money ran out so she talked her way into a job as an assistant carpenter, embodying the spirit of her father without even thinking twice about it. After all, he'd taught her all he knew.

She let herself smile at the memory of the first time he put a drill in her hand. The power she felt because of his trust in her. The gift he'd given her: self-sufficiency, in any situation. How prescient he'd been to do that.

Meanwhile, they walked, and walked, and walked.

Orchid and Camilla took turns finding animals to eat. Sometimes they went days without catching anything. Other times they'd get lucky and get birds or squirrels. Ava had become more helpful, finding plants that were edible, now that the landscape was getting lusher.

One afternoon they saw smoke in the distance, above the trees. Camilla looked at her and said, "Another wildfire?"

"It looks too small," Orchid said, her heart starting to race with excitement. "Controlled. It's a campfire." The smoke was in a single column.

"Do you think it's them?" Camilla nearly yelped.

"The rags point the other way," Max said.

"It could be them," Orchid said, ignoring Max.

"We should go look," said Camilla.

"Wait," Ava said. "Is that safe? What if they're dangerous?"

"What if they think *you're* dangerous?" Brook said.

"What if I just go check it out?" Orchid said. "They'll never see me."

They couldn't stop her. She went as quietly as she could through the forest until she heard the sounds of people talking. She hid behind trees and knelt in the brush as she got closer and closer. She could hear singing, smell meat cooking. There were a lot of people here.

But as she got closer, close enough to see some of them, she realized they were strangers. She didn't recognize a single person. It was odd, though, how even strangers could look familiar; peering through the bushes she could see the hardship etched into the lines on their faces, the complicated stories they held in their stooped spines. People were people. These just weren't hers.

She snuck back out as quietly as she'd come. When she reached the others, she simply shook her head. "Not them," she said. Camilla frowned, but didn't say anything.

Ava raised an eyebrow. "Shall we continue?" And they did.

They saw a few more settlements along the way, and even though none of them were the community they were looking for, it was a relief. They weren't the only humans left alive.

Orchid, eventually, stopped counting time. They'd covered so much ground. Every time she thought they'd lost track of Parker's little red rags, they'd find another, and keep going.

Everything hurt, all the time. But she didn't complain. None of them did. A grim sort of resolve settled over them.

It was clear that Camilla and Max had stopped fucking. Orchid guessed they were just too tired.

Eventually the forest and mountains began to give way to a flatter, more tundra-like terrain, an alien landscape of rock and—to her surprise—the occasional flurry of snow. It was getting colder and colder. While they were walking, the cold was nice, but at night they had to huddle close to one another around the fire to keep warm, to keep alive. Their clothes were fraying, turning to rags that hung around their bodies. She wondered if this was how the original humans lived. She felt like a cave person.

One night after Brook fell asleep sandwiched between Max and Camilla, Ava whispered, “I feel like we’re going to die out here.”

“I know,” Orchid said. “If we weren’t following this damn T-shirt trail I’d say we should just stop and set up shop somewhere.”

“Why *are* we so committed to finding them?” Ava asked. “At this point, it’s kind of like . . . ?” She trailed off.

“I owe it to Camilla to reunite her with her dad,” Orchid said. “She left him to wait for me. But”—she paused, searching Ava’s face in the light from the fire—“that doesn’t mean you owe it to her. You two can break off any time you’d like. You’re not stuck with me.”

“Don’t be ridiculous,” Ava said. “We’d be even more fucked without you.”

“Happy to keep you alive as long as I can,” Orchid said, while feeling sad that this was her purpose.

To her surprise, Ava rested her head on Orchid’s shoulder and sighed. Orchid stayed as still as possible, afraid if she moved, Ava would realize she was being affectionate.

“I want to forgive you,” Ava whispered into Orchid’s ear. Her breath made Orchid shiver.

“So forgive me,” she whispered back.

“Okay,” Ava said. As easy as that.

Orchid buried her face in Ava’s hair so that Ava wouldn’t be able to tell that she was crying. She didn’t want to have to explain the tears. She didn’t really have words for them.

She felt Ava’s skin growing hot, just like it used to do when they touched. “Warm enough now?” she asked, and Ava laughed, quietly, trying not to wake the others up.

“God, I missed you,” Orchid said.

“I know you did,” Ava said. “I missed you, too.”

“I don’t expect anything,” Orchid said.

Ava pulled away then, and lay down on her side, not a rejection but an invitation. Orchid lay behind her, the big spoon. Ava's butt pressed into her pelvis. Orchid wrapped an arm around Ava's torso and pulled her close.

A few of Ava's greasy curls made their way into Orchid's mouth as she inhaled the smell of her; her scalp caked in sweat and smoke and dirt and the lingering remains of something floral, maybe gardenia.

Then Ava turned her head back toward Orchid's face, and their mouths collided. Orchid felt her whole body tighten. She gripped Ava hard, kept her eyes open, felt tense and alert, not wanting to overstep or mistake what was happening. But Ava had chosen this, had made it happen. Had turned her head toward Orchid, not away, had made their lips meet. She could feel Ava relaxing in her arms, pressing into her more, as though this kiss was somehow soothing her, making her feel more safe. Even as their lips parted and Ava's tongue grazed Orchid's, Orchid found she couldn't stop ruminating on the difference in how their bodies felt; Orchid, stiff as a plank of wood, and Ava, softening like butter.

"What's wrong?" Ava whispered into her mouth, feeling her tension. "I thought you wanted this."

"More than you could possibly know," Orchid whispered back. "So much so that it terrifies me."

Ava wriggled around in her arms until they were facing each other, noses touching. "What are you afraid of?"

"I just want to be sure that this is what *you* want, too. That you would want it even if we weren't the only two lesbians left on earth."

Ava laughed, covering her mouth to conceal the sound.

"I guess we'll never know," Ava said.

She was teasing, but it made Orchid bristle. "Too soon," she said.

"Oh, come on," Ava said. She slipped a cold hand up the back of Orchid's shirt, warming her fingers under the ragged band of Orchid's sports bra. "You know I don't do anything I don't want to do. Not anymore."

This, Orchid found, was oddly comforting, or maybe it was just the intoxicating pressure of Ava's fingers on her skin.

"Want to go behind a rock or something?" Orchid said.

"Absolutely," said Ava. Orchid was on her feet in a matter of seconds, pulling Ava with her and leading her a few feet into the darkness, around the side of a large boulder, where they could pretend to have something that resembled privacy.

The nighttime roar of bug song was drowning out the snores from their little crew. Above them, a sliver of moon looked like an old yellow nail clipping.

Ava leaned against the rock and Orchid fell to her knees in front of her, ignoring the pinch of pain as her skin hit the rocky ground. She lifted Ava's dirty mauve tunic and started kissing Ava's stomach, which felt more hollowed out than she remembered, but softer, too, with skin that was pliable. She wanted to bite her, wanted to open her mouth wide enough that she'd be able to fit all of Ava inside of it, where she could keep her safe forever, but Ava dug her hands into Orchid's hair and pulled her head away. Orchid looked up at her, questioning, and before she could say anything Ava was on her knees, too, so they were eye level. Ava pressed her hands into Orchid's chest. The earth tilted and Orchid fell onto her back, Ava pushing her into the ground with a kind of assertiveness Orchid had never known her to have.

It made her smile, even while they kissed.

Ava smiled back. "Can I please touch you?"

"I think I might die if you don't," Orchid said, and as Ava pressed her hand down into where Orchid ached with longing, she felt decades of regret begin to ebb, replaced with a blinding pleasure that filled all her saddest, darkest places like white-hot sunshine. She gave in to it, in to Ava, allowed herself to be tended to. She reached for Ava a few times, trying hard to wedge her hand between Ava and her own thigh, but found Ava wouldn't let her.

"You first," Ava insisted, not allowing her in, though Orchid's fingers were almost itchy with how badly they wanted to be on her.

"Is this payback?" Orchid managed to say, though her breath was coming faster and faster and talking was hard. She knew it was, before the answer came. Payback for all the years they'd spent together with Orchid never getting fully naked, literally or otherwise, always pushing Ava's hands away, never letting herself be out of control.

But Ava shook her head. "Not payback. I just need you to be vulnerable first. So I know you're not going to clam up on me."

"The opposite," Orchid whispered. She guided Ava's fingers inside of her then, pressing the heel of Ava's palm into her, proof of her willingness to change, of her desperation to be known, fully. Ava gasped. She'd never touched Orchid this deeply, not once in their five years together when they were so young and naive. Orchid felt Ava's legs tighten around hers and they moved together like that, Ava riding her thigh while her fingers curled deeper inside Orchid, expertly thrumming the spot that was swelling like a sponge, letting Orchid know that she'd done this perhaps many times before, that just because Orchid had left didn't mean this part of Ava's life had ended. If anything, Orchid leaving allowed Ava's love life to continue, to expand, to take her places Orchid hadn't been able to. There had been other lovers who were more receptive than Orchid had been, and as Ava continued to deftly hit the bull's-eyes of Orchid's pleasure centers, Orchid found she didn't feel jealous but grateful—that other women had cared for Ava, had been open to her, while she was gone.

But she was scared to finish. Her orgasm loomed large in the shadows, threatening to destabilize her completely. She tried to hold it at bay. "Not yet," she whispered.

"Just let it go," Ava urged, and Orchid wasn't sure if it was the words or simply the sound of Ava's voice that unlocked the pressure building inside her. She split open. Her muscles contracted so tightly around Ava's hand that she heard Ava laugh and say, "Ow," but the sound of it felt far away and faint over the ringing in her ears.

Ava collapsed on top of her, and they lay like that, clutching each other with what remained of their strength.

"Hey," Ava said finally, still slightly out of breath. "I just have to tell you. I don't care what Max says about how amazing Kelly Green was. I don't know how anyone could leave their kid . . ." She paused, as if she wasn't sure how to say it. "I don't know how anyone could leave *you*."

Orchid had never felt so raw. "I can't believe you still feel like that, after I abandoned you."

"You did what you were taught to," Ava said, more gently than Orchid felt she deserved. "I can't really fault you for that."

When they finally stumbled back in the darkness to where the others lay, they were sticky and stinking and glowing, weak and spent after so much had been released between them. Orchid slept better that night than she had in a very long time.

A few days later, thanks to the flat expanse of the terrain, they saw in the distance a sight that to Orchid was definitely evidence of aliens: a perfectly round lake.

"Wait," Ava said, sounding excited. "I know where we are."

"You do?" Camilla and Brook said at the same time.

"Mars?" Orchid asked.

"It's a crater lake. Fuck, I can't remember what it's called, but it's famous! Wait. This is so cool . . ." She was talking faster now, her excitement overwhelming her, and Orchid couldn't help but smile at how endearing it was.

"This is amazing," she was saying. "This lake, it has some of the purest fresh water in the entire world, because its sources are rain and snow. It's not connected to any other water sources, like no streams underground or anything. And it has fish! It's famous for being full of fish. It used to ice over, but I bet it doesn't anymore."

Then Ava's face fell. "But we shouldn't have been able to get here by land."

"What do you mean?"

"I mean, I remember you had to fly here or take a boat. We should have had to cross a bunch of big rivers and lakes by now. They must have dried up."

"We knew that would happen, though, right?" Max asked. "This is what was predicted?"

"Yeah," she said, sounding sad. "I guess I just . . . had hoped it wouldn't? I don't know. I thought maybe with the Inside Project, with the end of fossil fuels, that it wouldn't get to this point."

"But it means we could get here," Camilla said, pointing toward the crater lake, always looking for the bright side. "That's not so bad."

"I just worry about what else it means," Ava said. "What has been underwater that is now exposed."

"Can we worry about that later, Mom?" Brook said.

"I mean, the lake sounds like a great place to settle," Orchid said. "Maybe . . . ?"

Even the weather had leveled out, becoming springlike, and though the ground was often almost lunar, there'd been some more greenery between the rocks recently, and more birds, too. She'd started to suspect they were in bear country, but wasn't worried; the bears would likely be more afraid of them than anything. Still, she continued to hang their food from the trees. Just because she wasn't afraid of them didn't mean she wanted to share her food with them. She *was* worried about the possibility of wolves, but hadn't said so. She didn't want to freak anyone out.

"It would be an incredible place to settle," Ava said. "It really would be. This is what I was talking about—how the poles might become tropical again. We're getting pretty far up there."

"This doesn't feel tropical." Brook shivered.

"It feels better than being in the middle of a forest fire," Max said.

"Let's go," Orchid said. "I have a good feeling about this. Besides, how many red rags do we really think Parker has left?"

They were giddy as they approached the crater lake. It was still a few miles off, but they kept finding red scraps, coming more frequently now, stuck between rocks, as though Parker had been excited, too.

Orchid couldn't help imagining where the meteor that made the crater had come from. What planets did it whiz by on its journey to the place in Northern Canada where it collided with the earth and then filled with water and eventually fish? She had an odd and surprising feeling of purpose, as though it was only because she'd been open to wonder and fear that she was able to find this spot that spoke of other, unknowable places.

The lake in the distance, the crater that contained it, the meteor that made the crater, the endless universe where the meteor was from: it was all connected. More importantly, *she* was connected to it all, to this world and the worlds beyond it, in all their vast mystery.

When they were close enough to see how clear and blue the water was, Camilla shielded her eyes from the sun, pointed to the left, and gasped, "Oh my god. I can see them. I can see my dad."

JUNE 1, 2041

Rick:

Let's drop the pretenses.

I know that you've read all my letters to Orchid. And I can't imagine that you've let her see them. I know what this is now. I know whose hands have been holding my words. Hello.

And perhaps also hello to whoever is going to screen this letter before it leaves the facility. I promise there won't be anything here you'd care about. Or believe.

Rick, I'm writing to you from my room in the asylum where they're keeping me. Maybe you know that already.

I was on the New Jersey Turnpike, about an hour outside of New York, when they got me. The sound of sirens and the whir of helicopters, the flashing lights, the parting of traffic to let the cops through; I immediately knew they were coming for me. It's not paranoia if you're right.

Anyway, it was terrifying, just so you know. I thought they were going to shoot me right then and there. Did you want me to feel terrified? Did you want me to think I was going to die? Did it make you feel better?

The men arresting me said things about conspiracy to kidnap a minor, trafficking classified information, collaborating with domestic terrorists. I suppose that is one way of looking at all of this.

It was naive of me to write down that I was crossing the country, that I was heading to her. I see that now. I was just so hopeful and excited to be returning home. I wanted Orchid to know it was real. I didn't mean to provide you—and them—with instructions for how to find me.

When they dragged me out of my car and handcuffed me, someone read me my rights, but it was clearly just a formality, in case there were bystanders filming.

I wasn't held in jail. I was immediately brought here, put into a hospital gown, locked in a room. I'm let out for ten minutes a day to see the sun. There are guards and doctors, but no one will answer my questions. I've not been allowed a phone call. If I get too upset they give me more drugs. I know that I am a political prisoner, but what they tell me is that I'm a danger to myself and society. A team of doctors will decide when I can be released. I have no rights, is the truth of the matter. I'm lucky to even have my own room, though it's windowless, more like a coffin. I feel I'm becoming a vampire.

It doesn't surprise me that they're letting me write to you. If anything it confirms my suspicions that it's you who turned me in. They know that nothing I could say to you would convince you to help me.

Of course, they're going to read this before it gets to you. But there's not much I could say at this point that would need to be censored. I've said it all.

What I will say is this: I was put in an impossible situation by the terrible circumstances of my whole life, and I did the best I could. Maybe you don't believe me, but I am sorry that I hurt you in the process. Both of you.

Rick, if there's any chance you could forgive me enough to let me see Orchid, I do think you could convince them to allow me one visitor. I want nothing more than to look at her face, even if it's for the last time. I want to see how she's grown and how beautiful I know she's become.

I also want you to know that I did love you. I did trust you. I did want a family with you. All the things that you wanted for us, I wanted, too.

But you have to understand that you and I, we were doomed from the beginning. There's no way a relationship survives such an imbalance of power. You should not have become my guardian. You should have advocated for me to be liberated from the guardianship in general. I don't know why that didn't occur to either of us.

I don't even fault you for cheating. I don't really care about all the girls in your phone. I understand how desire works: you can't desire what you already have. And you had me. You had my life in your hands. You had my freedom, my agency. There was nothing left of me for you to want. So of course you wanted other people. I get it.

I just wish that you had that same empathy for me. That you could understand why I had to leave and that I was always going to come back. I wish that you had let me maintain a relationship with Orchid while I was gone. A girl needs her mother. I could have been there for her, over the phone, in text, email. Instead you cut me off the second I did something you didn't like. If anything justifies the fact that I left, it's how you acted when I did.

Rick, we're at war. The enemy is the changing climate; or, rather, the people turning a blind eye to the change, speeding it up with their selfish decisions. We all have a responsibility to fight. And if I was a man going off to war, I would have been a hero. But I was a woman going off to fight *for* humanity, not with it, and so I'm the villain.

Listen: I expect to spend the rest of my life here. I'm okay with it. I've done all I can for the world. But I need you to know that something big is coming. A shift in how humanity exists on this earth. A lot of people are going to die. Power grids are going to be shut off, the old modes of transportation—cars, trains, planes, even boats—will have nothing to run on. The agricultural industries will fall apart. The government will limit its support to a certain class of people. A class that you and I are not part of. I gave my life to the cause. But it's happening no matter what.

Everything I wrote to Orchid is real. You have to believe me. I know it all sounds insane. Like the conspiracy theory of a madwoman. But you don't actually think I'm crazy, right? Even though you let them lock me in here?

Regardless of what you believe, I need Orchid to survive. And I know you do, too. No matter how much you hate me, we will always have this in common.

I need you to teach her everything you know about survival so that she's prepared to live without the comforts of modernity. Teach her to hunt, to grow food, to build shelters. Make sure if she's ever on her own that she'll be okay. This is the only thing I'll ever ask of you again. If you don't know how to teach her, go to the library. Get some books. Put in the effort. It's worth it.

The world will turn upside down before you know it. There's nothing left to do but adapt. Orchid is brave. She learns quickly. She'll need you, at first, but I hope that you can help her need you less, because one day you'll be gone and she'll be left with the memory of you and, hopefully, the knowledge you've imparted. Please teach her well. Please remind her that I love her, even though I left. That I left because I love her. That I hope someday she is blessed enough to love someone as much as I love her.

When I sat down to write this, I imagined ending on a "Fuck you." But now that I'm at the end, I don't feel so angry at you. You did what you felt was right to protect our daughter. Maybe you really do think I'm a crazy person trying to kidnap her. I can't fault you for keeping her safe, even if it's only safe from the idea you have of me. So, Rick, fuck you. But also thank you. For being her parent when I couldn't.

Stay safe out there. For her sake.

Kelly

10

BROOK

2078

THERE WAS SO MUCH FOR BROOK TO BE DAZZLED BY, once they found the people they were looking for. The little houses they'd built into the rock and the earth, nearly camouflaged completely into the landscape but for the wooden doors and the little makeshift chimneys pumping plumes of smoke into the sky. The sky—a smogless blue like she'd never seen. It made her heart ache to look at it. It was as though pollution had somehow not reached this place. Clothes were drying on lines between houses, a million different colors and materials, waving like flags. Wild blueberries grew between boulders.

She took in the distinct oniony smell of human bodies and the fishy odor coming from stews that cooked over flames. The pleasant din of conversation, of laughter, of the clattering of pots and pans, the sloshing of water. The slapping of children's bare feet on the hard ground as they chased one another around. Like something from the past; humans returned to their most wild state.

How ironic that it was not the past but the present, as though the age of advanced technology was simply a detour from some sort of true purpose, from living in harmony with the earth.

And the people. Oh, the people! So many different faces to study, so many new voices and accents to listen to. The people had rushed around them, once they'd seen them coming, hugging Orchid and Camilla and touching Ava and Brook gently, welcoming them, walking them toward the place where they'd decided to settle. There was something dreamlike about finally getting to where they were going. She kept wondering if she was about to wake up.

She watched as Camilla's father held her, rocking her, crying into her shoulder, and felt a rush of jealousy and longing. This was the kind of reunion she'd never get to have with July.

"Dad, this is Brook. She needs to use the off-grid to call someone who Shelby might know," Camilla said, pulling away from her father long enough to make introductions, but Brook noticed he was still clutching her as though she might vaporize.

"You can use it whenever you'd like," he said kindly.

Brook turned to Ava. "Now? Can we call her now?"

"I need a minute," Ava said. "I'm sorry. I just . . ." She paused. "I don't know if I'm ready to have my heart broken again. We don't know what Camilla's sister will say."

"Fine," Brook said, giving in, because now that they had a way to reach July, she felt less rushed about it. They'd call when they were both ready. It didn't have to be right this second. She wondered if Ava was putting it off for Brook's benefit. If her mother had sensed how overwhelmed she was before Brook had the words for it.

The other people all wanted to know about Inside, about how they'd escaped and then survived the journey north, but Brook, and Ava for that matter, were so tired that Parker eventually intervened and said, "Let them rest. There's time for stories later."

"Thank you," Ava said, and Brook felt relieved that she'd get to stay quiet a little longer, taking it all in.

The urge to count everything around her was prickling, but it felt different now that they were here. She began to tally the people not out of a need to feel in control but out of a sense of awe, a kind of surrender to the vastness and beauty of the earth, to its multitudes.

"We found a landfill full of clothes," Parker said. "Come, I'll take you to where we're keeping what we've salvaged."

Brook, Ava, Orchid, Max, and Camilla followed her to the back of a hut where someone was sorting clothes into piles. There were jeans, T-shirts, sneakers, boots, jackets, sweaters. Brook had never seen such variety.

She took off her canvas shoes, which were falling apart, and peeled her socks off her feet. She had lost a few toenails somewhere along the way, and her bare toes were blue and purple. Her heels were unrecognizable, covered with calluses and blisters.

"You need boots for those paws," Orchid said.

Ava's eyes were wet as she touched something purple and fuzzy and whispered, "This feels like cashmere."

Parker smiled. "And the best part, it'll actually get cold enough to wear it."

Orchid handed Brook a pair of blue jeans. "These'll fit you," she said. Brook had never worn pants with a button or a zipper and as she squeezed into them, she wasn't sure she liked the feeling of the metal against her skin. But she liked how tight they were, how sturdy the material was. This could protect her better than the soft linens, which were ripped around the ankles from branches and thorns that had scratched up her skin.

"Do you want us to wash what you had on?" Parker asked, once they were all changed.

Orchid nodded, thanking her. "I've had this T-shirt since the year 2052," she said, tugging off her shirt and tossing it to Parker.

"I think I got that for you," Ava said.

"You did. That's why it lasted this long. You always got me the expensive shit."

"I'd rather bury mine," Brook interrupted them. "I never want to see these things again."

She realized this was an awkward thing to say by the way everyone turned to look at her, but she was strong in her resolve. "This is a new life, Mom. We have to commit."

"I agree," Ava said. "Let's bury all of our stuff and start over."

"I have something I'd like to bury, too," Max said.

"We'll make a ceremony of it," said Camilla.

First, though, they bathed in clear, cold water from the crater lake that was brought to them in buckets. They were given privacy—Camilla and Max were lent one hut, Orchid another, and Ava and Brook in a third one—where they shivered around small fires and sponged themselves clean.

"I do miss showering," Brook said, after she'd scrubbed the last of the dirt from her toes.

Ava laughed. "I knew you would."

As they dried off with clean rags, Brook averted her gaze from Ava's body, though she couldn't help noticing that there was more to Ava now; though she was thin from too much walking and not enough eating, her skin rippled and moved in a way that struck Brook as beautiful, even while she felt embarrassed at their nakedness.

"Someday you'll be old, too," Ava said, smiling, drying her hair.

"You're not old," she replied.

"I meant that in a good way. I love that you will get to grow old. That we made it here. What a gift, you know? Most people weren't so lucky."

Brook nodded. She did know.

"Hey," Ava said. "How would you feel about living in your own space?"

"Fine, I guess," she said, though the thought made her a little nervous, a little lonely. "Are you going to live with Orchid?"

"I think I want to try it," Ava said. "I think it might be good."

"She loves you," Brook replied.

"I know." Ava nodded. "I think I love her, too. I think I always have."

"You should tell her."

"I will, at some point." Ava laughed. "When I'm ready."

"Don't make her wait too long," Brook said. "Life is short, you know?"

Ava pulled her into a hug. "It's short, but it's also long," she said. Brook hugged her back, as tightly as she could. Life *was* long, she thought. Hers had already contained so many chapters, and she had the feeling it was only just beginning. When they finally pulled away, it was Ava who let go first.

That night, after they'd eaten from the salmon and caribou stew the community prepared and figured out where they'd all sleep until they could build homes of their own, Orchid dug a hole in the ground.

In it went two mauve tunics, two pairs of mauve pants, two pairs of canvas shoes. Max tossed in something that looked like a little bundle of herbs. Camilla added the red strips of fabric that she'd saved along their trek north.

They all helped bury their things, each taking a fistful of cool earth and tossing it into the hole, until just a small mound, like a grave, remained.

"Amen," said Max. "And good riddance."

Brook felt lighter when she lay down on a bed made of clothing scraps and animal furs, her mother already snoring on the other side of the one-room hut they'd share for now.

She didn't dream that first night. As soon as she closed her eyes she was swallowed by darkness, and then morning—the light filtering through the ceiling made of branches, the sounds of people talking and starting their day—came too soon. Brook could hear her mother's voice talking to Orchid in low tones just outside the door.

Ava sounded softer, more loving than she had when they first found Orchid mangled on the side of the highway. Brook was glad for this. Orchid might not be the perfect person for her mom, but she was *here,* and maybe after all was said and done, that could be enough.

She wondered if there was a person here for *her.* What it might look like to have a love of her own. Someone who wasn't July or her mother. She'd never felt ready for that kind of love before, but she was curious. She wondered how she'd behave if someone adored her, treasured her. If it would change how she felt in the world.

Brook stretched, taking stock of how her body felt. It was almost as though her feet were bracing for more walking, though logically she knew the journey was over. *An object in motion remains in motion,* she thought to herself, wondering what it might feel like to finally stop running away.

When she felt ready, with Camilla's help, Brook would turn the dials on Camilla's off-grid that would allow her to reach a woman named Shelby, and Shelby would answer, and then run as fast as she could through the glass tunnels of the Inside in Auckland until she found July. Brook would hear Shelby's footsteps hitting the ground as loud as if she were running beside her.

"It's Brook," Shelby would yell so loudly that Brook would jump, and then finally she'd hear July's voice on the other end, quieter and almost nervous: "Hello? Is it really you?"

Through tears and static, she'd discover that July, too, had found a new sort of family on the other side of the world; Shelby had become a kind of mother to her, but because July was, after all, the most magnetic person Brook would ever know, she also already had tons of friends. Everyone who knew July loved her, as Brook had. Well—maybe not as Brook had. There was a chance no one would ever love either girl as much as they loved each other, but that was okay with Brook. She didn't know if she wanted to replicate it. She didn't really need to. Instead, she and July called each other almost every day on the clunky device that Camilla lent her, trying to describe their lives to each other, taking turns falling asleep to the sound of each other's voice, just as they used to.

Soon, after they felt more settled and had a grasp of what their lives would look like in this new place, Ava would talk to Orchid about living together, and Brook would watch what it looked like to have an old love rekindled, turned into something new.

Over time, Orchid would teach Brook how to build and repair shelters in the rocky land they now called home. Camilla would teach her how to fish in the giant circle of fresh crater water that glittered in the sun. At Ava's continued and gentle urging, Max would let go of the superstition that the technological knowledge they harbored would lead to the kind of abuses of power they'd grown up with, and would teach everyone how to make this pocket of the world safer, with cleaner air and flood-safe houses. When other groups of people passed through, they'd share the knowledge with them, too. This is how the majority of humans left on earth would learn to live in an irreversibly changed climate; not through the billionaire-funded structures that sheltered a select few, but through the sharing of resources between people who cared, who wanted to do things differently and better.

Brook never fully stopped wanting to count the world around her, but it became less about keeping herself calm and more about her boundless curiosity. The world held so many wonders. She wanted to number and catalog them all so she could look at them, analyze them, try to understand her place among them.

In time she would begin to think of Orchid as her second mother, Camilla and Max as her siblings. Together they'd start a new life, a family who found one another at the ends of the earth. And she'd meet other people, experience different kinds of family, of friendship. She'd be challenged in ways she never could have imagined, and while she slept by herself at night for a long, long time, she never felt alone again.

Eventually she craved intimacy more than she feared it, and to her surprise she fell in love, once, then twice, then several times. She loved fiercely and freely, once she let herself.

As they got older, Brook and July called each other less, but they never stopped completely. They never lost touch.

One day Brook would have a child who would grow up knowing and loving Aunt July, that nice lady who lived impossibly far away but somehow always seemed so close, the sound of her warm voice through the off-grid constant and familiar.

But all that was a long way off.

For now, in the ground, tucked in with Brook's old clothes, the B3k sprig Sterrett had given Max for good luck nestled deep in the soil, and after a few days the little seed pods that were hidden between its dried leaves began to swell.

A few days after that, the glistening morning dew turned to steam in the hot sun as it rose, and while the nutrients in the dirt found their way to the bloating seed pods, one of those pods split open.

A bright green tendril emerged from the split, reaching its way down into the soil; a little root, clinging to the earth, and then once it was secure it grew some more, curling back up, fighting toward the sunlight until it burst through the final layer of ground, as tender and precious as a wish, a sprout as determined to live as everything that came before it and would come after it. Soon it would grow leaves, and then it would flower, and the flowers would give way to small red beans.

But the plant would be oblivious to the humans who would eventually notice it, harvest it, learn to rely on it. It would only care about the warm sun, the fresh water, the soft earth; singularly focused on its one goal: to grow and then to keep growing, no matter what.

ACKNOWLEDGMENTS

Thank you times infinity to my incredible editor, Hannah O'Grady, for letting me write not one but two books about a bunch of queer people at the end of the world. Your belief in my work has changed my life.

Thank you to the entire team at St. Martin's Press: Amelia Beckerman, for getting this book into as many hands as possible; Dori Weintraub and Alyssa Gammello, for all the incredible publicity support; Jonathan Bush, for designing yet another stunning cover; Michael Storrings, for the creative direction; and Devan Norman, for the beautiful interior design. Thank you to Linda Sawicki for the copy edit (I'm sorry I still can't remember that "toward" doesn't have an *s* at the end). Thank you to Lauren Riebs, Layla Yuro, and Madeline Alsup for keeping the project moving forward. Thank you to the audiobook team: Claire Beyette, Ally Demeter, and Isabella Narvaez.

Thank you to Sarah Clark for the thoughtful authenticity read.

Thank you as always to my agent, Nicki Richesin, for encouraging me to keep writing within the world of YFTT and for making sure that I could.

Thank you to my sister, Miriam Jayaratna, for forever being the first eyes on everything I write, and for always giving the best edits; to Ilana Masad, for reading an early draft before driving us all the way to San Diego so we could discuss notes in the car; and to Terry Ferreira, for answering all my questions about what it was really like in various DIY activist spaces (those stories changed the shape of this book).

Thank you to the members of the Pink Door Writing Group—Alana

Levinson, Irina Gusin, Katie Heaney, and Ryan Yates—who dove deep into this story with me for an entire year. I literally couldn't have done it without you. The book is so much stronger because of your feedback.

Thank you to Lauren Cerand for your ongoing guidance and words of wisdom.

Thank you to my parents for a lifetime of encouragement.

Thank you to Wallace for everything, always. You're the best Book Wife a girl could ask for.

Finally, thank you to the book lovers, the librarians, the booksellers, and the writers who championed *Yours for the Taking* and whose support and enthusiasm meant I got to write a second book in the same world. I am forever grateful.

ABOUT THE AUTHOR

Lindsey Byrnes

Gabrielle Korn is the author of *Yours for the Taking* and *Everybody (Else) Is Perfect*, and the former editor in chief of *Nylon*. Her writing has been published across the internet since 2011, with bylines in *Literary Hub, InStyle, Domino, Oprah, Refinery29*, and more. Originally from New York, she now lives in Los Angeles with her wife, and together they run the Pink Door artist and writer residency.